THE CARRINGTON EFFECT:
A NOVEL OF HOPE

Andrew B. Dill

Disclaimer:
This book is purely a work of fiction. All names, characters, organizations, entities, institutions, establishments, products, devices, technologies, methods, techniques, municipalities, regions, locales, places and incidents either are products of the author's imagination or are used fictitiously. Any resemblance to actual names, organizations, entities, institutions, establishments, products, devices, technologies, methods, techniques, municipalities, regions, locales, places, incidents, events, or persons, living or dead, is entirely coincidental. This book is not intended to serve as an instructional guide; it is for entertainment purposes only. This book is not intended as a substitute for the medical advice of physicians. Neither the author nor the publisher shall be held liable or responsible to any person or entity with respect to any loss or incidental or consequential damages caused, or alleged to have been caused, directly or indirectly, by the information contained herein.

Cover art by: Robbin A. Dill

Copyright © 2013 Andrew B. Dill
All rights reserved.
ISBN: 0615856047
ISBN 13: 9780615856049

ARGENT JAEGER PRESS

For Della (1967-2013)
May The Lord God of Hosts bless you and keep you always. A portion of the proceeds from this book will be donated to children's cancer charities in honor of your selfless work to help those in need. We miss you.

AUTHOR'S FORWARD:

I would like to take a moment and thank all of my friends and family for putting up with me during my time spent writing this book. Your patience and steadfast support have enabled me to write my first work. It has been a labor of love, and it constitutes one and a half year's worth of thought and effort. I pray that each reader will see the truth inherent in this novel: that mankind can pull together despite the most terrifying of events. My life has been blessed by my family, my friends and colleagues, my patients, and most of all by my Lord.

Special note is made here to clarify my personal feelings towards one of the most disturbing aspects of this type of literary work. There are several instances of violence and suicide that occur within the larger framework of the novel. I personally would like to clarify that I neither condone nor condemn suicide. My religious views teach me that The Lord alone shall judge, but that He is also great in His mercies. I have debated for many months whether or not to include such events in my storyline and have prayed at length about the issue. I have consulted with numerous religious leaders from multiple denominations and faiths and have struggled with these issues of violence inherent in this type of novel. I have concluded that since real life itself often presents such terrible quandaries, good literature should imitate reality.

In addition, I would like to express my personal thanks to all of our men and women in uniform and in public service as well. Without the tireless support of our military, police and emergency management personnel, this could not be a free country, great and proud in its traditions. In the course of writing this novel, I realized that someone would have to be the bad guy. As members of the public service sectors, these professionals would be on the front line of any biological disaster, and by the very nature of their dedication to the cause of liberty, would be the first to become infected. As a former Air Force officer, I have only the greatest admiration and humble praise for our men and women who serve to protect us from the evils of the world. While any group will have a few bad apples, these organizations truly represent the thin blue line between safety and danger, oppression and freedom. I apologize if any writings herein offend any of our brave heroes who stand in the gap to defend us all from evil. You all have my eternal gratitude for allowing me the freedom to live, worship, speak and write as I have been blessed to do. Thank you for your sacrifices for the cause of liberty. I stand forever in your debt. God bless you all.

I would like to thank the tireless defenders of liberty and freedom here in Tennessee, without whom I would not have had the freedom to write this very book: the Tennessee National Guard-278th Armored Cavalry, the Police Forces of Gallatin, Hendersonville, Goodlettsville, Nashville, the Sumner County Emergency Management Agency, and all medical, fire and emergency agencies of our beautiful state. I would like to thank the Armed Forces of our great nation, and specifically the 5th Special Forces Group, 82nd Airborne, and the USAF. Thanks to the Sumner County Amateur Radio Association and ARES as well. Thanks to the personnel and staff of Sumner Medical Group, for enduring endless hours of dedicated effort making the lives of our patients better. I could not work without you all. You are truly a godsend to me, and I speak for all of the partners when I say that we are a better community because of your effort. Thanks to my partners and friends for everything that you do to make our community bright.

Thanks to my family for enduring late nights of endless timelines, research, edits and revisions. Thanks to my wife, Robbin: I could not live without your love! The cover photography and art is amazing. To my daughter, you have the best ideas; I am amazed everyday with your brilliance! To my mother, Judy Dill, thanks Mom! You are the living embodiment of the The Bard! I could not have survived this without your help. Thanks to my patients, who are the greatest subject matter experts in the world: your advice has led to this book.

To Deane Blake and his incredible family, where do I start? Without your inspiration, this book would never have been created. Your steadfast friendship, advice, encouragement and trust have led to this final product. It was born on that fateful day in Spring and I am forever grateful. I cannot wait to read your upcoming book! Your honor and integrity shine as a light for the rest of us to follow. To all of my friends whose names are withheld to protect the innocent (or not-so-innocent!), I am also forever in your debt! Any inaccuracies or errors are, of course, my own.

Most of all, I wish to thank my Lord and Savior, Jesus Christ The Righteous. Without Your love, I would have fallen long ago. You preserve me and keep me. You make me new. I am forever unto the end of time in Your debt. You hold me in the palm of Your hand. I shall always sing praises to Your Holy name, for otherwise the rocks would cry out!

    Andrew B. Dill, M.D.

Character list, in family or organizational order (parents first, relationships and professions where applicable):

Angus Gunn — Family Physician, former USAF
Gwenn Gunn — Home-maker, Angus' wife
  kids:
    Katherine "Kate" Gunn — Tessa Washington's best friend
    Joshua Gunn

Margaret Gunn — Retired Teacher, Angus' mother

Matt Mackenzie — Family Physician, former US Navy
Beth Mackenzie — Pediatrician, Matt's wife
  kids:
    Madison Mackenzie, Kimberly Mackenzie, Sean Mackenzie

Carlos Corpuz — Pulmonologist, from The Philippines
Cecelia Corpuz — Home-maker Carlos' wife
  kids:
    Rafael Corpuz, Roberto Corpuz

John Calvin — Undertaker, former USAF
Denise Calvin — Executive Banker, John's wife
  kids:
    Hailey Calvin, Luke Calvin, Stacy Calvin

Darryl Washington	Finance Manager, former USAF
Simone Washington	Home-maker, Darryl's wife
kids:	
Susane Washington	disabled
Tessa Washington	Kate Gunn's best friend
Jesse Washington	Darryl's middle child, Martial Arts Instructor
Samantha Washington	Home-maker, Jesse's wife
baby:	
Julia Washington	
Cleo Johnson	Jesse's best friend
Scott Rees	Park Ranger
Stephanie Rees	Teacher, Scott's wife
daughter:	
Erin Rees	
Justin Clearwater	Gallatin Police Officer, EMT, ER Tech
Francesca Clearwater Schultz	Nurse, Justin's sister
Lucien Tulley	Electrophysiology Technician, owner of Tulley Farm
Abigail Tulley	Lucien's wife
kids:	
Samuel "Sam" Tulley, Evi Tulley, Donovan Tulley, Sean Tulley	

Grace Winifred, Josh Winifred (siblings)

Doug McKnight   Computer engineer
Anastasia McKnight   Teacher, Doug's wife
  kids:
    Eliza McKnight, Chet McKnight, Stella McKnight

Samuel "Sam" Wallace   Nurse, owner of cattle ranch
Carolyn Wallace   Home-maker, Sam's wife
  adult kids:
    Trey Wallace   Gun salesman, former USAF
    Jessica Wallace   Secretary, ex-wife of Jim Summers

Jim Summers   Recovering alcoholic, Construction Worker, ex-husband of Jessica Wallace
  Kids:
    Sarah and Becky

Janet "Pirelli" Bledsoe   Medical Technician for Dr. Gunn
Thomas Bledsoe   Construction Worker, Pirelli's husband
  kids:
    Sophie Bledsoe, James Bledsoe

Chloe Pearl   Nurse for Dr. Gunn
  grandkids:
    Mattie Smith, Rebecca Smith

Edward "Ed" Douglass — Probation Officer
Issac Ferguson Davis — Accountant, student of the gun
   Issac's team:
      Jack Sutherland — Corporate Lawyer
      Harold "Judge" Simpson — County Judge
      Clay Masterson — A.C. Repairman
      Jonathan Burke — Truck Driver
      Eli Smith — History Professor
      Nathan Ford — Vanderbilt EMT
      Luke Dodson — Factory Machinist, former US Army Sniper

Trey Nellis — Gallatin Mechanic
Charlie Blake — General Surgeon
Mitchell O'Shaughnessy — Podiatrist

This is the plague with which the Lord will strike all the nations that fought against Jerusalem: Their flesh will rot while they are still standing on their feet, their eyes will rot in their sockets, and their tongues will rot in their mouths. On that day people will be stricken by the Lord with great panic. They will seize each other by the hand and attack one another.
Zechariah 14:12-13 NIV

Be sober, be vigilant; because your adversary the devil walks about like a roaring lion, seeking whom he may devour.
1 Peter 5:8 NKJV

PROLOGUE

Dawn broke over the ruined facade of the once famous eatery, its glass shattered in mute testimony to the violent upheavals of the very recent past. Reflections of a bright age, promise within its grasp, now darkened by the cloud of madness that had descended upon the earth. In the shadows, shattered glass reflected the darkness like the broken dreams of a naive and weak world, self-absorbed in its own presumed superiority. The crushing weight of the death of that world, ancient in its wonder, weighed heavily upon the man, like a fading dream upon his awakening to the harsh, brutal reality that all of this could have been prevented. Or at least planned for.

Angus cursed under his breath, "Where the hell is Justin?" He waited, crouched under the cover of the establishment's tables, his face blackened with the soot of the fires burning in the mall's hallways. His breath came slowly and evenly, one of the positive effects of his daily yoga. Amazing that he was still able to do ten minutes a day, even now. Almost every day. His bad back was to blame, an old injury on labor and delivery in residency training, a dozen or so years ago.

His brief military career had prepared him for the possibility that things could go wrong, sometimes really, really wrong. After family practice residency, he had volunteered for the Air Force and he had started his training at the rank of Captain. It seemed the military counted being yelled at by surgeons and working 110 hours per week in medical school as time served.

He had been a Major in the USAF and family physician for his base in California and his extra duties had included a two and a half year stint as the Base's Clinical Response Team Chief, a job he had both loved and hated. He always laughed at the duty requirements listed in the personnel manual: "To maintain unit mission readiness during a disaster contingency." Ha! To translate into plain English, his job was to keep his friends in his unit alive during an end of the world event. He and his base trained for wildfires, floods, and other natural disasters found in the local Northern California region. But they also trained for EMP events, terrorist bombings, nuclear catastrophes and biological contagion. And that last type of event was the thing that had kept him up at night for the two and a half year period that he held the job.

He could remember, with surprise, the first time he received a Department of Defense, or DOD email detailing the most recent figures for the possible spread patterns for worldwide emerging diseases. None of the data that he reviewed that day had ever been, or ever would be on the news. He would never be able to tell anyone any of the details of those reports. And none of it was conducive to restful sleep. Plagues started for a number of reasons. The reports never explained whether the diseases being tracked were bioweapons intentionally released for small scale testing, accidental lab releases or naturally occurring germs either transitioning from animal species to our own or evolving from prior infectious diseases already present in humans.

He would frequently wake up in a cold sweat, his wife Gwenn concerned over his worry. He told her what he could, what he was allowed to tell. Work was stressful, and she figured out enough to know that the world was a much more dangerous place than they had ever dreamed of in the beautiful East Tennessee town where their marriage had blossomed.

They had met at a mall clothier, working in the men's shoe department. He had brushed the hair from her forehead and won her heart. They had loved each other truly from the first day they met. They were together before he started medical school and they had their first child and adopted their second child and settled in the Nashville area after his military minimum service obligation was completed. They had settled in a small city just north of Nashville, and had been at peace with the world for several years before the madness had started. He no longer got the terrifying DOD Weekly Report. He no longer spent his days and nights rewriting Base Standard Operating Procedures for disaster contingencies. No longer did his thoughts turn to gas masks, level C suits, decontamination systems and antibiotic caches. He was a civilian. He slept well at night, the dreams of terror and fear forever behind him. Or so he thought.

A slobbering wail echoed through the darkened interior of the kitchen, sending chills of near panic through Angus. "Damn it, they're here!" he muttered under his breath again. A dark figure moved slowly towards the commotion at the front of the restaurant. Angus silently thanked God for His blessings. It appeared that the creature had not seen him yet.

She must have been beautiful at one time, before the infection had stripped the sanity from her mind and left a shell of raw edged emotion and psychosis. Her clothes were torn but mostly intact, the remains of a grisly feast still splashed across the dingy white of her designer blouse. Her high heeled shoes were still attached to her ankles and feet by the straps, the heels long since broken off.

They hated the light, but were not hurt by it. Most certainly weren't intelligent in the traditional sense, but could still think clearly enough to plan and coordinate efforts with more of their kind: to attack, gather food together, work for long term goals. The psychosis imparted by the plague hit each of the infected differently. You couldn't tell how much of their problem solving skill remained.

Suddenly, rocket fire shrieked across the parking lot; an overturned produce cart burst into flames. The heat of the explosion spread across Angus' neck, the heat of fear mixing with explosive impulse, causing sweat to bead on his brow. His plate armor carrier, and ACH helmet added to the sweltering conditions typical for a Nashville late summer. He keyed the mike of his 2 meter Ham radio handitalkie twice, a signal that could be heard by his team without giving away his position. The Yaesu radio complied, sending a double static break across the 144mhz band. Angus prayed again, this time asking that his distress signal be heard.

Concussions of small arms fire slapping through steel doors of cars and the rat tat tat of semiautomatic rifle fire rang through the air. Angus' radio crackled three times. His signal had been heard. He looked over the table that he was hiding beneath and saw three men in mixed civilian clothing firing AKs at a group of the infected walking out of the restaurant kitchen. The infected had no weapons save some kitchen knives and wooden rods, possibly banisters from the restaurant decor. One of the infected howled and charged headlong into the fire, 7.62x39 caliber rounds impacting its torso with pops of red spray. It continued running until it reached the line of men and stabbed the first directly in the chest. The man tried to scream but could not draw breath, the knife wedged into his sternum with incredible force.

His companion pointed his AK at the creature's head and fired, sending it slumping over, its brainpan rupturing like a watermelon dropped from a window. The third man screamed as several of the infected rushed forward, his shots impacting some, missing others. One of the infected was hit in the neck, grabbed the bleeding artery and fell sideways, its lifeblood emptying onto the pavement. Several more rocked back as the long barrelled RPK emptied its drum magazine in the group. More infected dropped as the man finished firing the RPK and threw it down, pulling what looked like a Mossberg 590 12 gauge shotgun from a backpack rifle sheath. The man cycled a round into the chamber just as one of the infected, a small Asian woman, lunged toward him, fingernails reaching out like claws. The buckshot round blew a tennis ball sized hole through the creature's upper chest, and it gasped a gurgling breath and fell forward onto the pavement. Fingernails grasped at the asphalt, then stopped. Several more men appeared, firing rifles and shotguns into the restaurant.

Angus ducked, just as gunfire zipped over his head. He held his position and heard the sound of more gunfire and screaming. Barked commands were heard and then silence, the racking of slides and the sounds of rifle magazines being exchanged. He could feel movement to his left, and he froze in the shadows. He heard trucks rumble and debris crunch as large tires rolled through the parking lot. Doors opened and shut, engines roaring to speed and smashing sounds that must be cars pushed to the sides as the trucks rumbled away.

The sounds receded into the distance and his ear mike chirped to life. "Echo 2, Foxtrot 1, Echo 2, Foxtrot 1."

Angus keyed his mike, "Roger Foxtrot 1, how copy?"

"Five by five. Await extraction, ETA three minutes."

"Roger wilco," Angus spoke through the mike as he glanced at his watch, marking the time mentally. Running footsteps sounded through the parking lot two minutes later and Angus peered over the table and saw Justin and John running at a trot, AR-15 rifles held muzzle down to the left side, at the low ready position, both scanning side to side as they ran. Angus yelled, "Snake, snake!"

"Palmetto!" was the extraction team leader's reply, as the footsteps approached. Angus slowly stood up, saw John glance his way, and key his mike, "Foxtrot 2, we have heavy, over."

"Roger that, Foxtrot 1, standby for exfil," they all heard over their ear buds.

Justin looked over as John took a knee facing the direction that they had come from. "Sorry man, we saw those guys come in and had to wait. We didn't know if they were cannibals or not, so we sat tight."

"You did the right thing, man. Don't worry about it, I'm good." Angus answered, trotting over to where John was kneeling. "Scared the hell out of me though! Thought you were goners. Glad you are O.K."

A large military truck appeared, rumbling through the parking lot, following the path cleared by the others. The Deuce and a Half maneuvered up and stopped just long enough for the three men to climb into the truck, and then rumbled down the street, engine revving up on the used motor oil filling its antiquated fuel tank. The sun continued its slow climb across the Middle Tennessee sky. The cicada chirping receded into the distance, a wild symphony for a dying culture, its bones bleaching in the sun, like some giant sea creature washed onto the barren shoals of an uncertain future.

Finally, brethren, whatever things are true, whatever things are noble, whatever things are just, whatever things are pure, whatever things are lovely, whatever things are of good report, if there is any virtue and if there is anything praiseworthy—meditate on these things.
—Philippians 4:8 NKJV

CHAPTER 1

Goodlettsville, TN
10 miles North of Nashville
Gunn House
June 4
8:37a.m.

"Katherine Gunn, where are you going?" Gwenn yelled, exasperated, from the top of the stairs. Gwenn Gunn sometimes started her day with a calm walk or a vigorous Zumba class, a nice stress relieving start to the morning. Today was not one of those days. Her home-schooled daughter, Katherine, was late to her martial arts training class, and had wandered off somewhere, probably investigating the life cycle of the rare and elusive South American Spotted Toad, or some new veterinary topic of interest. She was a tall girl, about 5'10" and had pale Celtic skin, long curly light brown hair and deep brown eyes. She was strong, stubborn and brilliant, shy, but very sweet, once you entered her inner circle. She was very beautiful, but so far had little interest in boys, as her path to veterinary school took precedence over all else, apparently including getting ready on time.

"In here, Mom!" she responded, assuming, as all teenagers do, that Mom would know automatically where "here" was located. Katherine, or Kate as she was called, ran from her laptop terminal to the stairwell. "Sorry, I was looking something up." She had in fact been researching the rare and elusive Ivory Billed Woodpecker. Debate raged on whether it was really extinct or not, and Kate loved a mystery, especially one related to biology.

"You're late!" Gwenn called

"Sorry, forgot the time!" Kate called. She was in fact already dressed for her mixed martial arts class, but the need to know more information about the animal in question had overridden her sense of time. "I'm leaving now!" she yelled, grabbing her purse and keys and trotting down the stairs into the garage to her early model Honda Pilot, a hand me down car from her mom. She punched the unlock button on the key fob, deactivated the home security system and enabled the remote garage door opener. Kate walked to the back hatch and tossed her regular clothes and makeup bag in the back, pushing the bug home bag to the side, to make room.

Every vehicle in the Gunn household had bug home bags, or B.H.B.s in the trunks. The idea was to carry enough gear to get you home, if a disaster occurred while you happened to be away from your house. "Bugging home" was different than "bugging out," in which one would evacuate his or her home in the event of an emergency, such as a fire, natural disaster, industrial accidental, riot or other upheaval. Bug out bags in the Gunn household were stored in the closet, near the door, and were much larger. They contained ten days of food, camping gear, weapons, tools, radios, and everything else that could be made to weigh less than 35 pounds and keep you alive and relatively comfortable if, for example, you had to leave your house after awakening naked at 2AM with the neighborhood on fire. There were also augmentational packs in the garage, basically Rubbermaid bins with even more food, electronics, gear, ammunition, and supplies to last an additional two weeks or more away from the house. Kate's BHB was a medium pack, weighing about twenty pounds, containing the minimum camping gear for an ultralight outing of three days, the time it would take her walking to get home from the furthest normal daily excursion. Her father, Angus, and her mother, Gwenn, had proportionally larger packs, given their respective ages and ability to legally carry firearms. Her younger brother, Joshua, had a pack of only ten pounds and an add-on pouch that could be attached to either of the adult's backpacks to hold the remaining nine extra pounds of his gear.

Kate punched the garage door opener and started the engine, flicking on the rear view camera. Her father had installed it when baby Joshua had been adopted, as fear of running over children had been forefront in their minds after a famous singer's child was accidentally killed by the family SUV. She backed out, heading to the dojo, loud Christian rock music playing, setting the mood for the day.

At 5'6", Gwenn was a beautiful, blonde haired, blue eyed forty one-year-old whose ancestry could be traced to England and primarily Norway. When the family went to EPCOT, she was stunned to find that all of the girls in the Norway exhibit looked like her siblings. She certainly had the look of a Viking maiden. Gwenn began her day homeschooling Joshua, her eight-year-old son. Kate was also home schooled and basically set her own schedule, as most of her high school topics were self-paced. Joshua was adopted from Taipei in Taiwan when he was an infant, the child of tribal Taiwanese parents who refused to abort him but were unable to feed another mouth in the family. Gwenn normally started him on his third grade routine after breakfast and then did chores in the afternoon since homeschooled children typically required less time in the classroom. Evenings and weekends were spent with her husband Angus and the family together, relaxing in the evenings, church every Sunday, Saturday for chores and activities with the family.

Gwenn had always been a practical woman. As a teenager she had witnessed hurricanes in the coastal South and had forever changed her views of society. She had seen firsthand the devastation that a natural disaster could bring, and she had seen on TV what happened in big cities when those dependent on the state for their well-being were cut off from the teat of welfare. The resulting riots, looting and terror pushed her to the belief that she must be able to protect herself no matter what the cost, and she must be able to protect her family. Her husband, Angus, had encouraged her to take self-defense classes and she had earned a Tennessee handgun carry permit. She rarely carried on her person, but did at least carry in her car. She had trained in a limited fashion with rifles, had a real fear of shotguns, and was a fairly good pistol shooter.

She had encouraged Katherine to practice archery with her father, as Kate was not yet old enough to carry a handgun. Kate had become an outstanding archer, since starting training at age eight and now could hit a tennis ball at thirty yards, with no bow sight. She was expert at compound, recurve and longbow respectively. She also had begun learning the AR-15 platform with her father and family friends and was progressing nicely. Gwenn had less interest with the rifles, but was passable at them. Little Joshua was already able to hit an orange at ten yards with his kid's bow. He had a Diamond Nuclear Ice, a kid's bow capable of launching a broad-head tipped arrow at speeds over 200 feet per second at the higher draw weights and half that at the lower weights. This enabled him to easily hunt small game now and he would be able to progress up the draw weights, as he grew. Today, math and spelling were the tactical subjects of the day for little Joshua.

Late that evening around, 8p.m., Angus returned from a late partners' meeting. He called before opening the garage door, in order to avoid setting off the zero delay alarm system always engaged at the house. His Honda Ridgeline was an effective truck and commuter vehicle combined. It was equipped with a truck bed and trunk underneath the bed. This allowed Angus to carry a robust bug home bag and survival equipment. He worked at his office about fifteen miles away and normally got home at six but today was a late meeting. Gwen deactivated the alarm after his call. The garage door opened and Angus pulled in, and he closed the door behind him. She opened the door into the garage and heard him call:

"Hey, it's me. Send Kate down, I've got a new machete to show her," Angus said.

"O.K." said Gwenn and then to Kate, "Come here, sweetie, Daddy's got a new toy he wants to brag on, I think. He's in the garage."

The door shut and then reopened and Kate came down the stairs. "Hi Daddy; missed you!" Kate said, hugging her daddy tightly.

"Hey squirt, love you" said Angus. "I got a new machete just like one that Matt got, it's called a parang. Look at it here; it's curved to keep it from hanging in the cut. Pretty neat, eh?"

Kate took the machete and removed it from the sheath, "It's got that goofball TV guy's name on it. But it has a good balance" she said. "Wonder how it would cut once you put an appleseed edge on it?"

A sword or machete could only cut as well as the edge that the tool was crafted with. A typical modern western cutting tool had either a chisel edge which ran straight from the cutting surface back perfectly flat, or a knife edge, which had a secondary steeper edge cut on the tip. Both of these worked well for shaving wood, or utility work, such as rope cutting or butchering and skinning. However, they would bind in the cut if attempting to say, lop off a tree limb or an opponent's limb. This is precisely why ancient samurai swords and, even medieval swords from the Dark Ages had rolled convex edges. These were not the paper-thin edges that could cut hair; rather, they were designed to allow the blade to continually push the cut material outward in a rolling fashion, away from the cut line itself. This is what allowed katanas and other swords made with this edge shape to literally slice directly through limbs and torsos with such little effort. Tatami mats were used in modern times to simulate this, enabling the practitioners to make quite a dramatic presentation of the blade's ability.

In order to achieve an appleseed edge, the tool would have to be sharpened on a concave surface, such as a rare Japanese water stone ground with use for just such a purpose, or if one lacked the money, a simple sandpaper piece on a sponge that gave way under the pressure of use to achieve this edge. A belt sander was what Angus used, with extra slack in the belt to achieve the same result. So long as the sharpener was patient and did not let the metal heat up and lose temper, he could achieve the desired result in an afternoon, rather than days on a stone.

"You know, sweetie, I was just asking myself the same question," Angus said as he locked the truck and headed upstairs to dinner. He entered the kitchen with Kate, having left the parang in the garage on the workbench. Gwen did not like weapons on her kitchen table.

"Did you have a good day?" Gwenn asked, setting out dinner plates.

"Yes, sorry the meeting was so long. Love you. Thanks for dinner." he said, hugging his wife and eying the delicious-appearing pasta carbonara and salad waiting on the counter.

"Love you too, sweetie, no problem. We were late at the store anyway. Lots of people buying stuff. Saw this thing on the news about the pole shifting or something. Said everything would be OK, but seemed like a lot of people were buying stuff. Probably overreacting," Gwen said.

Gwen had initially tolerated the extra food stores that Angus had brought home and later, after living in California and seeing the New Orleans riots, embraced the idea of long term food storage. They currently had about nine months of dry canned food mostly at home, but about two months at two storage units as well out of town, in case of disaster. Gwenn's close friend had been the Mormon wife of one of Angus' best friends in the Air Force when they had lived in California. The Mormons had food storage down to a science and their help had been invaluable.

At forty, Angus was a tall 6'2" brown haired, deep brown eyed, pale-skinned man who was trim after months working off the usual American male's spare tire. He had previously really let himself go after the Air Force and gotten up to 226 pounds. His current 198 pounds was partly the result of his concern for fitness as part of an overall survival strategy. He was always concerned that if a disaster occurred, he would not be fit enough to cope with the physical requirements that would be suddenly placed upon him.

He was of medium strength, not particularly fast, had moderately poor hearing in his left ear due to childhood ear infections, and had vertigo related to head movement for the same reason. But he knew a fair bit of Muai Tai, knife and sword fighting from his time studying the medieval period arts, and he was an exceptional rifle and pistol shot. He regularly could hit, under time stress, eight-inch plates at 25 yards with any pistol he owned, including his pocket 380, a feat that all of his friends could do now, thanks to the local dermatologist friend who showed them all that it was possible.

They still laughed about the day that they saw the skin doctor hitting the plates with his tiny pistol. They asked him if he had ever read gun magazines, as the authors claimed such a shot could not be done with the diminutive pieces. The man just said "no" and kept hitting the target with his pocket 380. Angus took notice and began practicing what amounted to a head shot at 25 yards with everything he owned. It only seemed practical.

Angus enjoyed accurate rifles. His DPMS Mini-SASS, a 5.56mm AR-15 clone with a heavy barrel and match trigger could group five shots in a dime at 100 yards. This was easy when he had a long range scope mounted. Right now, he had the gun set up as a long range unit, with a collapsible Ergo F-93 stock and Super Sniper 10x42mm tactical Mildot reticle. This configuration enabled the gun to serve the role of a designated marksman rifle, or DMR. Though the gun was a heavy twelve pounds with scope, the barrel contour allowed it to fire many times before overheating, a feature that allowed it to engage many targets at once if needed.

His wife's Doublestar M4 carbine had a Midwest Industries extended length lightweight picatinny rail that allowed an inverted pistol light to be placed above and in line with the bore axis, in front of the front iron sight. It was set up with a Trijicon Tripower optic that displayed a red chevron over the target and could use batteries, ambient light or tritium to illuminate the sight. Angus also had a Doublestar 20" barreled AR-15 with collapsible butt stock similar to those used by the Canadian army. He liked the adjustable length of pull with longer barrel. He could use both of his ARs well while wearing body armor. This gun had a Trijicon Advanced Combat Optical Gunsight TA-33GH, a bombproof military grade optic with a tritium and ambient light illuminated green inverted horseshoe reticle. The illuminated scope allowed for very rapid target engagement out to about 500 yards, and improved close range target acquisition, but Angus' eyes could not make out targets with the 3-power scope beyond about 400 yards, and his DPMS had a better long range scope.

He also had a Savage .308 bolt action, a model 10-FCP-SR, with a ten round detachable box magazine, a brown digicam stock, bipod and TPS rings with an unusual scope choice: an SWFA Super Sniper 16x42 mm scope with Mildot reticle. This scope was a new production copy of an older mid 80's US Navy spec design, sold in Texas. It was a very durable and robust unit, without the variable power found in more recent designs. The optical clarity and specifications rivaled scopes costing three to four times as much, and the precision of the turret adjustments exceeded all comparably priced models. This was the reason Angus had chosen the unit. He needed quality and durability and simply could not afford a more expensive scope due to the large number of other items he felt that he needed for his preparedness supplies. Angus could also use this gun to shoot sub-half-inch five shot groups at 100 yards, and with the 16 power scope, the gun had been used by others to hit man sized targets to 1000 yards, though Angus had never taken it farther than 600 yards, due to the difficulty of finding a range long enough to shoot that distance.

"Stay. Good doggies," Angus said to his three large seventy-pound Golden Retrievers, all waiting expectantly on the rug, the youngest, Genevieve, howling in pleasure. "That's enough Vi-vi. I love you too," he said to the exuberant affection hound.

The oldest was Sarah, at thirteen, still vibrant due to good feeding, vet care and obviously the Lord's blessing. She had been adopted from a local pound with her brother Samson, when they were both ten years old. He had passed away at age eleven, but not before forever blessing the Gunn family with love and affection. He had made an indelible mark on the children, who knew now that he lived in heaven with the Lord Jesus now. Little Joshua had placed the first shovelful of dirt on the backyard grave that Angus had dug on the day he had passed.

Angus shed his grief on that day in tears and sweat. He left work in the middle of a clinic day to perform his duty as a father, digging the four foot deep hole by hand, each shovelful of earth cut from the land, a gracious thanksgiving of anguish, despair and thankfulness at the gift of Samson's life with them. Katherine had given a homily so sweet and touching that the entire family wept at his graveside. For the Gunns, as had always been their clan's way, family bonds ran deep, and pets were no less a part of the whole.

Penelope was next at eleven, a little fat, but vigorous as well. She had been with them since eight weeks of age and was fully bonded to the family. Angus always joked that Penelope would follow you into a fire, she was so faithful. The youngest was Genevieve, at eight, strong, playful and the most powerful of the group. She had been adopted at age six from a puppy mill where she had been bred since six months of age, abused and was living literally in a barn. So, the exuberance could be excused. She, of all the dogs, had a zest for life that could not be diminished.

Angus ran upstairs and changed clothes into shorts and a T-shirt for dinner. They lived in a modest suburban house, brick, in a neighborhood of houses that were quite similar. They were just outside of town, though still technically in the city limits. People in their town were honest, uncomplicated folk, mostly there due to the good weather, four real seasons, ample job opportunities, and pretty countryside. They were close to downtown Nashville and also close to the country as well. One could truly have his cake and eat it too in the Nashville area. This was by far the best place Angus had ever lived. Certainly, there were hot summers and fairly cold winters by Southern standards, but the job was so good and the people so friendly, that this was the ideal place for the Gunns to raise a family.

The community was tightly-knit and held together, even in disasters. When a tornado hit the area years ago, there was no looting, no rioting. Society here was civil. But things had changed some since that time. There were more people from out of the area moving in, as the Gunns had years ago. It would be hard to tell how the area might react now to another disaster.

Angus came to dinner and sat down. Kate led the prayer, as she always did, "Dear Lord, bless us on this heavenly day, forgive us our sins, and bless this food to the nourishment of our bodies, and us to thy further service. In Jesus' name, Amen."

Angus thought about what Gwenn had said about the polar shift, "You know, honey, that polar shift thing has happened many times in the past. It's called a geomagnetic reversal and it has been documented in the ocean bedrock, I think. Nobody knows what will happen, but the prevailing theory is that there will be a period of unpredictable magnetic behavior with five or six poles around the world at once. Would really wreak havoc on compasses."

"Daddy, wouldn't that throw off the Van Allen belt?" Kate asked.

"Hmmm. Let me think about that." Angus answered.

Gwen listened and noted, "I think you're right sweetie, it could affect that as the belts are there due to the polar magnetic fields. But how would that matter?"

Kate answered, "Well, I was reading on the Van Allen belt and it is what keeps solar wind off of us, mostly. The aurora borealis is an example of the energy getting through. That's high energy discharge plasma, or something caused by the solar wind hitting the upper atmosphere." Angus stopped eating.

"What's wrong sweetie?" Gwen asked.

"Sorry, I just remembered something I read once, probably nothing." Angus said, remembering a briefing in the USAF about high energy discharges and the upper atmosphere related to EMP, or electromagnetic pulse events. EMP events would occur when nuclear bombs were detonated, and if done at a high enough altitude, namely in space, they could send a wave of energy across a large area. This could wipe out a power grid over a continent if the power grid were unshielded. The US power grid was unshielded. Of course, no one knew how long the effect would be, second, minutes, months, years when the poles would be in a state of flux, or if they just popped over instantly, north changing to south. He did not want to worry his family needlessly. He needed to get more information. The Gunns finished their meal, watched their favorite family program and went to bed, Angus reassuring Gwen that he would look into it that week.

The time to repair a roof is when the sun is shining.
—John F. Kennedy, State of The Union Address, January 11, 1962

CHAPTER 2

Gallatin, TN
15 miles North of Nashville
Southern Family Medical Group
June 6
10:00a.m.

Matt Mackenzie walked into his office laughing a disgusted chortle, throwing papers onto his desk. Angus poked his head in, hearing the noise.

"What's wrong dude?" he asked Matt.

Matt Mackenzie was a strong man, of medium build, six feet even and 210 pounds of well-muscled ex-Navy doctor. He had been in the US Navy for eight years and had seen combat and the casualties of combat while in Iraq, at a small FOB, or Forward Operating Base, and hospital in-country. He was a Family Physician, trained at an excellent Navy residency. He had provided medical support for the US Marines fighting the war in Iraq. His experiences had marked him deeply. He used a keen, quick wit and ability to jest to cover the psychological trauma that he had both witnessed and experienced while in the service. One of his duties had been to perform triage assessments on the wounded when they arrived at the hospital by helicopter or Humvee. They would often arrive screaming in agony and he had to determine on the spot if they were able to be saved, right there on the landing pad.

Delayed casualties were the walking wounded: they could wait. Immediate were those badly wounded, but not beyond hope. They got immediate care, as the name suggested. Minimal could have a bandage slapped on and see the doc the next day even, or as time permitted. Expectant were those so severely wounded, that no amount of care, no matter how rapidly given could have any hope of saving them. Obviously, this depended on the facilities present in the hospital or clinic in which the unit was located at the time. Many times, soldiers and civilians arrived in this condition, burned so badly that they had no pain, or bodies so mangled by explosions that they were almost unrecognizable. Sometimes, Matt had to ID soldiers from bags of body parts, sometimes parts as small as handfuls gathered faithfully together in a sack for the medical officer to inspect.

While Angus knew much of the theoretical horrors of potential war and disease, in fact more than the others due to his job in Base medical preparedness, he had never stood on a helipad, bullets streaking past as he unloaded men's bodies, still alive despite full thickness burns that cooked the eyeballs like hard boiled eggs, while reassuring them, "It's OK man." He never had been shot at, or had RPGs fired at his hospital. Angus had held arteries closed with his fingers, trying to keep patients from bleeding to death and amputated the legs from screaming patients during trauma work in medical school. He had thanked God for the lives of his patients as he held their hands during their gentle passing, and he had screamed at God while pounding on the chests of patients taken too soon. But his own life had never been threatened during those events. In stark contrast, the sheer volume of injury, death and despair that Matt had seen was almost overwhelming. Angus was always impressed with the way Matt coped with what he had witnessed, as his own career in the Air Force had been performed in the States in safe, sterile American hospitals.

Matt lived in Hendersonville, in between Gallatin and Goodlettsville, in an upscale neighborhood that backed up on private farmland. His brick three story house was on a hill, had a view of the area, and was well shaded and screened by large oak trees. This allowed Matt to see what was going on in the neighborhood without most people seeing his house. It was an ideal location to fall back to in a disaster. In fact, it was the first location that the group would consider relocating to if their own homes were overrun or unsafe to occupy. An entire network of houses was available to use, as any member of the group would open their house to any other. But the Mackenzie house was the most centrally located. Matt was loved by the entire group, as his humor and generosity were truly disarming.

Matt loved all things German, and all things historical, and prided himself on his knowledge of military history. He loved his M1As and considered his new Palmetto Arms AR-15 a neat little carbine, but no replacement for an accurized Sage-stocked M1A with a Leupold optic. The .308 and .45 seemed more appropriate to him than the smaller 9mm and 5.56mm that most of the rest of the group used. Matt had no formal martial arts training, but was a hell of a street fighter and tough as nails in the many bar fights his Navy career had seen. He, like the rest of the group, had amassed a large store of provisions, including months' worth of food, medicine, survival equipment and he was an excellent shot with all of his weapons. He favored his Parang, a Southeast Asian machete and his SOG Tactical Tomahawk for hand to hand combat. He could launch either at a tree trunk with astonishing speed and accuracy. Today, Matt was mad as hell at the latest governmental intrusion into his business affairs.

"Have you seen the latest 'adjustment' in the pay for a 99214?" Matt answered, referring to the recent pay cut that the government had announced to all physicians seeing government insured patients. Of course, that included most of the patients that all doctors saw, as most people now were receiving some sort of government issued or mandated plan. Even the private plans simply emulated the new numbers from Uncle Sam.

"Yeah," replied Angus.

"What in the hell are we going to do? Let half the staff go? We can't keep this up; it's not sustainable," Matt said.

"I don't know man, I don't know. We can talk to them at the meeting and see if there is any maneuvering we can do, but that's really a problem. Hell, a lot of us voted the bastards in that did this to us. Even the quote unquote conservatives sold us out. I think they want third world care, I really do. I can't explain it, is it easier to control unhealthy people? Hell. Sorry, I shouldn't say that," Angus said. "Also, the system went down again. Tech can't figure it out. I couldn't use my tablet yesterday, Wi-Fi wouldn't work. "

Matt motioned for Angus to push the office door closed. You never really knew what folks would talk about in a small office, so

Angus promptly shut the door quietly. "This damned polar inversion crap is to blame. The EM fields keep getting F'd up every time the pole slides over. My cousin was camping in the Rockies and kept getting lost last week. His GPS was useless and the compass was actually moving in front of his eyes while he was standing still."

Angus answered, "Yeah, the news keeps saying not to worry, it's all O.K. But you and I know that's bunk. Hell, that's what they taught me to say when I was in, if I ever had to speak officially. Well, as long as that's all that happens, we should be fine on that end."

"What do you mean, 'as long as'?"

"Well, as long as the sun stays the same."

"What the hell does that mean? The sun is the sa... shit. You're talking about the sunspot question. Oh, that's not going to happen, the chances are slim to none," Matt referred to known recent increases in solar output and solar flare events.

"Yeah, I know." Angus answered. "But what if it did increase, and what if? Well anyway, that's too many what-ifs."

Matt thought for a minute, sipping the Twinning's Earl Grey tea in his mug. "We should still talk to the group. Make some Faraday cages," he said as he sipped another mouthful of the brew.

"I know you are right, it's just that it seems so unreal. But we are prepped for social upheaval, already, I know adding this will be minor. I'll talk to Carlos at lunch," Angus said as he quietly opened the door. He walked back to his office ten feet way and began reviewing the next patient's chart as the nurses began the check-in process.

Later that day, Carlos Corpuz sat down in the doctors' lounge, next to Angus. They were all watching Fox News and hearing about the latest blackout and net interruptions from the "normal geomagnetic phase shifting." Nothing to be concerned about, NASA had coordinated with representatives from the Energy Department and had a working plan in place.

"Angus," Carlos said.

"Carlos," said Angus. Carlos Corpuz was definitely a man of few words. He had grown up in the Philippines and had immigrated to the United States for Medical School. He was a sub-specialist in Pulmonary Medicine and one of Angus' and Matt's business partners. He was one of the hardest working men that Angus knew and had come to Middle Tennessee to find a home for his family. He took care of most of the inpatient work and ran the ICU with another Pulmonologist. He had come from the mean streets of Manila and was an expert in Arnis, a Filipino stick fighting martial art. Basically, give him a pair of three foot long sticks and he could beat the hell out of anyone within 5 feet in every direction at once.

When he had come to the US, it had taken him 11 years to gain his citizenship, so corrupt and inefficient were the immigration laws. A doctor, a producer to society, a hard working honest Catholic could not get his citizenship for 11 years. It astounded Angus. When he first met Angus, Carlos warned him of the need to defend gun rights, because in the Philippines, even knife, bow, and sword ownership were illegal, hence the need to use sticks to defend oneself. Once he became a citizen, he joined the NRA, the local gun club and earned his handgun carry permit.

Carlos was a tough man, honest and very sweet to his family. At a compact 5'6" and about 140 pounds soaking wet, he was unassuming. You did not want to underestimate him, however. In addition to his excellent hand to hand combat skills, since coming to the US, he had amassed a small arsenal of AR-15s, pistols and crossbows. He was expert with all of them, and challenged Angus for his expertise at long range precision. He was the most physically fit of his friends, known informally as "the group."

The group had formed slowly over time as Carlos had met different like-minded people. The friends he had made were all concerned about surviving the possible tumultuous events that could occur in this uncertain time. The term "survivalist" in Tennessee basically described about half of the population. Most people knew how to hunt, fish, and home can, and had a volunteer spirit. This was why it was called the "Volunteer State" so many had volunteered for military service. Angus, Carlos and Matt comprised the core of a group who enjoyed target shooting, camping, expanding their skill and a desire to keep their families safe, no matter the cost of supplies, training and vigilance. The phrase, "the price of freedom is eternal vigilance" rang true to every member. They had missed vacations, avoided the latest toys common to Americans such as watercraft and sports cars, in lieu of extra ammunition, weapons, training, food stores, communications, medicine and survival equipment. Some spouses were more onboard than others, but all agreed that these were prudent precautions in an uncertain time.

"What do we do about dis?" Carlos said in his terse, thick Filipino accent.

"Which part, the pay cut or the thing on the T.V.?" asked Angus.

Carlos peered over his glasses, a habit he had that made him look even more serious, if such a thing were possible for the most intense man in the hospital. "The thing on de T.V. We need to talk to de group." Carlos said, the Filipino accent deeply rolling his Rs.

"That's the same thing Matt said. I agree. I am worried that the 'unrelated story' about the sunspots may have more to it. It smacks of cover-up, just like the ones we did about China's, well... stuff I did before."

Carlos did not speak, but looked intently at Angus. He peered deeply into Angus' eyes without blinking for several seconds, and then glanced at his lunch tray. A small salad, with sparse dressing, a tiny piece of grilled chicken and raw broccoli on a side plate comprised his meal. He was efficient in the extreme, never wasting, never over-indulging. This in large part was why he was the most fit member of the group. His meticulous attention to detail was extraordinary, really. Even for a doctor. Carlos' look spoke volumes and Angus had known him long enough to know not to say more. This information would go to the group tonight.

Angus finished his large meal of chicken-fried steak with gravy, salad with ranch dressing, green beans, small portion of mashed potatoes without gravy, and unsweetened Lipton tea in his own camel-back bottle, ice brewed the night before by leaving two tea bags in the bottle in the fridge before retiring for the night. Angus always carried drinks with him, water and unsweetened tea in this fashion. He was frequently chided about it, questions of "what's in the bottle" asked with big cockeyed grins coming from the older associates he held. Always good for a laugh, but Angus always knew he had something to drink with him. Angus would have to lift weights tonight after walking and running with Katherine to work this off, but the doctor's lounge meal was quite good. Angus hated to hear most other people complain about the free food; it really galled him. Angus thought to himself that the meal was free, why should they complain? Also, Angus was a connoisseur of good meals, be they MREs or from a fine restaurant, and by connoisseur, he meant that he liked the food, not complained about it. Some people would complain about anything. No matter how bad the situation was, Angus always enjoyed his meals, maybe too much. No point in letting life get you down, despite all of the fear and worry it had to offer.

Three things cannot be long hidden: the sun, the moon, and the truth.
—Buddha

CHAPTER 3

Mid-Eastern Asia
Foothills of the Sacred Mountain
What is now called Mount Bell, Nanjing province, China
Approximately the latitude of Southern Florida
1060 B.C.E.

Wei knew that stories of dragons living in this region were older than the cultural memory of his people. He thought of these things, especially the man-faced dragon that was supposed to occupy the sacred mountain, as he slowly climbed, step after step. He had come seeking wisdom for his village, located many days away. Perhaps Zhulong, the Torch Shade, could provide him with the answers they so desperately needed. Famine had touched the village. The heat of the wind and dryness of the fields had led many to starve, unable to grow the subsistence crops the village needed. Still, he was terrified at the prospect of actually seeing such a deity. It had been many years since he had supposedly been seen. The elders of the village were vague on when it had happened last.

Wei stared into the sky, a silent prayer upon his lips, when he suddenly let out a gasp, and fell to the ground, dropping the bundle in his arms. Tears of joy and fear streamed from the young man's eyes. Rivulets of red light swirled across the sky, twisting and twining their way over the top of the holy mountain. What exquisite fate! The dragon god Zhulong had appeared at last!

Oahu Island
Mid Pacific
Fishing canoe 1 mile from shore
1400 C.E.

The small outrigger canoe rocked slowly in the dim light, its cargo of squid kept fresh in clay vessels, as the fishermen stared into the night, the calm breeze blowing across their tanned skin. Hiapo glanced upwards as the moon shone across the water. The fishing had gone well, their cowrie shell lures worked well in the moonlight to emulate the small fish that the squid were hunting. The night's catch was almost complete. Soon he would be back at the hearth, back to Ailana, his wife, and his sons in their small thatched cottage. It had been a good season of harvest from these bountiful waters. The gods shone their blessings upon them tonight. As Hiapo stared with contentment into the beautiful moon, something strange caught his eye.

A red shape, twisting and turning into a roiling chain appeared in the sky, across the surface of the moon, its red tentacles of evil-appearing light sinking closer, closer. Hiapo's mind went numb.

"Oh great Wakea, have we broken the kapu?" He screamed to the sky father, asking if somehow they had broken the taboo of over fishing.

The others in the boat wailed in agony, several dived into the water in terrified fear. The sky trembled with red menace, tendrils of current ran through the upper troposphere. The aurora, thought by the modern mind only to reach upper latitudes, sent ripples of reddish light through the night sky, causing further shrieks of agony as the helpless villagers began dumping the clay jars of fresh squid into the water. The solar event that the modern world understood as simple electrical discharge into the upper atmosphere, rarely reached these lower latitudes, as the force required for such a southern excursion of their flow seemed almost unimaginable. In fact, it would not recur in this region again until 1859, the first time this was recorded by so called "modern man."

Undisclosed location
Suburb of Atlanta
Verlhk Biological
Security Station, Main entrance
June 6
12:06p.m.

The front gate camera monitor rotated to the left and Dirk Feierabend sat behind his monitoring station watching the car enter. Dirk sighed. He was bored out of his mind. Cindy, his girlfriend, wanted him to come for the weekend and he was stuck here on duty again. His boss, Mr. Feldman, had control of the duty roster and had stuck him with every weekend shift all month. He was sick of the crap, but this was the best job he could get after he washed out of the Coast Guard.

He had wanted to see the country and he had a good handle on boating, and his first month of training had gone well. It was his ticket out of his childhood home. He was from Michigan, the backwoods, a town no one had heard of and had spent weekends sailing with his grandfather as a kid. He figured that could help with the Coast Guard. Besides, he liked the idea of being in charge of other people. He did really well for the first month and then he was supposed to be at a training event early one Monday morning and had gotten drunk the night before and passed out in the barracks. He was summarily kicked out of training the next day when his C.O. found him sprawled out on his bunk. None of the other guys would go near him as he had threatened several of them after being picked on in the beginning. So they had left him there during the morning run.

After that, he left the Lakes region and came to Georgia, to Atlanta. He liked the city and thought he could make a fresh start. Private security for this firm had little requirements, less training and he had lied about his prior Coast Guard experience. He was quickly hired, because not many people wanted the job, but it surely beat flipping burgers. He was a strong, muscular man, dark hair, medium build and large biceps, as he constantly lifted weights. Somewhat of a bully, but very capable with the ladies, he had managed to easily attract a young red haired wildcat who liked long weekends away in cheap motels. Cindy was tall, in fact just taller than he was, and she wore heels usually, which intensified the effect.

Here, sitting in the Verlhk Biological security station, it was all he could think of, with her out on a Wednesday night. This particular Verlhk Biological laboratory was located in a small six story nondescript office building in an office park that looked just like every other office park around Atlanta: brick and stucco walls, functional glass and drywall interiors, boring beyond words. The geeks that came in and out of the place were just as boring as the location. At least he got to leave the security desk several times a day to make rounds. The company apparently worked on vaccines and was afraid that other companies would steal their product ideas. This was some kind of research and development lab. It was located in Atlanta because they had to work with the Centers for Disease Control, known as the C.D.C., on their vaccines, so Dirk had been told. They had all of the usual laboratory type equipment up on the fifth and sixth floors, and the rest was just office space, secretaries everywhere. At least some of them were hot. Some even winked at him as he made his rounds during the day shift. On night shifts, he was stuck with boring darkened office spaces: kinda creepy actually, with all the frankenware and Dr. Demento type equipment. He didn't know what any of it did, and he really didn't care. Just so long as he wrote in his log book and checked his gates, nobody cared. He got his paycheck and that was that.

What Dirk didn't realize was the real extent of the connections between the C.D.C. and Verlhk Biological. Verlhk was involved in more than just vaccines, and recently had been awarded a contract for an "in plain sight" Department of Defense advanced research initiative. This new initiative had taken the higher security risk research and decentralized it to hide it better from foreign countries prying eyes. The Chinese had apparently so fully infiltrated the larger companies typically involved in biological research, that the higher the security placed on a site, the more attention that the Chinese paid to it, and there had already been several serious security breaches at top secret sites across the nation. As with the atomic laboratory breaches of years past, the prospect of losing more secrets was obviously very concerning to top brass at the Pentagon.

This new "in plain sight" initiative followed models in Britain during and after World War II, and had so far successfully avoided information loss to the Chinese and other threatening nations. It did, however, increase the risk of inadvertent leaks involving the local populace. In the past, loss of laptops at the Veterans Affairs offices that contained thousands of social security numbers and other confidential information highlighted concern over these types of local information leaks. The decision had been made to keep all nonessential personnel at these facilities fully in the dark over the real aims of the research. Non essential personnel at Verlhk included security.

Dirk was unaware of the real reason that the sixth floor lab doors were always under electronic locks, controlled from a central station. All he knew was that his hot babe would find a new guy if he couldn't take her out Friday night. She would tell him she was having a "girl's night out." His hot babe, out with friends, ha! Yeah right. A girl like that wouldn't stay alone for long, and he was stuck here while his asshole boss spent "family time" with his "special needs" kid, some kind of retard obviously. This was bullshit. He had to figure something out for this weekend.

Solar Corona
Center of Solar System
Location of the Sun's "atmosphere"
June 6
20:31GMT

The corona surged with intense energy, coils of magnetic force lines twisting and turning in the agony of the solar surface. The giant sheets of plasma writhing in constant bending and looping, covering areas larger than the planet Earth itself. Suddenly, one band compressed and then spiraled outward, sending an enormous tendril of pure solar material coursing with unimaginable energy outward, both ends tethered to the photosphere, the visible surface of the sun. When viewed from Earth this would appear as a sunspot, a darkening of the surface of the kind first observed in 1859 by astronomer Richard Carrington. But no one on Earth would see it until eight minutes later, as this distance was so vast, that even light, the fastest thing in the universe, took that long to cover the distance.

The solar wind was full of many particles and waves of radiation: most traveled much more slowly than photons. The swirl of energy suddenly broke its tethers to the photosphere and began hurtling outward along the solar equatorial axis. The solar flare would be visible within a few minutes to synchronous satellites in orbit between earth and the sun, moments after that, solar observers around the planet would be aware that a very large solar flare was headed to Earth. This happened many times a year and usually did not raise any cause for alarm. In fact, the news had already reported on increased solar activity over the past few weeks. The government scientific establishment feared nothing, as they knew that the Van Allen belts protected them fully from the stellar onslaught. They would sleep easily tonight, knowing that within forty to sixty hours, when the flare hit the Earth, there might be some minor power outages, and some satellite disruptions, but nothing more serious.

A prudent man foresees evil and hides himself; The simple pass on and are punished.
—Proverbs 27:12 NKJV

CHAPTER 4

Glasgow, KY
15 miles North of Gallatin, TN
Eternal Serenity Family Funeral Parlor
June 6
2:03p.m.

John Calvin was an unassuming man. Six feet tall, Caucasian, and well-muscled, he had a short trimmed goatee, much like the one Angus Gunn wore. He was having a quiet day today, which in his case was generally a good thing, as someone usually had to die for him to be busy. A devout Southern Baptist, he was the funeral home director of a small, new and beautifully appointed funeral home in quiet southern Kentucky, just across the border. He loved his job, and was very good at it.

He had been trained by Mormons in the trade after he left the US Air Force Civil Engineers. He had seen combat in Mogadishu and had been involved in several minor actions. He had been in Somalia when the Blackhawk helicopters carrying US Special forces had been shot down. He had seen things during that engagement that he wished he could forget, as he had been escorting a general across town when rogue Somali fighters tried to block their convoy. This action was at the periphery of the contact noted in the famous book and movie.

Still, he was haunted by nightmares of drawing down on the Somali citizen, who just happened to be trying to cross the road. John had been standing out of the open top of a Humvee aiming at anything that moved, when a young woman came out of an alleyway suddenly, moving fast. He had come within an instant of killing her before he realized that the bundle in her arms was an infant, not a weapon. He often awakened at night yelling out, reliving the event. Sometimes in the dream, the girl lay dead, the infant still clinging to her lifeless body; sometimes he awakened without shooting. He was a deeply religious man, and during wakeful hours, he thanked God that he hadn't killed the woman on that day, though his mind played tricks on him in his deepest, darkest dreams. He wondered if he really would have what it took to defend himself and his family if it ever came to actually firing at someone. His friends did not share this concern, for they had seen the hard light appear in his eyes in the past when John had been threatened once in a restaurant.

John had been walking into his favorite Mexican food establishment when the event occurred. He had been born and raised in Texas before he had joined the USAF and later had settled in Tennessee. As a result, he loved Mexican food. On that day, a scruffy looking man in leather biker clothes was walking out of the restaurant and had cat-called to John's wife and made a racial slur at John's oldest adopted daughter, a Guatemalan girl of deep brown skin tone.

Matt and Carlos were walking some distance behind John in the parking lot during the event. Everyone froze. Between the three men and their wives, five concealed handguns stood ready to be used in a life threatening emergency. Cat calling and racial slurs did not rise to that level, of course, and no one would have done anything about the rude jackass if he had stopped at that point. Everyone would have continued walking into the restaurant, or perhaps gone back to their cars and selected another venue for the evening meal. No handgun permit carrier in his right mind ever wanted a conflict. This was precisely the reason they did carry. They only wanted to be left alone, and should someone attack them, and they had no other option, the handgun could certainly keep them safe. But it was always, always a failure of de-escalation tactics when they had to be used. Sometimes walking away worked best, sometimes it didn't work at all. John turned and proceeded to walk back to his car, with his family in tow when the biker removed a small folding knife from his pocket, rapidly clicked it open and yelled, "I'm talking to you boy!"

Matt and Carlos motioned to their families to silently return to their cars, and prepared for the worst, reaching for their concealed weapons, but stopping shy of drawing. They were both over 20 yards away, but could clearly see John's face when he turned back towards the knife-wielding man.

Matt's blood went cold and Carlos held his breath when they saw the steely eyed, cold, dead look in John's eyes. He had no facial expression, no anger, no rage, no remorse in those eyes. Only cold, calculating thought. John stared, unblinking into the eyes of the biker.

In martial arts, there is a tactic in which an opponent's next move can be determined by careful study of the eyes. The eyes will flicker and flit towards the area from which the next attacking move will come. To avoid this, one can learn to use "soft eyes." This technique removes all emotion from the eyes, and leaves a soft glare, with no discerning emotion, not unlike a crocodile or other predatory animal, and is also seen in the criminally insane, who lack all remorse. It is terrifying to witness, and can truly unnerve those who witness it. Some will say that this person has "seen the elephant" when describing such a facial expression, and this was precisely the look that gently covered John's face. John had experienced much racism towards his family before, but never physical threat.

The biker blinked, once, then three times rapidly. He stammered, muttered something unintelligible and fumbled with putting the knife back in his pocket, nearly taking the end of his index finger off in the rush to close the blade one-handed. Carlos and Matt saw the sweat beading on the brow of the biker glistening in the streetlights that illuminated the parking lot in their warm mercury-vapor glow. Everyone stood perfectly still as the biker moved rapidly away to his hog located at the other end of the parking lot. The rumble of the engine was actually comforting as it receded into the distance. Matt and Carlos had no doubts about John after witnessing that event, but John still questioned himself. He was his own worst critic.

John's wife, Denise Calvin, was a personal banker who worked with executive accounts in downtown Nashville. They lived in a small, beautiful home just two blocks from the Gallatin Memorial Hospital. He always joked that Angus could always walk to his house if need be in an emergency. John's children were all adopted. Hailey Calvin was 14, from Guatemala, twelve-year-old Luke Calvin, and eleven-year-old Stacy Calvin were from Panama. John and Denise were unable to have children of their own, but were so full of love that their family had bloomed, thanks to efforts internationally by the state department and funding from many local churches to pave the way for adoption agencies, set up to cater to those like the Calvins who wanted to enlarge their families through international adoption. Denise had helped many others in this process even before arranging her own family, so dedicated was she to the process.

John's experience with the Mormons or Church of Latter Day Saints, LDS for short, had opened his eyes to the world of preparedness. John had always hated religious bigotry in all forms, and while doctrinal differences caused some of the members of his church to develop hatred of the LDS, John loved them. He was truly devout, perhaps the most devout of the group, and he saw tolerance as part of his Christian mission. He saw that the Mormons truly put their money where their mouth was, supporting charitable causes of all types. And because John allowed for proper LDS burial rites, something some bigoted directors would not, John was well loved by the Mormon community.

Mormons preached and practiced a life of preparedness in all forms. The duty of every Mormon was to have ready a one-year food supply, a three month monetary supply and a preparedness to help all of those around them in need who were less fortunate. Angus had also worked with the LDS while in the Air Force, and the two men's experiences had helped push the group towards better preparedness. Every group member's family had a one year supply of food and supplies or was actively working towards that goal. The group had also engaged in firearms, first aid, land navigation, radio communication and survival training. Many group members even shared this information and training with the community at large, hosting fairs and exhibitions for each of these skill sets. As the region suffered occasional storms and tornadic activity, this was a welcomed offering that the community sincerely appreciated.

John was somewhat unsettled today, as he had spoken with Angus earlier in the week and had been doing internet research on solar flares and geomagnetic reversals in preparation for tonight's upcoming group meeting. What he had uncovered was truly remarkable, and frightening. While his group had been preparing against all manner of disasters including civil unrest, pandemic flu, earthquakes, nuclear and chemical disasters, among others, the concept of a global EMP event was not one that they had collectively considered. This was definitely something to bring to the group tonight. As a rule, group members would divide topics, do in-depth research, and then share their findings, thus saving time and effort. Angus, being less of a physical leader and more of a scholar, would usually divide the topics to prep amongst the group, although he always read everything himself. Angus had asked John to review solar and geomagnetic info for the meeting. Even though Angus would have read it all himself, other group members always came up with ideas that Angus would miss. This allowed for the most efficient and productive meeting possible as every member was expert in different fields. Tonight would be a real eye-opener.

Tulley Farm
Five miles north of Gallatin, TN
June 6
3:09p.m.

Clouds drifted slowly in the stifling heat. Lucien Albert Tulley waited as he sipped his organic coffee on the front porch. His wife, Abigail Rose Tulley was in the kitchen, thinking about what to make for dinner for the family. The Tulleys had four kids, all home schooled, most still teenagers. Lucien was 51 years old, bald as a Q ball, stocky, strong as an ox and had a bear hug that could squeeze a grin out of anyone. Abigail was younger at 48 years old. She was of medium build, brown hair and light brown eyes and had a smile that could calm a sea, and frequently did with her four older children. Her maiden name was Clancy, which in Ancient Irish Gaelic meant "red haired fighter."

Lucien had studied electro physiology in college and had spent a year in Japan, where, among other things, he began his life-long study of Bushido, the warrior's way of the samurai. He felt in his Celtic bones a connection to the Zen philosophy, and while a devout Protestant nondenominational Christian, he truly felt a calling to live a more Eastern life. He really did believe that the term samurai meant "those who serve their master," and Lucien considered Jesus Christ his personal master. He believed in the seven pillars of rectitude, courage, benevolence, respect, honesty, honor and loyalty. On these seven virtues hung all of his sense of self-worth and he believed with all of his heart that the Lord Jesus Christ had directed his way to Japan to learn these things.

So ingrained were these teachings in his family, they actually believed that they were American samurai, ready to serve the will of the Lord. Every family member trained with katana, wakizashi, bow (though they felt that the modern compound bow was more practical than the traditional asymmetrical Yumi style bow), and in hand to hand martial arts. They were also preppers and tried their best to live off the one hundred acres that they were blessed with. They had extensive weapons and medical training and could match anyone in the group with their primitive skill sets.

Right now, his children had completed target practice today and they had just put up the collection of Marlin, Winchester, and Walther .22 rifles that they had completed cleaning about five minutes ago. They always kept their gear in immaculate condition. Next would usually be a run and land navigation exercise with full pack and gear, but due to the heat, they had started to wander towards the property's creek to start some bokken training. Bokken were training swords simulating the weight and feel of both katana and wakizashi. The models used were foam padded to prevent injury. It was still better than a run in this weather, given the cooling effect of the shade trees and creek flow.

The oldest child was Samuel Owen Tulley, 21, a tall, handsome brown haired, brown eyed fellow, thin and lean with a quirky smile. He was a worship leader with the local church and spent his summers camping in Colorado where he went to school. He had just finished Air Force Basic training for the Air Reserves, and was an Airman now. He would be working with communications equipment next year, but was not trained in that yet. He was engaged to a beautiful local girl, the marriage set for next fall. He wanted to arrange a proper home for her first. Like his father, he believed in the old values.

The next was Evi Adaira Tulley, a beautiful, sprightly girl of 19. She was pursuing school at a local college and had not decided on her future plans yet. Despite her small frame, she was the best martial artist and archer in the group. She was of medium height, had long brown hair and deep, dark brown eyes.

At eighteen years old, Donovan Corey Tulley was the quickest wit and the fastest runner of the group. While he lacked the smirking grin that Samuel used to charm the ladies, he was strikingly handsome with darker skin and curly hair, cropped close to his chiseled facial features. His name in Ancient Irish Gaelic meant "dark warrior of the hollow," and the name fit. Sean Liam Tulley, "God's gracious gift," in Gaelic was the youngest at seventeen, his blond hair and blue eyes making him quite a striking figure.

The teenagers slashed and parried on the lawn, their foam blades cutting powerful arcs, slashing and blocking with each new maneuver. Lucien sighed. He sometimes wished that he were more fit and younger. Didn't everyone at his age? He thought about all of the work he had done preparing his kids and wife for an apocalypse that would probably never come. But he knew that time spent in these arts kept them away from drugs, sex, and the evils of the society that he had largely rejected. He prayed a prayer of thanksgiving to the Lord and felt a sudden calm release of tension as he always did when he knew the prayer had been heard. The Lord spoke to him often, usually in his dreams, but occasionally in his waking hours.

Cooking smells proceeding from the kitchen drew his attention. The smells of roasting meat and fresh bread baked from scratch were enough to force him from his chair on the porch and into the house to thank his wife. He had gotten home early from work today. There would be a large group of people coming for dinner. Tonight there was a group meeting.

Looking like a cross between his namesake and a giant Golden Retriever on steroids, Aslan, his 150 pound Great Pyrenees came running up with his 120 pound sister, Lucy, smelling the cooking. Aslan might be bigger, but Lucy's bark was far deeper and more fierce. They both howled with joy, smiling with the eternal belief that one day, maybe today, they would get some fresh bread! They seemed quite satisfied still with the large scoops of high grade dog food that Lucien heaped into their bowls.

The Tulleys lived on a one hundred acre farm, about two thirds wooded, just a few miles outside of town. A long ridge line separated them from the view of Gallatin, and they could stand on the ridge on clear days and gaze at the town, thankful for the distance. Lucien joked that the property should be called "Blackberry Acres," due to its large abundance of the wild fruit. Abigail made an excellent cobbler, worthy of the delicious fruit God had granted them.

Practice seemed to be winding down now, the time now closer to five PM. The kids unsuited and ran upstairs, jostling for the first showers. Lucien answered the phone as it rang. It was Edward Douglass, one of the group's friends, who had apparently spoken to Angus and wanted to attend the meeting. Lucien had already agreed, but Edward was a singular man of principle and would never arrive uninvited to someone's house. Lucien reassured him that he was always welcome at any time, as everyone was in the Tulley House.

Spence Creek State Park
10 miles Northeast of Gallatin, TN
Rees house
June 6
4:03p.m.

Officer Scott Rees was finishing his rounds at the state park as his wife texted him on his phone. He never had good call reception at the location where he worked at the state park. She had reminded him that he was supposed to be at the meeting tonight at the Tulley's place. He had not forgotten, but had to finish up his rounds at the park before he could join the group. Apparently this was some kind of urgent meeting and he never missed those. Angus and Matt were all up about something and he needed to know what.

Scott was a 58-year-old man of medium height with gray hair and well-muscled frame. He was a lean and fit man, had poor hearing and eyesight, requiring glasses to see well since fifth grade. None of these issues prevented him from serving very well as a park ranger. He was basically the police officer for his local state park. He was Sheriff and police department rolled into one. He worked hard, despite the inadequate pay and benefits and a boss who made him cringe. The man sought out every possible avenue to avoid work and thus, all of the work went to Scott.

Scott had a beautiful family. His gorgeous wife of 53, Stephanie, was a highly intelligent eighth grade teacher who was a real math whiz and looked closer to 40, with light brown hair and eyes and a trim figure. His daughter Erin, age 25, was similar in appearance to her mom, and a free spirit who spent lots of time camping and hiking out west, frequently in Montana. Scott felt that he had a blessed life. He loved his job, loved the location in which he worked, loved his family and loved his community. He was very pleased to have met Angus who had introduced him to the group. He had taken to the prepper's life like a duck to water. He had already amassed an entire complement of interceptor body armor systems and rifle protective plates for himself and his wife, and had outfitted them with the finest AR-15s made, the Colt 6920, the gun by which all other AR type rifles judged themselves.

The AR rifle stood for "Armalite rifle," and the design had been sold to Colt decades ago. The Colt remained truer to the original design, save that you could not interchange Colt parts with other brands due to proprietary part sizes. This was the result of a longstanding feud with other AR brands, but the net result was that Colt had arguably the most reliable AR ever built. Gun makers had been modifying the design for decades, adding piston systems, using space age parts, changing every dimension in every conceivable way. And while some makers had improved one feature or another, such as accuracy or weight, modularity or interchangeability, none had ever been able to definitively prove their make as superior to the Colt in a head to head test.

Really, there were many good makes, some better than others, but the "gold standard," the one set by the military trials was the Colt. The parts were better built, with better materials and tighter, more consistent tolerances than most of the competitors. This was why Scott had chosen them. Even though they cost $200-300 more than the cheaper models, he felt his life was worth that small sum at least. He did not have double the price needed to get a comparably reliable piston gun, and frankly did not see the point as all of the testing showed the piston designs to be equivalent, not superior, as long as the Colt was run with proper lubrication. The AR had gotten a bad reputation in the Vietnam War due to total lack of maintenance and a change in ammunition that proved to cause catastrophic failures. These issues had long since been resolved and many owners of more complex designs had fallen back to the simpler Colt design. To be fair, several other companies such as Daniel Defense, Lewis Machine and Tool and others had managed to replicate the reliability of the Colt and even some lesser names, such as DPMS, which Angus used, had greatly improved their reliability under the aggressive market forces which drove the industry. It was perhaps the best time in American history to buy fairly inexpensive guns that were far more robust and reliable than their predecessors.

Compared to twenty years ago, the $1100-1600 gun market provided an inflation adjusted screaming deal, despite the seemingly high outlay. With proper parts support, these guns would last a lifetime and with maintenance, could hold up to conditions thought impossible a decade earlier.

Scott and Angus had chosen the same style of body armor. They had chosen the Interceptor Body Armor by Point Blank Industries. This was identical to the fist armor issued by the US Army to its troops in Gulf War Two and used during the first waves of involvement in Afghanistan and Iraq. It had quite recently been supplanted by some more modular designs, several competing companies making similar units, but this was by far the most common unit in service to date. Improvements in the new units included ability to remove the vests by simply pulling a tab down. This was useful if the soldier were drowning in water under the heavy load. The newer units also included more room for rifle protective plates, and the main armor was fully resistant to shrapnel and shot and pistol fire, but required ceramic/aramid fiber plates to be added to stop incoming rifle rounds. The addition of side plate pockets and the elimination of the underlying soft armor in the new plates was a trade off in some of the newer designs. The soldier would now be more protected with less weight from rifle fire, but be more susceptible to grenades, bomb fragments and shotgun and pistol fire. As rifles were the most common small arms battlefield threat, many units, such as special operations forces and the US Marines chose these plate-only designs. But the Army faced I.E.D.s or improvised explosive devices as the main threat and they retained the IBA, and similar hybrid soft armor/plate armor designs.

The IBA consisted of a shell of Kevlar woven soft body panels that were modular and could be independently removed and replaced. These were housed in an open front, Velcro fastened, heavy duty nylon cover, patterned in any of a number of colors. Scott's were in woodland, the green, brown, and black version that was used prior to changing to the newer pale green and white digital pattern that was universally despised as it seemed to stick out like a sore thumb in any terrain, unless covered with dirt. Scott wondered why the Army ever accepted the new design. While the newest Multicam brand was very effective, and consisted of a lighter brown, blended with light green, white, dark brown and several other colors, it was also about twice the price. The woodland camo and the Mulitcam were considered equally ideal for the Tennessee region in which they lived. John Calvin had led the group in testing the various patterns and the results showed each worked very well in this region, in fact, better than many civilian hunting patterns, surprisingly.

The IBA shell covered the entire torso from all angles and had a front neck protector that no one could use, as this piece made it impossible to bend your chin down when you wore it. It also had flaps that covered the groin and upper arms, and the left and right sides of the neck and the entire shoulder girdle. This was almost exactly equivalent to level IIIa soft armor and was flexible and could stop all common pistol rounds up to 9mm ball ammo fired at 1400 feet per second out of a submachine gun. It could stop shotgun rounds and every other conceivable common pistol rounds, even the vaunted .44 magnum and .357 magnums, so durable was the Kevlar weave. It was also extremely hot, like wearing a twenty pound trash bag a third of an inch thick. Scott thought this was more practical for a civilian as most people had access to shotguns and pistols and rifles, while common were not the main threat in some areas. This soft armor covered so much of the body, that a police officer would be well protected from common lethal threats.

In addition to the soft armor, pockets were designed into the vest to align heavier rifle plates covering the front and back of the torso. Even side plates could be added to the exterior if desired, though the weight at that level would exceed forty pounds. Scott stuck with basic front and back rifle plates for his vests. They were 10 x12 inches across and 7/8ths of an inch thick. They weighed 8 pounds each, 16 pounds for the pair. This put the vest's weight at 36 pounds before any ammunition and accessories were attached to the vest's front. These particular plates were level III/IV multi-hit and could stop numerous rounds of rifles caliber hits at point blank range up to and including the rare .30-06 armor piercing rounds. They could stop all US legal common rounds used in ARs, AKs, almost every conceivable hunting load including, .308, 5.56x45 light armor piercing SS109 rounds that contained a steel core to penetrate cold war Russian armor, even 45-70 loads that could knock down a buffalo from hundreds of yards would stop cold in these plates. Certainly 50 BMG sniper and machine gun rounds would penetrate the vests like a hot knife through butter and there were 7.62x54R rounds available overseas that were designed to penetrate lesser level III plates, but the level IV rating assured that it would take either two hits in the same hole of a standard round or a 50 BMG to penetrate these plates.

One online test showed the plates stopped eleven of sixteen spaced rifle hits, the only ones getting through were late in the test, when several rounds entered weakened sections that had stopped prior bullets.

They were truly amazing devices and the recent influx in government funds into the industry had made them very inexpensive. Two plates cost less than a mid-grade hunting rifle. These plates were slightly heavier than the original SAPI or Small Arms Protective Inserts that Angus used in his IBA vest, but were significantly less expensive and were better rated, as the SAPIs would stop almost all of the rifle threats, but could not withstand the .30-06 AP rounds. Angus, as his plates were 11x14 inches and only weighed 5.8 pounds each, was better served with the slightly less effective but lighter SAPI plates as these covered his larger torso area.

While heavy, the vests allowed protection, and place to keep your ammunition magazines and radios, knives, first aid kits, and sometimes even side arms. This was the military standard, and once again, that was what Scott wanted. His helmets were the standard issue ACH, advanced combat helmet designed to stop all of the pistol, shotgun and shrapnel threats that the soft level IIIa armor of the vest was used for. While rifle rounds would usually penetrate unless they glanced off at an angle, there was no technology available to get direct rifle protection in any helmet. These were padded, cushioned, and once you got used to them, fairly comfortable. The "steel pots" of yesteryear were long gone.

Scott's standard load included six 30 round AR-15 magazines; actually they were M-16 magazines, and they were legal to use (one could not use an M-16 rifle or any parts unless you paid a tax stamp and had special permission from the government). These magazines were arranged on the front of the vest along with a radio, knife, three pistol magazines and a first aid kit. The total weight of the loaded vest was 42 pounds, not counting helmet and belt with pistol, small backpack and rifle. Scott wore it all of the time, and was in excellent physical shape, as could be imagined. His wife's rig was similar, with only two-thirds the ammunition so that she could tolerate the load. She did aggressive aerobic workouts to stay in shape and remain capable of carrying this load.

The group largely had the exact same setup for their similar vests and carried the same basic combat load. They had prepared this system based on copying the US Army and the Marines, each selecting gear that fit them best. The first aid kit that was common to all of the group members was a modified US Army IFAK, or Improved First Aid Kit. It was a marvel of utility and simplicity. It allowed a soldier to immediately access lifesaving supplies, enabling him or her to rapidly treat any gunshot, amputation, burn, or blast wound in seconds. The group modified them by replacing the ugly light sage green and white digicam pouches with more appropriate subdued patterns of woodland, Multicam, or coyote brown and they added rapid clotting agents such a Quickclot that could stop battlefield blood loss almost instantly. Had these advances been available in the past, many lives would have been saved in combat. Scott felt better knowing that he had planned for his and his wife's safety. His daughter never really got into the preparedness stuff, but he was convinced that she would eventually come around and he would buy her the same equipment. Right now, she was in Montana camping with friends on a horse ranch.

Scott also had the obligatory expensive bird hunting shotguns that were part and parcel to this region and he kept a standard issue Remington 870 12 gauge shotgun and an older FN FAL .308 rifle that he had built from a kit in the house as well. He and his wife used Glocks, his a model 22 in .40 Smith and Wesson, a standard police issued sidearm, and Stephanie's a model 19 in 9mm, each holding 15 rounds plus the one in the chamber. He liked having extra equipment. His Colt ARs had advanced optical sights as well as lights attached to illuminate threats. His had a Trijicon TA-11GH 3.5 power magnified optic that placed a green horseshoe shaped reticle over the target using only tritium or ambient light, requiring no batteries. Stephanie's AR had an Aimpoint Comp M2 that was not magnified, but placed a battery illuminated red dot over the target. Its battery lasted 10 years on the lowest setting and about half that on the medium setting. These sights allowed very rapid target engagement, much faster than the standard iron sights used as backup sights on the guns. Each gun had a sling connected to the front and back, allowing rapid adjustment and carry of the weapons, hands free when needed. A sling was to a rifle as a holster was to a pistol, at least so went Scott's logic.

Scott finished his rounds and headed to the house to pick up Stephanie, as she liked to attend as many meetings as possible. Plus, he was worried about the tone in Angus' voice. He had heard that tone before, and it did not bode well for a peaceful topic tonight.

Go to the ant, you sluggard;
consider its ways and be wise!
It has no commander,
no overseer or ruler,
yet it stores its provisions in summer
and gathers its food at harvest.
—Proverbs 6:6-8 NIV

CHAPTER 5

County Private Gun Club
Outskirts of Gallatin, TN
June 6
4:03p.m.

The .308 caliber projectile tore from the steel hammer-forged barrel at just over 2600 feet per second, reaching the paper target at one-hundred yards in a tiny fraction of a second. The ear splitting crack was attenuated to just a thump by the military grade active hearing muffs that Justin wore under his ACH helmet. The round impacted in an area adjoining another hole made seconds ago by the previous incoming round. Five rounds of the match grade 175 grain Sierra Match King hand loaded cartridges had been sent to the target in just over one minute. The distance between the center of the holes the bullets made in the paper was just under 3/4 of an inch. If he slowed down, Justin Clearwater could shrink that group size to less than 1/2 of an inch for the five shots, but he liked to challenge himself under time stress. With hand loads like these: match grade bullets over 43 grains of Hogdon Varget powder using match grade cases reloaded in a RCBS Rock Chucker hand press with a match grade micrometer powder thrower and match grade micrometer adjustable dies, he could repeatedly make a soda can bounce across the ground at 300 yards. Shots past 600 yards were possible with this gun, a Remington SPS Tactical 20" .308 with a four round internal box magazine and a Leupold Mk4 Tactical Milling Reticle 3.5-10x40 with Badger Ordinance rings and bases. This gun was every bit as accurate as Angus' Savage, though about twice the price, and the two always joshed each other about which one was best. Each one loved his rifle. This scope had an M2 illuminated reticle and could easily be used at night.

Justin was a part time Gallatin Police Officer and a full time EMT at the county hospital. He was a fit, lean 28-year-old with a youthful smile, brown hair and green eyes and was 5'7", 175 pounds. He was in very good physical shape and took his role as a GPD officer very seriously. He had amassed a small collection of firearms in addition to the .308, including his duty Glock model 21 in .45 ACP, holding 13+1 rounds, a Remington 870 police model 18 inch seven shot 12 gauge with Magpul stock and hand guard, a Ruger SR556 piston model AR-15 with an Aimpoint T-1 micro red dot sight in a Larue mount, with a 3x magnifier that could be swung of of the way to the side when the extra magnification was not needed. This was one of the same models used by security and police forces. Like the others in the group, Justin tried to make sure his gear was top-notch.

He was never in the armed forces, but would certainly have been a medic if he had been. He was very good with patients and was as tough on the force as he was polite in the E.R. He had never married and had no kids. He liked the free lifestyle and was not yet ready to settle down. He never felt the need to do much prepping, as he only had himself to take care of for now. He did have a very robust ammunition supply, as did all of the rest of the group members, and he kept all of his guns in his trunk at all times, so that they would be with him always. He did not have a large food or medication store, however. He was well trained and really enjoyed the martial arts and shooting. He was taking Krav Maga in town from a local expert. He thought that this tough style of fighting would serve him well if he ever needed it as a cop. He was expert with his ASP baton, and Kabar TDI backup knife.

His parents lived in North Carolina, on the Coast; he rarely saw them, but spoke to them every month. His older sister, Francesca Clearwater Schultz lived with her husband and two teenaged kids in town. Her husband worked at a local business and she was a nurse for Angus' medical group at their second campus across town where she took care of senior citizens in the clinic. Francesca and Justin got along well and loved each other as only siblings can. Their brother, James, lived in Oklahoma and they talked every week on an Internet video phone system.

Justin really liked horseback riding and he had struck up several friendships in the area with the mounted cops in the adjoining town of Hendersonville, where they kept their horses at a nearby stable just to the north of the local outdoor mall. Like all of the police in Gallatin, he had soft armor, level IIIa by Second Chance that he could wear under his police uniform shirt and unlike the GPD, he kept a pair of the same level III/IV multi hit rifle plates that Scott had in a less expensive Condor plate carrier. He could strap on the soft armor and wear the forest green colored vest with the plates in it when needed on duty, or he could actually remove the soft panels from the concealable carrier and insert them into the carrier underneath the plates in special pockets designed for the purpose. This vest, like all of the others, had the front pockets for the various items needed to continue defending yourself. It was a popular item and the Mackenzies all used the same vest and plates. Today, Justin was wearing his. He felt that practice should be as close to reality as possible.

Most of the group members came here to the private club to shoot, and often they set up informal matches. They also met at the Tulley Farm for more detailed events that could not be done at the formal range. They would engage in tactical scenarios of every kind imaginable, from close quarters battles, house entry, long range interdiction, to rally and retreat games. They also did sessions on fire making, water purification, aikido, Justin's Krav Maga and Carlos even taught the Arnis stick fighting. Basically, everyone taught everyone else what they knew and the knowledge of the group members compounded over time. They had become prepared well enough that they would give charitable lectures and donate food to several of the local churches. The local LDS church even invited them to speak in their sanctuary about tornado preparedness. Angus called his Mormon buddy from the Air Force before going and confirmed that suits and ties would be mandatory to avoid offending the deeply conservative parishioners. They were the only ones to arrive properly dressed. The parishioners held their tongues when the police, emergency services and fire departments all showed up casually dressed. That day, the group demonstrated the HAM radio system and talked to a contact over 100 miles away. The parishioners were impressed, but the group felt it was still a small thing compared to the extensive food storage help that the Mormons had given to them in the past.

Justin had been lying prone, or on his stomach, shooting the rifle over a backpack for support. He cleared the weapon and sat back on his haunches. He checked the range and noted that as usual, he was the only one present. Everyone else seemed to come on the weekend, but Justin was always working on the weekend, so, like Scott, Tuesday and Wednesday were his weekend. He cleared his weapon, strode the hundred yards to the target berm in a quick dash and retrieved his target stands. He packed up and headed to his house to wash up before tonight's meeting in an hour and a half. He would bring a loaf of organic bread from the store, just like Mrs. Tulley liked. Justin was a real boy scout when it came to protocol.

As he drove down the gravel road towards the gate, he pitched his helmet and ear protection into the passenger seat of his late model GMC Envoy. He thought of all that he had read about since Angus and Carlos called him about the meeting. It seemed incredible to think that the very sun that warmed the sky could turn his beautiful Detroit chariot into a useless hunk of steel. He really could not wrap his head around it, too great were the implications. He hoped it was all overkill. Angus tended to go off half-cocked sometimes. He remembered when an email went out telling everyone to meet immediately that night. He had missed the meeting, but Angus had sent the email in a panic when he figured out the real story behind one important recent event in the news. What he had uncovered was certainly disturbing, that the media would cover up such an important event, but it really did not directly impact them in Gallatin. He understood Angus' passion, but did not directly share it.

Still, he knew him well enough to trust that he had everybody's best interests at heart. In the past, the group had tried to influence the local government to prepare better for possible disasters that could occur, but the pleas always fell on deaf ears and the more they tried to help, the more they were labeled "survivalists," and so they had quit trying. They would help their families and anyone that would listen. Luckily, many other private citizens took these events seriously and would not present a drain on the system in a disaster. Justin wondered what would happen in the projects. They were in the center of town and literally next door to the hospital. Time would tell. With a quick shower, he should easily make the meeting on time. He pulled in, deactivated the house alarm, locked the SUV and ran inside. He could clean the guns tomorrow.

Gallatin, TN
15 miles North of Nashville
Southern Family Medical Group
June 6
5:30p.m.

"Mom, I've got to go, I'm late for a meeting! Yes, yes, I love you. I'm glad you're coming to visit for a week this month. Sounds like fun. Now let me go so I can finish up clinic and get out of here! The guys are going to kill me, I'm always late! Love you! Bye, talk to you tomorrow, bye!" Angus sighed and glanced at Chloe, his head nurse. "Sorry! Don't worry about that paperwork, just do the call backs in the morning, I know you have church."

"Thanks, Dr. Gunn. Have fun at your meeting," Chloe said as she grabbed her purse. She would be on time for Wednesday night church for a change. She had just enough time to get her grandkids from the sitter and head to the service.

Chloe Pearl lived in the small town of Portland about fifteen miles northwest of Gallatin. She was 48 years old, had light brown hair and eyes, a medium build and was a wonderful nurse. Patients loved her, she had 30 years of clinical experience and had learned every trick in the book to keep clinic running well. A nurse could make or break a doctor, and she knew it. Dr. Gunn had been her doctor for over five years and they worked well together. Chloe had divorced her ex-husband over his infidelity. She really did not think she ever wanted to be married again after that horror show.

She had custody of her grandkids, as her son was not reliable with them. She loved the responsibility and thinking of the two beautiful grade school girls made her beam with joy. She would come in to the office thirty minutes early tomorrow to finish the work. She headed to her car for the long drive up the ridge toward home. The summer was a good time to drive it, in the winter it was dangerous and icy, going from the valley to the plateau above. For a town this close, it was really a very rural route, with no one living or working much in the transitional region due to the topography.

Back at his desk, Angus frenetically punched keys into the computer, finishing his last note. He had already reviewed his labs, thanks be to God! He thought as he grabbed his EDC bag and raced out of the door, pausing long enough to shut off his tablet and PC. He forgot his water bottle in the fridge as usual and turned to snatch it out before restarting down the hallway of the small clinic. His bag was known in the gun circles as an EDC or everyday carry bag. Basically, whatever he needed with him every day went with him in the bag. Water and tea bottles made at home, pocket knife, flashlight, multitool, notebook, tablet, rain jacket, stethoscope, small HAM radio handitalkie with car antenna, and items needed for the day all went into the well-organized bag. If he were carrying a concealed weapon, he kept the extra ammo in the bag. He could even fit a small amount of groceries or lunch if needed. He used the bag, as the name suggested, every day.

He nearly ran George, the janitor, over as he raced down the hall, "Sorry George! Late for a meeting!" Angus called as George laughed and waved him off. George was a good man, in a town of good men. He was kind, gentle, hardworking and always had the place spotless by the next day. Angus always waved or spoke to him as he left. Everyone got along with George.

Angus bounded down the steps and into his waiting Honda Ridgeline. He turned the key, checked his rear view mirror, activated his review camera and pulled out of the parking lot, heading to the Tulley Farm. It was now 5:41. The meeting had started at 5:30 and as usual, he was late.

Tulley Farm
Five miles north of Gallatin, TN
June 6
5:50p.m.

"Sorry I'm late guys," Angus said as he entered the Tulleys' home through the side door. Lucien greeted him with a big bear hug and motioned for him to come inside.

"Don't worry about it. We know you run a little behind. We haven't started yet. We were about to eat," Lucien said. Smells of roasted pork chops filled the air and the scent of baked goods, possibly fresh bread, was delightful as well.

"Hey everybody," Angus said as he entered the living room of the small cottage. The room was full of familiar smiling faces.

Carlos Corpuz said "Welcome, Angus," in his typical condensed fashion.

Greetings went around, and Angus noted most of the group was here: Carlos, and Lucien, and all of the Tulleys, Justin Clearwater, Scott and Stephanie Rees, John Calvin, and Matt Mackenzie. In addition, a guest of the group was here, Edward Douglass.

Edward Douglass was a tall, strongly built man in his early fifties who worked as a probation officer for the county. Law enforcement by training, he was involved with another group of preppers in town. They were peripherally associated with Angus' group, and shared many of the same concerns. Edward liked his job, and was a very good shooter, preferring the M1A, an updated .308 M-14, and the 1911 .45ACP to the .223 ARs and smaller handgun calibers. He felt that these less powerful guns were just too anemic for his taste. Army be damned; they got it right in Korea as far as he was concerned. He was a seasoned veteran of prepping and had a full complement of equipment, right down to the night vision and Tactical Tailor plate carrier with the now ubiquitous Maxpro multihit rifle plates and year's food supply.

Angus sat down and thanked Abigail for the delicious plate of food she offered, pork chops, broccoli, cabbage, fresh bread and butter and mashed new potatoes. He was famished after a long day in clinic. Lucien started the meeting.

"Well, I think everybody knows why we came here tonight. Angus and Carlos and Matt have some concerns about solar activity they want to share. Guys, I'll turn it over to you."

Matt laughed as he looked at Angus, whose mouth was full of pork chop, and said, "Well, I'll start. We have been looking into this solar flare and geomagnetic reversal thing you've been seeing on the news. To boil it down, it's very bad news."

The room shifted some, Justin and Lucien looked at each other. The Tulley kids stared at the wall and kept quiet. Angus swallowed and said, "Sorry guys, but Matt is right. We have been prepping for a lot of stuff, but this may be the real deal. I hope I'm overreacting as usual, but if we are right, we will need a lot of Faraday cages."

Carlos touched his chin, and spoke in his usual cool, collected way "Guys, we have no choice. I tried talking to the new mayor and he didn't listen. Just looked at me."

Matt continued, "The data on the news is being skewed to show the less likely events that could occur. They are talking only about small blackouts, occasional satellite disruptions. But it could be much, much worse. The thing is, the sun's radiation is blocked by the Van Allen Belts that circle the globe. The auroras at the poles and in northern climates are the result of solar wind hitting the atmosphere, pretty to look at but hell on electronics, especially if it intensifies. We think of them as only hitting northern areas, but Angus here has found that they have been seen in the past in southern China, Egypt and Hawaii! That's a heck of a lot more potent than we first thought. This guy, Carrington saw one in 1859 and recorded the first solar flare hours before. Hawaii at night lit up like the daytime, the natural aurora was so intense. Five times the worst recorded one since."

Edward piped up, "So what's that got to do with the geomagnetic thing?"

Angus spoke, "Everything. You see, during the geomagnetic reversal, the poles switch north and south."

Edward said, "O.K. I'll hold my compass upside down, so what?"

Matt spoke next," Normally, that's right, big whoopetie doo! But the thing is that the rotation of the Earth's core is what produces the Van Allen belts, the 'radiation shield of the Earth' if you will. And during a polar reversal, it stops working right."

"And goes haywire," Justin completed.

"Yeah," said Angus

"Crap. HOW haywire?" asked Edward.

Matt spoke next, "Well, we don't know. Somewhere between a tiny ten second blip and a thousand years with no protection…"

"Why haven't they told us this," asked Sean Tulley, the youngest and most passionate of the Tulley Clan, "Sorry."

"It's O.K. I feel the same way Sean. The thing is likely to last a few days, best scientific guess of the solar experts. When it reverses, the Earth will literally have five or six, 'mini poles' none of which will protect us from the solar output. One of the videos I found was that Asian scientist always on TV, the guy with the gray hair, he said we were in for a 'solar tsunami,' and that if we didn't prepare, Western Society would crumble. Think Global EMP. All things electronic will fry, over the entire planet, as the sun rises in each region. You see, if the solar flares continue like they are predicted to do, and the geomagnetic reversal hits at the same time, there will be increased radiation and no protection. See, all the solar flare models are based on a working Van Allen Belt. If it's gone, we are toast, if a big flare hits the same day. Even a little one would become a big one, no belt, no shield, bad ju ju."

Silence filled the room.

"In other words, let's get some Faraday cages built. Now," Matt finished.

Carlos spoke next, "Look, if we are overreacting, we'll have fun building them anyway." Carlos had a dry sense of humor.

"So the 'unrelated news' about these things, not so unrelated," Justin said. He had read the data himself, but wanted confirmation.

Angus set his teeth, "Yeah."

"I mean, the history of Egypt and China seeing the aurora is really ancient, myth and stuff," Angus offered.

"But 1859 is not, and lots of tropical locations got the aurora. Well documented in the modern age. I mean that thing would fuck us... Sorry Abigail," Scott said

"It's OK," Abigail said

Scott continued, "I mean, mess us up real bad if a Carrington level event hits again, even without the loss of the Van Allen belt. With no belt? And the Carrington event happened in several waves, just like these minor solar flares are now on the news. Jesus, help us! We need to get those boxes built."

An EMP event, or electromagnetic pulse event either made by a nuclear bomb or the sun or other phenomenon, or made in the lab, produces a buildup of electrons in metal exposed to it. It basically fries anything with a computer chip. Old, pre-computer stuff would work fine, what they called "solid state," vacuum tubes and such. You could shield against it though, by containing the electronic item in a fully metal lined box, insulated from the item inside. Then the pulse is carried over the surface of the box, the way lighting hits your car or plane and doesn't kill you inside. All of the people in the room fully understood this as they had discussed it before when prepping for a traditional EMP attack from nuclear war or isolated event. They all knew the Chinese had planned on using a space based EMP if we ever went to war with them, and so they had an idea of where to start.

The problem was, if society had the lights permanently turned off, and had to rebuild the power grid from scratch, which is exactly what the solar storm promised to cause, then very bad things would happen. Surface delivery of groceries, gasoline, medicine, everything would instantly stop.

Dead in its tracks. Nothing. No groceries, no pharmacy, no gasoline. All kaput. Then would come riots as people fought for the two to three days' worth of supplies left in each town. The producers of goods would no longer be able to produce. And anyone with a special medical need would be done in very short order. No pacemakers, no oxygen, no insulin. Most people didn't have more than two weeks of food in their cabinets, some lived hand to mouth, especially in "assisted housing," the government's euphemism for welfare housing. Social chaos would ensue, within seven to nine meals. Everyone in the room also understood this as well as the fact that the most dangerous thing in any disaster was the crowd, not the disaster itself. The second wave was often worse than the first. America was too young and rebellious and had too many different kinds of people with disparate cultures to bond together well during a real crisis. Certainly Taiwan, Japan, China, some European regions were honor bound to follow the law, even when there was no law. There were places that would survive, just not the U.S. or most of rest of the developed world. This was bad news indeed.

The rest of the meal was finished, with apple pie for dessert and coffee, excellent as always. Each person went home. Angus paused before he left and thanked Lucien and Abigail, and spoke to Lucien, "I will tell the Washingtons when I drive home tonight. They have to be ready too, with their daughter." Angus made his goodbyes and drove off.

Angus had been referring to a family that formed really a group of their own. They lived in Bethpage and were some of the finest humans Angus had ever met. Darryl Washington was ex USAF security forces, and ran a local finance company. He was honorable to the extreme and a lifelong friend of Angus; Darryl's daughter Tessa was also Katherine Gunn's best friend. On the way home, Angus called his old friend and let him know their concerns. Not surprisingly, they were just finishing their last Faraday cage and had already prepped for this, seeing the news and wondering about it themselves.

"Yeah man, this thing has got me paying attention!" Darryl laughed because he had been picking up the phone to call Angus when it rang.

"Good deal, man. I worry about you guys," Angus felt better knowing this, because one of the Washington's daughters had Cerebral Palsy and would need the supplies prepared ahead.

"Do you think this could really happen?" Darryl asked, a concerned smile clear in his voice.

"Yeah. I do." Angus replied, steering his Ridgeline down the two lane track of Long Hollow Pike, pastureland streaming by in the dark. Angus knew this stretch of road by heart. He could see the farms and neighborhoods in his mind's eye as they passed each one. It was so amazing, the power to cover a day's walk in twenty-five minutes. Small world. Made so by technology.

"I really hate it when you say things like that. But I know you would never waste our time on this. I also know that you haven't been wrong on this stuff in the past. Like that swine flu stuff. You knew that it wouldn't be fatal, and that the coverage from the news made it seem worse than it was. I do remember though when you warned me about the 'cry wolf' phenomenon. That everybody would blow off the big one because the media over-blew minor things all the time," Darryl said.

"I sure hope I'm wrong on this Darryl. I really do. It sucks sometimes thinking about the way the county, and the country for that matter, take their safety for granted. I mean. I know the USAF knows a lot more than they let on. And God knows what higher branches of the government know. They are all so afraid of a panic, that they never tell the real story. I think it would help people realize how truly dangerous this planet is. Sorry for venting."

"No sweat, my brother from another mother."

"Yeah man!" Angus replied. He really liked Darryl, and the camaraderie lifted his spirits some. Still, lots to do. He'd be up half the night putting gear into ammo boxes. He had purchased a crate of night vision containers at a local gun show years ago, with just this in mind. The NVG, or night vision gear, cases were simply ammo cans lined with one and a half inch foam padding. This protected the gear from rough handling, but also, when the hermetically sealed lids were closed, created a Faraday cage. Angus would first place his electronics in a ziplock bag, then wrap aluminum foil around it and then place them in the metal can. This, in effect, was a Faraday cage within another Faraday cage. Angus did not believe in leaving things to chance. "We need to get together and do another range day. It's been awhile since I've shot my new rifle."

"Maybe we can do it next month," Darryl replied.

"Sounds good. Tell Simone 'hi' for me," Angus referred to Mrs. Washington.

"I will man. Try to cheer up. I can hear the worry in your voice."

"Yes sir. Roger wilco," Angus replied. "Talk you you this weekend."

"Goodnight man, hug Gwenn for me."

"Will do, my friend. See you then. Bye." Angus drove home in a funk, radio tuned to the local Christian station, praying for guidance.

> *By the pricking of my thumbs, Something wicked this way comes.*
> —William Shakespeare. <u>Macbeth.</u> 4.1.45-46

CHAPTER 6

Undisclosed location
Suburb of Atlanta
Verhk Biological
Security Station, Main entrance
June 7
9:21a.m.

The brown delivery truck was double parked at the front gate. Dirk could see it on his monitors at the desk of the security station. Here we go, he thought as he saw the usual svelte form advancing from the back of the truck with a dolly full of packages. The trim blonde who appeared at the desk a few seconds later leaned over the counter and gently slid her digital clipboard to Dirk, her pen in the corner of her mouth, breathing out slightly with pursed lips. Dirk wanted to swallow hard, but controlled his impulse to drool on the counter and howl out loud. Jenni, the delivery girl, always got the attention of everyone in the security station.

"Hey there, stranger," she cooed over the tall desk as she smirked and twiddled the pen in the corner of her mouth, "Sign here, big boy." She pointed at the clipboard's digital screen, not taking her eyes off of Dirk's flexing biceps. He paused, the tension was thick enough to cut with a knife.

"Hey there, yourself, sugar," he replied. Only in the Deep South could a man get away with what could amount to sexual harassment in any other part of the country. Besides, he thought, it was only harassment if she didn't want it.

"Whatcha got there?" he asked, deliberately looking at her ass while pretending to examine the packages.

"Don't know. Something for the fifth floor. Plus the usual stuff." She referred to the usual parcels that were delivered every week to the office. This was part of her regular route, and she paid attention to the normal flow of her packages. She enjoyed the mornings, Dirk was hot and she'd been teasing him for weeks now, he was just too hot in that uniform, and those pecs! Oh my Gawd! She really didn't give a damn about the parcels, she just wanted to see him drool over her. Maybe this weekend she could get him to ask her out. Oh well, she thought.

"Hmmm... fifth floor, yeah, it's the right tag on the address. Box is kinda big," Dirk said, looking at the two by two by one foot box.

"Yeah, looks like a sample of something, it feels like styrofoam inside. They use these sizes to ship stuff they have to keep cold'" she said, still leaning on the counter.

Dirk sighed. What a hottie! Dammit. "Checks out, you are good to go," he said as he reached under the counter and pressed the release for the elevator lock. The higher floors required authorization for entry and deliveries were sent up by the carrier as he could not be spared to run packages up. She winked and rolled the dolly onto the opening elevator.

"Thanks!" she said.

Dirk smirked and nodded. He would still get a nice view of that ass when she left in a minute.

Jenni delivered the packages to the fifth floor first, as the elevator was set for that once the security guy had unlocked it. She dropped off the box to some red haired geek and then headed down and delivered the rest to the third floor, as usual.

Brad Johansson took the box back to the lab after taking it from the delivery lady. Whew! Damn, what a woman, he thought as he handed the box to the lab assistant. He wanted to get to know that one, but they rarely got deliveries to the fifth floor from that company. Oh well.

"Brad, hand me that pair of scissors," said Beth Hinton as she took the package. She put it on her desk and took the scissors handed to her and opened the box. She saw the styrofoam and said, "Hmmm, must be a new sample."

She thanked Brad and headed into the lab with her new prize. Unbeknownst to anyone else in the office on the lower floors, or in the local area, Beth and her team had been working on a government funded mandate started by the Recovery Act. It allocated funding for government projects, including work to help prevent the spread of bio-weapons. One of the ways Verlhk was doing that work was to actually produce some of the toxins and parts of the biological agents to study their effects. This was really about vaccinating people to possible new viral plagues that could be mass produced.

Verlhk's management figured if some jihadist in the Middle East genetically altered an existing plague, they would already be one step ahead of them in producing the cure. And the more things they created that were lethal, the greater the chance of having the right treatment or cure. So, they changed the DNA in predictable ways, such as increasing the lethality or communicability of known strains, things that terrorists were likely to do. That way, if anyone attacked the US, or any other country for that matter, Verlhk could rapidly supply the cure. And supplying the cure meant making a lot of doses, and a lot of doses meant a lot of money. And making money was what Verlhk was all about.

Beth put on a pair of gloves and placed the package in the biocontainment hood, turned on the vents and filters and opened the styrofoam and looked in the package. She removed three vials that were tightly wrapped and contained in biohazard bags, and opened the bags and read the number listed on the sides. The vials all read "RL773P-12."

Excellent. She called Ben, her chief lab assistant, over to her station. "Ben, come here. We've got the new Rhaboviradae antigen markers. The delivery came. Email Greg and let him know it arrived."

Ben poked his head around the corner. "Cool, once we get the wild type samples from corporate, we can start doing the comparative analysis."

In nature, organisms adapted to their environment by altering their DNA by what for all intents and purposes was a genetic crap shoot. If the random modification worked better, then the organism would succeed more than its original genetic predecessors, and would take over the niche in the environment. If the change was deleterious, then it died out, thus leaving room for the other, more efficient organisms. Man was able to directly alter genes in organisms by either selective breeding, as with animal and plant stocks, or say, beer yeast, or by direct genetic recombination. This direct method could yield entirely new things: E. Coli bacteria that grew plastic or drugs for industry, plasmid DNA that could be forced into bacteria to induce resistance to antibiotics. Given enough time, anything could be modified.

Verlhk had been working on a series of known plagues: anthrax, tularemia, pneumonic plague, rabies, and Q fever. Each of these organisms were deadly in their own right, but the government mission was to prevent modified bioweapons from being used against us. So they had modified each of these to make them better to use as a weapon. Some agents had been successfully made more lethal and some had been made more contagious, some both, though the latter was very hard to achieve. Usually, when a contagious organism becomes more lethal, it also becomes less contagious, and vice versa. Ebola was highly lethal and contagious, but this was an exception to the rule. It had jumped from another animal species into humans and was so fast acting that it would burn itself out before spreading very far.

Flu and colds, on the other hand were highly contagious and much less lethal. This is the ideal state for an organism. It allows it to persist in the environment and does not kill the host body. Colds are perhaps the best evolved of all human viruses for this reason.

Wild rabies occurs in several varieties, or strains. Three common types are found in the US. They were capable of infecting any mammal. Pigs, goats, sheep, cows, lions, tigers, chipmunks, squirrels, bats, cows, raccoons, dogs, cats, humans and all other mammals are able to be infected. The virus enters the host body, often via a bite, sometimes by ingestion through the gut. Once it enters, the surface proteins bind to the host cell and the virus sends a payload of genetic material, in this case RNA, into the cell. The genetic material seizes control of the cell and forces it to produce the very genetic materials, and surface proteins required to make new virus particles, called virions.

The rabies virus then sends the surface proteins into the lipid bilayer cell membrane of the host. Genetic material compacts into a package and nears the outer host cell membrane and presses against the surface, creating a new package of RNA surrounded by host membrane studded with surface viral proteins. It uses the skin of the infected cell as a cloak or skin to wrap its deadly viral RNA package into, and then "buds off," pinching the host cell membrane off and stealing part of the host cell membrane in the process. This repeats innumerable times with each host cell.

The virion of the rabies virus is shaped like a bullet, specifically like a 9mm hollow point bullet, waiting to drive its next deadly payload into an adjoining, hapless cell. This brush fire of repeated transmission of RNA and self-replication starts slowly and gradually builds over the days and weeks of the infection to reach a fever pitch, a crescendo of agony and death for the host. The unstoppable rage and biting seen in its hapless victims serves to spread the virus to new hosts. Just as parasites and fungal infections in nature cause certain ant species to move their zombiefied bodies towards new host ants, this virus causes the host to bite and spread the new invasion troops to new host bodies.

The Verlhk lab group's job here was to compare the surface antigens of the wild type, naturally occurring rabies virus commonly found in nature against the heavily genetically modified version "RL773P-12." This virus was somewhat of a failure, a laboratory dead end. It had been modified from naturally occurring rabies to become more contagious, in this case, contagious by airborne transmission. However, as with the common cold, it had become much less lethal, at least in the mammal test subjects that had been infected with the strain. Oh, they would bark, drool, snarl, try to bite each other, but most of the animal subjects didn't die from it. The main difference was that they did not display as much of the classic hydrophobia, and were therefore able to drink and eat fairly normally. If anything, they seemed to eat large amount of food rapidly.

In a similar fashion to what had happened with other viruses, the new surface protein that they had genetically engineered had caused a reduction in the hydrophobia seen in normal rabies. A team of researchers had, in recent years, modified the deadly H5N1 bird flu virus to become able to be transmitted via the nasal passages more easily, as the original virus required passage into the deep lung tissue. Once the change in the surface protein was made, the new flu virus was significantly less lethal than its wild type predecessor. The same change in the binding affinity that allowed the new rabies virions to pass by aerosol transmission more readily also reduced their affinity to the neural pathways responsible for the fatal hydrophobic reaction. It had also reduced the likelihood of the fatal arrhythmias and uncontrolled hypertension seen in victims of normal rabies.

They had kept the subjects for up to 3 months before automatic destruction and the death rate varied by species, but was in the 20% range on average. This strain was still seen as a possible agent that a terrorist might construct and therefore Verlhk pursued it fully. After all, Uncle Sam was paying the bills and he had unlimited pockets for this type of work.

Beth's lab was secretly a BSL-2, or Biosafety level 2 lab in accordance with the CDC guidelines. These stated that work could be done on nonlethal agents to humans that pose risk of minor disease. Many BSL-2 labs had been authorized to work on common deadly agents, as long as the lab followed rigorous protocol, as the BSL-3 labs were far more expensive to construct and operate. Since they were primarily a think tank, and were only handling the antigenic surfaces of the organisms, not the entire organisms themselves, a BSL-2 rating was really overkill for their work, according to the CDC guidelines. They did not handle the actual organisms themselves, and the antigenic parts they handled were only the "skin" of the pathogen, not capable of producing disease, but what the body needed to manufacture antibodies to fight the disease. They did not do any of the vaccine production, only send analyses of the differences in the wild versus genetically modified versions to the main office. Other labs would make the actual vaccines. Beth thought of their work as "pure" science, and her humanist belief structure reveled in the glory of the new knowledge that they had already obtained during their short time here.

The samples were cold, a frozen gel pack placed on each side in the shipping container. The samples were always kept cold and she sealed the samples into another biohazard bag and once safe, placed them into a separate freezer unit and locked the door, placing the key on the table next to the unit. Locking it was overkill as well, as the outer doors to the lab were on an electronic lock and nobody could get in here anyway. They would have to wait for the next shipment from corporate as they needed the wild type rabies antigenic samples to compare with these, in order to catalog the differences prior to vaccine production. Beth turned her attention to her email and began typing, sending an email to her life partner, Dwayne, to tell him to stop by the organic market to get her favorite chili sauce for the night's meal. She was planning on quite a weekend, with friends from her college dorm days in town.

What Beth didn't realize, was that the corporate headquarters' lab tech had been drunk the night before he sent the samples. He had been sleeping off a hangover when two very dangerous things happened. First, his boss caught him and yelled at him for sleeping on the job, and second, the hottest babe in the office pool walked by and flirted with him. She liked the rebellious type, and saw the way he recovered from the scolding. Between the shock of anger and the heat of desire, by the time he went into the lab to mail the samples to the Atlanta lab, he was quite distracted.

What Beth had quite safely and sterilely placed in the freezer was not the inert, dead antigenic skin of the new rabies virus. Instead, it was the entire living sample, RL773-P12, the rabies virus Verlhk had genetically altered to be highly contagious through airborne spread.

These late eclipses in the sun and moon portend no good to us.
—William Shakespeare. King Lear. 1.2.100

CHAPTER 7

Goodlettsville, TN
10 miles North of Nashville
Gunn House
June 8
5:07a.m.

Light. Silence. A rumble of terrific power broke the stillness. Terror and agony screamed outward and threatened to tear the very fabric of spacetime itself. A spinning echo of fear, once and before, waiting to be again. A rending of all that has been. A falling away. A dying time like none before. Running. Screaming. The world turning and collapsing on itself, the weight of years of neglect and prosperity. Arrogance and self-assuredness refusing to believe the truth that all of the power that was theirs had now gone. Agonizing realization that all was lost. Bodies piling up, rotting away. The vestiges of a once great and now forgotten race, ancient in their wonders, as dead now as all of the kingdoms that had passed before them. Ultimate in their belief that they could accomplish anything. Disbelieving unto the end of all things.

Angus was standing on a hilltop overlooking the once great city, now a smoldering ruin. A shell of greatness, broken over the knee of a natural world gone mad in rage. A rage so unstoppable that the sheer terror of it ripped at the thin shell of sanity that so precariously covered the minds of those who had survived. Sweat and grime mixed on the brow of the man, utterly alone in this wilderness of fear and unknowing. How could this have happened? How could we not have been ready? Why?

Angus' mind was collapsing into itself, devoid of reason. His mind could not hold this understanding. It was more than one human could bear. The weight of his grief drove him to his knees. Hot tears streamed down his cheeks and mixed in the ashes at his feet.

A new sound emerged from the ruined city. A scratching, rattling sound. A chattering of teeth, unnatural in its intensity. A devouring noise. Fear began to pulsate through Angus.

Movement. Slowly at first, then faster. Bodies crawling, moving in a dance of death. A choreography of terror. Faces rent asunder. Skulls crushed. Bones crumpling as they held the weight of the dead. Necks turning and popping as evil intent surged through the wasteland of death.

Hunger. Thirst. The things began crawling up the hill towards Angus. Fingernails scrabbled at the rubble, pulling the lifeless forms inexorably toward the helpless man, terror bright in his eyes. A gleam of horrific fear. Nooooo!

"Angus! Wake up!" Gwenn yelled.

Angus sat bolt upright in his bed, sweat soaked into the Egyptian cotton sheets, his wife Gwenn shaking his arm violently. "You were yelling. Are you O.K.?" she asked, a look of fear furrowing her brow.

Angus stared blankly at her, calm slowly returning to his mind, still experiencing the prior terror in receding waves. His mind began to function again, the paralysis of horror fading away in the lamplight, the beautiful face of his wife now smiling at him.

"You have another one of those dreams?" she asked.

"Yeah, sorry. I didn't mean to scare you. What was I saying?" Angus replied.

"Nothing intelligible. You were just moaning really loud. I thought you were done with those now that we're not in anymore" she said, referring to the nightmares that he had when he was in the Air Force and had to deal with all of the disaster prepping for the base.

Angus had had several dreams over the past few weeks. Always the same. He had told her about the ruined city. The dust and the terror. But the dead were new. "There were dead people this time. They were trying to kill me."

"You should quit reading that zombie stuff. And that show is really good, but it scares me too."

"You're probably right, but this was so real. I was running and then everything collapsed like before, and then I was looking out over the city ruins, just like before in the other dreams. But then there were dead bodies everywhere and they came to life and started up the hill I was standing on. Scared the hell out of me. Sorry."

"Its OK. Snuggle with me. You've got a half hour before the alarm goes off," Gwenn said as she hugged her husband. Angus kissed her brow and moved over to the middle of the bed away from the sweat-soaked portion of the sheets. He dozed off smelling the fruity conditioner of Gwenn's hair. He loved his wife. She was a truly good woman.

Bethpage, TN
5 miles East of Gallatin
Washington House
June 8
12:10p.m.

Darryl pulled up the drive into his new house. Well, it was new to him. He was now living a dream that he had seen years ago, when he was trapped by the confines of the small Southern town of Gallatin. He had wanted his whole life to be a part of the countryside, "landed gentry," if you will. His Air Force career in Security Forces had led him to the conclusion that people were crazy, and would do anything in a desperate situation. This is ultimately what made him feel claustrophobic in cities and drove him to this country property.

"Hey Babe," he called after his wife Simone, a 49-year-old short haired beautiful Black woman of slim build and medium height.

"Home for the day or just lunch?" Simone asked.

"The day. I figured we needed to set the rest of the stuff up and the office was slow, so we closed early." Darryl was a meticulous man, 51, Black, medium height, strong and lean. His exercise regimens included long runs into the countryside and aggressive weight based aerobics. He spent a lot of time shooting. Now that he had property, he had constructed his own 75 yard target range in the back yard.

They were joined by their son Jesse, 27, who lived down the road and their daughter Tessa, 16, who was an expert archer and best friends with Kate Gunn. Their oldest daughter Susanne, was 24 and had severe cerebral palsy. Simone and Darryl had dedicated their lives to protecting their innocent daughter and she had become the soul of the family. She was able to communicate through pre-vocalizations and required help with almost every aspect of her life. She was far more intelligent than most passersby would realize. Those, like Angus Gunn, her doctor, could attest to this. Anyone who took the time to get to know her soon realized the depths of thought that occupied her mind. Darryl had made it his mission to protect her at all cost. He had spare wheelchairs, defensive embankments, extra food, medication, body armor, armored vehicle doors, rapid escape plans, bug out systems and off-site storage duplicates of the originals, all custom tailored to fit her needs. He would never leave her behind.

Her laughter and smiles bound the family in ways that families without a special needs member could never fully understand. He thanked Almighty God for the strength of will that they had been given to turn tragedy into such a blessing. She was truly the most loved person in her community.

Darryl had used his funds very carefully to stock a large amount of ammunition and weapons based on the AK rifle system. He had a variety of the simple, rugged rifles and thousands of rounds of the inexpensive, but very deadly ammunition for these. He made sure to include both the lighter AK-47 style Bulgarian rifles as well as the larger, more expensive RPK variety, in his case a Chinese version that was more expensive, but of a higher quality that some of the domestically refurbished models. These larger semi autos were originally light machine guns, and could sustain a higher rate of fire. He had converted some of these with the Slide Fire Solutions AK bump fire stock that allowed the inertia of the gun to carry the next round into the chamber for what amounted to legal fully automatic fire. The BATFE, the government agency that policed such matters, had declared it legal as it required the user to press his non firing arm forward to engage the device, thereby making it a semi auto, albeit, one that fired very fast. Like thirteen rounds a second fast. The stock design allowed for aimed fire and made the bump fire mode practical for serious use. Darryl had stockpiled and loaded dozens of the durable, inexpensive 30 round curved metal magazines that worked in both rifle types. His current aim was to procure long range sniper rifles, but this goal was a long term one that would have to wait for funding, as he had recently upgraded the groups food and medicine stores.

Jesse Washington, Darryl's son, had a wife, Samantha, age 25, and a new daughter Julia, who was 11 months old. Jesse was a black belt in Karate. At 5'8" and 145 pounds he was smaller than his father, but could take him down almost every time in sparring, despite Darryl's superior strength. Cleo Johnson, also 27 years old, was Jesse's best friend and shared his passion for the martial arts. He spent so much time at the house, that Darryl jested that he had two sons. The truth was certainly no joke, as Cleo was as dedicated to the Washington family as Jesse was. Cleo's family had died in a car accident when he was in college, and he saw the Washingtons as his family now.

Gun ownership was somewhat of a rite of passage into adulthood for the Washingtons. When Jesse turned 21, Darryl gave his son a Desert Eagle .44 magnum semi auto pistol. The gun held an incredible nine rounds of the devastating .44 magnum cartridge, eight in the magazine, plus one in the chamber. The gas system of the weapon allowed for reduced recoil and easy shooting for those strong enough to hold its considerable weight. Tessa would receive a pistol of her own at 21 as well. For now, she was pleased with her Matthews Monster MR5 compound bow, one of the world's fastest bows. It could launch its carbon spined arrows at an incredible 360 feet per second at the maximum 80 pound draw weight that she used.

Though she had a petite figure, she had incredibly strong upper back muscles from her years in ballet. Many thin ballet stars could easily hold up a 100 pound dancer on their palm. To her, this draw weight was actually easier, given its 80% draw weight let off, or reduction, seen at full draw. This enabled her to hold a fraction of that immense weight easily and quietly when aiming the technological marvel of composite honeycombed material.

Her bow draw weight was actually higher than anyone else's in the group, although for sheer speed of shooting, no one could surpass Kate Gunn, as she watched too many movies. At least that's what Tessa told herself when her best friend could launch three arrows in as a many seconds in practice, a feat made harder by the much more complicated arrow rest systems used in her modern bows. Older style longbows and recurves were far faster for most people to shoot, given the utter simplicity of the design and rest. You usually just threw the arrow onto the rest of center cut wood or angled your bow to allow the index finger to hold the arrow in place.

Kate still eschewed the greater accuracy of the mechanical string releases for the speed and familiarity of her gloved fingers. She also refused, quite stubbornly, to use sights on her bows. Tessa called it "using the force," usually calling her friend a goofball at the same time. Both girls had astonishing skill with the bow and could place ten arrows onto a soda can at fifty yards with monotonous regularity. Angus Gunn had started them with archery, and they had surpassed him within a few years. Tessa and Kate were lifelong best friends and spent most of their free time together as both were home schooled, this was a considerable amount of time, given their natural efficiency with their work.

A lunch of tuna fish sandwiches and pickles was finished and then the family settled into their usual weekend routine, but not before spending two hours finalizing their electronics protecting faraday cages. They had used copper mesh wire and wrapped these around plastic containers to hold all of their spare electronics to protect them against any EMP damage. Darryl figured that about half of the equipment fit in and allowed the rest to be used. Cellphones and computers were not placed in them, as without the Internet, they were much less useful. He planned on grilling steaks tonight to reward his crew for their help.

Atlanta suburbs
Club Veranza
15 miles from Verlhk Biological
June 8
11:55p.m.

"Shut up Frank, you're an asshole!" Dirk yelled halfheartedly at the bartender, grinning at the man's slack jawed appraisal of his girlfriend's tight figure. She wore high heeled wedge sandals, glittering blue, skin-tight hot pants and a flouncy black top. Her hoop earrings dangled five inches and her red hair was wavy and carefully teased to look unkempt. Music thrummed loudly through the club. Women and men both gyrated wildly to the Eurotech beat, while lights alternated color and direction highlighting the club walls with deep shadow.

Cindy leaned closer to him, her mouth hanging open, the smell of cheap whiskey and smoke clung to her breath as she leaned in to bite Dirk's ear. He looked away, always the cool guy. She grabbed his ass and squeezed, breathing hot and heavy into his ear, "Let's go Babe!" she yelled into his ear to cut through the noise. She pulled him towards the dance floor as he reluctantly followed. He always made them beg.

He had it made now. She wanted him so bad, this was gonna be a good night. He had figured out that if he made a digital loop recording of the camera tapes of him walking his rounds and changed the SD card in the security station, and then falsified his logs, no one would ever know that he had left. It had taken all night last night to make the video edit look good enough, but he had done it. Come Monday, no one would know. His shift change wouldn't happen until tomorrow morning at 8AM, and that would be plenty of time for Cindy. Oh yeah. Plenty of time.

He allowed himself to be dragged onto the dance floor and was just looking up at Cindy when suddenly the lights went out and the music stopped. There was about a half second of stunned silence and then people started bitching and complaining as the battery powered backup lights kicked on. The stale light of the backup lamps seared down across the dirty floor and hazy scene. The ambiance was utterly lost, like cold water on the face of a daydreamer. People milled about, started walking out and some yelled drunkenly at the DJ and bar staff.

"Shit!" Dirk said, ripping his hand out of Cindy's grasp.

"Ow, that hurt asshole!" Cindy yelled, pouting at the sudden change in his behavior. "What the hell was that for?"

"I've gotta go," Dirk said, wheeling away from his date.

"Where the hell are you going, dickhead?"

"I said, I'VE GOTTA GO BITCH!" Dirk screamed with uncharacteristic rage in his voice, as he shoved his way away from his girlfriend toward the exit. She stood rooted to the floor, stunned and unable to speak. He raced away, leaving her pouting, and shocked in the crowded bar. People looked on and started heading slowly towards the exit, not wanted to get involved.

Dirk raced down the street to his car, parked four blocks away, jumping a bush and railing to exit the club entrance. He was in a full panic. He looked around and saw that the streetlights were out, but the traffic lights were still working, partially at least. Yellow lights all over the district were flashing in monotonous synchrony. The flashing seemed to echo his own pounding pulse. If they found out he was gone, then he would be fucked for sure. They'd fire his ass, sure as shit. He did not want to lose this gig. He'd have to move back in with his mom while he tried to find work. Fuck that!

Dirk reached his sedan, opened the lock with the key fob and sat down, jamming the key into the ignition, gunning the engine and racing down the street. Mercifully, there was little traffic in the immediate post blackout confusion. It took him 45 minutes to reach the Verlhk Biological employee parking lot. He reached into his backseat and grabbed a duffle bag that contained his uniform and shoes and raced into the back door, punching the key fob lock and typing in the key code for the door of the building at the same time. His car horn honked, but nothing happened with the building door keypad. Shit, the power was out here too, he thought, reaching into his pocket to get his work keys. He inserted the correct door key into the door lock and turned the key. The door lock clicked and he pushed the door open. He raced to the locker room and slammed the door open and changed clothes in rapid succession, putting on his uniform and slicking his hair back. He checked himself in the mirror and sprayed mint into his mouth to cover the smell of alcohol. He threw his clothes into the duffle and slammed it into his locker and raced out to the security station.

Yes! He thought, no one else is here. He quickly removed the SD card from the camera system and placed the dubbed one into the slot. The time stamps had been the hardest thing to replicate. Luckily, some hacker type had free imaging software that was designed to do this for his video editing software. Amazing what you could find on the right Internet blog.

The building power was still out, so he could not check the tape. For some reason, the backup generators were not working. He was supposed to call in any disturbance in the power system to the home office, but if he did that, the SD card he had falsified would not make any sense. The tape ran for several hours more than he had been gone. What the hell was he going to do now? He stood and thought carefully. What if the power outage shorted out the system? That's it! He thought to himself as he grabbed the SD card out of the system and raced back out to his car. He unlocked it and grabbed the jumper cables and popped his hood, connecting them to the battery terminals. He clipped one of the other ends to the SD card and touched the other one rapidly to the card. Sparks flew and he jerked the lead back after a split second.

He unclipped the SD card, nearly burning his hand on the hot plastic. Good, it's not melted. It will look liked a power surge hit it! I'm not fucked! He sprinted back into the building and replaced the card into the unit. No one would be able to recover any data from the card and it would appear to be completely normal in a power surge.

He tried the desk telephone and it was dead. His cellphone had no bars here. There was no way to immediately report to home base, so he should just start back working now and pretend like he had been here all along. He would have to check the other floors. He grabbed a flashlight from behind the desk and raced up the stairs.

When he reached the fifth floor it was 1:45a.m. He walked up to the electronic door and stared at the blank panels. This section was always locked by the system. The door was cracked open. He had never seen this before and his mind reeled, trying to figure out what had happened. Did somebody go in? Oh that's great! Just fucking great! He thought and then remembered the safety briefing when he was hired. The upper floors had a safety fire system that automatically opened the doors in the event of a power failure. That way no one would burn alive trying to get the door open if there were a fire and the power was knocked out. Battery backups disengaged the locks and popped the doors open as an automatic fail safe.

He walked into the lab and shined his flashlight around. Maybe the surge had already messed up enough to cover his tracks. Power from a surge would travel often quite randomly through a large building like this one and frankly, this lab spooked him. Still, he was curious what the hell they did up here. He cautiously advanced into the dark, not sure what to expect. Tablet computers connected to plugs and notes lay on the counters, lab equipment was neatly organized on the counters. Microscopes and slides were arranged in certain areas, file cabinets nearby remained closed. A refrigerator was located next to a sink in which several beakers were in a drying rack. He was dying to know what the hell they kept in there. He saw a key on the counter and looked at the fridge door and saw the lock and took the key and opened the lock, swinging open the door and shined his flashlight inside. Multiple glass and plastic vials were kept on racks. He reached in and pulled one out, looking at the label. RL773-P12 was printed on the side of the glass sample, a red rubber stopper inserted into the top. Inside was a Clearwatery liquid.

Suddenly, the lights came back on. Dirk lurched backwards, his half drunken mind reeling at the shock of the sudden brightness from the room. His hand went slack as gravity took the vial and pulled it inexorably toward the black tiled floor. It spun, end over end in a graceful pirouette, smashing into the floor, its contents streaming out onto the black tile.

"Yes sir. That's correct, sir. Everything is fine here. Yes sir. The power went out and the phone was out. I couldn't get a cell signal either. You too. Yes sir, thank you sir. Good bye, sir." Dirk hung up the land line and sighed in relief. It was 2:01a.m. and he was sitting back at his desk on the first floor.

He had panicked when the vial had broken, but he was usually a quick thinker. He realized that the vial's label was still intact and that there were identical glass vials on the counter next to the fridge. He grabbed a pair of blue nitrile gloves out of a box on the counter, who the hell knew what that stuff was, and carefully picked up every piece of glass off of the floor and placed them in a small trash bag. He used his flashlight to scan the floor for fragments and he thought he got every one of them. He then took a very small paper towel and wiped up the liquid and squeezed what he could into a new vial, adding some tap water and very carefully removing the label from the broken vial and replacing it onto the new one. When he was finished, he was certain that no one could tell them apart. He took the trash bag and added the gloves and paper towel and wrapped them into a second trash bag. Unless they counted the plastic bags or vials, they would never know. There were no cameras in this lab.

When he drove home in the morning after his shift, he threw the bag into the river and kept driving. He was free and clear. Even if that damned bitch never called him again, he didn't care. She liked it rough anyway and he could probably turn it all around if he played his cards right. He drove home and showered and slipped into his bed, whiskey bottle still open on the counter. He would begin infecting others within three days.

In the fields of observation chance favors only the prepared mind.
—Louis Pasteur, Lecture, University of Lille, December 7, 1854

CHAPTER 8

McKnight Farm
4 miles north of Gallatin
June 9
7:32a.m.

Anastasia McKnight was awakened by the sound of her Great Pyrenees sheep dog barking. She looked over and the alarm clock was dead. She reached the lamp switch and flicked it. Nothing.

"Doug, wake up, power's out."

Grumbling, rolling over, "Humph... Sorry. What?" Doug replied.

"The power is out, sweetie," Anastasia repeated, rubbing her husband's massive shoulder. Anastasia was of medium height and build, with brown hair and eyes. She was a school teacher in a neighboring town, teaching agricultural sciences and was well versed in running their farm. She had a pilot's license and was certified on small Cessna four seater aircraft. The family had goats, sheep, a large barn, and a massive 150 pound sheep dog named Betsy that did an excellent job of keeping the coyotes from killing their animals, which they sold at market. They did well, considering their income from her job and her husband's work as a computer expert. He designed and managed websites for dozens of local businesses and governmental agencies. He basically had the keys to the city, having designed almost all of the local networks. He was well-liked and a popular figure in town.

Doug was a large man, almost completely bald, blue eyed, 6'1" and 260 pounds, 35 years old, overweight somewhat but with a massive upper torso and arms. He had been much heavier in the past and had lost over 50 pounds recently in an effort to improve his health that his doctor, Angus Gunn, had suggested. He would spend hours beating on his punching bags and lifting weights and walking around his 11 acre property as well, tending the animals. He spent most of his time managing his web-based business and knew that the time exercising was needed to keep fit. He could bench press well over 300 pounds and could lift a 200 pound man up a foot in the air at arm's length. He, like Angus, also suffered from an old back injury incurred during his youth when he had wrecked several race cars.

He was an expert driver and could pilot his Corvette through seemingly unbelievable maneuvers. He had avoided several accidents with his family using these skills, honed on the track in his youth. The skills learned from the near fatal events of his youth had prevented his family's demise on more than one occasion. He was, by far, the best driver in the group. He could pilot any on-road vehicle with aplomb. While there were others better at off-roading (he had gotten his F250 stuck more than once), no one he knew could match his on-road skill.

Like most everyone else in the group, he maintained a stash of at least six months of food, purchased at the Mormon cannery and kept in his basement, the cool earth sheltering his investment against starvation. He kept an advanced medicine chest and medical kit. He was a very proficient shooter as well. He and Angus would often compete pistol shooting, and they almost invariably tied. It was actually amazing to watch. No matter where they started, they always seemed to tie in any shooting contest. It was uncanny, and the first time they competed at plate racing, they stared in amazement at the results. They were competing to see who could most quickly knock down three 8 inch steel plates at 25 yards. Each would start at the outside and work towards the middle and whoever finished three first would continue to work on the opponent's side. Sometimes a shooter would clear all six plates, much to the chagrin of his or her opponent.

This was not so with Angus and Doug. The first time they ever competed, they tied the first round. They shook it off and prepared for the next round. They began again, the "boom/ping" sound of the percussion of fire of their identical Springfield XD-9 9mm service pistols occurring a few milliseconds before the pinging of the rounds impacting the soft steel falling plates. The second round resulted in a tie again, the last round of each sounding simultaneously. They paused and stared at each other, curious now. Everyone on the range had stopped shooting, watching with interest, as this had never happened before. Always, by the second round, one shooter would best the other. They reloaded, stood ready, and began again, and had the exact same, highly improbable result. They were in a dead heat, the final rounds impacting at exactly the same moment. They stopped and stared at each other, weapons still pointed safely down range, eyes wide this time, mouths open in shock. Heads started shaking, some nodded on the line, big grins slowly spreading through the crowd.

They knew good shooting when they saw it, and this was exceptional shooting. Both men cleared and holstered their pistols and shook hands, still grinning. A bond was formed that day that had lasted and been strengthened by the passage of time and effort.

Doug was one of the most generous men that Angus knew. He had once thrown his back out helping Angus move his eight foot tall pantry cabinets into the Gunn family prepping room. These large cabinets served to store his food supply and Angus simply could not move them himself. Doug never mentioned it, and Angus only knew about it from conferring with the local chiropractor who had informed him in a consult note, as this was part of Doug's medical record. Angus confronted Doug and Doug blew it off completely. He was loyal to a fault and would have done it again, even knowing his back would go out, so valuable were his friends to him.

Like Justin Clearwater, Doug preferred the Ruger SR-556 AR piston gun with an Aimpoint Comp M2 red dot optic, Surefire G2 Nitrolon light and single point sling. He stockpiled thousands of rounds of the military grade Federal M855 62 grain steel tip penetrator light armor piercing ammunition, among his other calibers. He frequented all of the local gun shows and the Internet for these bargains. Despite several periods of ammo shortages, he had been preparing for years and was well set. He had a Remington 870 police shotgun and several Springfield XD-9 and Glock 9mm pistols. Like everyone in the group, he had a pocket .380 that he carried concealed.

Anastasia preferred the Springfield XDs for defense and basically stayed away from the rifles. Both adults had full plate armor vests as well as the prior generation PASGT military helmets which were a level II equivalent, capable of stopping shotgun, fragmentation and pistol threats. Their home would be a bad bet for a midnight burglar.

Doug's long range tactical rifle was an FN TSR .308 bolt action rifle with a fluted 20 inch 1:12 twist rate barrel with a green Hogue over-molded stock. He had placed a Burris 4.5-14x 42mm scope with a ballistiplex reticle that was preset to allow for aiming rapidly at targets of varying ranges. While not as precise a scope in adjustment as the Leupolds or Super Snipers, this reticle allowed for very rapid target engagements out to around 500 yards, with no external adjustments of the scope. And while the other scopes could do the same thing with their Mildot systems, this Burris offered the adjustable power of the Leupold models at a third of the cost, allowing for use in a much closer shooting environment than the stock Super Sniper's fixed magnification. The scope was mounted in tough Burris Tactical rings, an excellent value for their durability. Using Black Hills 168 grain match ammunition, Doug routinely shot 0.75 inch or better groups at 100 yards, his moderately priced set up equaling the performance of much more expensive guns in the group.

Doug had bought, second hand, a large 50BMG sniper rifle from his relative who lived an hour away. The Barrett M82A1 weighed 42 pounds withs its 29" spring mounted, recoil absorbing barrel and heavy scope mounts and Leupold Mark 4 4.5-14x50mm scope with BORS, Barrett Optical Ranging System. The BORS was a computer that sat on the top of the Leupold scope and allowed the user to program in a series of variables such as wind, density altitude, temperature, elevation, bullet drag coefficient and weight, among others and keep those values saved in the system. When a target was ranged with laser rangefinder preferably or by optical comparison, the elevation turret of the scope was turned by hand. The BORS, attached physically to the scope, then displayed the distance that each click would cause the central zeroing point of the reticle to be aligned with.

For example, all of the data is programmed in at the beginning of the day, except for the distance. Then a target is ranged, using a laser range finder. The target might show "670 yards" on the range finder. The BORS would be turned on and would remember the settings already programmed into it and might display "100 yards" on its screen, having been set that way when sighting in the rifle. The shooter merely had to turn the elevation knob several turns, and as this was done, each click would bring up a slightly different setting, eventually reading "670 yards" or more likely a number likely very close, perhaps "672 yards" given that each click was a small, but discrete adjustment, not an infinite sliding scale. When the distance ranged, or a number as close as possible was reached on the setting, the shooter then looked through the scope, centered that target in the cross hairs and fired. If all of the variables were calculated correctly, the bullet would impact almost exactly where the cross hairs met. This process could be repeated as many times up and down as needed, without any loss of precision in the very expensive instrument, so high was the quality. The setting of the ring took only a few seconds and sped up the process of ranging to a point of military efficiency. It's was easily three to four times faster than anyone else's scope adjustment speed. A competent shooter could hit targets at three or four different ranges one at a time in less than two minutes, a feat that was unrivaled in this type of activity.

There were more accurate 50BMG rifles available, many from Barrett themselves, but no readily available models were ten round semi-automatics. You could fire all ten rounds from the magazine as fast as you could pull the trigger, and then reload then gun in seconds from another pre loaded magazine. This was true military grade firepower. The cartridge could literally destroy a modern car in seconds, driving the huge bullets several feet deep into the metal of the engine and transmission. The round could drive through sandbags that would stop every other common round in its tracks. The gun "turned cover into concealment," meaning that hiding behind a wall of concrete, dirt embankment or a tree would not protect you if the gun were fired at the obstacle.

The Hornady Amax 750 grain projectiles traveled at 2820 feet per second from the muzzle, and generated an astounding 13,241 foot pounds of energy. This was over five times more energy than a 175 grain .308 that traveled at slightly less speed, 2600 feet per second, yielding about 2600 feet pounds of energy at the muzzle, even this smaller cartridge was more than enough to instantly kill animals the size of an 800 pound elk out to 300 yards, and capable of human kills out to 1000 yards in the military theater of war. The longest recorded .308 kill was just over 1300 yards. The longest recorded 50BMG kill was over 2600 yards, with a Macmillan rifle, used by a Canadian sniper. Big game hunters had easily felled elephants with the round, the energy was double what the closest "elephant gun" could muster.

Terrorists who had been shot with the 50BMG or "50 cal," as it was commonly called, either with the Military Barrett or with the M2 Browning machine gun at ranges under 300 yards, usually had huge holes blown through their bodies. While the round would not blow arms and legs off, as in the movies, it was the most devastating small arms round in the US arsenal. When fired through machine guns with special armor piercing incendiary rounds, the 50BMG could take down fighter aircraft and helicopters, trucks, small armored vehicles and anything not specifically up-armored with either hardened metal plate armor or classified composite armor, only available to the military, each type weighing hundreds of pounds per vehicle side. The 50 BMG had more kinetic energy at 1000 yards than a .44 magnum pistol round had at point blank range. It was by far the most powerful gun any of the group members owned, and a great reassurance to Doug.

The gun itself was a 1.5 to 2M.O.A. or minute of angle gun: basically it could place all of its rounds in 2 inches at 100 yards, 10 inches at 500 yards and 20 inches at 1000 yards, though Doug had never shot it past 600 yards due to the lack of longer gun ranges to shoot in the area. He had sold an older truck to afford the ten thousand dollar price tag of the rifle, scope, ammunition and kit required to use it. He had a Bushnell ARC 1500 laser rangefinder, a bargain in comparison to use to range with. He would have liked to have Angus' Zeiss, but he simply had spent all of his available funds on the 50 cal. While only half as accurate as other rifles, it more than made up for this shortcoming in that the shooter could miss the center of a target by a foot or two and still neutralize it by effect of its massive trauma. Center mass aiming of this weapon almost guaranteed a kill shot. Even if the round were to miss the torso altogether and hit a limb or extremity, the enemy would almost certainly perish from the shock, tissue trauma and blood loss.

Doug prayed every week at church that he would never, ever have to use the device on a person, and that it could simply remain his favorite range toy. For that matter, every member of the group prayed that they would never have to defend themselves from anyone trying to hurt them. They all went to great lengths to avoid confrontation, from walking away from hecklers, to avoiding bad neighborhoods, from locking their doors, paying alarm companies to monitor their properties, adding extra deadbolts to their homes, to adding monitoring cameras easily seen by any would-be intruders. No one wanted to hurt anyone else. They all simply wanted to live in peace. Many of them prepared, with the silent prayer that this was all hopefully for nothing and that none of their fears would ever come to pass. Doug was a God-fearing man, and always took his family to the local Baptist church every Sunday.

Doug and Anastasia had three children. Eliza, 8 years old, was a spry, gregarious blonde with a beautiful smile. She had never met a stranger and would frequently lead in song the eighty plus member civic organization to which her daddy belonged. She had no stage fright whatsoever. Their four-year-old, Chet, a clone of his daddy, only one tenth his size and with the bushy brown hair that Doug had sported in his youth, was also a ham, never showing any fear really of anything. This led to much consternation on his mother's part, as he was a very active boy. The baby, Stella, was a gorgeous two-year-old, charming everyone with her blonde hair and blue eyes.

Doug sat up and said, "Hmmm. That's interesting. I wonder...," as he got up out of bed.

Anastasia looked at him and asked, "I wonder what?"

"I wonder if this was due to one of those solar flares that the group was talking about at the meeting I missed." Doug had been the only group member who was not at the meeting, but his neighbor, Lucien Tulley, had updated him the next day. The Tulley farm was at the end of his road, about a mile down and they frequently spoke.

Doug quickly explained the possible significance to his wife and she nodded in agreement. "Couldn't be a full blown one, because my cellphone still works. Man, that could have been bad. Nothing of ours are in those, what did you call them?"

"Faraday cages."

"Yeah, Faraday cages. We need to make those right now after breakfast. And what's Betsy on about this morning?" she said concerning her barking sheep dog.

"I don't see anything outside." Doug replied looking out the window. Probably a coyote or squirrel for that matter." He opened the porch door after disarming the house alarm and looked out onto the eight pasture acres that fed the goats and sheep. He did not see anything out of the ordinary. He had reflexively grabbed his 10-22 Ruger .22 Long rifle carbine in case there was an animal invader. He kept the little rifle on a shelf above the door, with a thumbprint locking device over the action, keeping it safe from little hands, but ready quickly when needed. Every group member with small children, or who had small children visit, had similar setups in their houses. Some even had gun safes on every level, ready in an instant to repel invaders, but safe from curious little fingers. The punch code safe had revolutionized child gun safety in these members' homes.

The 10-22 carbine was housed in a polymer stock made by Red Jacket, designed to be the "ultimate zombie killing 10-22," and made the rifle very compact and handy. Doug had applied for the tax stamp and purchased a small but highly effective sound suppressor for the gun, threaded to its factory barrel. This device, known incorrectly as a "silencer" could nevertheless make the gun so quiet that you could hear the bolt opening and closing when shooting it. It was quieter than most pellet guns. He liked the fact that he could dispatch an intruding animal without disturbing the neighbors at three AM when needed. The device cost more than the gun, but was worth it to Doug.

Betsy stopped barking and jogged over to Doug, head down, smiling at a job well done. "You goober," he said, vigorously scratching the giant pet's fur. She wagged her tail rapidly, her whole body getting into the act. Whatever malicious threat of impending doom was about to strike terror into the hearts of the McKnight household, it seemed to have shied away at the prospect of 150 pounds of angry fur and fang charging it down this morning.

Anastasia began the morning ritual of getting the kids up. Luckily, it was a Saturday and no one had missed school or work due to the power outage. Doug threw on some clothes, brushed his teeth and hair, put on some deodorant, dumped his pajamas on the bed and went down to the barn and fired up the second hand Yamaha generator that he had rigged in line with the house's power supply. He had so many favorable contacts in town, that it had been simple to barter computer work for a specialist to run line from the barn across the property. Doug loved his job. Also, the time he spent on the web at work allowed him to monitor current events for the rest of the group. He usually knew what was happening as it happened, sometimes before it happened. At least most of it. Some things the government certainly kept a lid on. Several of the group members had seen that first hand, when they had worked in the military in the past.

With the power back on, at least for the next eight hours, before the generator needed refilling, Doug set to the work of making the Faraday cages. He knew he should have done it the other day, but he just didn't have the time, and he frankly hoped that the whole thing was an overreaction. He took several ammo boxes out of the barn and began wiping them down. Next he grabbed a box of mylar foil computer bags, the kind used to store and ship laptops and hard drives. The metal foil was sealed into the plastic and prevented static discharge through the bags. He took them back to the garage and started loading nonessential backup electronics into them.

He loaded FRS or family radio service radios into them. These would serve for near range communication. He took an extra ICOM 2 meter band handi talkie and removed the battery pack and placed the unit, battery and charger into a bag. This would connect him to the larger group out to 10-15 miles when used with a high gain "fox hunting" antenna. He did not yet have the short wave monitoring radio or HF, High Frequency, Ham radios that he wanted for Christmas. These could allow for truly worldwide communication and could be arranged using a "near vertical incidence skywave" antenna and tuning to allow for 0-300 mile communication range. The radios on Humvees seen in the military that rested behind the vehicles parallel to the ground were good examples of this technology. They bounced their signal off the ionosphere in the upper atmosphere and it reflected back to earth covering an expanding swath of ground. This would be ideal, but the Barrett had tapped him out and the radios would have to wait. He took several cell phones, palm computers and laptops, along with several large bags of electronic parts and placed them in the mylar bags. He added battery chargers, small solar panels, watches, clocks, radios, LED flashlights, car electronic spare parts, starter coils, spark plugs and anything redundant that was electronic that he could find in his house. It took over two hours to collect the twenty bags worth of items, and he had about a compact truck bed's-worth of equipment spread throughout the house to go through. He had a lot of electronic gear as computers were his life and living.

He took a heat sealer designed for kitchen use and began to seal the Mylar bags closed. This melted the plastic and made continuous metal foil around the items. He then placed the bags into metal ammunition cans from various surplus supply houses that he frequented. Some were already lined with foam, others, he simply added 3/8" foam with a hot glue gun, roughly attaching them to the walls. He then dumped the Mylar bags full of gear into the cans and then sealed each lid, creating, in effect, double thick Faraday cages. He took a 3 foot tall aluminum metal trash can and lined it with a double layer of the foam and then placed most of the electronics he used on a daily basis into three small school sized backpacks, or book bags and then closed the lid, making sure the metal lid touched all the way around the lid circumference. It was new and undamaged and was a tight fit. He then placed the entire trash can into a steel garage storage cabinet lining one of the walls of the garage. It was not quite as tight a setup as the other units, but would allow easy, instant access to his stuff and probably provided comparable protection from EMP.

By now it was lunchtime and the power had come back on. He turned off the genset and prepared to protect it as well. He took four overlapping layers of 1/2 inch hole aluminum chicken wire and began using copper wire to tie the chicken wire together at intervals. He lined the inside of the wire with wool felt, with large vent holes cut into it. This could cover the generator and prevent the metal from touching the unit. This took well into the afternoon; the monotony of it strained his patience. He finally had enough to protect the generator and he went to the barn and covered the generator with the wire, tying the edges together in the same manner. He cut several access ports into the wire and tied those back down, so that he could fuel, operate and maintain the unit when needed. He ran heavy gauge grounding wire from the chicken wire mesh cover and attached it to a series of five four-foot rebar steel rods he had driven into the ground with a ten pound sledgehammer. It was very easy work for the big man. This would allow any EMP surge, even a lightning strike to cover the skin of the cage and be transmitted into the ground, leaving the equipment unharmed. He felt like he had done enough for now, and frankly, the remainder of his gear wouldn't fit into any container usable as a Faraday cage.

He went into the house and showered and turned on the news. It was all about the power outage and the "minor effect of the solar flare." There was "no need to panic, everything was returning to normal." He had heard that before. It was the same thing he expected them to say. Time would tell. Oh well, time for dinner, he thought, walking into the kitchen, daydreaming of a large burger and fries.

Hell is empty and all the devils are here.
—William Shakespeare. The Tempest. 1.2.253-254

CHAPTER 9

Undisclosed location
Suburb of Atlanta
Verlhk Biological
Security Station, Main entrance
June 14
2:12p.m.

The week had passed quickly enough for the Atlanta area inhabitants. The blackout had covered most of the West Coast, the South central US, the Midwest and parts of Mexico, and the Eastern part of Canada. It did not affect the Northeast or Pacific Northwest. The greatest population density in the US was not affected by it. It was very heterogenous in its effect. Certain areas went down, and others were totally unaffected. Atlanta, Miami, Charleston, Houston, Dallas, Albuquerque, and Los Angeles were the largest cities affected. It was a simple blackout for most, and luckily only a brownout for Los Angeles. Still, there had been rioting in the inner cities in Houston, Miami and

Atlanta. These were quelled very quickly and were very small scale; basically thugs out on Friday night looking for trouble and using the outage as an excuse to party.

Los Angeles was a different story. While the vast majority of Hispanic Americans decried violence and were the hardworking backbone of the community, some violent radicals sought political gain from the event. Even though there had been a brownout only, racial extremists in the community organized a march against "The Man," who had, in their minds, planned the outage as a "test of will" against "the Greater Latino Community." No one was really sure what that meant, but it seemed to sound good when the news anchors repeated the phrase endlessly with breathless 24 hour coverage.

The rioting had gone on for two days in full force and then on a smaller scale for two more days. The National Guard was finally called in and by Wednesday, had quelled the violence. Heat, politics, racism, hatred, and intolerance fertilized the young minds in the Southern California city and out of it grew a total disrespect for authority, along with an eager willingness to commit violence on anyone around. This evil influence along with the decades of entitlement mentality produced a powder keg of turmoil waiting to erupt with any minor or even potential disruption of services.

Luckily, the other major cities and smaller towns had power restored very rapidly, most that night or the next day at the latest. Disruptions in the Tennessee and Georgia region were very minor, similar to those seen with a simple thunderstorm. Power crews were experts at managing this type of event and no one had rioted in the smaller areas or suburbs. Life went on with smooth easiness in this region as it had for decades.

The events at the Verlhk research facility had been obscured by the frenetic activity of its night security guard. Dirk had succeeded in removing any traces of his tampering with the vial of unknown liquid in that strange refrigerator. The technicians still had not received the second, required wild type antigens to begin their comparative analysis. No one had even looked at the sample to notice the dilution that had been done. The outage had delayed normal work somewhat as several experiments had to be restarted due to the backup power systems not kicking in. It was a curious thing, seen in several areas, with similar effects. Certain power systems were less robust in managing the solar event.

The news did finally link the event to the solar flare activity. The weekend news cycle had centered on the breakup and social drama of a popular movie star and the couple's involvement with a new religious group that preached "free love and the love of God." All in one breath. You could, I guess, have your cake and eat it too with this church. At any rate, several pastors of the church had been caught in a sex sting with minors at a camp event in the recent past, and it had been revealed that the couple had attended the camp events where this had taken place. Speculation had been unending as to the possible connections between the Hollywood love nesters and the cult group.

Solar flare related disruptions had been predicted by several noted physicists in the recent news. All of this was ignored by the media. Even worse, because the events that it caused were so minor, all of the concern the scientific community had expressed was dispelled as fear-mongering. The populace took it as more evidence of overreaction on the part of anyone who actually attempted to prepare against these types of events.

The 24 hour news station ran a weeklong special on "Disaster Survivalists" and their assumed links to every kind of antigovernment, terrorist, racist and religious cult that they could find. Their attempts to prepare for disasters were portrayed as escapist philosophies for the socially inept. The equipment and supplies purchased were portrayed as if they were boondoggles that could throw these families into the poorhouse. The government was represented by psychiatrists, social workers, military leaders and police who all were quoted in support of anti-hoarding and anti-separatist laws. Several radical left wing senators and representatives had proposed such laws in Washington, including ones that would outlaw home schooling and the keeping more than two months of supplies such as food and ammunition in any one household. The network's ratings went through the roof. It was the most popular series that they had ever run and they planned on multiple spin-offs to continue the ratings trend. They had not had a hit like this since the moderate right wing news station had pulled most of their viewers away in an ongoing ratings war.

The backlash against preppers continued to grow and the events only served to strengthen the preppers' resolve that their efforts were very much needed, now more than before. This started to widen the schism between the "survivalists" and the "sheeple" to use each group's derogatory words for the other. The general populace felt that the preppers were dangerous and unpredictable and the preppers thought that the general populace was as unprepared to handle real dangers as a herd of sheep. This led to increasing distrust and separation between the two groups, though the preppers were rapidly gaining numbers in the West, the South and the rural nation as well, even in some large cities that were classically the liberal socialists domain, largely due to political backlash against the current national government. Luckily, there had been no violence committed on either side.

A car drove into view on one of Dirk's monitors. He had been granted leave tomorrow to attend an international conference on homeland security. The event would be held over a three day weekend in downtown Atlanta and members of security forces, police departments, private security firms, overseas governments, fire departments, homeland security workers, emergency management workers, and other similar business representatives were now traveling from all over the globe to meet in Atlanta to attend the meeting. There would be booths displaying the wares of over two hundred security product vendors, lectures on security related issues and hundreds of millions of dollars would exchange hands during this massive event, hosted by the US government in its effort to stamp out global and domestic terrorism.

Dirk had been recommended to go due to his "proper handling of an out of the box situation," referring to the power outage. In truth, the management thought he would do well to get out of the office for a few days, as his demeanor had recently worsened. He had become snippy and had actually yelled at a delivery girl who brought packages into the office. All week, he had shied away from others, sulking in his booth, hastily performing his duties with a mild smirk, scowl, or sometimes a completely blank face. He said that he had a cold, as his nose was running and he felt very feverish. But he came to work and didn't openly complain, so his boss decided to take the weekend shift himself. His boss didn't like big events anyway, and could at least talk to his family while on duty some.

Dirk looked at the monitor and saw the vehicle move across the screen. His mind wandered, thinking about the big conference tomorrow. A sneeze ripped from his nose as he used a tissue to wipe the thin line of saliva running from the corner of his mouth. He had been drooling on everything the last two days. He hadn't slept well and his dreams had been very erratic and strange. He couldn't concentrate worth a damn, either. And he had been sweating all day. He felt feverish and he would soak the sheets and then freeze in the cold wetness. He looked down at his hand and noticed the thin, fine twitch that had just started in his left fourth and fifth fingers. What the hell was this? He needed a break.

THIS GODDAMNED JOB! Fuckin-A! Where the hell did that come from? He thought, wondering at the mental outburst. He looked back at the screen and saw cats dancing across the screen. Cats with purple coats of fur and ears rotating in spirals on their heads. They were staring at him, those green eyes, rolling, rolling, rolling.... Shit!

What the hell was going on!?

Drool hung limp from his mouth as he sat staring at the screen, now blank. He heard a noise and snapped the tissue up, catching the line of saliva without seeing it. The employee passed out into the parking lot without looking at him. He began to stare at the back of the man's head. The man's brains were melting and running in gutters out of his ears, the gray yellow fluid, viscous like gelatinized snot. He kept walking out to his car, a mindless man, having left his mind at work.

The car door opened and the man began to get in, but teeth in the car door sprouted outward and chomped down viciously on the man, catching him on the neck and shins as he tried to sit down. Rivulets of blood ran down the man's neck and legs into his shoes, pooling up and spilling out and the car door began chewing its victim in a slow inexorable grinding motion. The man's eyes opened wide in horror and shock, looking directly at Dirk, unable to change their now fixed gaze. The glass wall and closed door leading out to the parking lot afforded Dirk a view of the agony, but kept the sound from entering the building. People walked past the gruesome scene and simply passed by.

Instantly, the scene shifted. The man seemed completely uninjured. He shut the car door and quietly drove off down the street.

What's happening to me!? Thought Dirk, as his mind raced ahead, thinking of the reason this must have happened. It must be Burt, his boss. The bastard wanted Cindy. The bitch must have been fucking him for weeks now. THAT'S WHY HE WANTS ME AT THE CONFERENCE! So he can go fuck her all night long. He made up that shit about his retard kid for sympathy. That's it! Chicks dig it when you have a softie heart! Fuckin-A man! He must have fucked with my mind with that magic protonic solution. The tip-top secret protonic amazing salt bath of destiny. Fuckin-A!

Dirk managed to finish out the shift, keeping the secret knowledge of his thoughts from everyone else. He went home and ate a jar of mayonnaise and burned his work uniform in the backyard. He slept in his bathtub in case the sensors in his brain were sending signals to the home base. They couldn't probe him here. Tomorrow would be his destiny. Tomorrow, tomorrow, tomorrow, tomorrow...

Wallace Farm
Outskirts of Portland, TN
10 miles Northeast of Gallatin
June 14
5:10p.m.

The dinner bell rang in the distance, as Samuel Wallace cleaned off his case knife. He stood in the shadow of a tall, ancient oak tree in front of his barn, staring with steely blue eyes towards the small white house, where his wife has just finished preparing the family meal. He was dressed in Carhartt long parts and a dark brown colored heavy cotton shirt, and worn out black and grey New Balance running shoes. This was his uniform outside of work. The clothes worked as well for his 57-year-old frame as anything else he had ever tried on. He could be recognized by anyone that knew him. He must have five sets of similar clothes.

Samuel worked as a nurse at Dr. Mackenzie's office, but his heart was here, in the rural Tennessee countryside. He hunted, fished, trapped, skinned and farmed in this, the place of his birth. His family had owned the land since the early 1800s, since they had come across the mountain to seek a new life. They had carved out a small piece of paradise here. They were never wealthy. There was no manor house or left over property carved up over the years by greedy children and siblings. There was just this, the same 300 acres that they had from the beginning. Nothing more, nothing less. To him, it was heaven.

He spent many weekends as a frontier re-enactor and could make a fire from flint and steel, preserve meat and cook over campfires. He could catch fish with string and an old spoon and could shoot a deer, or squirrel, for that matter, in the head from fifty paces with his musket. He was a frontiersman by heart. He felt he had been born into the wrong time.

He closed his knife and grabbed his hat and began walking towards the house, his mind running to cornbread and biscuits. His mouth watered, thinking of the food waiting for him in this, the house he had been born in. His son and daughter from his previous marriage would be here tonight. Thirty one-year-old Trey Wallace was, like his dad, of medium build and beginning to show grey in his brown hair. He collected things. Namely, he collected bullets. It was an old family joke about his lack of non-firearm related hobbies. He had been an AWACS operator in the US Air Force and had been stationed in Alaska where he had taken extensive survival training. He worked at a local gun store in a neighboring city now. He had even one-upped his father's trick of making acorn bread by instead memorizing all of the wild edible plants in North America. In fairness, his father did know all of the edible ones in Tennessee.

Jessica, Sam's 27-year-old, blonde-haired, green-eyed daughter, was divorced with three kids. She worked as a secretary at the headquarters of a locally based international Christian book store chain. Since her family was away with her ex-husband now, she liked to spend her weekends alone with her father and mother. Samuel's wife, Carolyn, was 44 and of medium build, blonde, with a beautiful, youthful smile. She was a dedicated home-maker. She had never smoked or drank and the years of good living had caught up to her. She looked much more 35 than 44.

Samuel had built a second cabin on the property to allow for more protection. The walls were reinforced with rammed earth and offered significant thermal and ballistic protection and would remain cool in the summer and warm in the winter. He had set up solar panels, hand crank wells, and a full inverter system for the farm. His barn was full of manual farm implements and he had a workshop full of old hand tools that comforted him, each one fit his palm like a glove. He felt that he was a blessed man indeed.

The smells from the kitchen were wafting toward him now as he approached the house, the scent of meats and vegetables and baked goods setting his mind to a prayer of thanksgiving. He felt a surge of hope in the midst of what he knew to be a troubled world. If beauty could survive here and honor could be taught and passed down, there was hope for the world. Somehow, he knew God was telling him something here. Somehow he felt hope would be needed soon...just maybe very soon.

Atlanta International Conference Center
Downtown Atlanta
Conference Center Exhibition Hall Floor
June 15
3:42p.m.

Dirk paced slowly across the floor of the center. He saw them all, staring at him. Their eyes burrowed holes into his brain. They were all talking, talking about him. They knew. They knew that he knew. Hunger, aching hunger and thirst.

He saw men in turbans, women in miniskirts, police in full uniform, military in uniform, business men and women in suits, Asian men in khaki pants and dark-colored short sleeved shirts. People from all over the world had converged by the thousands to participate in this landmark event. The basic goal of terrorist elimination was to be a global goal. Drool continued to run in rivulets, now down the corners of Dirk's mouth, his jaw now slack as his mind worked feverishly, billions of virions racing through the brain and spinal cord, attacking system after system. He felt his bowels loosen just as he turned toward the sound to his right.

A small security detail was coming across the floor, headed past where Dirk was standing, its obviously Arab dignitary flanked by a series of security men in dark suits forming a protective ring around the man. Dirk had been wandering around the convention all day long. He couldn't seem to remember why he was there. He just paced around and around, touching the display items, drooling on his shirt, sometimes growling low, under his breath if anyone got too close. He did not trust anyone now, not since the virus had begun to rewrite his neuro chemistry, warping his perceptions of time and space, increasing his limbic system's responses to stimuli. The rage centers of his brain were hyper-stimulated. Every motion around him was interpreted as a threat. His mouth had filled with drool. He was salivating at an increasing pace.

Unlike victims of wild type rabies, his brainstem had not been fully ravaged by the virus. The loss of the ability to swallow was the most likely cause of the hydrophobic reaction seen in rabies. The victim could not swallow correctly and therefore would do anything to keep water and any liquid or even solid out of the mouth. The victim would spit, choke, gag, vomit, or even run the other way if presented with water. But the genetic modification of the receptor proteins that enabled the increased airborne spread, also reduced the binding site affinity to the brainstem neurons that caused the very hydrophobia that contributed to the rapid death seen in wild-type victims. In addition, the cardiac arrhythmias that were so often fatal, were much less likely to happen due to the same change in binding affinity of the genetically engineered receptor subtypes. Dirk's lower brain functions remained intact, but his higher brain which controlled thought and suppressed emotional drive was a raging wave of neurotransmitters screaming though a sea of infecting virions, budding off one neuron, to the next and the next, the crescendo of infection sweeping him into the abyss of madness. The plague reached critical mass. The infection had completely saturated every functioning neuron.

As his bowels loosed fecal material though his undergarments and drool ran down his neck, soaking into his shirt, he turned and lunged at the oncoming group. His fingers ripped across the neck of the first guard, tearing the skin of his adam's apple away, revealing a whitish cartilage frame, with blood spraying outward. The man gurgled and grabbed at his ruined neck and fell sideways as Dirk's momentum carried him forward. His teeth were bared in a feral grin, slobber flying in every direction, splashing onto the floor, the walls, the men knocked backwards by the sudden attack. The dignitary's eyes went wide as Dirk's mouth snapped down onto his neck, teeth tearing a bright red jagged line across the left side of the man's jugular vein. Blood erupted and covered both men's upper chests and faces. The victim buckled under the savage onslaught and just as quickly, the enraged attacker was bounding down the hall, screaming and gurgling as blood and spittle ran down his chin, rage coursing through the shell of thought that once contained his mind. The man who had once been known as Dirk was no more, his body taken by the virus.

The brutal attacks continued with inhuman speed, a rabid animal charging through the conference hall, snapping, biting, and clawing its way through the crowd. Only seconds had elapsed and already ten people lay bleeding from the horrifying attacks. The creature stumbled into an opening in the crowd. Its clothes were covered in blood and saliva, the wet mixture streaming down from its teeth and mouth, the coppery smell of blood mixing with the sharp foul odor of the fecal material now ground into its undergarments and pants. Its jaws opened in a leering grin as it scanned the group and lunged again towards a police officer.

The crowd was now tearing away from the scene, knocking over tables and chairs, trampling each other in a desperate effort to flee from this crazed apparition. The specter of death loomed over the crowd. Already doomed, none realized the true horror of the scene. All day long, the man had passed from booth to booth, handling gear, fondling equipment, rubbing saliva and virions onto most of the surfaces in the conference hall. Thousands of people had already been exposed by touching these items or by inhaling the breath of the man as he had walked from booth to booth, spreading the deadly airborne plague. This had been occurring all week, since about the third day the man had been exposed by the broken vial at the lab. As in many other viruses, this disease spread before the symptoms appeared. Not everyone who was exposed would become infected. No disease outside of science fiction could claim that honor, but over two thirds exposed would become infected.

The police officer had seen the initial attack and already had his Taser in his hand. The rabid creature lunged and the Taser discharged its spikes, both catching onto the clothing of the creature. Arcs of current ran out and the effect was immediate, as the lunge stopped midway and the beast crashed to the ground. The police man breathed a sigh and advanced slowly. The infected man lay sideways, a stinking heap of flesh and bodily fluids, most from his victims. The officer's gaze wavered momentarily to the side as the crowd surged.

In that instant, the thing lurched sideways, the Taser darts still attached, the device remaining in the officer's hands as the plastic housing jerked out of the front of the gun and dragged on the ground behind the creature. Two shots rang out, followed by three more as two Atlanta PD officers discharged their weapons into the infected man's torso. It stumbled forward, screaming in rage and kept moving forward toward the officers. Behind them, several bystanders froze in a panic, pressed against the surging crowd, now smashing windows to evacuate the hall. The beast's blood was running down its chest and mid-abdomen as it hobbled forward. Repeated fire echoed in the chamber as the two officers emptied their standard issue Smith and Wesson M&P .40 caliber pistols into the thing's body. A total of 20 of the 32 rounds fired went into its torso and head, finally ending the terror.

Blood pooled across the floor, soaking into the carpet of the convention center hall. Blood dripped from the walls of nearby booths; the deadly mist clung to the clothing and surfaces for several feet in every direction. The event would be closed to the public. The cancellation of the remaining lectures and exhibits meant that all of the travelers would have more time to spend in Atlanta. They would tour the area, eat at restaurants, sleep in hotels. They would soon be returning to their cities of origin, in the U.S. and all around the world. And the virus would travel with them, circling the globe within 24 hours of the first flight leaving the convention city. The formal investigation would never release its findings to the general public. Inquiries like this usually took months, and there simply would not be time.

Occurring in such a high profile place, and involving a Saudi dignitary, who had already bled to death, the events would fill the news for days. The official story was of a "lone wolf homegrown terrorist with mental illness" who had attacked the Arab man out of "racist bigotry." A tall thin man with a khaki tactical pants and a white shirt stared into the devastation, furrowed brow betraying his deep concern over the scene. On the back of his white polo knit shirt were emblazoned the words "Sumner County EMS." Standing next to him, also in casual police gear, a shorter, red-haired, younger man looked on, his expression blank in shock. The navy blue shirt he wore read "Gallatin Police Department."

Self-reliance, the height and perfection of man, is reliance on God.
—Ralph Waldo Emerson, *The Fugitive Slave Law*

CHAPTER 10

Gallatin, TN
15 miles North of Nashville
Southern Family Medical Group
June 17
7:12p.m.

"Hey there, Dr. Corpuz. How's it going?" George asked Carlos as he strode out of the office down the hall after a long day.

"Doing great, George," Carlos answered. George was the night janitor and well-liked by everyone. "You have a good weekend?"

"Yes Sir! Went to Atlanta to visit family. Had a great time" George's family had a reunion every five years and it was a big family. They always rented space at a local hotel in Atlanta and this year they had gone downtown and seen the lights. It was a wonderful reunion this year.

"Have a great evening man," Carlos said as he left the building. What a nice guy, he thought.

Times Square
New York City
June 19th
1:32p.m.

People walked through the crowd, sneezing and wiping their brows. This summer cold was ridiculous, thought most New Yorkers. It had come suddenly, as do most of these things. Some people had even been to the hospital. There was a rumor on Internet social media sites that some of the people had West Nile virus and had gone nuts. West Nile had been seen in NYC before and terrified most of its inhabitants. Scary jungle disease in the big city.

As several people walked through the crows, virions of the genetically altered rabies virus passed easily among them, spreading from mere breath, inhaled into the unsuspecting nasal passages of new hosts. An era of unprecedentedly rapid air travel had allowed the plague to span the globe in a day. There were infected now in four continents, in two hundred major cities around the globe. And it had been only four days. Some were already hallucinating, going to the ERs or mental hospitals, this younger generation being more "in touch" with their psychiatric health. The plague had reached as far as Australia now, its tendrils of infection spreading. Members of the lab at Verlhk biological were already showing signs of aberrant behavior, being the first to be exposed to patient zero, who had unwittingly infected himself with the plague. The crescendo would not be seen yet, but the wave of death was coming, its roar slowly building. The tiny bullet shaped vessels of destruction floated through the air in respiratory droplets and in saliva into new hosts everywhere, around the world, in this new global economy. Inside the world's prosperity were held the very seeds of its own destruction. A young tourist placed his hand on a railing that had just been seeded with the salivary secretions of an infected host. The boy rubbed his nose with the hand and instantly doomed himself and those around him. The plague continued, the populace unaware of its real nature.

Los Angeles
City center
June 21
6:17p.m.

Ricky walked along the edge of the crowd, his heart beginning to beat faster, the chanting of the crowd washing over him. His saliva was flowing rapidly, drool dripping onto his chin. Others in the crowd seemed to be in a similar state, enchanted by the rhetoric of the speaker, his megaphone blaring political slogans against the perceived injustice against the little man.

He did not understand the words, which at first seemed odd, but as his anger grew, he forgot what he was angry about. He stared at the crowd next to him, slack jawed in a fevered sweat, his eyes unfocused as neurons were steadily losing the battle with the bullet shaped virions. His limbic system was taking control of his consciousness, its raw emotion overwhelming reason. Rage, anger, hate and all of the raw animal emotions brimmed to the surface, washing away all reason in a sea of biochemical lust.

Suddenly a rock flew across the crowd, striking the speaker in the head. Blood poured from his scalp as the sudden thud and following silence echoed across the minds of the bystanders. The moment of terrible silence ensued, and then three figures raced onto the small, hastily erected stage. Screams of mortal agony and writhing pain seared into the minds of the onlookers as the hooded figures began tearing the man apart, pulling and biting with savage ferocity. Their rage had no focus, they were mad with fury, attacking everyone in the crowd. A melee ensued, trampling feet crushing those in their way. Blood spattered across Ricky's face and he sank his teeth into the woman's neck in front of him. The orgy of terror and death had begun and would not stop until the police department and the National Guard began shooting and killing the protestors, their response uncharacteristic for civil servants. They, too, were slowly losing the battle of will against the virus. A state of emergency would ensue with a total media blackout enforced by the governor, his Homeland Security troops cordoning off the city as it began to burn in a hellish nightmare of fear and terror.

The outside world was told of political riots of epic proportions to cover the truth, the truth that had only recently dawned on the government, its research teams uncovering the facts less than 48 hours ago. Internet videos from cellphones would leak out despite all of the social media site content related to it being automatically blocked, a benefit of the "Internet off-switch" asked for by the recent president and granted amidst an uproar of protest. A crackdown on any information related to the riots, now going on in several major cities went into overdrive. Cover stories of political unrest and natural disasters were dutifully assigned to each new event as it occurred.

Around the globe, rioting and crime sprees became so common that the news cycle could not keep up with them as they occurred. They became as common as traffic accidents and in fact, in some places, more common. The rural communities were not yet as hard hit, being farther from the regions of rapid air travel, and having fewer residents who did travel as far from home. But even here the effects were just starting to be felt, and as time passed, more and more crime and illness began to spread through the entire country. In foreign countries, the picture was harder to ascertain, as the media coverage was spotty at best.

The government began to understand more or less what was happening and they began to attempt to filter information "to prevent a panic." They knew that the modified rabies virus now was the cause of the events and that the plague was spreading. They had identified the diluted sample in the freezer that patient zero had altered. The entire Verlhk lab had been closed down and hundreds of officials from the CDC had begun to work on the problem. Verlhk had modified the virus based on instructions from the administration. They were the very lab that was to produce an experimental vaccine for the infection, and now half of their staff were infected and quarantined. Work to produce a viable vaccine was underway, but there simply would not be enough time to complete the work on creating the vaccine, much less producing enough of it to protect the population. That was the work the Verhlk had already been paid to do. The unintentional release came so early in the processes of vaccine study that there now was no way to speed up the steps. They wouldn't even have time to test if the standard wild type vaccine would be effective, as the typical results from animal trials would requires weeks at a minimum, weeks that they simply did not have. The government was running out of time with each new city that fell prey to the spread of the disease.

Online bloggers were arrested, shut down, some simply disappeared overnight. Anyone using cellphones to broadcast footage of the events was tracked using the cell signals and shut down, but the videos went viral and the government began to systematically threaten every news agency with the Patriot Act to keep the news reporters reading the officially approved cover stories. Articles would appear on web pages reporting the actual events and then immediately they would disappear within hours. The NSA spent its entire allotment of computer time tracking sites and shutting down non-official reports and viral videos.

Still, people emailed and called each other, and the word was beginning to spread that people were getting sick and that there were riots and crimes waves everywhere. The government simply could not keep up with the sheer volume of communication that was occurring. Arrests of private citizens for talking to family members about the real events began, but the much ballyhooed "FEMA camps" that the conspiracy theorists worried about day and night could not be staffed to contain the number of people that would have to be detained to prevent the information from spreading.

The camps were real. They were simply not meant to round up the entire population as some had thought. They were a containment method for controlling isolated disease outbreaks. If only one city were affected by a plague, the system would probably have worked. The FEMA system could cordon off the area and evacuate the population to the defined camp areas and keep the contagion from spreading. They simply could not handle every major city being affected at basically the same time. How could they have enough staff to contain everyone in the country? While the conspiracy theorists were certainly right about the fact that the government did have some fairly nefarious plans that could be put in place rapidly during a national emergency, the government simply was not omniscient, omnipotent and omnipresent.

By now, Atlanta, Los Angeles, Dallas, Houston, Milwaukee, Miami, Portland, Washington D.C., New York City, Chicago, and several smaller cities were experiencing riots and had been completely or partially isolated and cordoned off. Various cover stories were used to explain the events, from West Nile in New York City to power outages and looting in Miami. So information spilled out, and people were overlooked. The administration realized they were fighting a losing battle and their efforts began to weaken after only a few days, so great were the number of simultaneous regions affected. Containment now was impossible.

Gallatin, TN
15 miles North of Nashville
Southern Family Medical Group
June 21
6:32p.m.

Angus turned off his computer and carefully took off his yellow disposable apron and nitrile gloves, placing them in the biohazard container behind his desk. He used alcohol based hand sanitizer gel to sterilize his hands and then gingerly removed the N95 mask from his face and placed it also in the biohazard trash can. The practice had been seeing a large number of what appeared to be a type of summer flu virus. Angus was not sure what it was and never was much for overreacting and notifying the CDC of every little thing that came through. After all, he had spent several years in the Air Force preparing for much more serious plagues and disasters. But, since he had kids and a wife at home, he had instituted the same simple precautions for infection prevention that he had previously used during the swine flu pandemic. That event, or nonevent as it were, was fresh in his mind.

Still, just because the symptoms of salivary secretions and fever seemed mild, he didn't feel like giving any new colds to his family. All of his staff were required to do the same thing as well. No eating or socializing. All telephones and surfaces were wiped with sanitizing cloths after each shift, and after any droplet contamination from any patient. The simple universal precautions were cheap and easy to follow. He called out to his technicians and nurse and told them to go home and thanked them for their work today. They had seen thirty patients and it had been a good day. Most were routine follow ups, but about half had complained of this summer virus.

Two cases of psychosis had presented. One was a new patient who appeared to have longstanding paranoid schizophrenia, though he had no records to confirm this yet. This was a fairly common event in any doctor's office as these patients tended to hop from doctor to doctor, the disease causing fear and distrust that interfered with the normal doctor-patient relationship. However, one really worried him. One of his regular patients had been in a car accident after hallucinating seeing a school bus on fire in front of her car. The accident was very minor, but now he had started a dementia work up on the 61-year-old female. He really liked the patient and worried for her, as it could be the start of a serious dementia, and at the younger end of the spectrum. The neuro psychiatric testing next month would help elucidate the cause and then he could plan an appropriate treatment. Still, he hated dementia, having lost two grandparents to it, and felt sadness for the patient's suffering. Angus said a brief prayer of thanks and prayed for the healing of his patients and headed home after rewashing his hands with chlorhexidine soap for the thirtieth time today. He would need some lotion to prevent dry skin, he thought as he headed out of the door.

Bethpage, TN
Rouges Fork Road
7 miles Northeast of Gallatin
June 21
11:47p.m.

The Dodge Charger Police cruiser screamed down the narrow rural road, lights and sirens blaring. Officer Mattfield was in hot pursuit of a homicide suspect, the cruiser gaining on the older bondo covered truck. The road twisted and turned as the chase continued. This was not his first rodeo. He was an experienced officer in the force and piloted his vehicle with adept control. He called in, "Station, this is seventeen, in pursuit of suspect, over."

"Copy seventeen, continue pursuit, over," the dispatcher replied. "No reserve units available, over."

"Roger that." There had been a veritable crime wave in town this week. He didn't know if it was the heat, or a new street drug, but this was ridiculous. Ever since returning from Atlanta, he had been tired, some summer flu, he guessed. Probably picked it up on the plane. He had vivid memories of standing and watching the horrific scene unfold at the convention center. He and Judd Clarke, one of his buddies in the Emergency Management in Sumner County had represented the community at the event. It had been a good trip till the murders there. It was the craziest thing he had ever seen.

He had nightmares about it, and his temper had even been off some. He had yelled at his wife for nothing last night. He figured it was akin to a combat stress reaction and such events were better understood now. Guys frequently got snippy after crap went down. The debrief had helped. But still, the nightmares. So real. Sometimes, he even thought he saw it during the day. Shut up man, concentrate on the road. You can't let that crap worm its way into your brain, you'll lose your cool and get killed or kicked to desk work for a month. Still, he had seen something. And heard stuff. Shit. Anyway, gotta catch this asshole.

The road wound ahead. He would need to slow to make the turn. The red, rusted truck in front of him suddenly veered off to the right and almost lost control, barely regaining the roadway as the vehicle's speed approached ninety miles an hour.

Suddenly a flash of light appeared in Mattfield's vision. A large object descended from the sky, tendrils of light reaching through the glass, pure blue electric evil. What the fuck! The officer slammed on the brakes as the tendrils of light penetrated the windshield and began burrowing into the skin of his hand, still holding the wheel.

"Jesus!" he cried out as the cruiser veered left and the left front tire left the roadway. The increased drag of the rocketing vehicle caused the back to rotate rapidly to the right, spinning the car 180 degrees and launching it into the air, all four tires leaving the road. The car shot through the air as if from a catapult and impacted with full velocity into a large, ancient oak tree lining the left side of the road. The sudden deceleration crushed the back half of the vehicle like a paper box and the officer's aorta ripped from the lining that held it attached to the inside of the man's chest, tearing the vessel along ten inches of its length. The weight of the blood in the thick vessel had overwhelmed the strength of its fibrous attachment to the retroperitoneum, and the man's life blood coursed unstoppably into his torso and abdomen. The impact tore his left retina from its attachment and the meningial covering of the brain was rent into shreds simultaneously. The 100 G force impact had instantly killed the man. His body slumped in the seat, radio still blaring, the cruisers lights flashing, the siren ripped off and thrown onto the pavement somewhere. The rusted truck continued to speed away, rocketing into the distance. Crows sitting on a nearby fence cawed hoarsely at the vehicle, smoke and dust now settling back to the earth in silent testimony to the recent violence.

Attacks and episodes of insanity were beginning to pop up in random areas around the world. The rate of initial events was not high enough to raise any suspicion as insanity was unfortunately a common modern ailment. Each death, attack and abnormal event was simply labeled according to its type and the police, military, emergency services workers, and medical crews did not suspect anything odd. Murder, even horrific murder, was a fact of life throughout the world. The marching dance of death had begun, its light footfalls not noticed amidst the chaos and flurry of everyday life.

Blow the trumpet in Zion,
And sound an alarm in My holy mountain!
Let all the inhabitants of the land tremble;
For the day of the Lord is coming,
For it is at hand:
A day of darkness and gloominess,
A day of clouds and thick darkness,
Like the morning clouds spread over the mountains.
A people come, great and strong,
The like of whom has never been;
Nor will there ever be any such after them,
Even for many successive generations.
—Joel 2:1-2 NKJV

CHAPTER 11

Gallatin, TN
15 miles North of Nashville
Southern Family Medical Group
June 22
8:20p.m.

Matt Mackenzie was just closing his laptop when he heard an unusual noise, and then a loud thump. What the hell is that, he thought as he shut off his laptop. He was late getting home as he had been signing orders from the local nursing home. He was ready for some chow, in this case homemade chili in the fridge that he had made last night for his family. It was always better the next day. He washed his hands thoroughly again. He had already disposed of his protective garments two hours before settling in for the month's worth of work he had just caught up on. His tech and nurse had gone home two hours ago, and Matt was alone in the clinic, except for the cleaning crew. Usually one or two guys would come and clean after the day was done. Trustworthy people and really thorough cleaners.

But, what the hell was that noise? Matt heard it again, like a cat wailing, way, way down the hallway. The sound was so unnatural that it sent chills down his spine. What the hell? He moved slowly, down the corridor of the office towards the main hallway. He paused, frozen in his tracks. The door from the main hallway was opening slowly, a soft shuffling scrabbling coming from behind, as if the figure opening the door was leaning onto it to support its weight.

"Hello, are you O.K.?" Matt called out, feeling concern for whoever was opening the door. They obviously needed help, maybe that's what the cry was. Matt started to advance towards the opening door, when abject terror seized him. A long bloody butcher knife became visible moving past the edge of the door. The wailing sounded again. A gurgling, wrenching sound shrieked down the corridor. A weathered, dark skinned hand was holding the knife, its fingers covered in fresh blood, still dripping onto the tile floor.

Matt froze, unable to move his feet, this ex-Navy officer with extensive casualty care experience, riveted to his place, so terrifying was the scene. The knife-wielding man moved into view, the door banging hard into his shoulder, then slammed shut as the ominous figure blocked the exit. The man slobbered and coughed lightly, he was staring at Matt, but did not appear to have recognized that a person was in his field of view.

"George! What the hell happened to you?!" said Matt, stunned at recognizing the beloved member of the night shift cleaning crew. How could this be the man Matt had seen only a few days ago? George's face was contorted, his eyes sunken, hair unkempt, blood ran from his nostrils and covered his teeth and hands.

"Gurbgle, haaaaagghhhhh!" the creature that had once been the cleaning man roared, its grinding breath hissing into the sounds. No longer capable of words, the beast had realized that Matt was in front of him. Through whatever fog of confusion or complex array of hallucinations, the presence of a human had registered in the mad creature's consciousness. It started hobbling at a horrible speed, directly towards Matt, its movement like a macabre dance of horrible intent. Arms flailing, teeth bared, it charged in a sideways crab crawl racing towards the terrified doctor.

Blam! Blamblamblam! Blamblamblam! Cracked the tiny pocket .380 Smith and Wesson Bodyguard pistol. Matt had emptied the six rounds in the magazine plus one in the chamber in less than 2 seconds, his mind not registering the hits. He had no time to actuate the laser on the unit, only to point shoot at the lethal threat blocking his safe exit.

The crazed monster lay bleeding on the floor of the short hallway, four small holes in its torso and three in its face and forehead. Matt had reacted with his concealed weapons training. He had not had time to even warn the attacker, the attack was so sudden and so close. If Matt had hesitated, he would have had a large butcher knife imbedded in his body, or worse. That thing looked like it had blood on its teeth, like it had been EATING something, or…someone? How could this be? What had he done? Shit!

He looked at the body and saw no signs of life, then he leaped over the limp form and stumbled into the main hallway of the office and ran towards the front desk phones. He did not see anyone else in the office. He scrambled to a phone and dialed 911.

"911, what is the nature of your emergency?" asked the operator.

"A crazy man just tried to kill me with a knife and I had to shoot him! Please help me!" answered Matt, his normally calm demeanor shaken to the core. His sympathetic nervous system had reacted instantly during the event and now his adrenal glands were kicking in. Most people thought that adrenalin was what allowed for feats of athletic ability during an unexpected emergency, but that hormone actually took about two minutes to take effect. The nervous system had instantly kicked in and Matt had experienced a phenomenon known as tachypsychia, in which the time experienced by the person affected appears to move very slowly. Matt had been able to draw from concealment, aim and fire the entire contents of the tiny pistol within a moment. Now his hands and arms were shaking as his body suffered the aftereffects of the hormone and sympathetic neurotransmitter dump.

"Could you repeat that sir?" asked the operator.

"Yes, a crazy guy just attacked me with a knife and lunged at me and just tried to kill me." Matt said, his voice shaking, "I had to shoot him to keep him from killing me. I think he is dead. Please send help!"

"Thank you, sir." The operator confirmed his address and then asked, "are you injured sir?"

"I don't think so."

"Do you require medical assistance?" asked the operator.

"No ma'am."

"Please stay on the line, I have dispatched an officer to your location and and an ambulance as well. Do you understand?"

"Yes ma'am, thanks," Matt replied, his voice settling down some. His breathing was still coming in waves. He remained on the phone for two minutes as the elevator door opened and a police officer entered the hallway. Matt had already placed his now empty gun on the counter and was over ten feet away from it when the officer, with his own hand on his sidearm, asked, "Are you O.K. sir?"

"I think so, sir."

"The officer is here ma'am," he said to the 911 dispatcher.

"Understood. Please hang up and follow the officer's instructions."

"Yes ma'am," he said and promptly hung up the phone.

"Please step this way, sir," the officer asked politely.

Matt stepped the way the officer indicated. The officer asked him if he had any weapons and then took Matt's pistol, confirming with Matt that the weapon had been used. Matt replied in the affirmative and the officer asked to see the body. When stepping around the counter Matt nearly tripped over another body, blood made his shoes slip.

The other member of the night cleaning staff lay dead at Matt's feet, blood soaking through the clothes. "Sir, this isn't him. This isn't the guy I had to shoot. The guy that attacked me is in there," he said pointed towards the separate hallway. The officer asked Matt to stay put and went over to the crime scene, made several calls into his radio and retuned to Matt.

"I've got to take you downtown, and I have to confiscate the firearm used in the incident. Do you understand?"

"Yes sir. Thank you for coming so soon."

A brief interrogation followed in which Matt repeated his statements to the policeman. He thought the man was trying to kill him, the man had a bloody knife, he didn't have time or a way to run and he thought the man was crazy and going to kill him. Two more officers appeared in the elevator, along with a hospital guard and several plain clothes officers. Cameras flashed and bags were taken out to catalogue the event. EMS crews arrived and loaded the two bodies onto gurneys to be taken to the morgue.

Matt followed the police officer down the elevator. He had called his office manager to come up and had asked her to remain in the office while the police and EMS were cleaning up. She had called the cleaning crew to come in and scrub the blood off the floors. The owner had been stunned at the apparent turn of events. It seemed that George was his most reliable employee. The very idea that he would murder his coworker and try to murder the doctor was unthinkable. Matt sat in the back of the Dodge Charger police cruiser as they drove the short three-block drive to the police station. They parked in the police officer's lot and they got out and walked into the back door of the station. There were cars everywhere, double parked and people yelling and arguing in the parking lot.

Matt had been past the station on a number of occasions, driving home or meeting with friends at a nearby restaurant. He had never seen people in the parking lot. Several of them were rubbing runny noses and had spit running down corners of their mouths. Some had vacant stares. Matt reflexively reached into his pocket and pulled out a fresh N95 mask and slipped it on and sanitized his hands with a bottle of pocket hand gel. The officer raised an eyebrow but said nothing.

"Been seeing this flu thing all week; don't want to catch it and miss work. Sorry, occupational hazard, I guess," Matt said in response.

The officer nodded and grinned. "Where can I get one of those?"

Matt reached into his pocket and pulled out the last one he had and handed it to the officer, "Hardware store, also get some gloves and hand gel."

The officer nodded thanks. They went inside and the scene was utter chaos. People were lined up against the walls, yelling and talking loud. This seemed like New York City Metro, not little old Gallatin. They entered a room and pushed some people aside who glared at them cutting in line. Matt was processed with digital fingerprints and had to remove his mask for a mug shot. He replaced it immediately.

The shift leader, a Lieutenant, shook hands with Matt, peering curiously at the mask.

"Sorry, occupational risk with this flu going around. Can't work if I'm laid up," said Matt.

"That's actually a good idea," said the supervisor. "Look, I read the report and talked to Jones here," he said referring to the officer who had reported to the scene. "This seems cut and dried. You were attacked by a guy with a bloody knife who charged you after stabbing his buddy. The path reports will probably confirm it was the buddy's blood on the knife and that explains the sound you heard. Off the record, you did everybody a favor. Guy seems to have snapped. Freakin maniac, if you ask me."

Matt looked around at the dozens of people arguing in the room and raised an eyebrow.

"Yeah. Seems to be going around. We've had sixteen murders in the last week. What the hell is going on? I don't know, but I don't have time to process you. Listen, the DA will have the last word on whether or not you will be prosecuted, but I see no reason to hold you. We will contact you if we need anything. Do not leave town. Is that clear?" the Lieutenant stated.

"Yes Sir, of course Sir," Matt replied. "I understand. Thank you for your help. I have never had this happen before."

"I can see that. You were Navy right?"

"Yeah. I was in Iraq and saw stuff, but I've never had to defend myself."

"Don't talk to anyone about it. Just shut up about it and get a lawyer for the civil suit, if one comes," the officer said, referring to the likely wrongful death lawsuit that would almost inevitably be filed by the family of the attacker. More misery to endure.

"Yes Sir," Matt nodded and Officer Jones touched his arm and led him back out to the parking lot. He rode back to the office in silence and thanked the officer. Then he checked on the office and his manager had everything cleaned up and was staring, shellshocked at the floor. Matt apologized and she shook it off, smiling. He thanked her and drove home, his nerves still wound tight. It would be a long night.

Castalian Springs, TN
7 miles East of Gallatin
The Clarke's Residence
June 23
9:07a.m.

Hummingbirds buzzed contentedly at the stand of feeders in the backyard as the slow Southern Saturday began. Several neighbors were mowing their yards, anxious to get the large amount of mowing done before it got too hot. Yards in this area were big, several acres usually. A group of older women were sitting together on a nearby front porch taking about life, food and mainly the neighbors' business. This was a typical Southern weekend morning. The sun was out, a smattering of light clouds drifted lazily through the blue sky. The morning temperature was in the mid-eighties, typical for this time of year. It would probably be 95 degrees by one o'clock. This was a beautiful place, shallow rolling hills, covered in green grass, tulip poplars and water oaks mixing with some occasional cedar stands. Pasture land stood occupied with a small cluster of beef cattle. Barns littered the countryside, most working farms with intermixed small houses and trailers. For many, this was a piece of heaven on Earth.

Inside the house, however, was another place entirely. Judd Clarke had not been himself the last few days. He was a Christian man, a devout Southern Baptist. He did not drink, smoke, or use drugs. He loved his family and his dogs and cats and had been a dedicated community man. Joining Sumner County Emergency Management made sense to him, a way to protect the community and serve his country. He was a true patriot.

But ever since returning from Atlanta, he had not been the same. It all started with a runny nose and fevers and chills. Nothing severe, but more like a common summer cold. If that were all, he wouldn't have thought anything of it. But then came the visions. He had been seeing things, things he knew were not real. People standing in his kitchen, people standing in the shower with him, dogs on the rooftops of neighbors houses growling and snarling at him. He started hearing things as well. He heard voices at night, under the sheets.

He had been hard to be around as well. He had become increasingly agitated. He had argued so much with his wife, that she had suggested that she visit her mom in Alabama. He couldn't understand why he was yelling all of the time either. He had asked for a few days of sick leave and they were granted. He was due to return to work on Monday.

For the past two days he had become convinced that he was losing his mind. He had increasingly violent thoughts, and spent hours weeping, sobbing uncontrollably at the shame he felt for his murderous desires. How could he have become such a monster? He had daydreamed of murdering his family with an axe. He did not understand from where this had come. As he sat on the floor of his kitchen, he felt his control slipping away. Nothing anyone could do would help. He would end up like that monster in Atlanta.

Nooooooo! His mind screamed. He couldn't let that happen. He couldn't be responsible for hurting anyone. He had to hide from them in case he tried to kill them. He imagined feeding on the dead bodies of those he murdered. The visions were so real! He began sobbing again. He saw spiders crawling on his skin, his sanity ebbing away like the tide. He saw knives appear, sprouting from his skin, like hair follicles, spreading down into his hands. Blood dripped from the walls of the house and a hole opened up in the kitchen floor. A man with red skin and two small horns sprouting from the forehead and a long red tail began walking up from hell itself, swirling fear and loathing emanating from him like thick fog on the water.

"You are mine!" screamed Beelzebub, "I command you to destroy!" laughed the old demon, a throaty, belly laugh that shook him to his core. Judd began foaming at the mouth and howling like a dog. Like a wolfman. Fur began to sprout from his skin, his canine teeth enlarging. He could not control it anymore. He was changing into a monster.

Tears streamed down from his cheeks, splashing onto the hardwood floor of the kitchen. Reality and hallucination warred with each other, like alternating bicycle spokes spun up to speed, the real world a tiny fractal pattern dancing in front of his eyes. He saw the Ruger .357 Magnum stutter into and out of existence, its stainless steel frame reflecting the light of the beautiful summer morning. Church was tomorrow. The pastor would be giving a sermon on Abraham's near sacrifice of Isaac.

The monster within him began to pant, blood lust entered his veins and he began moving towards the kitchen door. The neighbor's three-year-old twins would be in their backyard now, playing with the family dog. Hunger, insatiable hunger. His fangs dripped poison now, his eyes involuting into sockets of fire. Burning lust for flesh consumed his mind. He would feast.

Noooooooo!!!!!!

The last vestige of humanity clung to life in a sea of madness. He could make his arms move. The beast within fought desperately for control of his body. His legs started for the door and the man's body fell face down to the floor, his chin smashing into the hardwood, blood erupting from his teeth and gums as the jaws smashed together, crushing part of his lip that was caught in between. The sudden jolt of pain turned the tide. His sane mind forced his arms and legs to writhe towards the counter, away from the door. The Devil screamed at him, "Feast on the flesh of the young!" The deep rumbling voice shook the floor of the house, "I command you to murder!"

In the center of his agony, a still, small voice called, "I am with you. I have forgiven you." Clarity spilled into his mind like a shock of ice water in his veins. The figure of a man in a robe appeared, his dark hair shorter than the paintings suggested. His stocky, weathered features were stark and dusty, the olive skin reflecting the morning light. His eyes seared into Judd's soul, a compassion so overwhelming that he became lost in the warmth and completeness of it.

"I have already carried this burden for you," He said. "You must have faith, for I am with you now and until the end of time. I have counted the hairs upon your head and have known you while you were in your mother's womb. I knitted you together from the dust, and I am with you now, Judd Clarke."

Fear and anguish fled from his wracked frame, the terrifying image of death and cannibalistic lust still swirled around him like a storm, threatening at any moment to break through the solitary control. A piercing light from His eyes struck Judd, pouring strength into him at the last, here at the end of all things. The shells of his body and mind were ruined. The virions raced through his last remaining uninfected nerves, budding off new particles to force chaos upon his mind, to wrench control from his consciousness and hand it over to the reptilian part of his brainstem and limbic system.

One chance left. One solitary action to prevent rabid destruction. Rage, rage against the chaos. Rage, rage against the dying of the light. Fight, damn you, fight! He cried out in his mind. He looked clearly into the kitchen and a small window of reality opened up. The swirl of evil lust tore at his flesh like wind-blown debris. The vacuum of chaos began to pull him backwards towards the door, the three-year-old girls and their babysitting grandmother laughing in the sunshine, oblivious to the desperate struggle occurring only yards away.

Judd's hand shot out onto the countertop, finding the steel and placing fingers on the rubber and rosewood grip.

"Arrrggggggghhhhhhh!" screamed the figure of the devil, his fangs showing, his red skin stretched tight over the horrible visage. "You shall not deprive me! He is mine!"

Light shot across the room with a violence unequaled. Streams of flesh began to burn from the chief demon's skin, a horrible wailing vomited forth from its lungs. The Carpenter stood, the light pouring from his body and garments, his arms raised, a stern, compassionate voice rang out clear and true, "It is time, my son. Rest now: you shall be with me always."

With all of his remaining strength of will, Judd forced the hammer back and slowly moved the four inch barrel towards his temple. The demon clung to him, shaking his weakened frame, driving claws into his flesh and mind, prying as hard as he could against the steel device. The bore of the weapon rested across the man's upper ear. The demon shrieked the loudest noise the man had ever heard, painfully jarring his ear drums. A smile flashed across Judd's countenance, and he turned his head so that the bullet would exit his head safely, away from the neighbors. Peace at last.

"I'm coming Father," said Judd as the last uninfected neural pathway activated the right index finger's flexor muscles, engaging the sear of the weapon, the hammer falling onto the striker bar and transmitting the kinetic energy to the firing pin, detonating the round's primer. The Speer .357 Magnum 125 grain Gold Dot Hollow Point rocketed though Judd's head, just above the ear and it began to mushroom back, destroying roughly fifty percent of his brain matter, exploding out the opposite left side and slamming deeply into a wooden beam in the ceiling.

Judd's body slumped to the floor, half of his head sprayed upon the ceiling, the madness defeated by a superhuman force of will and love. The young girls and their grandmother paused at the loud noise and walked towards the low fence. They would never know the love and self-sacrifice that their neighbor had shown them on that day. The days ahead would be dark and evil, but on this day, terror had died at the hands of faith.

As stars with trains of fire and dews of blood,
Disasters in the sun; and the moist star
Upon whose influence Neptune's empire stands
Was sick almost to doomsday with eclipse:
And even the like precurse of fierce events,
As harbingers preceding still the fates
And prologue to the omen coming on,
Have heaven and earth together demonstrated
Unto our climatures and countrymen.
—William Shakespeare. Hamlet. 1.1.130-138

CHAPTER 12

Solar Corona
Center of Solar System
Location of the Sun's "atmosphere"
June 27
13:32GMT

The plasma ball continued churning as it had for millennia. Balls of liquid energy stretched outward into thick bands of solar material, threatening to rupture off again as they had recently done before. Differential bands of rotating plasma shifted from side to side, the seething engine of the solar system writhing in constant movement. Solar activity is never fully predictable. The gas ball that powers our solar system is massive in comparison to our planet. Flares of energy often are larger than the planets at which they are flung. The solar wind had picked up intensity since the first flare several weeks ago. The churning mix of electromagnetic energy had experienced a recent shift in intensity. Many scientists on earth had been ignoring the input of the sun when calculating effects of climate change, claiming the entire change in global temperature was solely due to the input of human activity in order to justify political and behavioral regime change.

Whatever the role of human pollution on the environment and the temperature changes was not fully clear. However, it was clear that the solar output was increasing over the year. Sunspot activity had dramatically increased over the past few weeks. The first flare produced only a minor impact upon the earth. Already several more flares had launched harmlessly into space, aimed well away from the earth. It was good luck indeed. But luck does not always hold.

Gallatin, TN
15 miles North of Nashville
Summer County Regional Hospital
June 29
6:32a.m.

Carlos Corpuz clicked rapidly through the patient's electronic medical record. He was searching for any data that could help shed light on the patient's true diagnosis. This patient was like dozens more with similar symptoms. They had fevers, chills, rhinorrhea, fatigue, hallucinations and irritability. None of them seemed to have anything in common. They were from a large geographic region. Furthermore, his colleagues in nearby hospitals were seeing the same thing. Thousands of sick people with similar effects. What the hell was it? He couldn't get any reply from the CDC. He had been trying all week. Several of the patients had died in comas. Several more had to be shipped to psychiatric units due to the extremely violent behavior.

Frankly, this was not adding up. Angus' crazy theory scared him, but he was starting to think that there might be something to it. After all, he had studied stuff like this in the Air Force. But, could there really have been a release of an encephalitis virus? It seemed so improbable. But, then again, so did the hospital filling up with dozens of patients with the same symptom set. They had no treatment. The labs could not identify the cause. The Infectious Disease group had been stumped as well. None of the serological tests for anthrax, Japanese encephalitis, influenza, rabies, West Nile virus or any other tested entities had returned positive on any patient. There had been an occasional false positive that was refuted by confirmatory testing. He thought he had uncovered it all when the Lyme titer of one patient was positive, but the follow up assay was clearly negative, so he was still in the dark.

Thinking of darkness, his mind turned to the recent attack on one of the nurses. One of the patients now in the psychiatric ward of a nearby specialty center had violently attacked one of the floor nurses, screaming at her and nearly beating her to death when she tried to draw blood. She was doing well, but had been given time off to recover. It was scary, the way some of the patients looked at him when he came to examine them.

The hospital would not allow anyone to carry a concealed weapon, thinking that the "no guns" sign would somehow magically prevent criminals from bringing guns into the building. This was, of course, the ultimate in liberal logic. No criminal who was intent on murder would care about violating the rules on a sign! All the signs did was prevent law abiding citizens from carrying their concealed handguns. The effects of this backwards logic had played out multiple times in the news over the years. Criminals had specifically targeted areas that disallowed guns. They knew there could be no resistance from their victims. The signs might as well say "only police and criminals are allowed to carry here" because that's what really happened when these policies went into effect. The gun community called these places "victim disarmament zones" and Carlos felt quite disarmed thinking of the wall upon wall of blank or openly hostile stares coming from the overfilled rooms of sick patients.

Davis house
3 miles North of Gallatin
June 30
2:30p.m.

Thudding feet and radio chatter sounded down the property. Static and the sounds of gear gently rattling as the two men moved in unison, each covering the other's flank. Silence. Then the sound of a bolt cocking in the distance.

"Thwack! Thwack, thwack!" sounded the airsoft pellets as they ricocheted off of the back of the house. The two men rolled sideways, one to the left, one to the right, coming up square onto the targeted structure. Their replica Glocks came up in unison as they simultaneously stormed the last distance to the house, sweat beading on their faces and soaking into their woodland pattern BDU, or battle dress uniforms and Tactical Tailor plate carriers. They rapidly entered the back door as a hail of airsoft pellets rained down from the side yard, missing them by inches.

Breath came heavy as the men zigged and zagged into the kitchen and living room, heading directly for the bedroom, airsoft fire now streaming down the hallway. A dummy flashbang canister sailed through the air towards the shooter, Edward Douglass' pitch was true and the canister bounced off the vest of the defender.

"Shit Ed, you got me!" Jack Sutherland said, the man unslung his replica airsoft Steyr AUG and walked down the hallway, "You're just too damned fast. I couldn't hit you."

"You sure tried, Jack," Edward replied, a sideways grin spreading on his face. "Nearly got Issac."

"The hell he did. He nearly got you," replied Issac Fergusson Davis. Issac was a lean man, with a powerful upper torso, striking features and a medium thick salt and pepper goatee and thick graying hair. He was an accountant in town and best friends with Edward. "Now help me vacuum up these damned pellets!"

"Yes ma'am," said the two other men in unison, saluting backwards and clicking their heels together. These men had known each other for years, decades in the case of Ed and Issac. Their humor ran the gauntlet. They were members of another society dedicated to improving their chances of survival. Their spouses thought of it as a boy's club, and really it was. They pooled their resources, planned group purchases of equipment, and like today, trained together. Several other men were involved as well. They met at a local steakhouse to discuss their latest activities. Most were members of the police force, but Issac was never in the military or police. He had more training than any of them, however. He had joined Frontsight training center as a lifetime member, and spent time every year flying to the Southwest for week-long training events. He had amassed more hours in combat training than any police officer in town, and he thanked the Lord that he had never had to use the training.

Issac was 51 years old and had been born in the blizzard of the century, in a home birth with only his family there to help. He had endured a rough childhood, but had come out a polished gem. There was no man alive who was more of a genteel Southerner than Issac Fergusson Davis. The gentleman exuded good taste and civility. He only drank good single malt scotch and his house was an exact duplicate of the home of Jefferson Davis, no relation, the President of the Confederacy.

Issac had a daughter who was always traveling. She was now in Montana hiking with friends. He was always glad when Angie was back in town, she was the light of his life. He had been married once and previously divorced, and now had met a beautiful woman in town, a nurse, and was just starting to date again, after the shock of the previous divorce. He was learning to trust again, very slowly.

The men all laughed and proceeded to clean the place up and settle in for some chow. The TV news blared reports of more rioting and looting, caused by various natural disasters and "political unrest." The men believed nothing of it, but had intensified their training efforts in response to it. They only hoped that they could be ready to defend liberty, God forbid, when and if the time came. After dinner, the men chatted some and Issac said goodnight and Jack and Edward headed home to their respective clans and Issac turned in for the night. Hopefully, he could get some sleep; nightmares of crumbling cities had filled his dreams lately. He prayed that this time of danger would pass, and then drifted off into a restless sleep, a foreboding sense of dread haunting his dreams.

Sam's Coffee House
Duluth, North Dakota
June 30
4:57p.m.

    Patrons entered at their leisure and sat down to a very nice cup of joe. Sam had retired years ago, but the new owner had kept the establishment's name. It had been one of the best places in the area for really good coffee. Today was nothing special- lots of paying customers. Chelsea Swanson was just starting her shift and swung her apron on when she walked into the coffee shop.
    People looked very happy. It was a nice town, with nice people. One of the Sheriff's deputies was sitting at a back table. John had just come back from a big convention down south and she was looking forward to serving him coffee. She always had had a thing for men in uniform. Now that he was back, he would be bored and looking for the thrill he had left in the big city. Tonight might be her lucky night.
    She moseyed, strutted really, over to the table and looked at the handsome young man's face. He had his head down in his hands. She blinked and licked her lips, preparing to ask what he wanted to order, the sugar daddy. He did not stir.

He was alone at the table, which was odd as he usually sat with one of his buddies from the station. Come to think of it, she had never seen him alone at any time in the past. Maybe he was here for her and wanted to be alone! Her heart raced and the muscles in her neck tightened, preparing to speak. He looked up, perhaps sensing the disturbance in the local air currents.

Her voice froze. The man before her was nothing like the beautiful, handsome young buck she wanted between her thighs. Drool hung from his lips, his face contorted into a grimace of pain and agony. His fingers were covered in blood, dried and caking on the palms. His mouth quivered as her body froze in horror and overwhelming fear. Her lack of understanding warred with her desire to survive the next moment. He looked...well, he looked like a beast. The eyes did not seem to recognize that a person was standing in front of him, as if the image did not register on the brain. Slowly, the pupils narrowed, as a laser would, focusing on its target. Its arms swung out, lashing forth like predatory talons, reaching, reaching for her throat.

Her mind's eye flashed back to the training, her weeks of unending training, the mixed martial arts that her former boyfriend had put her through. She had only done it to get laid, and now it came flooding back. Her back muscles tensed as her torso whipped backwards and the clawing fingers missed her by inches. She tumbled back and rolled under the counter and came up behind the register as her eyes coped with the disbelief that her mind experienced.

Images of horror flooded into her vision. Blood spattered as the attack, initially aimed at her, shifted to a young girl at the counter. Teeth sank into the neck as screams of unbelieving horror echoed through the small diner. Again and again, the teeth bit into flesh, the mob of people trampling one another, as each new victim fell to the terrifying speed and fury of the attacker.

A shot rang out, as an armed civilian fired at the deputy. The bullet penetrated the upper chest wall, just an inch above the level IIIA concealed vest. The deputy flung himself, like a leopard onto the concealed permit holder's body and bit deeply into the man's scalp as he futilely emptied his revolver into the officer's soft armor vest, its Kevlar folds stopping each new round. The officer's blood still poured from the hole in his upper chest, just below the neck.

Several more shots rang out as two more concealed weapons permit holders fired their weapons into the crazed officer's body, two head shots finally ending the orgy of destruction. Seventeen more people were now infected from bites or blood spatter and injury. The orgy of death had only just begun.

Back Alley
Miami, Florida
June 30
8:33p.m.

Mathias quickened his pace, as he advanced through the failing light. He did not like the sound of the footsteps behind him. It sounded like several people following him. The footfalls sounded, well... wrong. They just didn't seem right. He couldn't explain it, but the cadence was off, as if the feet were inhuman. He was early for Sonny's birthday party and took the alley to save time walking from his parking place. He should have walked the long way. Oh well. He jogged the last few yards into the apartment and opened the back door, closing it behind him as he stepped inside. His friend always left the door open when he expected guests.

The scene inside shocked Mathias. Plates were smashed, food left out to rot covered the counters. The smell was overwhelming. What was Sonny doing? Banging sounded on the back door. Then, something else. Scratching? Mathias opened the door.

"Sonny!?" Mathias said as he stared in disbelief at his friend's face. Drool ran down from his chin as the vacant eyes glowered at him. Behind him, several more people stood and lumbered forward. Too late, Mathias tried to shut the door.

Screams of agony filled the alleyway, awakening neighbors as more people came through the alley, some with bite marks on their hands and arms, others without a mark. But all drooling and staring vacantly. The setting sun's rays faded as the screams stopped and quiet returned to the street and alleyway, the blood now appearing black on the floor of the dingy apartment as it flowed out onto the stained carpet.

Groups of antigovernment protestors were able to shut down a news broadcast and send their own signal this week. They claimed that there was a coverup of the "real facts" and that some type of governmentally created plague was the true cause of the disruptions. Three small solar flares hit the Earth in rapid succession over the weekend. They hit different parts of the Earth, based on the areas exposed to the sunlight at the time they struck. They were very short-lived and did not cause any blackouts. The media ran a story and had round table talks on how minor the effects of a solar flare "really were," and how anyone "overreacting to them" was a "survivalist type," and clearly not mentally stable. One popular technology magazine even went so far as to claim that there never would be any kind of doomsday, of any kind. The evidence that they used was the lack of any prior doomsday events during our technological lifetime. Their logic stated that because an event had never happened, therefore it would never happen. Of course they ignored all of the actual disasters of the earth prior to the past century.

The people went about their business unaware that the flares had pushed away almost all of the solar wind in between the sun and Earth. Scientists predicted that the solar events would now decline and were on the way back down to a lower intensity. All but one, an Asian physicist, frequently on cable TV shows, who said we should be very concerned. He had previously made comments about the Earth potentially suffering a "solar tsunami." Just as in 1859, the pathway from the sun to the Earth had been cleared by smaller previously occurring solar flares.

The plague continued to infect new victims around the world. The world's medical system was straining under the weight of the infected, as the numbers continued to rise. US hospitals were starting to fill to capacity, and jails and mental wards had been totally full for several days by now, the infected patients' violent behavior causing a huge public health threat. People were finally starting to notice something might be wrong. Word on social media was getting around; the sheer numbers of people talking about it overwhelmed the government's censorship system. People were starting to catch on to the truth. Societal resources could barely contain the victims, but as in many prior plague events, the system seemed to be muddling through somehow. How long this could continue, and how long the media could effectively cover it up remained to be seen.

Goodlettsville, TN
10 miles North of Nashville
Gunn House
July 2
4:32a.m.

Angus stood on the hill, the desolation of the city in front of him was complete and utter. Devoid of life, devoid of hope, a dull matte gray film of ash covered everything, mixing in the gentle breeze to form swirling eddies of lost potential. All that was once, is now gone. The death of the empire had sent shock waves of emptiness through the land, echoing into the oblivion to which it was now consigned. Its rotting carcass like some great humpbacked beast, crushed under the weight of its own shame: shame for not preparing and preventing its own ruin.

Hot ash and sweat mixed on Angus' skin, making him a grey man in a grey landscape. Fear and uncertainty tugged at his neck, causing him to look about the destroyed landscape. Rumblings and creakings caught his attention. No, not that. Please not that.

Torn bodies twisted as form upon form began to writhe in the rhythm of their agony, reborn once more in the image of death. The macabre dance had begun. Angus froze, rooted to the spot, terror holding him firm to the ground, his sweat turning cold against the breeze that wafted by, carrying the scent of decay. The ruined bodies continued their marionette twistings, clambering inch by inch towards the helpless man, saliva streaming from cracked lips as the wail of hunger pierced the silent landscape.

Please, Lord Jesus, no! Angus wailed inside of his own mind, unable to speak, so great was the horror that he witnessed. The dead were crawling inexorably towards him, mouths snapping and tongues wiggling in grim anticipation of the dark feast. Please God, help me!

A tiny light, far in the distance opened in the clouds. Angus held his breath and waited for the inevitable pain and anguish. The beasts were moving closer and closer. The light spread out across the horizon, the dead things oblivious to its movement. The image of the sunrise, so beautiful that no music on Earth could contain its majesty, held Angus' rapt attention, despite his desperate fear. A blaring, deep sound, so deep and powerful that it was as if the foundations of the universe had shifted. Again, the blaring sounded, a trumpet of wonder, roaring its noise across the wasteland.

The beasts stopped and turned away from Angus, towards the sound, the light burning their undead eyes. Slowly, the light grew, the beasts frozen in their curiosity at the new stimulus. Light streamed from the heavens down onto Angus and the beasts. Everywhere it touched his skin, Angus felt a renewing hope wash through him. Everywhere the light touched the dead things, the corpses burst into flames, their rending growls of agony signaling their second death, flames shooting out from their moribund flesh. Ashes remained.

A voice sounded across the land, so deep and natural and magnificent it was as if the very foundation of the mountains was speaking,

"Angus, I have heard your cry," the voice rolling like thunder across the heavens.

Angus could not stand, and his weakened knees buckled as he fell forward onto his face, tears of joy streaming down his cheeks. He knew these were the Words of Creation, the Voice of the Heavens, and the Song of Salvation. He could not bear the beauty of their intonation. He wept, sobbing for breath amidst the ash strewn landscape, every fiber of his being rocked with the heaving grief and joy.

"Angus, my people shall not be abandoned. I shall provide them a way," the voice of the Creator sounded across the world. It was as if all of the energy, matter and substance of the universe were contained within the sound.

Angus tried to speak, choked on ash and fell silent again, awaiting his judgement. His unworthiness clung to him like a cloak of shame, like grime working its way under his fingernails and into his pores. For the last time, the voice spoke: words of life, words of hope, words of terrifying clarity.

"Angus, hear these words and believe: I will raise up a leader amongst my people, I shall crown him king and he shall have the blessing and favor of the Lord. Joshua shall lead my people."

His breath escaped him and darkness enveloped him as he fell from the heights, down, down and into his bed. He sat up slowly, breath still coming in heaving waves, the presence of the Lord still close on his skin, the echo of the words still ringing in his ears.

Gwenn sat up and reached across the bed and touched Angus' arm. "Are you O.K.?"

Angus grabbed her arm and squeezed it, "Maybe. Just maybe..."

She should have died hereafter;
There would have been a time for such a word.
Tomorrow, and tomorrow, and tomorrow,
Creeps in this petty pace from day to day,
To the last syllable of recorded time;
And all our yesterdays have lighted fools
The way to dusty death. Out, out, brief candle!
Life's but a walking shadow, a poor player
That struts and frets his hour upon the stage
And then is heard no more. It is a tale
Told by an idiot, full of sound and fury
Signifying nothing.
—William Shakespeare. <u>Macbeth.</u> 5.5.17-28

CHAPTER 13

Gallatin, TN
15 miles North of Nashville
Southern Family Medical Group
July 3
8:42a.m.

Angus toyed with the compass in his hand, thinking about how primal a thing basic navigation was. A tool like this was amazing; it could tell anyone all of the four cardinal directions and every degree in between. Well, usually it could. Today, it was moving all over the place. It would jump from one direction to another, seemingly randomly. Normally of course, it would point to the magnetic north pole, but today, it seemed to have a mind of its own. If he did not know better, he would have thought that he were in an area of high magnetic ore, or other similar interfering metal. But he knew that his office was free of those types of interference. It looked like the geomagnetic pole had finally begun shifting and the Van Allen belts were on a hiatus. He'd better call his family. Luckily, his mom, Margaret Gunn was visiting from South Carolina. She would be having fun now with the family at home, so Angus felt good about that.

He picked up the phone and checked his watch. He had a few minutes until the patient showed up. It was a late morning. He called his brother, Nick Gunn. Nick was 46 and lived in Alexandria, Virginia and worked in Washington D.C. for a worldwide legal firm. He had been in the army for the G.I. Bill and had a very pragmatic way about him. Nick's family still lived in Texas and he would continue to go home every weekend until his youngest graduated from high school, when the family would then also move to Virginia. Not many could pull off that kind of life, but Nick was the most disciplined man Angus knew. He had taken Latin as his second language just because it was hard and he wanted a challenge. Stoic in the extreme and as tough as nails, as a child he had tripped on the neighbor's slick lawn and impaled his knee on a three pronged sprinkler. He calmly unscrewed the sprinkler and held the metal device in his knee and limped to the front door of the neighbor's house and rang the doorbell. The dermatologist had answered the door, fainted upon seeing the injury and his wife had taken Nick to the E.R.

The phone rang. "Hello," Nick answered.

"Hey man," Angus said.

"Angus. Good to hear from you. I was just about to call you."

"Really? What's going on?"

"Well, there have been some concerning things going on here in this area. I wanted you to tell Mom not to visit after she leaves Nashville." Margaret Gunn had planned on seeing Nick next after her visit with Angus.

"Like what kind of things?" Angus asked, the unspoken "O.K. You're scaring me because you never get upset about anything and think that everything survival related is romantic, self-aggrandizing BS" hanging in the silence.

"They've cordoned off downtown."

"What!?" Angus replied in shock. He knew there had been similar events in other cities, but never the Capitol. Also, the other cities' events had been publicized on the news with various cover stories. Now this wasn't even on the news, which meant that they weren't even trying to pretend now. This was seriously bad.

"I think it's the plague. They've had men in biohazard suits all week going around, taking people away. I'm only calling now because I don't want Mom to come and I am planning on leaving today to fly home. I thought you might know something, and needed to know this as well," Nick said.

"Shit. Sorry, I don't know anything specific, but this whole thing is going down like scenarios we planned for when I was in the service. I figure they know what it is and don't have a ready treatment or cure, otherwise they would be issuing it by now. I think something got out of their control, maybe an accidental release of some kind. I mean, they had an inadvertent release of Tularemia at Texas Tech in

2007, in which the school's bio weapons research lab got a live sample shipped to them instead of a neutralized one. They had been working on new vaccines and the government accidentally sent live, weapons grade agent instead of the requested dead, heat killed agent. The lab tech popped the tube open and everyone in the lab got sick and nearly died a few days later. I mean, that's easy to treat with antibiotics, but this one, well, we don't know what to do with it."

"I can tell you what it isn't. It's not flu, meningitis, West Nile, Lyme disease, equine encephalitis, malaria, smallpox, tularemia, or any of about ten other things we checked. All those serologies are negative. It's like something out of a movie or book; sounds stupid, I know. The hospital is overrun with patients complaining of fever, chills, muscle aches and hallucinations. They are violent. I mean really violent. Scary. I'm glad I am doing outpatient only now. Not as many through the clinic; most go straight to the E.R."

Nick replied, concern deep in his voice, "That's roughly what my other doctor friends have told me as well. At any rate, I am going to head to the airport later today and fly home. I am flying out of Richmond, away from the city. Be careful,"

"Yeah, that's a good idea. Listen, I am also very concerned about this solar flare activity. I called to warn you that the power could go out. It's happened before, in 1859. I read about it since we had the outage a few weeks ago. I know the news says it's no big deal, but just the same, be careful. And put your electronics in a Faraday cage, like we talked about. It'll protect them, I hope. You may want to consider driving, but I don't know," Angus said. Suddenly that lights in the office started browning out. What the hell? "Nick, our lights are dimming."

"The power's on here, so it's probably.... Well, wait a minute; we are having a brownout too. Listen, I'll..." The line went ominously dead; the silence of the lost signal echoed through Angus' consciousness.

The power flickered and then went completely black. The fluorescent light above Angus' desk crackled and exploded, the lexan shield catching the glass debris as Angus ducked involuntarily. Cries of shock and fear echoed from the direction of the clinic. Smoke gently rose from the vents on the back of his flat screen computer monitor. In the hallway, the overhead lighting had crackled and smashed apart as well. A thin, ozone laden mist hung in the air. Angus' hair had been standing on end for a moment and the the sensation now receded.

Angus stood up and hung up the dead phone. He looked at his watch, it was dead, the digital readout was blank and the second hand frozen at 9:01:33. He walked into the office and the nurses were vainly trying to turn on their flashlights, which were dead as well. The battery powered radio and wall clock were dead. All of the computers screens were black. Smoke drifted up from all of the monitors. The hallway was dark and Angus said, "Chloe, we are canceling clinic today. Go home anyway you can. We have the first patient here. Ask them to reschedule another day when the power is up. Please take Pirelli with you." Janet "Pirelli" Bledsoe was their medical technician. A young woman in her late twenties, she and her ten-year-older husband and kids from a prior marriage lived in Portland near Chloe.

"What's happening, Dr. Gunn?"

"I don't know, but I bet your car doesn't work. You will likely have to walk. Here, take all of the drinks out of my fridge and food out of our snack area. Did you get the bug home bag I suggested?"

"Yes, I have a book-bag with some stuff in it. But, it's at home on the counter. I didn't put it in my car. You really mean we have to walk home?"

"You'll know in a minute," Angus replied. "Godspeed. Good luck and don't stop to help or talk to anyone please. Just do it."

She looked at him with real fear in her eyes. And then she nodded and hugged him on the shoulder.

Angus called over to the nurses' station, "Sam, I need a favor..." Angus called Samuel Wallace, his other nurse technician and spoke with him for a moment, then shook his hand. He then turned and left straight away following the other nurses.

Angus stepped to the window and the entire town, as far as he could see from the third floor of the office building was out of power. All of the cars had stopped, drivers were slowly getting out, some were talking to each other. He returned inside and went to talk to his other partners to come up with a plan. Several were out of town and most would be coming in from the nursing homes and the hospital after doing rounds. He couldn't find Matt or anyone else. He told the office manager to cancel all clinics till the power was back on then he started back towards his office, reassuring his staff as he went by, asking everyone to remain calm and head home however they could. Most just stared at him over this comment. He did not waste breath explaining it. Most wouldn't believe it. Anyway they would know one way or the other soon enough if their cars didn't crank. This was just not something most people had ever heard of, and he did not have time to convince a dozen people right now. They all nodded and started gathering their things.

If this really was a full-on solar flare or coronal mass ejection with no Van Allen belt protection, then nothing electronic that had been exposed would ever work again. Only new circuits built to replace the damaged ones would do the job. That could, well would take years. Right now he would need to talk to Gwenn and see how she was doing. He had a Faraday cage in his truck with a Ham radio set and walkie talkies and flashlights in it. He would have to get to the parking garage. He walked into his office and looked out of the window again. Perhaps ten to twenty minutes had passed.

He looked out at the drivers who had been peacefully talking just moments ago. He could not hear yelling through the fixed window, but he saw some of them shoving each other. He looked towards the hospital and he saw several people run out, eyes and mouths wide, their terror completely mute behind the glass. Behind them staggered several people in hospital gowns. Smoke billowed from the hospital.

Gallatin, TN
15 miles North of Nashville
Summer County Regional Hospital
July 3
9:01a.m.

Matt Mackenzie clicked the computer and it died, along with all of the lights. A loud pop sounded from behind the old style CRT monitor and he ducked as shards of glass spayed out from an overhead recessed incandescent light. The smell of ozone and thin metallic smoke hung in the air. What the hell? He wondered. The emergency lights did not kick on, his watch light did not work. He heard a commotion and yelling. It was nearly pitch black in the section he was in. He joked with a nurse and then asked if everybody was O.K. The staff at this station seemed fine. Several were trying flashlights and cell phones that all appeared dead. He sat for a minute and waited for the emergency light to kick on. He was just sitting there quietly when a door to a patient room opened and light spilled in. He immediately wished it hadn't opened as he stood quietly and very quickly up and then froze in place. Several heads poked out from the door, glassy eyes unfocused. The patients walked out of the room past him, appearing not to see him. He then heard screaming and smelled smoke. He ducked and ran down the hallway, knocking down something in the way. It grabbed at him and he heard a frothy guttural sound. Panic rose within his throat.

He back-kicked hard and whoever had his foot grunted, and let go, he felt the crunch of possibly teeth on his heel. He ran further and tore open the door to the room where the smoke appeared to be coming from. Flames were billowing from a patient bed, the patient still strapped on the bed in restraints. Another patient stood right in front of the bed, the flames singeing his hair and eyebrows, a still lit cigarette lighter in his hand.

"Dumbly, bubbly! Dumbly numbly! Bubbly fumbly! Hee Hee Hee Hee Hee!!" the patient screamed at the top of his lungs. "Burn, bitch, burn!!"

The patient on the bed heaved once and then slumped down, the flames consuming the victim's body. Matt stood, stunned. The arsonist turned and was frothing at the mouth, his face half burned off. The monstrosity opened its arms fell in a spectacular backflip right onto the burning bed. It danced and writhed in the flame, and then stood up and started towards the door at a run, body and clothing on fire.

Matt ducked and rolled to the side, the madman barely missing him. Matt then stood and ran to the hallway. The creature was still running, grabbing others, and hugging them, cackling one second and then screaming in agony in alternating fits of madness. The flames spread to everything and everyone who was in the way. The flaming madman turned and leaped down a stairwell and disappeared from sight. Matt looked down the hallway to see if he could help anyone, looking side to side in the half light, when a large fat man in a hospital gown burst through the hallway and lunged at him, teeth bared, spittle running down his chin. Matt skidded down and turned, his knee contacting directly into the man's crotch, his knee crushing the man's testicles. The man slumped down and filled the hallway. Three more forms appeared behind him, glazed eyes staring directly at Matt, hunger in each eye, faces blank with apathy. They slowly advanced, fingernails curling into claws, as the flames started spreading down the hallway, lighting the patients' demonic visages.

"Screw this!" Matt said as he hurled himself backwards and down the nearest stairwell. He knocked over another man who was dressed in a tee shirt and jeans. He looked at the man's face. It appeared stunned, but normal.

"Sorry! You O.K.?," Matt said to the stricken man.

"Fine. You knocked the hell out of me though," the man replied.

"I didn't mean to. We've got to get out, it's all on fire up there."

The man nodded and followed Matt down the stairs into the lobby. It was a scene of utter chaos. People were running every direction. Some were yelling, some were fighting, clawing at each other and screaming. Some were just standing there, others running past. A child was standing in the walkway just outside the glass of the front entrance, mute, frozen. The boy turned his head to the side, just as a large 1950s Ford Pickup smashed him into the glass and barreled into the lobby. The boy's body spread out over the hood and then slumped under the vehicle as it smashed headlong into the reception desk. Smoke billowed from its hood, the driver thrown forward, his body hanging halfway out of the broken glass, slumped on the hood.

Matt looked for the child's body but could not see it in the chaos. The man he had run into in the stairwell was gone, nowhere in sight. He had no weapon, no medical gear, and no idea who to help. He ran outside and looked up at the hospital. It seemed to be about twenty minutes later, but he had no way to know the time. Thick smoke was pouring out of the broken windows of the third and fourth floors. A figure leaped out of a window and disappeared from view before striking the ground. What in the hell was going on? He had to find Angus. He raced through the narrow lane between the hospital and medical office building. People were tearing out of the building now, running in every direction. He looked down the hall as he entered and saw a tall brown haired man striding his direction.

"Matt, thank God you're O.K.!" Angus said as he met the man. "We've got to get people out."

"Let's go to the E.R. entrance. It's on a lower floor!" Matt replied as they both set off running in their loafers and dress clothes, racing towards the side entrance of the hospital.

Gallatin, TN
15 miles North of Nashville
Corner of neighborhood behind hospital
July 3
9:01a.m.

John Calvin turned the key in the ignition again. He was dressed in shorts and a Hawaiian shirt and loafers. He was just leaving his house for their annual Disney vacation. The kids in the back dressed in casual T shirts as well. No reaction by the pricey imported minivan. He looked at his watch. The second hand had stopped. He picked up his cellphone. Black screen. Oh no.

He looked at his wife Denise and she looked back.

"O.K. Kids, we need to try to get this car out of the road," he said, looking again at his wife. Fear furrowed her brow, but now, in front of the kids was not the time to ask questions.

"What's wrong, Daddy?" asked 14-year-old Hailey.

"I don't know, sweetie, but we need to move the car over so people can get past. Let's all get out and push it over."

Everybody complied and they quickly pushed the useless heap of metal over to the side. He looked up at the sky. It had been about 9AM when the power went out; his watch was frozen at the time. "I hope Angus wasn't right, but it sure looks that way," he said to Denise.

He asked the family to go ahead and walk the two blocks back to the house. He rolled most of the suitcases himself, but could not get all of them. He let his kids in the house, and he and Denise walked back to the car to get the rest.

"You mean right about the solar thing?" Denise asked

"Yeah."

"Really. Car breaks down and you think a solar flare caused it?"

"Check your cellphone, and look at the stoplights," he replied.

She looked at both and sure enough, they were dead. "Hmmm, O.K. that's creepy. Maybe you are right."

They walked back to the van and unloaded the last suitcases and rolled them back to the house. When he turned to enter the house, he saw smoke billowing into the sky from the direction of the hospital.

Fear and concern darkened his face. He turned to Denise. "Get the bugout bags in the Deuce," he said referring to their bugout vehicle, and old, pre-computer, multifueled military vehicle. "I've got to help Angus; there will be people trapped."

She looked at the smoke and ran into the house calling out instructions to her kids in rapid fire order. He dashed down the street, his muscular legs pumping hard as he approached the E.R. door.

Gallatin, TN
15 miles North of Nashville
Summer County Regional Hospital
Top of parking garage
July 3
9:45a.m.

Angus had raced up the stairs and bounded to his Honda Ridgeline. He tried the keyfob and then manually unlocked it when the fob didn't work. The vehicle wouldn't start, no matter how many times he tried. He knew this would be the case, but had to make the attempt. He opened the trunk, under the bed of the pickup and removed several bags. The Ridgeline had a separate car trunk under the short pickup bed. He took out his bug home bag and body armor vest. He removed an ammo box and removed its contents. He was taking a risk here in that the flare might not be over. But at the rate these animals were attacking, he didn't have a choice, he had to warn Gwenn.

He and several other people had helped as many as they could out of the E.R. exit and then he had left the guys and run up here to try a contact. He had dodged the infected so far, and most were either in the building burning or had already run well out into town in every direction. His 2 meter handitalkie sparked to life! Praise God from whom all blessings flow! It worked! Hopefully Gwenn had opened up her gear as well when the power went out.

Angus plugged in the fox hunting high gain directional antenna along the compass point he knew to lead to home. He did this from memory and practice, as the actual compass was useless now except to reference for azimuth direction if you already knew the direction of true north or were referencing known landmarks on a map held in relation to the land viewed. The compass was useless for finding a direction at this point, so was GPS for that matter. Angus bet the satellites had already fried to a crisp by this time.

The channel was already set for simplex comm. "Lima Lima Lima, how copy over?" Angus said. During normal comm, Ham radio operators were forbidden to use any code of any type. Every user was rigidly required to self-identify every ten minutes. Needless to say, these were not ordinary times. The Gunns had long since set up a code for emergencies and this code was highly urgent.

No response. Dammit! He tried again, three more times and on the fourth try, "Roger that, four by four, audible but weak. Are you O.K.?" Gwenn asked.

"Not injured. Matt and I are headed for his house on foot. Everything's out, the solar flare must have hit big. You have to get out immediately and get Betsy and get everybody to Matt's house ASAP. There are infected people killing everybody here," Angus said, referring to "Betsy," the family bug out vehicle, a deuce and a half nearly identical to John Calvin's. They were pre computer and should run no matter what kind of EMP or solar event occurred, just like the old truck now resting in the hospital lobby.

"Repeat last," Gwenn replied.

"Infected patients have burned down the hospital and are running through the streets killing everyone they find. People are coming out of their cars and houses and doing the same. How copy?"

"Four by four. What do you mean, killing everybody? Over."

"The building is burning to the ground. Matt and John and Justin and I are O.K., but we have had to dodge and defend against the people who have this new disease. They've all gone insane and are killing people with knife, and fire and their bare hands, and teeth. They are biting people. You have got to get out of there."

"Oh my God. Angus, Kate is at the archery megamart."

"What? When did she go!?"

"She left this morning with Tessa. Simone called and asked if it was O.K. The two of them would have been there for half an hour shooting. We have to get them. I will take Betsy and go get her now."

"NO. YOU CAN'T!" screamed Angus

"The hell I can't. That's my daughter!" replied Gwenn. "I am leaving now!"

"You'll never make it. The roads will be jammed, the infected people everywhere will be out. You'll get killed and likely eaten."

"I can't leave her there!" Gwenn sobbed into the mike.

"Meet us at Matt's and we will all convey in a group. Then you won't die for nothing. You have to protect Joshua. You know this. Kate is tough as hell. We made her that way. And Tessa is with her. You would be alone, with an eight-year-old boy and your mother in law. Over."

"Shit, your mom is in town shopping for antiques. It's near the storage center where Betsy is. I'll get her and she can ride shotgun. We will come to Matt's and regroup. Over."

"O.K. I love you. Do not go near anyone. The infected people seem to have lost whatever was holding them together once the power went out and nothing works. Also, regular people may try to kill you for our stuff. Take the bug out bags for everybody there. I'll get mine later and get the rest of the stuff. We'll get Kate and then get to the retreat. John is already heading that way to secure it. This is no shit the real deal, everything we practiced. Get out in fifteen minutes. Tell Joshua I love him. God protect you. I love you, over."

"Roger that. I love you too. Where are you? Are you heading with Matt now? Over."

"Affirmative, Matt and I are walking together. I am on the roof of the parking garage to get a signal. Won't work on the ground till we are a lot closer. I'll call you as we approach. Take the handie talkie and leave it on an earbud so you can hear me when I call. It will be a few hours, I guess. Over."

"Roger last. Am heading to town for Betsy and Margaret. Over." Gwenn said

"Roger that, out." Angus replied

"Out." echoed Gwenn.

While on the roof, Angus changed clothes into Mulitcam tactical BDUs right down to his grey underwear and socks and brown Asolo boots. No one was there. He worried only about one of those maniacs coming up. Matt would have his gear ready by now. He looked out and saw the fire spreading to the office building that housed his practice and to several outlying buildings. Screams echoed in the distance. Gallatin was burning.

Gallatin, TN
15 miles North of Nashville
Summer County Regional Hospital
Emergency Room parking lot
July 3
9:50a.m.

Angus checked the Tag Formula watch that he had kept in the Faraday cage and noted the time. He told everyone. Justin Clearwater coughed and thanked him. Edward Douglass had seen the smoke and had run the four blocks from the courthouse. He had helped Angus and Matt pull several people from the burning building. The Fire Department could not respond, as their equipment didn't work anymore, but the firefighters themselves had arrived with some medical equipment and had taken over caring for those injured that had been saved. By this time, other buildings were catching fire, spreading from the main inferno at the hospital. The low income housing behind the hospital had erupted into chaos as some of the infected patients went rampaging through it. Gunfire could now be heard, along with political slogans being chanted out and generally more yelling and screaming. This was fast becoming a very dangerous place.

Justin, John, Ed, Angus and Matt stared at each other. They were all in some partial state of shock. Matt and Angus had been able to change into new clothes, and had less soot on their faces as they had changed, Matt into woodland BDUs and Angus into his Multicam. The two were now fully kitted out, each had an Eberlestock backpack containing a rifle and now with open-carried Springfield XDs, Angus' in 9mm, Matt's in .45 ACP, both in tactical drop leg holsters. Time for subtlety was apparently over. Each had on a plate carrier in forest green. As both men talked, they took off their packs and removed their rifles from the backpack scabbards and loaded the rifles. Matt carried an M4 profile AR-15 and Angus had a Marlin Guide Gun GBL in 45-70, each man's vest rigged for the specific rifle. They loaded and slung their rifles on two point slings across the chest.

"Matt and I are heading to his house. I reached Gwenn and she will meet us there. Kate and Tessa are at the downtown archery range. We will have to mount a rescue effort once we can provide enough shooters," Angus said, his voice calm and neutral despite the anguish in his heart. Everyone could, and probably would lose loved ones soon.

"I will go to 'the hotel,' and set everything up, Denise is already working on loading the deuce and a half. I'll leave immediately. You guys come when you can. Ed, door's open," John Calvin said speaking to the group members and then to Edward Douglass.

"Yeah," said all of the other guys simultaneously.

"Thanks for the vote of confidence guys, but I need to stay here. Somebody's got to set Gallatin back up. I am going to head to the Sheriff's office now that the firemen are here," Ed stated, turning to go, "You guys be careful." With that he shook hands, thanked them and left, walking briskly back to the courthouse and Sheriff's office.

"I'm going to get to the GPD," stated Justin, referring to the Gallatin Police Department," I need to get changed into uniform and see if they have an incident command set up. If possible, I will join you guys later, but I have a job to do now, just like Ed. Once it settles out, I want to try and get your daughter and her friend out, but I've sworn to help here in town first."

"I understand and appreciate the offer. I know what you have to do. I knew what I had to do, but now my business and workplace are burning to the ground. Matt and I will get her out, I'm sure," Angus said.

"I hope Scott, Carlos, Doug, and Lucien are O.K. We don't have time to do a net now, but can try at dusk like in the drills we did before," Matt said, referring to a multiuser Ham radio chat that the group set up and would try at dusk, as they all had saved the gear in their Faraday Cages.

"You're right. Lord Bless us and all of the friends. Help us all in our time of need. Keep us safe and watch over us now and forever more, Amen," Angus said, turning and racking the lever of his Marlin Guide Gun, cycling a 325 grain Hornady Lever Evolution cartridge into the camber, six more behind it as he slid a replacement into the tube from his vest.

"And Lord help those who get in the way," Justin said looking at the grim determination of the father preparing to trek across any distance, face any risk, and kill any enemy to save his daughter.

"Let's go," Angus said.

So when the last and dreadful hour
This crumbling pageant shall devour,
The trumpet shall be heard on high,
The dead shall live, the living die,
And Music shall untune the sky
—John Dryden, "A Song for St. Cecilia's Day"

CHAPTER 14

Bethpage, TN
5 miles East of Gallatin
Washington House
July 3
9:01a.m.

Darryl Washington was sitting in his living room, resting. He had been taking a family day today to be at home. He did this every month just to try to catch up. Nothing planned, no agenda. Then, the power went out, the incandescent lights popped and the fluorescent kitchen light shattered. He could still make out the page of the book he had been reading. He paused.

Oh Lord God in Heaven. Tessa!

He leaped up from the couch the instant he noted that not only was the power out, but that his watch was dead. He careened into the bedroom and yelled out, "Everybody, we're moving out!"

Feet came running into the kitchen. "Darryl?" Simone Washington called out, her tone filled with concern.

"It's the solar flare we were worried about. Check your electronics. All I have found are dead. Don't open the cages! Might not be over for a while; no way to know. We've got to get Tessa!" Darryl responded.

Simone paused and looked at her husband, deep concern etched upon her face. Tessa was at the archery range with Kate Gunn and that area would be totally without power, no way to drive the fifteen or more miles back. This was serious. They would have to get their gear and get out now to go get her.

"Go get her. Jesse will have to stay here with us for perimeter security. We can't man the house with fewer people, and somebody has to be with Susanne," Simone said.

"I know, I agree. Get the body armor and gear out, set up a perimeter and the LP/OP and keep a low profile," Darryl said referring to the listening post/observation post that he had constructed on their land to monitor the property without being observed. Preparing their homestead to defend against looters was a major concern to the Washingtons.

"Tessa will likely head for the Mackenzie place. It's a lot closer than here and while we aren't members of their group, that's where Kate would go if I were her. Their whole group will be there and the railroad runs almost right to the area. I'll meet up with the Gunns and their group and we will go get them together if they haven't already left to get them. If so, then I'll just follow, on foot if I have to. I don't know when or if I'll be back. If I return, it will be with Tessa, though. I promise, one way or another.

Darryl grabbed his Bulgarian AK-47 semi-auto clone and his Interceptor Body Armor vest and slung it on over his jeans and black cotton long sleeved dress shirt, the sleeves half rolled up as he usually did when he was in his casual mode. He threw off his loafers and slid on black USAF combat boots and laced them. Simone handed him a small three day pack filled with supplies, a fresh loaf of bread, navel oranges, a block of farm fresh cheese and paper towels. She kissed him, squeezed his hand and he raced out to the old F250 Ford diesel truck. He prayed a silent prayer that it would work. When he popped the hood, he could see a low glow from the wiring.

He dropped the hood and cranked the engine easily. The radio was useless, and he was glad the windows were manual. The increased current had made the glow plugs pre-warm, just as it had increased the power of telegraph lines in 1859. Craziest damned thing, he thought. The vehicle rumbled to life and tore out of the driveway, its twin still in the drive, the family looking on out of the window. He looked back in the truck bed and king cab back seat and mentally counted the gear he had stowed there, including extra weapons, food, water, repair gear, and he thanked God for his benevolence. It was going to be a long day.

Hendersonville, TN
Halfway between Gallatin and Goodlettsville
3 miles from Mackenzie House
July 3
9:01 a.m.

Carlos Corpus was sitting at the breakfast table with his family on his day off from work. He was sipping good coffee. He had run this morning with his sons as usual, and had just now finished a light omelette for breakfast.

The lights went out, and the compact fluorescent bulbs all popped simultaneously, sending glass onto the floor all over the house. Carlos looked around and checked his watch. The watch was dead. He walked into the living room and the TV was dead as well. So were his cellphone and iPad. Dammit. Angus was right.

He returned to the kitchen and started laying out a plan for the family. Hopefully, none of it would be needed. They began setting out gear and filling packs. It was quiet and peaceful on their private neighborhood road.

Outdoorsman's Proshop Warehouse
Attached to Country Music Mall
East Nashville, TN
July 3
8:59a.m.

Left arm tensed in an outward push, right arm bent full, index fingertip touching the right corner of her lip, her rhomboids powerfully contracting against the 70 pounds of pressure stored in the matrix of synthetic limbs, cams and string, she held her breath gently. Her mind traced the arc of flight that the carbon fiber shafted arrow would follow upon release, having seen this thousands of times. The unity of bow and archer was complete, the pinnacle of early man's adoption of technology, reborn in a modern composite form. The world fell away, walls disappearing, the lane floor replaced with a grassy hill, the roof dissolving into gently shifting clouds and dappled sunlight, the target replaced with a stag Elk, turned ninety degrees to the hunter. Its own breath was in sync with hers, held in anticipation of the release.

Her forearm muscles began to relax and the string tension began pulling forward against the fingers of her right hand, the string clearing her gloved fingers. Most archers now used mechanical releases and mechanical sighting systems to improve their aim and release. Kate Gunn would have neither. From the first bow her father ever gave her at age five, she had asked him to "take that thing out of the way, I can't see the target," referring to the front bow sight found on most bows now. Kate was an instinctive shooter, she felt where the arrow would go, before it ever left the string.

The arrow cleared the string and rest and rocketed towards the target, porpoising through the air in the archer's paradox, the frequency of the oscillations rapidly increasing as the arrow covered the thirty yards in a seeming instant. The arrow struck the center of the black one inch dot placed there for it to hit. This distance was much too close to shoot more than one arrow at the same point as the later arrows would hit and destroy the first. A row of nine other black one inch dots were lined up on the target, each one pierced by an identical black shaft.

Kate felt good when she knew the arrow had hit. This was always before the shot was completed. When she hit, it was as if the world lined up and its secrets fell from the sky.

Tessa smirked, "Show off," and rolled her eyes.

"Not showin' off if it's real skill! Besides, I wouldn't want you to feel like I let you win like last week," Kate replied to groans on her friend's part.

"I beat you fair and square last week!"

"Whatever makes you feel better, girl," Kate joshed back. Tessa smacked her on the shoulder and grinned. Suddenly, the lights went out. Static pops could be head all over the store as recessed lighting snapped and a thin ozone smell permeated the air. No emergency lights came on. "That's odd," Kate said. "The emergency lights are out. My flashlight's out too, and my cellphone's dead." She had tried both with no result.

Tessa touched Kate's back and said, "It's pitch black in here. Let's back out slowly. Leave your arrows for now."

"Hey! What's going on here?" Kate yelled to the employees.

"Hey, who's there? Y'all O.K. back in there?" one of the archery guys yelled.

"Yeah, we're good, just can't see a damned thing!" yelled Tessa.

Distant booms shook the building, the ground shaking beneath their feet. The girls dashed to the window opposite of the front entrance, keeping in the middle lane of the store to try not to trip in the half dark. They looked up, towards the airport. Their hearts both froze at the sight.

In the direction of the airport, to the South, a large commercial aircraft was falling sideways, the wings rolling casually over to the left. It appeared to have been just taking off when the power went out. The aircraft bent over at an impossible angle, and then disappeared from view behind the hillside and hotels blocking the view. New explosions rocked the ground like small earthquakes. A loud shuddering series of large booms echoed across town. Cars filled the freeway. Some had struck one another, while others were just sitting in traffic, immobile. The owners were like little dots in the distance, getting out to survey the damage. Some were throwing their hands up, other sat on their hoods.

"You girls O.K.?" a store clerk asked, "That's terrible out there. I'm sorry y'all had to see that. I'm sorry, but we can't seem to get the power on, and I know you've got a dozen of your arrows down the lane. Maybe we can help you see them to get 'em out of the arrow block." He motioned to another employee.

The girls looked over and saw a small flame. One of the employees had a cigarette lighter lit. He walked over and Kate looked at the small flame and had an idea. "Hey, grab me one of those camping lanterns man, I'll buy it cash, right now. I've been wanting one anyway with Dad into all that EMP stuff he talks about." She handed the clerk three twenties and he nodded.

"You want the butane one, I guess. May be a minute on the change, they're $44.99 plus tax and the cylinder is $4.95, O.K.?"

"Sounds great. Just crack one open so I can go get my arrows," Kate said, smiling at the young man. He ran as quick as he could, stumbling a little in the dark. He came back in a second with the stove and lit it for her after attaching the fuel cylinder.

He showed her how to work it and then said, "Not usually store policy, but don't know what else to do."

Two dark figures could be seen outside, walking sideways and stumbling towards the front door. Three more behind them were wandering around as well.

"What the hell?" Tessa said, both girls freezing as Kate lowered the flame to a dim light and hid it under the shelf to block the light. The mall attached to the outdoors store would not open for another hour roughly. It was almost 9a.m. when the lights went out, and that was about five minutes ago. The only people who were in the area would be in this store, which opened at 8a.m. to accommodate the higher popularity and sales margins than the regular mall's customer base. This had been a sore point for the mall, which always lagged in sales to the outdoor giant. Good prices and great service kept them hopping at the sales counter, and features like free unlimited archery lane usage for regular customers didn't hurt. The girls usually shopped here for that reason.

Kate didn't like the looks on the faces of the people in the parking lot. And she liked their ataxic gait even less. Human physiology was one of her home school pre-vet classes and she had paid attention when her father had taught her the neurology section. The shuffling movement could indicate drug use, motor cortex damage, other neurological disease or possible this new infection sweeping thought the country. Her dad had warned her about violent behavior after the nurse was attacked at the hospital. She never got filtered data on anything since she was a home schooled, very mature, early starter in everything. Her parents treated her with more respect than most and gave her more freedom as a result of her trustworthiness. She knew all about the concerns of the group. She knew, as did Tessa, that the lights would probably never come back on, unless they were rebuilt. And she knew that her car wouldn't work and that likely no one else in the store would have any idea what was going on.

Suddenly, there was a cry of strangled anguish in the back. Kate turned up the light and the girls raced towards the noise. As they came around the corner, they saw legs kicking lightly against the floor. They rounded the corner and saw an older gentleman, a store employee, sprawled out on the ground clutching his chest. He had ripped the top buttons off of his shirt in his anguish. There, on the upper left rib cage was the unmistakable round subdermal imprint of a pacemaker or automated implantable defibrillator.

The man was gasping for air as two employees attached a AED, or automated external defibrillator to his chest. They knew exactly what to do, and this did not appear to surprise them much. "Come on Joe, we'll get it!" one of them said, offering support. "You always hated that damned thing ever since they put it in your chest. You said it knocked you on your ass when it went off on you. What's it doing now?"

"Nothing...." squeaked the pitiful figure, "My heart's gone aflutter and it ain't workin' no more...can't breathe... Usually...kicks in before this, keep my heart running right." The man clenched his chest as the others placed the AED down and pressed the big yellow button on the front. Nothing happened. They tried again. Nothing.

The man gasped and one of the employees smacked the plastic AED box onto the floor hard three times and pressed the button again. Nothing. The man started CPR and the compression elicited a groan of pain from the afflicted man.

He gasped, "It's no use, Sam. You tried. Doc warned me CPR wouldn't work, only this thing could save me," he said rubbing his fingertips over the disc imprint on his chest. "Plum gave out with... with that last of whatever killed the lights...heard... 'bout...'bout that EMP or solar flare them newsies kept lying about... Bastards. Now they... now they killed us all." He paused, looked up at the younger man's face and said, "tell Martha...tell her I love her..."

Tears streamed down the younger man's cheeks. The older man gasped and smiled, his eyes glazed over and he jerked upwards once more. His hand fell from the place on his left chest that he had been clutching. The pupils dilated and his cheeks relaxed, all of the agony was done, his last breath rattling outward from the thin frame and narrow ribs, never more to suffer again.

The group of employees stood up, shock in their eyes as one turned to the side. A man was standing there, fingers curled into claw like grips, saliva dripping down the front of his chin. His eyes were unfocused. His breathing was shallow and rapid, like an animal that was in new and unfamiliar surroundings.

"Mr. Mathewson?" the clerk said, obviously recognizing the customer. The man was dressed in a striped dress shirt, stained with what looked like mustard and something brown, maybe dried barbecue sauce. There were small tears on his skin and clothing, as if he had walked all night through a field of brush. His hair was unkempt, his glasses hung from one ear over the face, dangling at an odd angle over the mouth.

The noise seemed to have startled the person. The pupils narrowed in focus and a low growl emanated from its throat. Suddenly, it lunged, scrabbling hard fingernails towards the clerk, the man throwing up his hands to defend himself. The men all jumped into the fray as the girls noticed several other people wandering in to the store. The fight seemed to be attracting attention.

Kate and Tessa tore themselves away and ran for the archery lane. Kate turned up the light in her hands and raced down the lane, grabbing the arrows as fast as she could and stuffing the broad-head tipped carbon tubes as fast as she safely could into her hip quiver, which she was still wearing when the power went out. Tessa reached behind the counter and pulled out her own bow, the brown camouflaged alloy and composite riser slipping into her hand

Screaming echoed from the store and yelling mixed with the sound, terrifying both girls. For all of the well-meaning intentions of the Store management, they would not allow employees to conceal carry their handguns. This disarmament philosophy was a noted trend in the late twentieth and early twenty-first centuries, fostered by decades of unopposed liberal intrusion into the classroom. None of the store employees had a gun.

The click of a folding knife being deployed could be heard, then the ripping sound of flesh being rent. One of the employees stood up from the fight, blood dripping down his hand and wrist. At his feet lay the patron, his abdomen pouring blood onto the carpet. The employees stared, stunned at the scene.

The knife wielding employee turned and bumped into a woman, also disheveled, covered in leaf litter and with matted hair. She screamed a burbling wail and sank her teeth into the man's nose and ripped her head sideways, tearing the nose off. The man let out a muffled cry, unable to intonate correctly without his nose as the woman's hand shot out and clutched the man's throat and fell forward onto the struggling man's body.

Before they hit the ground, the woman's teeth sank into the man's neck and blood shot out, covering her face. The man went limp and the creature stood up and stared into the eyes of the remaining two employees. They froze in terror and turned to run, only to see three more figures loping up the aisle. One knocked over a stand of fishing poles as he made a bee-line towards the gun counter, keys shaking in his hands. He reached the counter and furiously struggled with the locks on a shotgun rack, trying desperately to find the right key, his hands shaking like a leaf. A small framed Hispanic man ran towards him, slobbering, a gobbling noise wrenching itself from his mouth. In his hand he had a tire iron, swinging it with vicious intent. Just as he was about to leap the counter and attack the clerk, a thin black arrow sailed into and through his torso, from the left to the right side. The man stopped, blood pouring down both sides of his ribcage, just below the heart, green color of bile mixing with the bleeding, indicating that the arrow had pierced the liver or gallbladder. Despite such intense trauma, the man began running towards Tessa, as she struggled to fit the next arrow to her string, fear shaking her hands and preventing the normally fluid motion. She screamed. The man was nearly upon her, blood now mixing with the spittle on his jaw, tire iron discarded, hands and fingers out in a rage filled charge of fury.

Thwift...thwift...thwift. Three arrows pierced the figure's chest in rapid sequence. Each arrow struck into and through the upper torso, cracking ribs and rupturing the mediastinal great arteries. Unable to effectively oxygenate the body now, the man stumbled, gouts of blood now vomiting forth from his mouth, and pouring out of the three new holes in the chest, blood still running out of the first holes in the sides of his torso. His body struck the ground and he reached a quavering hand and began to crawl towards Tessa, shock causing both girls to be rooted to the spot.

As the bloody man still crawled towards them, the other employee screamed as two figures bore down on him, clubbing him to death with what looked like iron skillets. They wailed and moaned as their hands smashed down on the chubby man's arms and head and neck, his helpless cries ceasing as one pan crushed his skull. The creatures dropped the skillets and turned to the girls and the clerk, still struggling with the keys.

A hail of arrows descended upon the two figures, roughly forty-yards away. Fully eight arrows flew in a matter of seconds, five from the black Bowtech and three from the brown Matthews. Tessa had regained her composure and her fingers found the hip quiver quickly as she restrung her next arrow. The two creatures lay in a tumbled heap. One had one arrow hole in the chest, the arrow passing through, two arrows in the neck and a fourth in the head, all stopped halfway through their transit by the skull and vertebrae. The other had three arrow holes though the upper chest and one lodged in the forehead, arrow almost fully through, piercing both front and back skull plates stopped only at the fletching. This last was from Tessa's eighty pound draw Matthews Monster MR5, its draw weight exceeding most compounds bows on the market.

Kate had shot one arrow into each chest and three more into the head and neck of the attacker on the right, while Tessa finished off the one on the right, finally stopping it with the head shot. The attacker on the carpet in front of them had bled out after crawling five more feet. Tessa turned to the side and vomited. Kate just stood there, breath coming in and out slowly. They had both been deer hunting and had butchered hogs with Tessa's dad. Those had been bloody events, certainly, but nothing like having to defend one's self against a human. Even an insane one, or in this case several. Kate felt her eyes bore into the scene, the neurons of her occipital cortex burning the images deep into her subconscious. She was the first person in her family who had ever killed another human, and she would never be the same.

The two girls and the clerk behind the gun counter were the only people left in the store, everyone else must have fled, or been attacked without the girls realizing it, as there had been a smattering of customers and a couple of managers there when the chaos had erupted. Tessa wiped her mouth off and stood up. She turned to her best friend and they hugged each other and wept. They regained their composure after a couple of minutes, and began to look around. Kate's fingers burned. She had not had time to put her shooting glove back on before the attack ensued, and the fast flight spectra fiber string had abraded her skin somewhat. Luckily she did a lot of work with her hands and was fairly mentally tough. She looked around the scene.

Bodies littered the floor, the pooling blood and vomit and expelled fecal material almost made Kate swoon. The girls walked over to the clerk behind the gun counter. He behaved as if he could not see them. His hands kept frenetically fidgeting with the keys trying to get the locking rack off of the shotguns. Kate touched his arm. Hot tears flooded down the young man's face. His black hair and thick mutton chop sideburns covered a terrified face. He was somewhat overweight and of medium build. The man stopped trying the keys and turned to look at the girls.

Kate spoke clearly, "Are you O.K.?"

The man nodded. He paused and then smiled. Despite all of the terror, these were two very beautiful girls, and they had just saved his life.

"I need to buy some stuff. Is that O.K.? I have my checkbook and some cash. I figure with the power out you can't take my credit card." Because she was very reliable, her dad had set her up with her own account attached to the family account.

The man thought for a moment, "Yeah, the check would work fine. I can hand write it up. I've done that procedure before. I guess I'll have to close the store then. Looks like I'm it for today."

"Thank you, we will get started now. Why don't you get us all a bottled water or something? I'll be about five minutes." Kate handed him two $1 bills. The man nodded, wiped his cheeks and walked to the drink fridge.

Kate turned to Tessa, "This must be the solar event our dads have been on about this month. It really just happened. We need to get you some gear, we're going to have to walk home, and I've already got my bug home bag in the trunk. But you don't have yours because we took my car, not yours. I'll get the stuff and you can pay me back later, I don't think dad will care.

They rapidly collected a kit, forest green pack and gear for Tessa. They got first aid gear in a small pack, added several Quickclot packs for treatment of life threatening bleeding, added fire making and survival gear, a curved Parang machete just like the one Angus Gunn had, a tactical tomahawk and freeze-dried food and small camping stove and fuel cylinder. Also several granola bars and granola cereal with powdered milk. The girls were too young to own firearms, and even though they had their own rifles and pistols at home, they had to settle with their bows and the bladed tools for defense.

They went to the floor of the store and Tessa wouldn't let Kate retrieve her arrows. She pointed out that they had no easy way to sterilize them here and that spending a couple of hundred bucks on new arrows and broad heads made more sense now, especially if money wouldn't be worth anything in a day or two anyway. They each got a dozen new arrows, matched to their current set. The clerk cut them to length using a hand tool, as the electric cutter was out of commission, and he attached their favorite broadheads for them with glue-in inserts. They filed their quivers, Kate had now twenty-two arrows, and Tessa had twenty-three.

Kate bought a ghillie blanket large enough to cover two people. She thought they might hide under it, if they needed to disappear suddenly. The blanket was thick, but lightweight mesh, covered with burlap strips, and could be dragged over an area to pick up leaves and sticks. After this procedure, it could appear as part of the surroundings. They paid the clerk with Kate's check, drank their water and ripped off all of the packaging from the new gear and piled it into the pack for Tessa. Kate thanked the clerk and he gave her a handwritten receipt.

"Thanks back there. I thought I was a goner," the man said, a little sheepishly. "I don't know what the hell happened to those people. Like freakin' zombies!"

"Well, I don't know either, but my dad says it's an infection that makes them violent. Stay away from them; you could catch it," she motioned to the bodies. "I understand if you have to call the cops on us for having to... do that." She motioned towards the dead.

"Hell with that: you saved my ass. Leave it alone. Where are you girls going?"

"Home. And, thanks." Kate left it with a serious look, not wanting company. The girls walked back out of the store and headed outside.

"We need to get away from all of those people on the interstate there. There is a railroad line that runs on the other side of the river. My dad made me remember all of the rail line locations in the area. Said we could use them to travel by without attracting attention," Tessa said. She changed her brown long sleeved T shirt for a civilian camouflage long sleeved shirt, and kept her olive drab tactical pants and hiking boots.

The girls jogged to Kate's older model Honda Pilot. Kate manually unlocked the tailgate as the key fob was dead. She tore off her pink T shirt and dark blue jeans and put on woodland camo BDUs and put back on her brown hiking boots. She reattached her hip quiver and grabbed her bug home bag and took about half of her purse contents and placed them into the bag. She smeared black and green face paint on roughly at an angle to break up her facial outline. She drank the water in her cup from the front seat and left a short coded note in case anyone found the car and needed to find them later.

She tossed an extra water bottle from the trunk into her own pack, giving her three liters now, plus what she just drank. She tossed the last water bottles to Tessa, giving her two liters. They could always purify more later or find a tap if needed. They set off south at a brisk walk. It was hard to say the time, but she guessed an hour had passed. Unlike her dad, she had not made a Faraday cage for her car to store electronics in. A watch and radio would have been nice. They would try for the pedestrian bridge south of the mall. They would have to dodge anyone walking off of the freeway.

Random gunshots started to crack and boom in the distance in several directions. They saw smoke rising from new fires, also in several areas. The smell of burning tires filled their noses, the acrid smoke choking them as they passed the freeway entrance to the mall. Tessa looked out over the scene, the recent terror filling her mind, threatening to take control of her sanity. It would be a long trip north, she felt. Smoke drifted over the frontage road and rolled across, into the distance to the river, running through the heart of downtown and East Nashville. The girls began their epic trek home, their dreams of a normal future slipping away with each new horror. Kate mouthed a silent prayer of thanks, as they jogged quickly towards the foot bridge.

Wild, dark times are rumbling toward us, and the prophet who wishes to write a new apocalypse will have to invent entirely new beasts, and beasts so terrible that the ancient animal symbols of St. John will seem like cooing doves and cupids in comparison.

—Heinrich Heine, "Lutetia; or, Paris." From the Augsberg Gazette, 12, VII, 1842

CHAPTER 15

Goodlettsville, TN
10 miles North of Nashville
Gunn House
July 3
9:48a.m.

Gwenn ended the radio contact with Angus and headed into the kitchen. She grabbed water bottles and began pulling out the bug out bags. She reviewed the contents on the master list and adjusted some of Joshua's clothing for size. She was moving fast, worried about her daughter. She looked out of all of the windows and did not see anything out of the ordinary, given that the power was out. She noticed neighbors checking their generators, scratching their heads. Some were walking the neighborhood with their dogs. It seemed that the power outage was a good excuse to wander the neighborhood.

She called the dogs and Joshua and realized she didn't need to turn off the alarm to open the back door. She opened the door and let the dogs out, not looking into the yard, having just surveyed it only two minutes earlier. The dogs stopped short of the yard. Their hair was bristling and the electric current of fear rippled through the air. Gwenn looked up towards the back yard, Joshua at her side, hugging her shoulder. There was a man in the backyard.

Gallatin, TN
Downtown
West of the hospital
July 3
10:10a.m.

Angus and Matt walked carefully along the sidewalk, spaced ten meters apart, rifles slung on their chests, ready for any attack. Engine noises started down the main street and the men ducked behind cover as three white Ford F250 Sumner County Emergency Management trucks blasted past, one smashing into the rear fender of a dead sedan in the road. The owner shook his fist at the truck, but it did not slow down. What the hell was that all about? Angus wondered as he came out from behind the mailbox and checked the street. No one had bothered them since they left the hospital. Nothing said "don't screw with me" better than tactical gear and a slung rifle, Angus thought as he walked on, keeping up a brisk walk towards Hendersonville.

Tulley Farm
Five miles north of Gallatin, TN
July 3
10:15a.m.

Lucien stared in amazement at the sight. His family was lined up on the ridge of their property overlooking the town. The flames spread out over the eastern parts of Gallatin, fueled by the inferno that had been the hospital. The town was burning. They were too far away at five miles to see any detail, but it was clear that this was an epic disaster. None of their equipment had worked, except what they took out of their Faraday cages forty five minutes after the event. It had been a risk. He knew that flares could come in waves and last hours sometimes. They had not attempted to call anyone, but did confirm that that the Ham radios and flashlights did work. They had returned the gear to the cages after confirming that they worked.

Lucien stared at the horizon. The shadow of his wakizashi handle ran across his right deltoid. His entire family was in full gear, plate carriers, Japanese short swords, rifles slung, and helmets. He heard a whistle behind him, a bird sound, and turned from the scene of chaos.

Donovan Tulley stood up from the ground and dropped his ghillie blanket at his feet. He had appeared to be a bush five seconds ago. "The McKnights are here," he said, pointing to the roadway behind them, where the entire McKnight family walked with bug out bags and a contingent of sheep, goats and a large working dog, a Great Pyrenees.

"God bless us all. We're going to need it," Lucien spoke to himself. "Sean, welcome our guests," he said to his youngest. The young man slung his rifle on his shoulder and quietly walked down the hill, hands up in a greeting gesture.

Continual Living Advancement Clinic
Gallatin, TN
South of the hospital
July 3
10:03a.m.

Francesca Clearwater Schultz stared out of the window in dismay. The power had gone out over an hour ago, and they had just finished arranging walking transportation for their last patients to get home. The staff had made arrangements with the next door neighbor, a medical supply house. They had borrowed several wheelchairs and divided volunteers to walk the folks home. The owner had trusted them with the honor system; he always was a good and decent man. There were several patients who had already left and several who were leaving now to walk to nearby houses and nursing homes in town. Only one lady from Hendersonville remained and had not been very appreciative of the efforts to help her out. Francesca frankly didn't care if she walked home by herself, the biddy. You try to help some people and they don't appreciate it.

She had been wondering how she would get home. She figured her husband would come to get her somehow, but she had been so distracted by getting the patients home that she had not really had time to think it through.

Right now, her attention was rapt, as she looked through the window. A truck had slammed on the brakes, just shy of ramming into a school bus when the power had gone out. The kids had been sitting next to the bus for about an hour, in the shade. She had worried about getting them home as well, but it looked like the bus driver was doing a great job organizing them, and she had been too busy at this point to help. The driver of the truck had been sitting behind the wheel for all of this time, smoking several cigarettes patiently.

But now, he was not being so patient. He was standing in front of the bus driver shaking his arms at the man who was nodding his head and backing away slowly. What the heck? The man stormed back to his truck and retrieved a large revolver and aimed it at the bus driver. Time froze as Francesca remembered her training. She had been to an excellent concealed handgun course and regularly carried a pistol in her car, as she was excluded from carrying one in the building. She raced towards the door through the pharmacy which led into the parking lot. As she passed the clinic and leaped across the pharmacy exit, she heard a loud bang, followed by screaming children. Nooooooo!

She emerged into the parking lot, her long brown hair streaming in the wind as her hands actuated the key fob in her hand. Nothing! Crap, even the car power is out! Her mind spun at the implications of that fact, but she did not have time to think. Her eyes moved to the side as the car came up in front of her. The man was pointing the gun at the kids, the bus driver lying bleeding on the pavement, empty eyes staring at the sun.

"HEY ASSHOLE, OVER HERE!" she called out, just as the hammer came down. The man turned the shot, distracted. The round punched into the concrete, inches from a screaming ten-year-old boy, sobbing and wailing in terror.

She shoved the key into the car door lock and turned. It opened. Thank God! She reached into the car for the glove box as the first round punched a hole clear through the passenger door, making her ears ring, her face burning as micro-impacts of steel and glass debris blasted into her cheeks and eyes. Burning pain radiated from her face, reddened by the exercise and anger.

She flipped the glove box open and grabbed the Kel Tec .32 caliber pistol out of its holster, and dove back out of the car. Her body rolled over the hood as the madman took aim at her torso. She prayed a silent prayer, prayed for strength for what must be done. The target was twenty yards away, a very difficult shot for the diminutive auto. She had hit eight inch plates at twenty five yards before, under slow fire, about half the time. Never under time pressure. The sights lined up just as the insane man's gun went off.

Pain seared through her upper torso, her vision started to fade. The .357 magnum 125 grain hollow point bullet had rammed through her epigastrium, tearing a hole out of her lower cardiac muscle, the bullet exiting through her mid back near the spine, to the right side. Her lifeblood began emptying onto the steel hood of her small sedan. Please God, help me, she thought.

She focused all of her life energy and began methodically emptying the seven rounds, one round from the chamber, and six from the magazine. Shots rang out and began impacting the madman's chest. Blood sprayed out of his nose and mouth as he heaved under the lung and heart shots. Four of the seven rounds of the little .32 in the tiny gun struck home. The madman staggered towards her, foamy blood running in rivulets down his chin, running out of his mouth and nose, and down his shirt, his breath heaving in frothy waves. He staggered ten, twenty, twenty five feet, fired another round into the car wheel well, his aim low, and he collapsed onto the ground.

Francesca tried to breath; waves of unbelievable pain echoed through her body as her life trickled away. Then, the pain disappeared. She slumped onto the hood of the car, her hand still locked onto the pistol. She still embraced the tiny lifesaving tool as her vision faded. The world went white and the struggle was over.

The nurses swarmed out of the clinic. Francesca's co-workers sobbed in grief. Two of the women shook with horror and shock at the sudden loss of their closest friend. Hot tears streamed down their faces as they collapsed on the sidewalk, unable to move, unable to breathe. Wails of shuddering disbelief tore from their throats. Only seconds had passed since the insane events had started. They funneled the children into the clinic, holding the helpless students. Each one was safe and whole, as the opponents lay dead, players in a battle of selfless good against utter evil that would play out many times in the coming days. One of the nurses conferred with her friends and began the short run to the police station. Her brother would need to know. And they would need help. They would all need help.

Spence Creek State Park
10 miles Northeast of Gallatin, TN
Rees house
July 3
10:01a.m.

A light breeze rustled the leaves of a nearby water oak tree. Scott Rees stared at the figure walking slowly up the drive towards the house. The power had been out for some time now, perhaps an hour. He had not relished knowing that the group's predictions had been right concerning the solar activity, but he had at least put away some electronic goods into cages for their protection. He was without any contact from his boss and simply had fallen back to a plan B of defending the park. Most of his life was spent doing this in one way or another anyway, so it seemed the logical thing to do.

Dealing with assholes in the park had been another matter entirely, however. Several groups of campers were stranded on the premises and there had been almost immediate friction when they realized that their electronics would not work. Some of them did not comprehend that most of the world did not camp with air conditioned trailers, but might actually camp in a tent with a sleeping bag. Most did not have enough food to last more than a few days. This was certainly going to be an interesting week.

And now this lady was walking, really slowly, up the drive. What the heck did she want? He wondered. Was she actually drooling? He knew what he would do if that were a dog moseying up on him, but this was a person, one of the people he was sworn to protect. The woman kept walking, staring at him at an angle, jaw open, to the side. This was getting majorly weird now. She was close enough to see more clearly. She had on a loose pair of jeans and tee shirt that was stained with something black. She kept ambling up.

"Ma'am, can I help you?" Scott called out. No response.

"Hello, anything I can do for you? Do you need any help? The public campgrounds are the other direction."

The woman stopped.

"Hello?" Scott started to ask another question when he looked at the woman. Her eyes were a yellowish color and drool ran from her lips, down the corners of her mouth. What the hell!? He started to back away, when she suddenly lunged from ten feet away, covering the distance in less than a second. Like a rabid dog, she snarled and her fangs were out.

Scott reeled backwards as the woman lunged forward at him, her teeth sinking into his left forearm. He drew simultaneously, and fired the Glock 22 at point blank range, the .40 caliber slug tearing into the woman's torso, a body contact shot.

His ears rang as he realized that she was literally unaffected by the round hitting her torso. She opened her jaws for another bite, and Scott kicked her hard in the groin, her body sailing back against the viscous blow. She hit the ground and stood up just as fast, her arms rolling like a marionette doll, controlled by an evil impulse to bite. She snarled and lunged for his neck, teeth bared with his blood now running down her lips. Terror filled Scott's mind as the monstrous form curled forward to attack.

Multiple shots rang out from the Glock, the woman, buffeting backwards under the hail of fire, the last two upper center mass shots causing blood to erupt from her mouth and nose. Blood ran down her chest in rivulets, her shirt torn by the hail of fire, now soaking through with her lifeblood. She staggered forward as Scott backed up again. She covered three feet and collapsed face down in the dirt of the driveway, her fingers still flexing for a few moments before stopping.

Scott holstered the Glock and grabbed the bleeding left forearm with his right hand. He glanced at the immobile form once again to confirm no movement and then ran to the house, his wife Stephanie already opening the door in surprise at the shots fired. She had a 12 gauge Benelli Super Black Eagle loaded with buckshot in her hands already, not knowing what to expect. Scott raced to the sink and turned on the faucet. Nothing. No water pressure from the electrically controlled well. He tore off the lid of a one gallon drinking water jug and poured the entire contents onto the wound, roughly scrubbing the wound with the kitchen soap bar. Blood oozed out of the shallow wound. He followed with a bottle of iodine, yelled several choice curse words, and then followed with half the contents of a second gallon water bottle. Stephanie inspected the wound, and did not see any debris, and then bandaged it with sterile gauze and antibiotic ointment. The bleeding had stopped.

"What the hell was that? She bit you?!" Stephanie asked in dismay after the wound care had been completed. "You better take some antibiotics. Angus said these kind of bites can get really nasty. I can't believe you were bitten in the arm by a camper!"

"I don't know. She was crazy looking. I didn't know what she was going to do, but this shocked me. I'm just glad she didn't go for the jugular." Scott stared at the floor. It had been a long time since he had had to kill anyone in the line of duty. He didn't like it any more now. The paperwork burden would be immense. He dreaded the inevitable trial, civil suit, months of agony waiting for the judgment, and mandatory time off work. He hated it all. He reached into the kitchen cabinet and pulled out a bottle of Augmentin and took the first dose. Angus Gunn was his doctor and had taught everyone in the group what to take and when, and he remembered that this one was for bites of mammals, including humans. Oh well, at least he had some. Walking to the pharmacy ten miles away would have really ruined his day! Scott sat down and nibbled a donut from breakfast and thought about what the power being out really meant. He was not sure, but he worried about what would be next as he asked Stephanie to get the bug out bags ready. Just in case.

North Water Ave
Northern Gallatin
July 3
10:04a.m.

Samuel Wallace paced himself. He had to keep up the pace as fast as he thought the girls would be able to cover ground without tiring them out too quickly. He was frankly nervous in town, and they had quite a few miles to cover before they reached the open county between Gallatin and Portland. This was going well so far. At least the girls had running shoes on. This would be miserable if they were wearing heels.

Sam turned around and looked at his six. The girls were walking quickly, two feet behind him. They looked up and nodded at him, slightly out of breath, but not complaining. They had walked for about an hour, he figured, and were nearing the cutoff to get to the Portland highway. It was still several miles until they would be out of town. He hated the city, and felt naked here. There was nowhere to hide if someone saw them.

They had gone to the parking lot right after Dr. Gunn had closed the office, and he had changed clothes in his car. The girls wore their scrubs, as they didn't have any other clothes with them. Sam had a bug home bag in his trunk, a small book bag with an assortment of tools. He wore his usual Carhartt clothing now with running shoes. He had given Pirelli an oversized camo T-shirt to wear instead of the pink scrub top she had worn to work. At least her scrub pants were black. Chloe had on a navy blue scrub set, and it was muted enough not to matter. The girls had their purses and water bottles and food stuffed in them that Dr. Gunn had given them before they left. They were loaded down and switched shoulders every twenty minutes or so.

So far they had been ignored by everyone that they passed. Smoke drifted across the road in front of them as they hurried down the edge of the lane. There was no clear path and they wove in and out between cars that were stranded in the lane. No electric sounds were heard. Gunshots occasionally echoed to the edges of their hearing, mostly behind them, thank God. Sometimes there would be a scream, or series of screams, but they were so far away that they sounded more animalistic than human. Every time they heard this, they increased their pace. It was becoming very unnerving. But the noises served to keep them moving fairly fast.

Sam took a swig of water and looked at the sun. This was the only way left to tell the time of day and cardinal direction, as his watch and compass were useless, left back at his truck. He heard a noise in the distance, a rumbling. An engine! Somebody had an engine, no...two engines running, sounded like Ford diesels!

Man! This could be really good, or really bad, he thought. He stopped and listened intently. The noise was coming from behind. He motioned to the girls towards the tree to their right. There was an empty lot to the right side, near a small repair shop. The large tree had branches that ran down to the ground and was surrounded by a thick, dense hedge, making excellent cover. The girls turned and ducked into the empty lot and ran underneath the branches of the oak tree. Sam followed. They all got down and Sam whispered for them to put their faces down. They complied and just then two white Sumner County Emergency Management trucks whizzed by, nearly smashing into several of the abandoned cars.

What the hell was that? Sam thought for a moment. Maybe they were responding to an emergency. They obviously had some EMP-proof vehicles. Still, the thought worried him. All of the smoke and gunshots were the other way. What were they doing?

The trucks slammed to a stop in front of a small ramshackle house. Two men jumped out of each truck, pistols drawn. The two in the front truck ran inside the house and gunfire erupted. The other two looked nervously around, holding their pistols in both hands. Sam could see the drool running in thin rivulets down the corner of the nearer man's lip. His eyes appeared glazed over, a blank expression on his young face. He could not see the face of the other man. Just then, Chloe let out a gasp.

The two that had entered the house appeared at the doorway, dragging out an old woman, her clothes stained with blood across the lower abdomen. She was sobbing unintelligibly. Her moaning wails pierced the air as the two men dragged her by the hair. She half walked, half stumbled onto her front porch. The men then stopped and threw her the remaining ten feet of the porch and onto the grassy front yard three steps down the front walk. She landed, sprawled out on her back, a screech of agony ripped from her tormented lips, her graying hair flying wildly, her tears matting the hair, now streaked with flecks of dirt and grass from the fall. Her nightgown lifted up as she fell, revealing legs stained with varicose veins. One of her slippers had come off during the attack. Sam cursed under his breath. His .45 Colt was on the night stand at home, doing him no good here. Still, four against one, he would never make it if he attacked. He could probably get one or two of them with his knife, and die trying. He couldn't do that, he had promised Dr. Gunn to get the girls back to Portland.

Pirelli started sobbing quietly; Chloe shook with rage and horror, tears streaming from her eyes as they watched the horror unfolding in front of them. She had seen many awful things in her thirty years as a nurse, but never anything like this. The sheer weight of agony, the cosmic injustice of this event overwhelmed her mind's ability to comprehend. Pirelli vomited once, her stomach heaving uncontrollably. One of the guards glanced in their direction and the three froze. His stare revealed a vacant expression. He started to walk towards them, when two shots rang out. He stopped and turned back towards the house. The front guard had fired his pistol into the helpless woman's form.

Sam froze in horror. They had murdered this helpless woman. Her form lay motionless. Sam could not see her eyes from his vantage point. The other EMS worker walked, staggering towards the dead form. He unbuckled his belt, his excitement revealed by the bulge in his pants. Drool ran from his chin, his eyes wild in a vacuous rage. He knelt in front of the dead woman's form and lifted the nightgown. Sam looked away. The girls stared at the dirt in front of them, silent tears streaming down their cheeks. Sam hugged each one close, his own face wet with tears, his shame at not being able to stop this madness exploding forth from his mind. He sobbed quietly, praying to the Lord God of Hosts to take this memory from his mind.

Before the throne of the Almighty, man will be judged not by his acts but by his intentions. For God alone reads our hearts.
—Mahatma Gandhi

CHAPTER 16

Goodlettsville, TN
10 miles North of Nashville
Gunn House
July 3
9:49a.m.

Gwenn stared motionless into the backyard. Little Joshua held her legs and looked out from behind her left side, staring, blinking into the bright day. A man in a tattered business suit stood in the yard, not thirty feet from them. His face was a mask of contorted rage, his breath coming in heaving gasps, through clenched teeth, saliva running from the corners of his mouth. His eyes burned a dull glow, a rage unspeakable in its horror. Gwenn was a full five feet from the door to the house, the glass storm door shut, standing on the weathered deck, three steps up from the yard. She had no weapon.

The man turned and stared at the helpless mother and child, his hands by his side. His suit was a brown pin stripe, covered in grass and woody debris. It looked as if he had crawled through the brush for miles. His expensive-appearing leather dress shoes were covered in muck and grass, matted to the turned-up cuffs of the tailored suit pants he wore. Small tears and rips appeared over the entire suit, the tie still hanging in shreds from the man's neck, one button of the Oxford white shirt missing, now stained brown with sweat, muck and grime.

The man's right hand was hidden behind his leg, a black congealed substance covering his clothing to the elbow. The hand lifted. A large Bowie knife was clutched in the claw-like appendage, its surface covered with the same congealed black substance. The creature opened its lips, the hot breath foaming spittle through the clenched teeth. The teeth opened and a howl of animal lust and rage roared from its mouth. Gwenn's heart skipped a beat as the monster tensed and leaped forward, racing towards them, arms raised, knife thrusting forward. Gwenn grabbed Joshua and reached for the door, a desperate attempt to put distance in between her little boy and this thing that lunged forth from the bowels of Hell. *Dear God, save us!* She thought.

Her mind sped up, tachypsychia kicking in as her actions appeared to slow down. *The dogs!* She thought as her right hand reached for the door, still three feet away, left hand clutching Joshua to her side. The thing's speed was incredible; it had already covered half the distance before Gwenn could even reach the door handle. They weren't going to make it.

She looked down with her heart full of compassion at Sarah and Genevieve who both cowered away from the man, their eyes full of terror at the same realization that they could not match this threat. While reaching for the door, Gwenn started praying, her last moments on Earth, she thought, should be spent with the One who gave her life.

Her thoughts were coming in rapid waves, her life flashing before her eyes: childhood dance recitals, her baptism, her future husband brushing the hair from her forehead the day they met, her wedding, the birth of her daughter, meeting Joshua's mother. A low growl started, deep and powerful. Gwenn turned her head towards the noise as her body still moved towards the door. Penelope's hackles stood up, her teeth bared as the deep, throaty growl echoed through the backyard. The infected man was ten feet away and started to leap towards the helpless family. Penelope's body tensed as every fiber of her being focused on the threat to her pack. Surging energy rippled through her body as the dog's muscles strained against the wood of the deck. Her body lunged forward, teeth open, a deep rumbling sound roaring out of her throat as she sailed through the air, five feet off the ground. The creature leaped in the same moment, knife out forward, teeth snarling, spittle flying outward as hideous infected rage met valor beyond the comprehension of man.

Penelope had been adopted when she was eight weeks old, from a breeder in Georgia. She had been the Gunn's only pet at the time. She had hiked mountains with her masters, traveled across continents, slept at their feet camping, and guarded their dwellings since puppyhood. She had bonded to her pack family more closely than most dogs ever would. She had witnessed the adoption of Joshua and had never been more than ten feet from his side for the majority of that time. Her bond to the Gunn Clan was complete, her life was so intertwined with their lives that she could not tell where one began and the other ended. She knew when family members were sad before they knew it themselves. She would comfort anyone in grief, warm the feet of anyone who felt lonely, and felt the power of her family's love at the heart of her being. Angus had prayed to the Lord for a guardian for his family, and when he had adopted Penelope, he knew that his prayer had been answered.

When Penelope had sensed the intruder in her pack's domain, she knew that this represented a terrible threat to her pack. The smell was wrong. She had been smelling things for weeks now. Strange things, bad things. She knew something was wrong. This was not a person. This was death come to visit havoc upon her dwelling. She could not allow it. The calm voice of The Master told her to protect her pack. The Creator spoke words of strength. Usually, the voice told her to kiss or nuzzle someone in the pack. The voice that had been with her since her birth spoke now, loud in her mind. The command was not to nurture. It was to attack. Defend. Protect. She could not fail. He was with her now. She leaped forth, teeth bared, mind fully focused on this monster that charged towards her pack.

Gwenn stared in shock as the large eighty-pound Golden Retriever leaped from the deck. A gurgling howl ripped from the throat of the infected man as he leaped forward at the same moment. The two met in midair, their bodies locked in a pirouette of desperate energy, the clash of mindless rage against valiant, selfless devotion. The knife pierced the dog's chest at the same moment that her fangs clamped down on the right side of the infected man's throat, her teeth ripping free a chunk of tissue the size of a softball. Both bodies hurled away from the deck, the power of the dog's leap knocking the man's body backwards like a bowling pin hit by a sledgehammer. The infected man splayed backwards, the knife coming out of his hand as he reached for the place where his neck had been, blood erupting forth in massive waves, vomiting outward from its nose and mouth and tearing like a wave from the three inch gap in the right carotid and jugular, the vile fluid rippling down, soaking his clothing and spreading in a wave outward through the neatly trimmed grass of the yard.

Penelope lay sideways where she had landed, ten feet past the intruder as she had tumbled after their collision. The impact had knocked the wind out of her and she heaved for breath, her own blood streaming on to the grass. She coughed and her own blood mixed with the blood of the vile intruder that she had slain, dribbling from her jaws. Her eyes blinked as she looked back towards the deck, her family huddled against the wood, safe from the monster that lay on the grass, its form limp and harmless. She had done it; she had saved her pack. Pain now coursed through her, her chest heaving where the knife had torn a hole through her lung and pulmonary vessels.

Gwenn stood and looked at the scene. The infected man's face was rigid, blood still running out of the hole in his neck, the knife lying three feet away. She let go of Joshua and spoke, "Stay here. Don't move."

He nodded, his face unsure as he had not had time to process what had just happened, the suddenness of the event outstripping his young mind's comprehension. Genevieve and Sarah nuzzled him as Gwenn ran out into the yard. Gwenn looked at the intruder and saw his fingers clutch and then release, his chest was still. She kicked the knife ten feet away and kicked the man's chest. Nothing.

She turned to her beloved pet, the dog's form limp and heaving. She ran to Penelope, tears starting at the corners of her eyes as she saw the blood on the dog's chest. God no! Tears streamed down her face as the agony of understanding washed over her. No, no, no!

The dog looked up, peace on her face. Her breath came in shallow gasps, her eyes started to become unfocused. Tears mixed with blood and fur as Gwenn sobbed into the beautiful dog's mane. Gwenn's chest heaved as her breath came in waves, grief washing over her.

"I love you, Penelope," she said as the faithful dog lifted her head towards the pack leader. The dog's gaze focused on her owner as her chest heaved once more and then stopped, the beautiful light of understanding fading from her deep brown eyes.

Penelope stared at Gwenn, her owner also looking into her eyes. Love surged through the dog's heart as her vision started to fade. A voice spoke into her mind. The deep, calm voice of her Creator spoke words of thanks, of appreciation, of gratitude. As her mind faded away from this world, and her owner's tears dropped onto her fur, she clearly heard the Master again. The voice that had been with her since her birth clearly resounded through her mind, "Well done, my good and faithful servant."

Hendersonville, TN
Corpuz house
Halfway between Gallatin and Goodlettsville
3 miles from Mackenzie House
July 3
10:34a.m.

Carlos was sitting reading a medical journal. They had just finished packing their gear. It was hot inside the house, but the windows and doors were opened, and Carlos was from the Philippines. He was used to the heat. He stopped reading. Was that a noise? Hmmmm. Again, he heard a soft noise, like someone trying to be quiet. His family was spread throughout the beautiful house on the ground floor, the upper floors being too hot to occupy with the AC out. Probably one of his sons was goofing off. Still, he felt the hair on the back of his neck prickle. His time in Manila had increased his situations awareness to a higher degree than most Americans.

Again, soft noises. This is no good, he thought. He reached for the Rock River Carbine and racked a round into the chamber, correctly locking back the charging handle and pressing the bolt release to ensure a proper chambering. The 62 grain M855 round slammed home into the chamber. Carlos stood and called out, "Hello, Roberto? Is that you?" referring to his youngest son, the one most likely to be sneaking around.

No answer. Then, faintly from the other end of the house, "Hey Dad, we're over here."

Before Carlos could answer, a tall white man with a hooded jacket appeared from around a corner in the room. His football jersey, faded jeans and black hoodie were all three sizes too big. Carlos froze and pulled the AR to his shoulder, sling dangling to the front.

"Who are you!?" he demanded, and the large form smiled a wicked smile, staring at him with evil intent.

"Shut up, sand nigger!" the man yelled as his right hand started to come up, a large blued revolver coming into view, it's eight inch barrel gleaming in the morning light.

Dios mio! Thought Carlos as reflex took over. The AR raised to his cheek, the Eotech sight coming into view, even before the rifle was fully into his cheek hold. Carlos thumbed the safety release as the rifle swung up, the intruder's pistol almost up to vertical. The AR boomed three times in rapid succession. The intruder's arm dropped down, the pistol clattering to the floor. Blood blossomed from the man's upper chest and forehead. Two small bloody holes appeared in the sternum, three inches apart, and one small hole trickled a tiny rivulet of blood from the lower center of his forehead, between his brows.

The man collapsed like a marionette with its strings suddenly cut. Carlos' ears rang as pain seared through his ear drums. He could not hear anything, the intense concussions of the 5.56mm cartridges impacting and damaging his eardrums. He lowered the now smoking rifle and stared in disbelief at the scene in front of him. The man lay dead in his living room. His family rushed into the room, shock on their faces as well.

Gallatin Police Department
Gallatin, TN
Basement level
July 3
10:40a.m.

Justin Clearwater rummaged through his gear locker and put his uniform on. It had been a terrible day so far. He looked in the mirror and could barely see his grime covered face through the dim light of the candle he had used to light the room. It was pitch dark down here, as the power was out. He finished getting his gear together and closed the locker. He was walking past the weapon locker when he heard load voices on the floor above. He walked up the stairs to see what was going on.

"Goddammit Johnnie, I've told you already, we're not going through town to 'eradicate' this thing, or whatever the hell you call it!" shouted the Gallatin Police Chief to one of his Lieutenants.

"Chief, we've got to stop it! The motherfuckers'll kill us all, kill us ALL!" Lieutenant John Jeffries said, motioning with his arms out. A thin line of snot ran down his nose onto his chin. His left arm was shaking in a mild tremor.

Several of the GPD officers were standing behind him. Some were holding shotguns and AR-15 carbines that had been issued a few years ago. The men standing there in a group had been close friends with the recently deceased officer Mattfield. He had wrecked his cruiser chasing a homicide suspect. It had been all over the newspapers. The group shared the late week night shift and because of the crazy hours spent most of their free time together. They had always had a deep camaraderie and since his death, many of the crew had been on edge. Normally, they would not be here in the morning, but the chief had asked for double shifts for the past week due to the severe increase in crime plaguing the city. The men had been up for about eighteen hours now. They appeared in no mood to be calmed.

Ever since Mattfield died, several of them had gotten into fistfights with some other shift members. Justin figured at first it must be the sheer stress of the situation that they were all in, but now that he looked at them together, another horrifying thought crossed his mind.

The Lieutenant rubbed the snot and spit from his mouth with the back of his hand. Several others in the group had drool running onto their chins, and some of them had drooping expressions. A couple of them had been out sick yesterday, but had staggered into the station late last night, complaining about "summer flu." Several GPD officers were AWOL, or absent without leave. The dispatchers had been unable to reach them and their whereabouts were unknown.

Since the power had been out, officers were checking in on foot for orders. The wave of escaping infected from the hospital had been met by some rookies who had shot a number of them, before the rest escaped, fleeing in every direction. There had been no containment, as they simply ran in every direction and would not respond to commands. The vehicular units had all returned to the station on foot for instruction, and this group seemed to have their own idea of what to do.

Several of the night crew began grumbling, some coughed and others fidgeted with their firearms. A couple of day shift officers walked up behind the chief. The night shift guys swayed on the spot and turned and walked out.

What the hell was that? Justin was considering what this anger meant, what the saliva and drooping expressions meant, when suddenly a police cruiser smashed through the front door. The Chief was knocked down to the floor. He hit his head hard and did not move. Gunfire erupted through the windshield of the Dodge as several officers in the station fell, rifle bullets tearing through their soft concealed body armor.

Justin dived for cover under a desk and shimmied over to the chief. He checked his carotid pulse. Nothing. The chief was dead. Return pistol fire echoed across the hallways and shotgun blasts deafened Justin as he scrambled back under the desk. He pulled out his Glock and popped up over the desk.

A tall nightshift officer loomed over the desk, shotgun in hand, aimed directly at the place Justin had stood up. The gun discharged before Justin could level his pistol. The triple ought buckshot blasted into Justin's chest, just below the sternum, tearing through his shirt and smashing into the trauma plate of Kevlar wrapped stainless steel. The nine .36 caliber pellets ripped through the stainless steel layer and buried themselves into the level II concealed Kevlar vest, tearing through half the strands of polymer weave, snapping hundreds of small, woven fibers, each one over five times the tensile strength of steel. The pellets stopped in the vest, not penetrating, but the kinetic energy of the impact was akin to a sledgehammer to the upper belly.

Justin's lower ribcage suffered a tiny crack and bruising to the outer upper diaphragm and upper abdominal wall musculature. Justin collapsed to the ground, breath knocked out of him, almost completely unconscious. Another officer engaged the attacker and shot him in the neck and head, the shotgun wielding maniac falling to the side holding his neck. The battle raged on, about twenty officers on each side, a running fight through the station.

Justin stirred slightly and looked up. His lower chest and upper belly hurt like he had been punched in a street fight. He rolled to one side and found his Glock that he had dropped. The night shift crew was gaining the upper hand and was moving through the office, gunning down officers and civilian workers as they moved forward. Justin looked towards the wall where the cruiser had punched through and his heart stopped.

The lieutenant who had yelled at the chief had a gasoline can in one hand and a satchel in the other. He dropped the satchel and from it pulled out a flash-bang grenade. He grabbed duct tape and several more flash-bangs and began taping them to the gas can as two other officers brought up more gas cans and setting them on the desk, while their colleagues continued murdering innocent bystanders and the resisting officers in the hall.

Justin ducked behind the door into the stairwell, his mind racing. He leaped down the darkened steps and opened the door into the weapons locker with his key by feel. It was pitch black in the concrete room. He grabbed the stub of candle that he had placed in his pocket earlier when dressing and lit it with his Bic lighter. He set it on the counter. He began to rummage thought the equipment lockers and found an NVG box. The NVG box, or night vision goggle box, was basically an ammo can that was foamed lined to protect the contents from shock and, being of military origin, also from enemy EMP. This was, in reality, a Faraday cage. He tore open the lids of three of the boxes and stuffed their contents, small binocular goggles, into a canvas gear bag he had fished out of a drawer. He reached over the counter and grabbed a handful of retired concealable soft armor vests as shoved them into the bag as well. He got ten of the precious vests, and then started dumping boxes of Speer Lawman .45ACP full metal jacket target ammunition and 12 gauge triple ought buckshot into the bag.

The battle raged on upstairs, gunfire echoing down the corridor. Screams could be heard as the infected night shift workers began laughing hysterically. This was insane, thought Justin as he headed for the exit. It was hopeless to go in that room. He realized when he had exited moments ago that he had no way to stop them, there were too many. And the surprise tactic of smashing the cruiser through the wall had completely knocked the day shift off balance. He could stay and die, or get out and help somewhere else later. He heard sounds of gasoline tanks sloshing around. My God, they were pouring out the contents. What the hell were they thinking?

Clearly, they weren't thinking. They had been infected by this, this plague that made them lose their minds. They were going to blow up the station. Why? Justin raced up the stairs and ducked down, as he passed the door to the main office. Gunfire still echoed past as the firefight continued. He shimmied to the front door, leaped out and raced down the sidewalk at a full run. He took cover behind a cruiser that was fifty yards away and started to look over the hood, when a massive blast knocked him backwards. Flames shot up and outward from the station, as a large fireball lurched upwards into the sky. Black smoke poured out of the remnants of the station. Justin's hearing was momentarily gone. His ears rang. He spun on his heels and sat down abruptly, dizziness forcing him to the ground. Blood leaked from his nose where the over pressure had damaged his mucous membranes. His vision blurred momentarily as the shock of the explosion slowly faded. Flame and smoke continued to billow up from the wreckage of the station. No one inside could have survived the blast. He looked around and several other GPD officers were walking towards the blaze, shocked expressions on each unsure face.

They made a survey of the scene and got as close to the flames as they dared, the heat searing their skin. They circled the station from every angle and there simply was no way in and there were no bodies or wounded on any side. Justin sighed as he walked back towards the parking lot where he had first taken cover.

He turned towards the sound of a running engine. A large Ford diesel rumbled down the street and came to a stop. Several GPD officers looked at it as a tall black man wearing sunglasses, a black shirt and blue jeans and a forest camo vest hopped out holding an AK in his right hand. One of the officers walked over to the man.

"I'm commandeering this truck in the name of..." said the officer, stopped in mid-sentence by the AK barrel now two inches from his chin. Sweat beaded from the officer's brow as he began to visibly shake, his hand frozen as it had begun to reach for the Glock on his belt. Two other officers had drawn their pistols on the man who calmly held the rifle leveled at the first officer's head.

"Tell your officers to lower their weapons and re-holster them very slowly," the black man calmly said, his voice calm and deep.

The first officer blinked and froze. Justin walked over slowly, recognizing Darryl, "I'd do what he says. I know this guy and whether or not you guys shoot him, he will take the head off of Smith here"

"What the hell, Clearwater? You can't just point a gun at a cop and walk!" the second officer said. "This is bullshit!"

"Look around Fred," Justin said to his colleague, nodding towards the ruined station and wreckage of the town. "Look, I know this guy. He is a close family friend, and I'm telling you now, he is about ten seconds from killing Smith. He's ex Air Force Security Forces and has killed men before. He is here for something important, obviously. Let him talk." He spoke to Darryl, "Come on man, let's cool it off here. Nobody's going to take your truck."

"I'm confiscating it!" yelled Smith

"Smith, I'll shoot you myself if you touch the damn truck, you dumbass!" Justin replied, "If you ask Mr. Washington here, he'll probably drive you wherever you want to go anyway. Don't be an idiot."

"O.K. O.K. I'm sorry. I won't touch your truck. Now could you get the AK out of my nose!?" Smith said to Darryl. "Guys, let's all lower the weapons at the same time, O.K. 'Mr. Washington'?" he said to everyone and then Darryl, sarcasm in his voice.

Everyone slowly lowered their guns. Justin breathed a quiet sigh. Darryl stared coldly at Smith. Smith blinked again, blood returning to his face slowly. The tension of the moment eased as Justin walked over to Darryl and shook his hand. Smith looked at Darryl.

"Could you give us a ride to the Hendersonville PD?" he begrudgingly asked.

"Of course, be glad to help. What the hell happened here?"

"Don't know, everybody's dead in the station. Some guy smashed a cruiser into the station and a bunch of officers started shooting everyone. Craziest damned thing I ever saw. Was walking over from downtown and saw the whole thing from a distance, ran here as fast as I could and the station blew up before I reached it," Smith said.

"I was inside and the night shift went ape shit and killed everybody and then blew themselves up. This is fucked up," Justin said.

Fire spread to the neighboring buildings. Gallatin continued to burn, as more and more buildings were in flames. People were walking in the streets now, many heading towards Hendersonville to the west, their belongings on their backs, or pulled in carts. Many were rubbing their noses and sniffling, drool running from their mouths and noses. Many vacant eyes followed the officers. The entire town was regrouping, and it looked like Hendersonville was the place most had decided on going. While some were heading out in other directions, likely towards family or friend's homes, there was a general wave of humanity heading west. Gunshots still echoed in the distance.

A middle aged woman walked up to the officers. She looked bedraggled and distraught. She looked at Officer Smith.

"Is there an officer Clearwater here?" she asked.

Smith pointed at Justin, "Right here ma'am."

The woman stared for a moment at the young officer. Tears welled up in her eyes. She walked towards Clearwater, her hands grasping his tightly as she reached him. Justin looked at her and saw the I.D. badge from his sister's medical office pinned on her shirt. His heart sank.

"Officer Clearwater, my name is Dusty. I work with Francesca...."

She recounted the tale of his sister's valor, squeezing his hands tightly as tears ran from her cheeks. He did not remember the exact words that she used, but years later he would remember that something changed in his mind, something snapped. A sea change occurred in him and he would never be the same. He had never had a family of his own. He had been very close with his sister and always expected her to be there.

Tears streamed from his eyes as he stared at the ground. He nodded at the woman, unable to speak. Darryl reached over and walked the woman away from Justin, giving him space. Justin sank to the ground, heaving sobs wrenching from his lungs. He screamed in emotional agony, sobs of uncontrolled rage and loss tearing through his frame, pushing aside the pain in his ears and chest. He sat on the sidewalk for several minutes while the blazing inferno that was the station spread to the nearby downtown buildings. The fire department officers across the street stood with shovels and watched the blaze, helpless to act without power. Gallatin was burning to the ground.

Darryl walked over and sat Indian style in front of Justin, his calm, slow breathing anchoring Justin's mind into the rhythm. Calmness returned to his thoughts. The town was on fire. Crazy infected people ran around murdering as they went. Order had been destroyed. He could grieve properly later. Right now, he had to find his center.

Darryl looked calmly at his friend, "I need your help."

Justin wiped the tears from his eyes with the back of his hand and nodded at Darryl. No words yet.

"My daughter is with Kate Gunn at the archery store downtown. I have to go get her and I need help. I figured your group would head out to get Kate. The hospital and surrounding buildings are all on fire, you can't even get close to it, so I figured some of you guys might be here."

Justin nodded. He had known about the girls, and that Angus was going to get them. "Angus told us that he was going to get them. I told them I had duty here I had to report for."

Darryl looked at the inferno where the station used to be.

"Yeah, not much duty now," Justin said, laughing a bitter laugh.

Justin looked at Smith, "Gather the guys up, man. Let's go and regroup. The whole town has already evacuated. We need to have half of the force stay here and regroup with the Sherriff and half come to Hendersonville, as that is where everyone seems to be going. We'll ride with Darryl." He looked at Darryl for permission.

Darryl nodded, "What's in the bag?"

"Insurance, and bartering tokens," said Justin smiling a thin smile at his friend. He opened the bag and showed him the contents and they both stood up stiffly.

Darryl bear hugged Justin and shook his hand firmly, looking him in the eyes, lowering his sunglasses to reveal his deep brown eyes. "I'm praying for you, man. She died saving kids, man. She's with Jesus now. Never forget that."

Justin fought back new tears and turned away, motioning the other officers into the backseats and truck bed of the aging Ford. Darryl hopped into the driver's seat and Justin hopped into the front passenger seat. Darryl gunned the engine and then headed out, the firemen still staring blankly at the wall of flame that engulfed the entire downtown now.

Infected be the air whereon they ride,
And damned all those that trust them.
—William Shakespeare. Macbeth. 4.1.138

CHAPTER 17

Gallatin, TN
West of downtown
July 3
11:01a.m.

A loud boom echoed from behind the two men. A black fireball rose into the distant sky. Matt and Angus stopped walking and turned towards the blast. They stared at each other, silent concern etched on their faces. They continued on, walking towards the outskirts of town, heading towards the Mackenzie place. They froze as another loud engine sound came from the street behind them. They dived for cover in a culvert on the side of the road. As they neared the freeway junction, this part of the town had few trees, occasional houses and small churches

A white truck roared into the driveway of a small brick house and slammed on the brakes. Two Sumner County Emergency Management workers leaped from the truck and ran to the door, slamming their shoulders into the front door twice before it gave way, splinters flying as the wood cracked behind the deadbolt. The men poured inside. Shots were fired, a scream and then silence. Another EMS truck pulled in the drive and two other men staggered out of it. The men wiped drool from their mouths onto the backs of their hands. One scratched himself and spit drool onto the ground. They began walking up to the house casually, as the men inside the house re-emerged, dragging the body of a young girl, her light brown skin glistening in the sun. The girl's limp form hung grotesquely as the EMS man dragged her by her shirt onto the grass of the front yard.

Angus and Matt stared in disgust at the scene. Anger boiled into rage. A righteous indignation flooded through the men as the scene unfolded. One of the men lit a rag on a stick and threw it into the house. Smoke started drifting out as the building slowly began to burn. The two men who had entered the house threw the girl's body down and began to pull off her leggings, her preteen form limply flopping, blood running from her chest where two bullet holes had ended her life. The man began to fumble with his belt and kicked the dead girl's legs apart.

"I've seen enough," Matt said, looking at Angus. Both men had sixteen-year-old daughters and a rage had spread through them while witnessing the injustice.

Angus was too enraged to speak, his lip quivering with emotion. He nodded and made hand signals towards the back of the trucks, indicating where Matt should go, while he pointed two fingers at his chest and motioned towards the side yard. Matt slapped Angus' shoulder and leaped from the ditch as Angus tore off, down the side of the road, headed for the side yard. Fear, hatred, anger and an overwhelming desire to kill flooded through Angus' mind as he covered the ground in seconds.

Matt, being faster and more fit, covered the ground twice as fast, coming up rapidly behind the EMS crew. Matt's AR-15 spoke several rounds in rapid succession. The EMS man who had been preparing to rape the dead girl looked up, three holes in his lower chest, blood running down his white short-sleeved issue polo shirt.

Amazingly, he stood up, coughed and drew his pistol, firing at Matt. The other men turned and one roared a guttural howl and charged Matt. Pistol fire slammed into the EMS trucks as Matt ducked back, just before the rounds hit. The rapist walked forward, firing his pistol, blood still pouring out of his chest.

Angus reached the side yard and leveled his Marlin to his shoulder, pausing to take aim, his body shielded by the brick corner of the now burning house. The EMS crew were pouring fire into Matt's position. Angus sighted on the nearest man and pulled the trigger. The .45-70 boomed, its 325 grain spire-tip bullet ripping into the upper torso of the man, entering under the armpit and mushrooming as it tore through the upper heart and great vessels at over 1900 feet per second. The temporary wound cavity stretched seven inches laterally in every direction stopping only at the inner margin of the ribcage, destroying the man's lungs, esophagus and heart. The bullet exited through the man's left arm, shattering the upper humerus, the arm now hanging by threads of torn muscle tissue. The infected man's body dropped like a stone, crumpling under the massive injury.

Two of the remaining men turned and fired at Angus, their rounds pinging of the brick wall and ricocheting outward. Angus levered another round into the rifle and prepared to fire. Matt reached around the passenger side of the truck and fired two rounds into the head of the man he had just shot. The man finally went down, pistol still firing as he went, rounds slamming into the trucks engine bay, the radiator blowing steam from the hits. The last stray round slammed into Matt's right upper arm, grazing a furrow across the surface, tearing out an inch deep trough, blood pouring out. Matt dropped the AR, his sling holding the rifle to the front of his body.

"Whiskey, whiskey, whiskey!" he hoarsely yelled, their group's code for having been hit by incoming fire.

Angus fired another round that missed, as the EMS man hit the dirt just before the shot. The two men had reloaded their pistols and were continuing firing, taking cover behind the bodies of the fallen comrades.

Matt grabbed his sling, pulled the adjustment out as far as it would go and switched to his left hand. The sling came up on his neck and he shouldered the rifle one handed, blood still streaming out of his right upper arm. He reached around the driver's side of the truck and started firing rapidly, seventeen rounds in four seconds, then ran like hell to Angus' position, emptying the magazine as Angus' big rifle boomed repeatedly, emptying his tube with five more rounds fired.

Matt dived for cover behind Angus. One of Matt's rounds had hit the closer EMS man's foot, and one of Angus' rounds had hit the others hand, blowing the pistol out onto the ground, and tearing off three of the man's fingers. Surprisingly, neither one yelled or appeared to be in any pain.

Angus and Matt started reloading and preparing to finish the job when they heard engine sounds. Two other EMS white trucks pulled into the drive, four more men got out, each one staggering forward, obviously infected, drool running down their chins, eyes red and unfocused.

The two doctors looked at each other, Matt holding pressure on his wound. The new EMS guys walked up to their comrades and pulled out their pistols. Matt and Angus ducked back and ran as hard as they could into the thick brush and fields near the house. The house blocked the view from the front yard. They ducked as they ran, the thick foliage camouflaging their retreat to the West. The EMS men fired several times in the direction of the house corner. Both men whispered silent prayers as they continued to run full tilt, brush snapping by them. They could no longer see the EMS crew as they began E and E, or escape and evasion. They stopped in a thicket and Matt ripped out his US Army IFAK, or improved first aid kit. He took gauze out and wiped his arm, the blood still oozing out. He slipped out a pouch of old style Quickclot and poured the powder on the injured skin, cursing quietly at the pain of the exothermic reaction. The bleeding instantly stopped and Angus helped him by stuffing gauze over it and wrapping it with tape from Matt's IFAK. One didn't use his own emergency supplies on someone else. That's why all of the group members had their own kits attached to their own vests.

Once they put some distance away from the road and the attackers, they would have to crawl, duck, hide and sneak to get out of this. They turned and ran another half mile through the brush listening to the EMS trucks rumbling down the roads in every direction. No one followed them on foot. It seemed that they could only think in terms of roads and vehicles. It would take forever to get to Matt's now, if they even made it there at all.

County Courthouse
Gallatin, TN
July 3
11:01a.m.

Edward Douglass was standing outside, helping to keep order at the courthouse. He had returned from helping at the hospital. When the power went out, many of the parolees decided to go to the courthouse to try and find out what was going on. There had been a crowd milling about and various deputies and officers were improvising a crowd control barrier. People had been fairly calm, but tension filled the air. A loud boom shattered the relative calm and a black fireball rose into the sky from behind city hall. Either the fire department or the police station just went up. Great, thought Ed as he turned and headed to the Sheriff's office, just behind the courthouse.

Unbeknownst to Ed and the others, small groups of infected were attacking people throughout the community. The fire at the hospital and police response had chased all of them into outlying areas. Clearly, the murders and attacks of the prior days and weeks had been a direct result of the infected losing control and murdering their neighbors and strangers alike.

They were now heading in every direction, out into the surrounding small communities, their numbers growing as more and more people succumbed to the effects of the infection. In their houses, confronted with no working power, a total loss in water pressure and no way to communicate, the infected snapped, the disease taking the last vestiges of their control away. The horde mentality would kick in and they would walk out into the street and wander around with the others. Fights would erupt amongst them, sometimes over a food item or simply for no reason at all.

Some people sat in their houses and just stopped moving. Some of these would sit and die of dehydration after several days, or be burned alive today in the fires that raged on through town. Some suffered worse fates as other infected people found them. Some died from gunshot wounds inflicted by the EMS crews; some committed suicide when they realized what was happening. Fully one-half of the residents of Gallatin and the greater Nashville area were now infected, and the contagion was still spreading, by bite and aerosol spread. Societal breakdown was almost complete, with only islands of law and order left intact. But these islands were growing smaller and fewer as the day progressed.

Rioting had started in downtown Nashville and in most major U.S. cities. Communication had completely broken down and none of the survivors would know for months what had happened. People in areas even only a few miles apart did not know the whereabouts of their loved ones. An almost instantaneous Dark Age had descended upon the Earth. Electronic communication methods had been used for more than 150 years. People could not yet conceive of the fact that no more electronic communication could occur until the entire network was rebuilt from scratch. Most still thought of this as a temporary event and fully expected the cavalry to arrive with the solution in the form of outside government intervention.

What they did not understand was that every city, county and town in the western hemisphere had just been blasted with a forty minute long solar flare that had saturated all of the electronic devices exposed to the sun at the time. The solar radiation had swirled well past the horizons of sunrise and sunset, coursing through the atmosphere in eddy currents, following the remnants of geomagnetic field lines. Three quarters of the globe was blasted with a mixture of high energy particles and cosmic rays, the Van Allen belts having effectively failed. The geomagnetic north pole had split and alternated every few seconds between five and six separate mini poles, each providing about ten to twenty percent of the previous configuration's prior field strength. The massive solar wave had compressed even this to about thirty percent of its intact field strength.

This left spotty regions of isolated partial protection, and regions of absolutely no protection. Mongolia was relatively protected, as were the Solomon islands, South Africa and parts of Northern Australia. China and Europe were under mini poles at the moment of impact, and the field lines concentrated the intense radiation into those regions, wiping out unshielded electronics completely. Each region's military forces remained intact, but were also dealing with increasing numbers of plague victims, rapidly spreading through each area.

All of the satellites in orbit, save a few military units, were instantly fried. Even the various country's military units, heavily shielded, could not establish communication linkages as the GPS, or global positioning system was utterly destroyed. The more robust Russian GLONASS system survived for a few more seconds before total system shutdown. The problem with many of the remaining satellites was that they used either one or the other GPS systems to maintain their orbit trajectories. Without this constantly required input, they had already begun to drift in or out of field. Some would burn up within days.

Martial law was established overnight in China, Russia and Western Europe. Soldiers used any means necessary to stop civilian unrest. Millions would die over the next week, both infected and uninfected as a direct result of the atrocities committed in the name of social order. Most of the events would neither be recorded or remembered, and most people witnessing them would die within the next month, and their memories would die with them, as there were almost no methods still available to electronically record the attacks on the populace.

Most would die of simple starvation over the next few weeks, but many would be murdered by either the infected or the military trying in vain to contain the infection. As with Swine Flu, the infection had already circled the globe within twenty four hours and had been slowly blossoming locally almost everywhere at once. Some remote, tiny islands far in the oceans would not see the plague for weeks or months, finally being exposed as survivors looked anywhere for sanctuary, carrying the seeds of their death with them. Rioting would begin on a global scale within hours as government services utterly failed around the planet.

The nurturing of the serf class, along with the concentration of power around oligarchical government-industry-media complexes relied on working power, services, and instant global communications to keep the citizenry placated. When all of the electronic functions of modern society collapsed simultaneously, the cabals that ruled the Earth could no longer keep order. People who lived hand to mouth and nursed from the teat of big government, now had no food, water, information, sanitation, medical care or any of the other myriad services previously available.

Within minutes of the power going out, citizens of Los Angeles, New Orleans, Chicago, Miami, Atlanta and several other cities began to riot in the streets. Without working vehicles, water cannons, stun guns and loudspeakers, the police forces could not even reach the affected regions, much less stop the tide of insanity. In areas where police were already concentrated, the only defenses available were simple firearms. Thousands would die in the first wave of riots at the hands of terrified police, outnumbered hundreds to one with no hope of reinforcements. Fires started in these cities from the looters and rioters. Without effective fire suppression, Gallatin's fate would be shared by most major cities. By the end of the day, half of the cities over one hundred thousand were on fire and burning to the ground. Waves of refugees would start out for the countryside, and would carry the infection with them as they began flooding into smaller towns. The mass exodus from Nashville had not started yet, but already small fires and mass rioting had begun around governmental service offices.

In downtown Gallatin, the fires were the main concern. There seemed nothing to be done, as the fire department could not mount an effective response without power. The number of buildings that had caught fire was staggering and they would soon simply have to leave the town to burn.

Edward walked into the Sheriff's office and nodded at the receptionist, still at her post, a candle burning to illuminate the work area. She had sheets of paper and pens everywhere. An incident command post was busily working, runners grabbing notes and running from room to room. Finally, someone was working against the tide here.

Just then a loud roar came from outside. Ed opened the door and looked out. Back at the crowd control station, dozens of citizens were screaming and chanting, pushing the barrier back. Shit, thought Ed, and his mind raced. Before he could react, the sheriff and two deputies raced past him, out the door and towards the rioters. As in most counties, the sheriff was an elected official, a politician at heart. He wouldn't want to disappoint his constituents.

Ed watched with growing concern as the sheriff reached the crowd and stood on the hood of a squad car behind the barrier. He began yelling into the crowd, trying to calm the situation. He was gesturing with his hands, uttering platitudes and reassurances when a single shot rang out from the crowd's direction. A lone man at the back of the crowd stood grinning. Ugly, poorly executed tattoos covered his arms, his white hair ran down his back in a ponytail, a bandana covered his head, red and white skulls replacing the more usual bandana pattern. In his hands, an old hunting rifle rested, a thin wisp of smoke curling from the end of the barrel.

The sheriff collapsed, blood blossoming from the center of his chest. His deputies grabbed him and prevented his head from hitting the car as he fell. Two officers at the crowd control line growled and pulled their pistols, firing wildly into the crowd. Others in the crowd returned fire and several thin, gaunt men actually leaped over the improvised barrier and stabbed frenetically at the mix of police trying to hold the crowd at bay. Civilians and police both fell and were trampled by the crowd, madness ensuing.

Ed leaped into the sheriff's office and bolted for the weapons room. He ran past the stunned receptionist, though the door, and grabbed an older Remington 12 gauge police special, loaded its four-round tube, racked the slide and loaded another round in the tube. He dumped the contents of two five-round boxes of buckshot into his left front pocket. He already had his Springfield Armory Loaded MC Operator 1911 .45ACP on his hip with two spare eight round Wilson

Combat magazines on the left side balancing his gear belt. In his right front pocket lived a Smith and Wesson Bodyguard .380 pocket semi auto.

He bolted back out the front door and the scene in front of him had dissolved into a swarming mass of chaos. Gunfire erupted from both sides, the dead littering the street, blood running into the gutter. The wounded crawled, moaning in agony as madness consumed the scene. A large, fat man with no shirt came charging past the barrier directly towards Ed. His belly flapped with the motion, a primitive greenish jailhouse type tattoo read "FUCK YOU" on his lower abdomen. He held an aluminum baseball bat in his giant right hand, fresh blood dripping from the shiny metal as he flew past the remaining officers.

Ed calmly shouldered the Remington and waited till the madman was clear of the mass of struggling humanity. Once he had a clear backstop of the brick bail bondsman's office, he touched off the first round of triple ought buckshot, the nine pellets impacting into the man's upper chest and neck. The man collapsed, the bat sailing down the side street, bouncing and pinging off of the asphalt for fifty more feet before resting against the curb.

Two more men cleared the barrier. One had blue hair and wore a faded leather jacket, despite the heat, and held a wicked looking machete, also blood stained, in his right hand. The other was a short, balding man with round glasses in overalls stained with paint. He had what appeared to be an old .22 semi-auto held in his hands. These two went down with a buckshot round each as well. Ed reloaded the shotgun tube from his pocket as the crowd scattered, a final officer falling to a gut shot from a silver medium frame revolver.

The shooter was a middle aged woman, dressed in black yoga pants, high heels and a flouncy blue tee shirt. She aimed the weapon at Ed and collapsed as her head exploded, a 230 grain .45 ACP hollow point rupturing her skull. Ed had transitioned to the pistol and held the shotgun still in his left hand by the front hand guard, the barrel safely pointed up. He had needed the tighter precision of the match grade pistol, given the fact that the woman stood in front of a dozen other people and Edward did not want the buckshot to go astray. He hated firing without a safe backstop, but would not stand there and allow himself to get shot by the criminal.

Ed re-holstered his .45 and shouldered the shotgun. With the four recent attackers stopped cold, the mood of the crowd had changed and their desire to riot was now waning rapidly. Ed walked forward and the crowd scattered in every direction, some running into alleyways of buildings on fire. It was impossible to tell how much of this erratic behavior was due to infection or sheer mob mentality in the uninfected. Regardless, order needed to be restored now.

Ed surveyed the scene of the fight. The sheriff and seven deputies were dead, their bodies sprawled out on the pavement. Three ancillary officers like himself were dead as well, along with the bailiff and about two dozen civilians, some still holding the knives, guns and other improvised weapons that they had used to murder the officers. Other weapons lay scattered about, a hodgepodge of implements. Most of these people had been parolees and were banned from gun ownership. Looks like that law didn't work too well, thought Ed, as he scanned the remaining personnel.

About a dozen ancillary personnel remained with two rookie deputies. The ranking members of the Sheriff's office had been wiped out in one fell swoop. Ed had seniority over all but the deputies here. He called the men over and conferred with them. The rookies seemed to have no desire to lead the group and asked him what to do.

"I'll tell you what to do," said a familiar voice.

Edward turned and saw his best friend in the whole world, Issac Ferguson Davis, standing behind him, plate carrier on over multicam camouflage BDUs and high top black combat boots, knees and elbows covered with Blackhawk brand olive drab pads. A katana was slung over his right shoulder in the style of the Tulleys, its stingray skin grip gleaming in the sun. Smoke drifted past as the man stood ready, his M1A SOCOM in a rifle scabbard attached to the left side of his Multicam patrol pack, his Tactical Tailor plate carrier loaded with six spare twenty round magazines. On his right thigh was a Safariland tactical holster with a Wilson Combat custom 1911 .45 ACP; on the left thigh was a tactical rig with spare 1911 mags and two smoke grenades. Slung over his chest and held in both hands was his Kel Tec KSG 12 gauge bullpup combat shotgun, two tubes of seven rounds each fixed under the imposing barrel, Aimpoint weapon sight and Surefire weaponlight now attached to the rail system of the shotgun. Issac had kept his electronics in Faraday cages at home and work, and had spares ready, even thinking of LED flashlights and weapon sights and lights that most had neglected to protect.

"Well, I'll be damned!" Edward exclaimed, "The cavalry really has arrived."

Behind Issac, seven other men stood ready in similar gear. They cut imposing figures, each man with grim determination set into his face.

"I was at the office and when the power went out it took me a minute to get ready. Sorry it took so long to get everybody ready. Did we miss anything?" Issac smirked, looking out over the field of battle. There were no injured left, the mad crowd had seen to that, stomping and crushing anyone who had fallen.

Ed sighed and vigorously shook his best friend's hand. The deputies looked on, concern wrinkling their brows. It was illegal in Tennessee to go about "armed." While a concealed carry state, the laws were very vague about open carry of long guns and had been interpreted in different ways. Ed looked over and rolled his eyes, reading clearly the thought of the two rookies. Here it comes, he thought.

One of the young men walked over. "I'm going to have to ask you all to disband and hand over those firearms."

Issac walked directly up to the officer. "You and what army going to carry out that threat?"

The officer gulped and breathed out through pursed lips. Ed walked up and gently touched Issac's arm. Issac relaxed the death grip on the shotgun, the whites of his knuckles had been showing.

"Listen, deputy, we are kind of short on officers, wouldn't you say?" Ed asked, a smile crossing his face.

"Yeah, definitely. But what are we going to do about the law here?" the deputy asked, a stern grimace on his young face.

"Now that's a good question," Ed said, and slowly laid out his plan, each side listening intently. Hands came off of weapons and handshakes and tight smiles spread through the groups and they each greeted the other side.

When bad men combine, the good must associate; else they will fall one by one, an unpitied sacrifice in a contemptible struggle.
—Edmund Burke, "Thoughts on the Cause of the Present Discontents"

CHAPTER 18

Cumberland River Pedestrian Bridge
East Nashville, TN
July 3
11:05a.m.

The girls walked slowly, careful not to make any sudden movements or noise. They had walked south of the mall area and had clambered down the embankment to the greenway and footbridge. They had successfully dodged the stranded motorists on the freeway. It had been touch and go, but most of them never even looked down the side roads. They seemed totally focused on the people, cars and events occurring on Briley Parkway itself. They had heard several shouting matches and more than one outbreak of gunfire.

People were now streaming into the mall area north of them. They had gotten out just before the wave of humanity sought refuge in a place that they recognized, a place they felt comfortable. Like moths drawn to a flame, the citizens on the roadway had realized they were near the mall and remembrances of food courts and smoothies and good coffee had convinced most that it would be better there than on the freeway. Some stubbornly stayed with their now useless vehicles, convinced that someone "in charge" would miraculously come to help.

Most simply did not realize that the dream was over. The Earth had awakened from its brief dream of near-utopia, when waves of energy from its own life-giving sun had set events in motion that would destroy the very fabric of society so carefully woven over the millennia. All of the plans and hope and aspirations of the naive populace would be crushed into dust over the coming days. No one was coming to help. No one could. They could only have helped themselves, but decades of dependence had stripped from most of them their ability to survive. The liberal, pacifistic society the government and media had so carefully cultivated had no skills of its own to intervene in preventing its own destruction. They were now like lambs led to the slaughter.

But that would change when they realized that the great beast of government that they suckled from was dying. When they smelled the decay and rot of its bloated corpse, they would awaken to the uncontrolled animal instincts that could not be removed from society. Most of American society by the early twenty first century had largely rejected previous moral and religious tenets as outdated and irrelevant. These prior systems had guarded against mankind's evil nature. These taboos and prohibitions were now long gone for over half of society: there was no overriding reason to act in a moral and ethical manner. Mob rule and self-preservation would override all other motivations. The peaceful would turn on themselves. They would eventually kill for a drink of water.

The man was sitting, his back against the south side of the bridge, his feet sticking out into the walkway. The bridge was not very wide, perhaps six to seven feet. They would have to risk going around the man. Despite intense study through Kate's eight-power Pentax binoculars, they could not determine if he was alive or dead.

The bridge led to a park with essentially no services. No one had attempted to go this way, which is precisely why the girls had chosen this place to cross. The man was a problem. He could simply be sleeping, or be a drunk who had passed out the night before, sleeping off a hangover. Something tickled Kate's and Tessa's minds, however, telling them that this was not the case. Both of them strung arrows rapidly as they approached.

He was overweight, in a dingy navy suit. He had slumped to the side of the bridge and his feet and arms were splayed out in an unnatural pose. The man was either sleeping deeply or was dead. They were now about thirty yards away, walking slowly, always keeping one foot still while moving to other, to try and prevent the bridge from swaying any during their movement. It seemed to be working well. Kate was looking ahead at the man, when her booted foot crunched down hard on a bottle.

Both girls froze, their hearts thumping hard in their chests, afraid to breathe too hard. The man stirred. The girls steadied their weight onto their left feet, bows coming up , preparing to shoot. Their three bladed broadheads glinted in the sun. Each girl wore a mask of control covering her fear, with her jaw set against the inevitable violence.

The feet of the man twitched and his head jerked suddenly up. They could see drool crusted on his chin, fresh new rivulets running own now as he started awake. His eyes were still shut, crusted eye matter covered both lid margins. His eyes slowly opened and seemed unfocused, his breathing quickened and the two girls remained frozen.

The man turned and stared at them, thirty yards away and his expression changed. His brow furrowed and his teeth clenched. He lifted himself up, rage and hatred in his stare. He stood and staggered two steps towards them. Fury and animal lust spread through him, his cheeks turning pink as he hyperventilated. His head began shaking with fury, frothy saliva now foaming from his mouth, he inhaled deeply and reared his head back, preparing to roar.

Two arrows simultaneously pierced his neck stopping the sound before it could be emitted. The beast jerked its head forward towards the girls, blood pouring out of its neck, the trachea and esophagus transacted. The left carotid artery and jugular vein sliced in half by the broad heads sunk up to the fletchings, still dangling out of the back of the man's neck, bobbing up and down as he ran wildly, turning to the left and right.

He wove around wildly, in impotent rage, as his clothes became saturated with his blood. The girls loosed another arrow each at the moving target. Tessa's shot pierced the upper torso, slamming into and transecting the thoracic spinal cord after passing through the center of the heart. Kate's shot went high a second later as the man fell down, piercing the upper lung under the clavicle on the left side and exiting through the back, glancing off of a rib, pirouetting dramatically into the air upward and down, sinking into the river with no noise. He dropped like a rag doll, the motor neurons to the lower body below the mid chest cut by Tessa's broadhead. He flopped his arms and gurgled for half a minute and then his jaw and eyes started working open and shut slowly, like a fish out of water on a riverbank awaiting the fisherman's knife.

The girls stood still and waited until he had quit moving. He finally stopped trying to breathe after a full two minutes. Blood pooled out over the concrete of the bridge. The girls nodded to each other and sprinted past, running up along the edges of the bridge, staying as far as possible from the beast. They continued running until they crossed to the other side of the river and immediately ducked into the bushes. They waited for a moment and caught their breath and scanned the area with the compact waterproof binoculars. The Pentax UCC models had a very high optical quality for the price and were very durable. They were identical to the ones Kate's dad used in his bug home bag. They did not see anyone else in the park area. They carefully took the trail North and prayed that they could get home safely. The sun steadily rose as the day became hotter. Remote sounds of gunshots echoed from the freeway and west towards downtown. They saw smoke in the remote distance. The river flowed silently to their right as they cautiously walked North, their hopes set on home.

Goodlettsville, TN
10 miles North of Nashville
Gunn House
July 3
12:01p.m.

Gwenn Gunn wiped the sweat from her brow and the tears from her eyes. She had just performed the most unpleasant task she could ever remember. Her beloved Penelope's body could not be left out for animals to ravage, or worse, for the infected to find, but she did not have time to bury her dog.

She had done all that she could. She had remembered her survival readings and the section on handling dead bodies in the long haired hippie man's book. It actually was excellent advice, and one most people would simply not explain. Most survival books talked about guns and medicine and how evil the government was, but this little gem of a book went into great detail on unpleasant, but essential topics.

She had first wrapped up the body in two fifty five gallon, industrial strength trash bags, and duct taped them as airtight as possible. She then moved the body near the deck, onto the concrete and covered it with the fire pit bowl, inverting it to conceal the body. She then covered the whole thing with loose bricks from under the deck. She simply did not have the arm strength to wield a pick axe and shovel to bury the dog. This way would allow Angus to return later and dig the hole, and keep both burrowing and walking animals off of the body for a few days at least.

It had taken only twenty minutes, much less than Angus had spent digging the grave for Samson, their prior pet. He had spent over two hours with the claylike soil. She turned into the house, little Joshua watching from the deck ten feet away. She smiled at him and could see tears running down his cheeks. She hugged him close. He still had not spoken since the event occurred, and Gwenn knew better than to push him to talk. He would when he was ready. God willing, they would still all be alive by then.

She went into the house and used the remainder of the water pressure to wash off and put on woodland camo BDUs and grey Asolo boots and then dressed Joshua in the same style of clothing. She placed his navy blue soft armor surplus police vest on him and fastened the Velcro. He was too young to handle the weight of a full set of plates, but this vest was a woman's small and weighed only two pounds. He put on his Commandolight level IIIa helmet, again a size adult small and grabbed his child bug out bag. It contained only a lightweight sleeping bag, lightweight 3/4 length sleeping mat, compass, two days of energy bars, 750 ml of water in a plastic canteen, a poncho that could serve as a sort of mini tent, headlamp and extra batteries in a mini Faraday cage, spoon and IFAK military grade first aid kit, and Simmons 8x21mm compact binoculars, and iodine water purification tablets. The pack weighed only eight pounds and was easy for a small child to carry.

He knew how to use everything in the kit safely. He had had numerous outside courses on wilderness survival, children's first aid, navigation and had started escape and evasion and martial arts training with the group. With his pack, Joshua could make a cold camp, stay warm and dry, hide from view effectively, get drinkable water, scout ahead for threats with the binoculars, and eat for up to two days at the least without requiring adult intervention. He was not yet ready for a knife or fire making supplies, but that would come in time. Yes, should the worst come to pass, he would be lonely and terrified, but it was unacceptable to the Gunns to consider any other emergency plan for their children. They wanted their kids to survive, even if they themselves did not. They would do anything moral and legal to increase the odds in their favor.

The extra clothing and food he had were contained in a modular MOLLE sleeping bag pouch that Gwenn now attached to the front of her camouflaged Kelty bug out bag. The pack could be attached in seconds to either adult's or even Kate's pack. Whoever was alive in the house at any time could take the boy and go, in moments if need be. Gwenn's bug out bag was purposefully light and lean as she was not as powerful as the men in the group. By the time she had on a helmet and vest, she would have little capacity to carry a pack. Her pack had one change of clothing, three changes of underwear and socks, toiletries, ultralight camping equipment including a sub three ounce MSR butane stove. It did, however, include ten full days of food in the form of dehydrated Mountain House meals, Nature Valley Granola Bars and Quaker grits packets. About 2500 calories per day including drink mixes, and coffee with cream and sugar, all dehydrated and hermetically sealed. The pack weighed only fifteen pounds full, before Joshua's modular five pound unit was added. Shelter was only a military poncho, but that could be improved by bringing more containers if a vehicle or off road stroller were used to carry the extra weight. Their entire family system was modular.

Extra supplies were kept in the garage and bedroom closets in such a way that, depending on the time allowed and the method of travel, modular "augmentation packs" could be added to the bug out gear. This gear and Angus' pack would have to stay as Gwenn needed to travel on foot, and fast. Even the dogs had saddlebag style bug out bags. They were all identical and contained the same meds, food and water and feeding/water bowls, so that even if only one dog were able to lug a load, the rest could benefit. That was the case today, as Sarah was simply to old to carry her own pack. Genevieve carried one pack with about three days of food each for two dogs and a liter water bottle for them to share, along with the meds and canine first aid kit.

Gwenn secured the pack to the dog's back, and grabbed the original thousand count stock bottles of the dogs' seizure and thyroid meds. These were compact and weighed a few ounces and could get the two dogs through about three years, so long as they could find food. She grabbed her Springfield XD 9mm subcompact and holstered it in the cross draw holster mounted to the left side of the pack's waist belt and grabbed her AR-15 rifle. She loaded a magazine and chambered a round.

She stuffed her small purse into the top pocket of the pack, and then put on her custom Multicam plate carrier after inserting the multi-hit plates over the soft armor inserts. She kept the vest without the plates to use in case of tornados, an infinitely more common event than an apocalypse such as today. She slipped the pack on after making sure the main power breaker and gas lines were off. No point in burning the house down on the off chance the power ever came back on.

Angus would hopefully be able to return in the near future and collect more gear. She put on her helmet, a PASGT surplus model with a woodland cover. She walked out of the garage center door and locked it. She shouldered her pack after securing her son's on him. She clicked into the hip belt and adjusted the straps. The weight was heavy with the combat gear, but it was well distributed. She set off with her son and two remaining dogs, pushing the thought of Penelope's sacrifice out of her mind. She needed all of her concentration focused on getting to the storage unit without getting her or her remaining family killed. Always, the time worried her as she could not stop thinking of Kate downtown. The dogs would have to follow without a leash, they had to move now.

Sheriff's office
Gallatin, TN
July 3
12:03p.m.

Bustling activity spread through the building, runners taking written messages in and out of separate offices. Issac looked down at the forms he and his crew had just signed. He looked at the new star shaped badge on his plate carrier. This was a lot to take in at one time. He looked up as Ed entered the room.

"Don't get too comfortable, I need you to use that badge, not shine it up and stare at it," Ed said.

"Don't you get comfortable either," Issac said, looking at the new badge on Ed's shirt. All of them had been deputized on the spot by the ranking rookie deputy. Informal, maybe not even legal, but it was all that they had. They needed people to help, right now. The rookies had deferred to Ed now so much that he had become the de facto sheriff.

"How's it coming with the patrol unit?" Ed asked, referring to the foot patrol of Issac's men that had been sent out to survey damage.

"Not good, we are going to have to evacuate soon. The fires are getting closer. They could not find anyone left in any of the buildings. It's getting like a ghost town. They had no EMS contact. Also, they had to shoot several dogs that seemed to be rabid. Damnedest thing. About ten dogs just moseyed over and started to growl at the guys. Right on Main Street. Must have come from the projects behind the hospital is what they thought, no tags on any of them. Just walked calmly up and almost bit a couple of the guys. Went from normal to ape shit in about two seconds. They had to shoot the whole lot," Issac said. "Where do they keep the rabies vaccine, anyway? Is there somewhere other than the hospital, now that it's in flames?"

"I think the health department, but just don't let any damned dog bite you, O.K. We don't have time to deal with this shit, much less a dog bite," Ed said, turning to the door where a runner stood with paper in hand.

Several teenagers had appeared and volunteered to help. They had been ferrying messages between the courthouse and Sheriff's office, and units on patrol. Ed had taken charge of the incident command. The Gallatin Police Department had evacuated to Hendersonville at their police department. Several people had reported that today. Most of the residents of Gallatin had evacuated that way, so it actually made sense. The group here would have to leave soon as well, but Ed wanted to try to get some gear working and out of the way of the fire first. If they ever wanted to rebuild, it would have to be done.

"Send word to the salvage crew that we need any kind of working vehicles. At least get any hopefuls out of the way of the fire. Go," he said to the pimply faced teenager as he ran out of the door, note in hand.

Ed had asked two of the local church pastors to set up a food drive. They had been in their church offices when the power went out and there were about fifty volunteers now going door to door and just taking any food they found abandoned. They were piling it in the parking lot behind one of the churches next to the Sheriff's office. In total, they had about one hundred people who had remained and not evacuated Gallatin.

Then, there was the jail. This had been the most distasteful issue of the day, so far. He had been wondering what they would do with the prisoners, when a runner dashed in and breathlessly told the story of the events of the morning there. Apparently several of the guards had gone nuts and decided to implement "the final solution" with the prisoners.

Some were simply petty thieves. Certainly, there were violent criminals in the mix, but they had been the minority. The infected guards had shot all of the prisoners and several of the other guards who have valiantly tried to stop them. Then they appeared to have just shot each other after the deed was done. Now they had a jail full of the dead and no one to clean them up.

Then, there was the question of food and water. Where would they get enough for everyone? Also, where would they go when the rest of the town burned up? These concerns ran through his head as he surveyed the scene. At least he had people working. Among the new deputies were Issac's team members, men he had known for many years now. He looked out into the front hall and looked at the crew, standing at ease, awaiting their first assignment as new deputies.

Jack Sutherland, 57, was a local defense attorney who was divorced and had two kids who lived in New York City. He was Caucasian, tall, overweight but quite fit for his size. He carried a Saiga 12 gauge semi auto shotgun with its ten round magazines taking up a good portion of his chest rig's real estate. He was talking to the secretary, grinning and laughing.

Next to him was Nathan Ford, 29, a single EMT for Vanderbilt Hospital, the downtown tertiary care center. He was a helicopter pilot in his spare time as well. He was a black man of medium height and medium build. He had on the group's usual gear. They all were dressed in Multicam BDUs and Garmont desert combat boots. They all had

Tactical Tailor plate carriers with the same multi-hit level IV armor plates that Issac and many others used. These had been so inexpensive and effective, that most people had gone with them, having so many other things to buy. Each member had an ACH helmet with a Multicam cover and night vision goggles, or NVGs attached to the front on swing down mounts that would keep the units out of the way until needed. All of the guys had kept their electronics in Faraday cages after Edward had warned Issac of the danger. They had simply attached lights, lasers and NVGs onto the repeatable, modular mounts after the lights stopped glowing.

Each man, with few exceptions, had a Daniel Defense M-4 with integrated infrared laser target designators and illuminators, Surfire weaponlights and Aimpoint Micro red dot sights. They used Larue quick detachable mounts to remove and reattach the electronics without needing to re-sight in the equipment. Each carbine had a Surefire 60 round magazine and each member kept more 60 rounders on their vests and leg rigs for ready access to superior firepower when needed. All but one man had Wilson Combat 1911 custom .45 ACP pistols with Wilson Combat 8 round magazines. This way, they could all share gear in a firefight.

In addition to the regular gear of his group, Nathan carried an Ohio Ordnance M240-SLR, a .308 semi-auto machine gun, complete with British 100 round ammo bags, bipod, and an Elcan M145 3.4x illuminated optic that had ballistic compensation on the reticle out to 1200 yards. This was a very heavy weapon at over twenty pounds with ammo. He did not carry an M-4, but had a Mossberg 590 A1 combat shotgun with an 8 round tube instead.

Sitting on a bench was Luke Dodson, 26, a short single white man of 5'9", 160 pounds. He was an ex US Army sniper who worked now as a local factory machinist in training. He had all of the usual gear, and was leaning against his Savage M-110BA in .338 Lapua, its five round box magazine locked and loaded. The Super Sniper 16x42 scope on Seekins Precision rings easily getting him hits out to 1500 yards.

The 52 year old county judge, Harold "Judge" Simson sat next to him. Balding with brown eyes and black hair, he was nondescript and of medium height and build. His wife had passed away three years ago and his one son had moved to Berlin, Germany after the funeral. His son was working as an English teacher, and seemed to need the distance. He had all of the usual gear, plus a Taurus Judge 3 inch standard model loaded with Federal .410 5 pellet copper plated premium buckshot as a backup in a cross draw holster on his chest rig.

Standing next to them was Clay Masterson, 41, a handsome blonde haired, blue eyed man, his golden locks pulled back in a ponytail. He had moved a few years ago from Miami, seeking refuge from the big city. His ex-wife had remained in Miami after their divorce. They had no children, but Clay's brother lived in East Tennesee. Clay was also of medium height and build, and was a former Navy Corpsman who worked as an A.C. repairman now. He had the usual kit plus a Rock River M-4 style carbine in .458 SOCOM with standard Troy iron sights, a beast of a close quarters round. This cartridge copied the ballistics of the .45-70 in an AR platform, for a devastating punch.

He was talking to a tall white man with brown hair and green eyes. Jonathan Burke, 38, was a short haul truck driver. He lived with his wife and three kids in Gallatin. His family was helping now with the church food gathering. He also had the standard gear, but eschewed the standard pistol for a Para SuperHawg. This stainless steel .45ACP had a double stack 14 round magazine plus one in the chamber, a six inch barrel, and was capable of astounding accuracy. He had Trijicon tritium night sights mounts for night shooting. One inch groups at 25 yards were the norm, with easy head shots out to 50 yards in capable hands. And Jonathan certainly had capable hands. He carried a full ten extra magazines for this beast on his plate carrier and thigh rigs. For close range, he preferred the powerful pistol to his carbine and spent most weekends shooting at local pistol competitions, placing at or near the top each time. He had reloaded thousands of his favorite 230 grain hollowpoints.

At the other end of the room stood Eli Smith, a 35 year old, 6'3" white man with black hair in a buzzcut with piercing ice blue eyes. He also carried the group's usual gear. In his Eberlestock X1 rifle pack, he had a Springfiled M1A in a Sage M39 EMR stock with a Nightforce 3.5-15x50 NXS scope with an NPR1 reticle. This scope allowed for ballistic compensation past 800 yards. Unfortunately, the scope mounts he used did not allow for quick removal and the solar flare had shorted the electronics on the scope out, preventing him from using the illuminated reticle. The scope functioned perfectly in every other regard and could still be used at night, just without the illumination feature. This gun almost exactly copied the EMR rifle fielded with great effect by the US Marines. He carried extra twenty round magazines in a Specter Gear left leg thigh rig, saving the chest rig for his AR mags. Each man had brought a large duffel bag containing bug out gear. The bags were stowed in the corner of the room. Extra medical gear and tactical equipment were contained in two group duffles, each marked as such by the unit.

This group of men had basically spent their life savings on their gear. The equipment each man carried cost more than twenty thousand dollars per person, and in the cases of the men with specialty rifles, well more than thirty thousand dollars each. Ed looked at the crew and thought, all in all, that he was very lucky to have such a unit at his disposal. The guys had trained with him for years now and he knew them as well as Issac. They would see how well all that time and effort would pay off now that the shit had finally hit the fan.

The harder the conflict, the more glorious the triumph. What we obtain too cheap, we esteem too lightly; it is dearness only that gives everything its value.

—Thomas Paine, "The American Crisis"

CHAPTER 19

15 miles east of Gallatin
Calvin family Deuce and a half
July 3
12:07p.m.

The large vehicle rumbled onward, dodging the occasional stranded vehicle, the family inside concerned over the sight behind them. John Calvin drove while his daughter Hailey rode shotgun, her Doublestar M-4 aimed out the passenger window. She had trained to fire the weapon ambidextrously and he hoped that she would not have to use the skill. Denise and the other kids, Luke and Stacy were in the back, guarding the rear of the vehicle. They looked to the rear as they rumbled on at a pace of about 35 miles an hour, their gear stowed under nets and locked down with packing straps. Smoke billowed into the sky from the direction of their home, Gallatin. Huge streamers of black wisps spread out into the calm upper atmosphere.

John looked into his rear view mirror and thought of all that they had done there, his memories flooding back. It would never be the same. It looked like the city was burning to the ground. The calm weather ahead belied the coming storm of violence. The beautiful, hot ninety degree summer day seemed so peaceful, but they all knew that death could hide behind any vehicle, any tree. They lumbered on, sweat gently beaded on their foreheads, their armor vests and helmets making them hot in this weather. John prayed for safe travel as Denise, looking back towards the town, prayed for all those who were still in the area. Life would never be the same. The hot day slowly moved on, the sun beating down from the blue sky, the dreams of a future now lost slowly fading into oblivion.

Hendersonville, TN
Corpuz house
Halfway between Gallatin and Goodlettsville
3 miles from Mackenzie House
July 3
12:09p.m.

Carlos Corpuz finished examining their gear. They had prepared all of their bug out bags and had pulled up the family mountain bikes. The kids had rigged a bicycle each with extra gear in bags straddling the center bars of the bikes. They were weight matched on each side so the bikes could be easily pushed when walking and not become unstable. They resembled panniers in form and function. They had pulled out extra ammo, clothes, food and medical equipment and were saddling up, putting on their vests and packs. Each family member grabbed his bike by the handlebars and headed out into the driveway. Carlos locked the garage door, manually pulling it down and locking it from the inside. He then went out through the house's front door, after checking to ensure that the main breaker switch, water, sewer and gas lines were all shut off.

He put on his vest and bug out bag and grabbed his Rock River 20" stainless steel designated marksman rifle and handed his son Rafael the Rock River 16" stainless steel carbine and turned to look back at his house. It all seemed so unreal. They were actually leaving their home. They had lived here for nine years now, through many trials and tests, and The Lord had seen them through. But now, the voice in Carlos' head told him to leave, to leave now. He knew that God was speaking to him and he would not disobey the command. He turned away, his eyes glistening with emotion.

He set his jaw like flint and nodded at his wife Cecelia Corpuz and she smiled a thin smile and they both headed out, the kids in the middle of the marching column, their silent progress unnoticed by the neighbors who still hadn't come out of their house since the power went out. They started down the road towards the Mackenzie place and towards an unknown future. Carlos prayed for strength and felt the power of The Lord wash through him. He smiled, and laughed, the strength within was so great that he could not help himself.

He knew. He knew: The Lord Jesus would not abandon them. They were in the palm of His hand. His family looked at him, and he nodded, a terse motion, and then kissed Cecelia and tousled the hair of his boys, Rafael and Roberto, and they all turned back and headed down the road, their camouflage clothing and dark colored gear and bikes fading into the summer shrubbery, their progress silent as they carefully picked their way along the road.

Two miles from Long Hollow Pike
Northwest Gallatin
River bottom
July 3
1:32p.m.

Matt looked silently across Highway 109 North. A white truck shot by, the occupant looking out the passenger window with binoculars as the vehicle sped north. They were not visible from the road, having covered their faces with mud from the riverbank. The only way across was under the road, down the riverbank. Luckily, this time of year there had been a drought and the creek bed was nearly fully dry. They would have to go almost directly underneath the other truck that had positioned itself on the bridge. This was their riskiest move yet, and they would need luck and a little divine intervention to make it through. Matt and Angus each checked the other's gear for any noises or flashy areas of metal. Once the job was complete, the two men shook hands, looked each other in the eyes and quietly set off for the riverbank, their hearts beating faster as they approached the road.

North end of Shelby Bottoms Greenway
East Nashville, TN
July 3
1:25p.m.

The wind gently rustled the leaves of the bushes in which the girls were hiding. Kate and Tessa were frozen still, not daring to breathe as they surveyed the scene before them. Several men were quickly running into the house in front of the park walkway entrance. They were carrying televisions, electronics, jewelry and guns out of the house. No one appeared to be home. Several neighbors stood on their front porches, transfixed by the scene. This modest neighborhood seemed to be aloof to the robbery occurring directly in front of them. The men were laughing as they ran down the street with their new prizes, talking quickly to one another.

One of the male neighbors, an older black man, perhaps in his seventies, approached the thieves and yelled at them. The girls couldn't hear what was said. Suddenly one of the men, a tall Latino with a yellow tee shirt and baggy pants, pulled out a small pistol and fired once at the man. The man crumpled, yelling out in pain, as he clung desperately to his cane, unable to hold himself up. The men laughed and the shooter walked up and began kicking the helpless senior. He cried out in agony under the furious blows. The man stopped kicking and started to walk away. He turned and paused, then fired three rounds at the prostrate form, silencing his cries. A dark liquid began pooling onto the asphalt, the man's lifeblood spilling onto the pavement, his cane still clutched in his hands.

The girls stared, shocked at the scene. There were easily ten men carrying out the looting. They all could be armed. There was no way the two girls could survive against such odds without firearms. Even with them, Tessa thought, they would not likely survive the contact. Kate trembled in helpless rage, tears streaming silently down her cheeks. Her best friend in the whole world hugged her tightly and her eyes glistened with her own tears of shame, rage and hatred. She felt shame at not being able to stop this atrocity, rage at the men responsible and hatred for them and all of their kind. Something shifted inside her mind. As with Kate at the sports store, her thought patterns had forever changed. The girls had been violently thrust into adulthood on this day, their full realization of life's real horrors coming without warning.

The neighbors who had been standing on their porches had retreated into their houses, presumably either to hide or try to defend themselves. These men were essentially stealing garbage, the circuits having been fried this morning. They had murdered a man for worthless junk. What would they do with two young women? Kate shuddered at the thought. The girls sat under the bush and waited until the men had moved to another house down the street and out of view. They then withdrew silently and began walking around, toward the river bank. They would have to work their way north this way to get to the railroad. It would be a long walk home.

Happy Traveler Mini Storage
Goodlettsville, TN
July 3
1:30p.m.

Gwenn opened the door of the large military vehicle. She let Joshua into the passenger side of the bench and cranked the engine. The Deuce and a Half roared to life, its multi fuel engine revving well on the diesel in its tank. She had checked their cargo containers, opening each to assure everything was in place. Angus had attached the containers to the truck with a strong cable chain to avert theft. The dogs were loaded into makeshift beds in the back, locked in with their car harnesses to tie down anchors in the floor of the bed. Penelope's bed was empty. Gwenn choked back her anguish as she hurried to exit the storage area.

The gate of the mini storage had been closed and no one was in the office. She hated doing it, but had to get to her vehicle. Lives depended on it. She had jumped the fence and gotten the truck jack from the Deuce and had returned to the gate. She had Joshua hidden in the bushes with the bug out gear and dogs tied to a tree. They were on the edge of town, a 2.5 mile walk from the house.

Gwenn had used the Deuce's heavy jack to pry open the electronic gate, destroying the locking mechanism. She abhorred vandalism, but it was either this or drive the deuce through the gate at speed. She knew this would be much easier for the owner to fix, and she had left a note and $200 cash in the drop box. She hoped it would be enough, it was half of the cash she had.

Gwenn turned the large vehicle around and started towards the gate. She had planned on closing the gate after leaving, but as she looked out of the large front windshield, her heart stopped. Three figures, two men and one woman in torn clothing blocked the way, staggering forward, streams of un swallowed saliva running from their mouths.

Gwenn gunned the massive engine, exhaust billowing out of the muffler, the beast of a truck lurching forward. She had about one hundred feet to the exit gate. The figures staggered forward, now seeing her, the angry screams of the infected drowned out by the diesel roar of the engine. She looked at Joshua.

"Look away! Close your eyes!" she screamed.

Little eight-year-old Joshua started to cry, hot tears streaming down his beautiful Asian cheeks. He closed his eyes and pulled his legs up instinctively, covering his face with his knees. He sobbed bitterly at what he knew must be done. He was a good boy, a loving boy, but he would not see those things hurt his mommy or him. He knew that he would kill them if they tried to hurt his family. He had witnessed the entire attack and the death of his favorite dog, Penelope, and he knew that he did not want to see what was about to happen.

The huge forest camouflaged green truck reached twenty-five miles an hour as the infected figures roared and charged the front of the vehicle. They were so far gone that they did not even know to get out of the way, and this was what Gwenn had prayed for. The vehicle bumper caught the first two in the kneecaps, breaking their legs and sweeping them to the pavement, their lower legs crushed as the radiator screen smashed into their faces and torsos. The third was on the passenger side of the vehicle and missed being crushed.

The two in front disappeared from view as the huge vehicle burst out onto the road, knocking an abandoned sedan five feet out of the way, wheels screeching under the effort of the right turn. Movement to the right side caught Gwenn's eye. A man's head, covered in blood and saliva lifted up into view slowly, its eyes a study in madness. Rage and evil swirled in the eyelids and the pupils were constricted in a mask of hatred so intense that it burned into Gwenn's mind, threatening to overcome her will to fight. A partially crushed hand reached back to smash at the window. Little Joshua looked up from his knees, sensing danger, and stared directly into the abyss of the infected man's face, shock and horror filling his mind.

Before Gwenn could react, he reached into the center floor console and came up with Gwenn's Springfield XD 9mm pistol, aimed at the beast and fired three rapid shots. Joshua had been trained in the use of a .22 target pistol and this was very close in weight, if not recoil, yet, the boy did not drop the gun. The window shattered, sending glass into the cabin; the infected man fell from the car, dead with one of the three bullets through the head. Both mother and son were completely deaf now, ears ringing painfully. Gwenn drove another two hundred feet and gently stopped the truck. She reached over and gently took the pistol, keeping the muzzle in a safe direction. Joshua still had wet tears on his cheeks, but a grim resolve had settled into his countenance. Gwenn stowed the pistol in its fixed floor holster in the center compartment, and hugged Joshua. Her own tears now streaming silently down. Her little boy, the light of her life, now having to kill to survive.

If she had reached the pistol first, she might have hit him, and could have killed him, and certainly would have permanently damaged his hearing, even if the shot went well. As it stood, the fact that he shot with the muzzle towards the threat and away from both of them, the situation was actually safer, though she grieved at what he had been forced to do. She could start to hear things now, though her ears still rang, she knew from past experience that the effects would wear off in an hour or so.

"Are you O.K.?" she asked her little man.

"Yes Ma'am, I think so," he yelled. "I can't hear anything but ringing though."

"That's O.K., it will pass in an hour or so, "I love you. You saved us from that attacker. I'm sorry you had to do that. I love you very much!" Her voice quavered with emotion. She squeezed him so tightly that he thought his chest would burst. He hugged her back.

"I love you too, Mommy," he said, his face now set like flint. "I promised God that I wouldn't let them hurt you."

Gwenn sobbed into his shoulder, her body racked with guilt and anger at the situation. She blamed herself for not protecting him, not protecting his innocence. She prayed to the Lord Jesus for strength.

Joshua squeezed her neck and kissed her on the cheek. She wiped the glass from his cheeks and kissed him on the forehead. She sat back into the seat, dried her tears and assessed the road ahead. Some interspersed cars covered the roadway into downtown. She should be able to pick her way forward with care.

They saw no one as they drove into town. It was as if the place were abandoned. Goodlettsville was a small town, but near to a big city. It had a diverse mix of urbanites, suburbanites and rural citizens. Everyone got along very well, usually. Fifteen minutes of careful maneuvering of the huge truck led them in front of a row of shops. An antique store was directly in front of them. She killed the engine and grabbed her carbine and turned to Joshua. He looked at her and put on his helmet. He had placed it on the floor earlier and did not want to repeat the events of the morning. He slid on light brown tinted size small Crossfire shooting glasses for kids and small adults. They were hand me downs from his big sister, but he thought they looked cool. He should have had them on before and he would have been better protected from the glass.

"If I don't come back, you obviously know how to use the pistol. It has fourteen rounds left in it. O.K.?" she said, as she realized that Angus must have spent more time training him than he had let on. She knew he had spent a couple of days letting him shoot, but she still did not see him as ready for a pocket knife, much less a gun. This was a new world now. "Just remember the rules. Imagine all guns are always loaded. Don't point it at something you don't want to destroy. Keep your finger out of the trigger guard until ready to shoot. Be aware of your target and what's behind it. Got it?"

He recited the rules. He had memorized it when his daddy took him to the range this year in the Spring. His daddy would not let him touch the gun, until he could say the rules himself. Gwenn sighed and nodded.

She slung the rifle and walked into the store, her backup weapon light illuminating the room. The primary lights were of course all fried as they had been attached to the gun when the flare hit. She looked through the Trijicon Tripower red dot optic, seeing the red chevron glowing in the summer daylight filtering through the shop window. The optic's batteries and electronic system were fried, but the fiber optic light collector and tritium backups were working perfectly. The three dozen batteries Angus had bought were useless, but as long as the scope had daylight or even nighttime room light or reflected flashlight beams bounced off of walls, the fiber optic collectors worked to illuminate the chevron aiming point. Angus called this his "end of the world optic," and Gwenn was starting to see why.

No sound came from within the store. Boxes and tables were strewn out around the floor, their must have been a fight here. Shit! She thought Angus' mom might be gone. "Margaret!" she called.

"Margaret Gunn, do you hear me!?"

A rustling from the back could be heard. A large armoire door opened up and the tiny frame of Margaret Gunn, Angus' mom dropped gently into view. Another figure appeared, a small graying blonde woman.

"Saints alive! We sure are glad to see you, you pretty thing!" Margaret said in her thick South Carolina Southern drawl, hugging Gwenn's neck.

"Me too! This place is a wreck. Are you O.K.? And who's your friend?"

"This is Jadena. She is the proprietor of this establishment. We're fine, sugar. We just had to wait things out. Some very unruly visitors made quite a scene, quite a scene. Where are Joshua and Kate?" Margaret said, concern furrowing her brow. She was a small woman, 5'4" and 100 pounds soaking wet. She had suffered a car accident twenty years ago that nearly claimed her life and twenty three years of a bad marriage to the father of her children. She was a survivor: that was certain.

"Long story. Let's get in the truck, I'll catch you up. Jadena, you are welcome to come as well," Gwenn said. She was sure the rifle, helmet, camo clothes and body armor had surprised the woman, though she looked far too polite to ask. The women walked briskly back to the truck and Gwenn used her boot to sweep glass away from the seat and step of the truck. Joshua hopped out and hugged his grandmother.

Margaret walked quickly to her brand new Honda Pilot and tried the key fob. When it didn't work, she turned the key manually and got something out of the glove box. She went to the back hatch and turned the key in it and pulled up the hatch. She pulled out a small Rubbermaid bin and put it on the pavement. She closed and locked the SUV and returned to the Deuce. Gwenn took the Rubbermaid bin and placed it in the truck bed. Joshua had already hopped back in the truck. She then helped the women up the steps. The two small women squeezed tightly in next to Joshua on the massive bench seat. The shop owner went without a seatbelt.

Gwenn cranked the engine and asked the store owner if she wanted a ride perhaps to her house. The woman was very appreciative and directed them to the neighborhood across from the Gunn's house. They headed out and Gwenn told Margaret what had transpired so far. Margaret sobbed upon learning that Peneolpe had died. Margaret had a Golden Retriever of her own, now in a kennel in South Carolina. Gwenn wondered if part of the tears were due to the fact that she would likely never see the dog again. Gwenn thought of her own family in South Carolina and privately shared Margaret's grief. When Gwenn explained about Kate, Margaret had tears in her eyes, and could not speak.

They continued working their way up the cluttered road, Gwenn driving and explaining the implications of the solar event and the threat of the infected people. Gwenn told Margaret about the infection and danger. She did not yet mention the shooting that Joshua had to do. Gwenn suspected that Margaret had already figured it out. She had looked at the window, the glass, the blood on the outside of the door and had seen the new steeliness in the boy's eye. She knew. Later, when they were safe would be the time to talk. As Angus would say, to "debrief." Right now, they had to get to Hendersonville. And they had to get to Kate.

Indian Lake Police Horse Barn
Hendersonville, TN
July 3
2:02p.m.

Justin Clearwater hopped from the front passenger seat of the truck as it came to a stop. He had a canvas bag in his hands and walked briskly into the front of the barn. Darryl Washington got out and walked around his truck, surveying the area. Smoke could be seen billowing up from Hendersonville now. Large black plumes of smoke spread skyward from Gallatin, but fire also seemed to be starting in Hendersonville as well. The beautiful summer's day made him seem far removed from the terror he had already witnessed.

They had dropped off the Gallatin PD officers at the Hendersonville PD just now and had headed up this way. Justin had a thought concerning horses. After they dropped off the other police officers, Justin had mentioned that horses would be a good way to travel fast along the tight confines of a railway line. Darryl had assumed he would have to go on foot, as his vehicle would not fit down the railway, or along the side. He was glad of the suggestion as it would really speed up the travel downtown. Also, the animals could really be useful in other areas as well.

Justin entered the small stable office and was greeted by his longtime friend who ran the stable. He was amazed, with all of the chaos that the stable was still running.

"Bill! How's it going, my friend?" Justin asked, smiling broadly and shaking the man's hand.

"Goin' pretty well for an old man. What's all this ruckus in town? Bunch them boys been up here raising cane. Had to shoot one uv um. Body's out back. Sumbitch tried to bite me. Damnedest thing. Spitting all over the place. Iffin' it wuzza dog, ida thought it was rabid. Power's been out too, can't get my wristwatch to work either. Damnedest thing, I tell you. Horses is all stirred up. What can I do you for, Justin? You uns is always welcome here." Bill said, sitting on his stool at the door of the small room.

"Well Bill, you're pretty much on top of it. Same kinda stuff in town as well, just more of it," Justin replied, the man's comment about rabies got the EMT in him thinking. "I need a favor, for a good cause."

"Well that's something we might be able to help. Whatcha needing?"

"Bill, to cut clean to it, we need horses."

"Well, we don't normally sell them, of course these usually go to the Po-lice as you know," Bill said, referring to the arrangement he had with the Hendersonville Police Department. He sold them horses and stabled them as well. They were used in the outdoor malls and parks in the city, and were a very successful operation.

"I see your point, but this really is a question of life or death. You see, my two close friends, Darryl here and Dr. Gunn over in Gallatin, their daughters are stuck downtown in this mess. We need horses to go and get them out, because we think they're on the railroad line walking back. And I don't need to tell you what two pretty teenagers could risk walking through the town that sits between here and there."

"Well now, that changes things a bit. Whatcha got in mind?" the older man asked.

"Well, I know that you've got connections with the police here, so I have something I could trade you for. I figure three horses will do. I don't know if you know, but the others like the guy you shot, well, they've burned down the hospital in Gallatin. I almost died there this morning. I got smoke in my lungs and passed out at the ER. A good friend dragged me out before I would've died. Lots of people did die. The entire town is on fire and it looks like Hendersonville may be next." Justin looked out over the fields south towards town and saw the plumes of smoke continuing to rise steadily, with new tendrils appearing by the minute. He was glad they had dropped off the other full time officers there. It looked like they would need all the help they could get.

Justin continued, "So the night shift at the Gallatin PD went nuts and blew the building up and themselves and most of the other officers with them. I got some gear out before it blew. I have it here and can use it myself, but I figured you could pass it along to the Hendersonville P.D. in exchange for the horses."

Justin opened the bag and showed the man the priceless night vision equipment and ammunition. He had left the vests in the truck and had planned on keeping that for those that needed it later.

Bill looked the gear over and thought for a moment. He seemed to be quite the country chap, but actually was very well educated and the accent was almost an adaptation to the environment."Hmmm. Not sure what to think about that."

"Look, Bill, I tried to get people out before the building blew and got shot doing it. My vest stopped the round and now I have a couple of broken ribs for my effort. I couldn't get past the bastards shooting everyone. So I got equipment out. These are not ordinary times. Give them to the Hendersonville P.D., they will need them anyway. I've got to get horses or we will have a helluva walk, and they may not make it," Justin sighed at the end. He was played out, spent. He prayed for wisdom and strength, and felt his spirits rise.

"Puttin' it like that's different, I s'pose. Well, I've got these retired ones here. These three are older horses, just retired last week. The Po-lice don't have no more use of 'em and I was just going to sell them on the secondary market. Don't get much for 'em being as they are getting older. But the've still got good years in them, many years if cared for proper. If you like 'em, I'll take the trade in gear. I'll even saddle 'em up for you. I don't know how you kept NVGs working during an EMP event, but that's impressive. Priceless, really." Bill said, confirming Justin's understanding of the man's extensive knowledge base.

Bill just grinned at him and showed him to the barn. "These two have Percheron and Thoroughbred in them, both are 16.4 hands high, one is 22, the other is 17. The young one hates the shoeing. Normally don't retire them that young. Have to sedate him when the farrier comes by. By the way, you know they use rubber coated shoes, right. Keeps 'em quieter on the pavement. The other is mostly Tennessee Walker, with a good chunk of Quarter-horse in her. She's 19, slow and steady, 17 hands high. The've all been with the force for over ten years. You've got to show them a strong hand and keep your cool, they don't really have ground manners. Just used to you getting on straight away."

They arranged the trade and got the three mares and full set of tack and even food to get started. Justin had to throw in one of the vests for that deal. Bill liked the idea of getting shot and living to tell about it, and wouldn't take no for an answer when he heard Justin's story of how his vest had worked. Justin warned him it wasn't for rifles, just shotguns and pistols, and Bill paid attention. Justin helped saddle up the horses and being a very experienced rider had no trouble leading the other two. It was around 4:00 when they were done. Justin estimated the time, as his watch was useless.

He thanked Bill, warned him to watch for the crazy people and spoke with Darryl. They decided their best bet was to head for the Mackenzie house and get backup before attempting to get to the girls. Darryl had accepted that this would likely be the case, as things simply were not the same anymore. He knew Simone would understand. She had packed him a three-day pack from the start. They prayed together and thanked the Lord for His blessings and set out, Justin riding the young Percheron mix, correctly figuring the older mares would follow on a lead better. Darryl trailed slowly behind in the truck to keep from spooking the horses and to monitor from the rear.

You must not fear them, for the Lord your God Himself fights for you.
–Deuteronomy 3:22 NKJV

CHAPTER 20

Sheriff's office
Gallatin, TN
July 3rd
2:10p.m.

Several people in mechanic's attire were standing in the entrance of the Sheriff's office. Fires were still spreading throughout town now. The men and several women had on oil and grease stained overalls and were milling about waiting to speak with Edward. Some were chewing dip, others were wiping their hands with red rags. Ed walked up.

"Good afternoon, gentlemen. What have we got?" Ed asked in reference to his request that every able bodied mechanic or anyone with mechanical inclination start immediately finding some form of working transportation.

The men and women looked around amongst themselves, awaiting the materialization of a spokesperson. A short, lanky fellow with long brown hair to his neck stepped up, a cotton string bullet necklace hanging out of his coveralls.

"What's your name, son?" Ed asked. Always good to know somebody's name.

"Trey, Sir. Trey Nellis. Well, we've got several things for you. Probably be best for you to just come look," he said, motioning to the rear parking lot adjoining the jail.

Ed nodded and followed, Issac and his crew and several onlookers joining the cavalcade. They walked around the back into the back parking lot. Many people had moved the now useless police cruisers to the other end, leaving room for the new transportation. Two dozen mechanics had been hard at work. Several dozen more had scouted through town for hours to find what they could. Anytime they found anything of value, they asked for it for the sheriff, and if no one was home, which was most of the time, they left a note.

Ed looked out and sighed. Still, it was a hell of a lot better than he expected. In front of him was an odd assortment of vehicles. There were a number of different dirt bikes and motorcycles and several older cars and trucks. A 1955 Chevy Bel Air, rusted paint that appeared more brownish orange than any other particular color sat on the left, one of the female mechanics grinning, standing next to her prize.

"This one's mine. You can use it, so long as I drive," the young woman said, wiping her brow on her sleeve.

Ed nodded, "Absolutely. Thanks for the help."

He paused and looked around. People were gathering together around the scene. He realized that this was an important moment. "Gather everybody together!" he called out. Deputies jogged into the office and returned with the entire crew behind them. Everybody stopped and looked at him. He stood up on the curb to get a few inches up in the air. He looked around at those he knew and those he didn't. He had seen almost everybody at least once or twice. Gallatin was a small town.

"Listen up, everybody. We are not going to be taking anything from anyone who refuses to offer it. If we see something we need, we ask. Is that clear?"

Everybody nodded. Looks of serious understanding started to dawn on members of the group. There were about fifty people here. There were probably another fifty running around town at that moment trying to gather supplies.

"Get the word out to any people gathering supplies. There will be no stealing. Anybody that doesn't want to help out, that's their business. If we don't know who owns stuff, we leave notes and we pay market value for it. We will work out what to do once things cool off."

"Well, that's my truck over there!" said an older white man, pointing his fingers at a green older model Ford pickup. "And your goons stole it!"

Ed looked at the man. He stepped down and walked over to the man. He turned to the mechanics and nodded once. They tossed him the keys. He turned back to the owner and handed him the keys.

The older man snarled and snatched the keys from Ed's hand. He glowered at Ed. "You buncha thieves!"

"Mister, if anybody knew you were home, they wouldn't have taken the truck. Have you been listening?"

"You can go to hell! I'm taking my truck back, and suing the county and you with them!"

Ed steeled himself and crossed his arms, "Everybody listen up! This is the most important thing I'll say all day. This man here has every right to keep his personal property. You have seen us give his keys back and I apologize for the inconvenience. But, things aren't the same, and they aren't going to be the same, maybe ever. This was a solar event, likely global. That means nobody's coming to the rescue. It's just us. Everybody else has his own issues to deal with. Nobody is coming to help."

Silence greeted his comments. Some nodded. Some shook their heads. Some just stared blankly. A few women shed quiet tears. Two men walked off and did not return. The rest of the group waited. The older man still glowered at Ed.

"So, here's the deal. Anybody wants to help out, great. We've got your back. We need all the help we can get. Lord knows we can't survive this alone. The town is burning down. Crazy people are killing our neighbors. I don't claim to have any answers. But I will not stop working on this until we all get through it." Ed looked from face to face around the group, stopping with the obstreperous old man, still clutching his keys in a white knuckle grip.

"But, if anybody doesn't want to help, so be it. We can't tell you what to do. We only have the resources to get ourselves through this. So if anybody wants out, there's the way out." he pointed to the road. "If you don't want to be a part of the solution, then we aren't going to try and help you when your house burns down, or some psycho kills you. We just don't have enough resources."

"You can't threaten me! I'm a tax-paying citizen. I paid your salary and you have to help me!" The old man shook in rage.

"File a complaint. And no, I don't have to help you. According to Federal and Tennessee state emergency legal code, I can take everything you own, except your, guns, ammo, and reloading equipment. And you can thank the NRA for that one thing. I could take it all, right down to the clothes on your back. Don't believe me, look it up. Unless the library burned down, that is. Oh yeah, I don't think the Internet is going to be up for web surfing anymore either. We don't have to do a damned thing if the public good isn't served by it. And diverting equipment for one lone asshole is not in the priorities now. I won't set up a looting government. Everything taken will be by permission and paid for, if the owner is alive and can be located. It may take forever, but we are keeping records."

Ed looked directly at the man, "Look, we need the help. Last chance to join the crew."

The man spit on the sidewalk.

"Get out," Ed said as the man stormed past him and cranked up his engine and drove down the street and into the smoke of the fires. Ed turned back to the remaining vehicles. "Anybody else own any of these?" No one responded. He looked down the aisle.

A 1948 red Ford F1 pickup appeared to have been newly restored next to the '55 Chevy. Down the line was a black 1966 Chevelle convertible with the top down, and early seventies red Dodge Challenger with faded paint and several dings. It appeared to be a Hemi V8 if his memory served him correctly. Now, they were getting somewhere. Gallatin had a museum with some older cars in it as well, and some of these may have come from there. It's just as well, as the building was now on fire. So, better to use them than lose them, he thought. On the right was a white Chevy truck.

"What's that one," Ed asked, pointing to the right.

"It's a '72 Chevy C10 Cheyenne, a 350," Trey answered, "Drives great, full tank too!"

Next to the automobiles was an assortment of motorcycles, both on and off road styles. Ed walked down the line and read the tags. There was a Kawasaki KD 125, a Suzuki RM 125, an old Husqvarna 250 WR from the seventies, he guessed.

"That's a 1975 Husqvarna, the Hondas are '76 CR 125M and a '74 250 of the same. And that one on the side is a Yamaha Dt 250 from '74," Trey added, pleased with his work so far. "The cars and trucks work, but the bikes we had to push over here. Also, we are gonna have to get fuel for them. I need some guys to get spare gas cans and try to siphon out from the gas stations in town. I might be able to have the bikes ready in a couple of hours, but we gotta find the parts. We also found a bunch of bicycles as well, maybe twenty, mostly mountain bikes."

"Thanks Trey. Good work everybody. We will have to keep strict records of where all of this came from, as the county will have to reimburse everyone who owns this stuff," Ed said. "Let's get those parts going. And somebody get the church to bring over some food and reports of how much we recovered."

He was worried. Worried that they didn't have enough food or potable water. He was worried about the Sumner County EMS. He had heard reports today that they were looting and killing. They must have been infected by this thing. He would have to watch his people. The summer sun beat down on him as he slipped on his Tactical Tailor plate carrier. He had one of the runners retrieve it and his bug out bag from his truck. This was already the longest day in his recorded history, and it was only past lunch.

Three miles from Mackenzie house
Hendersonville, TN
July 3rd
2:14p.m.

The thick hedges on the side of the suburban lane provided good cover for the Corpuz family as they waited, hiding from the threat ahead. Each family member was praying silently as the scene before them unfolded. The death throes of modern society were just beginning, the shock waves spreading out as services failed. There, in front of them was a band of looters, dressed in casual clothes, slinging the homeowner's goods onto their shoulders, walking brazenly out into the street.

The house was a tall, stately mansion, its oak front door and Italian windows smashed in, goods thrown out onto the front yard. The metrosexual appearing owner literally shook in terror at the feet of one of the gang of looters. The pathetic man had blond hair, unkempt and too long for his head, splaying out into his eyes, copying the look of several famous country music stars. His significant other looked equally terrified, her jeans stained with dust, where they had been knocked down. She clung to her man, abject terror in her eyes. The gang continued pulling and throwing out their expensive finery onto the lawn, roaring with laughter.

Carlos had counted five of them in all. They appeared to be armed with an assortment of knives, clubs and machetes. He could see the one looming over the couple had a cheap shotgun held at port arms. The man spit on the woman and kicked the man in the legs hard. He continued to quake. Carlos was getting fed up with watching this.

He had immediately hidden his family at the first sign of the looters running down the street. He had planned on moving on when they became distracted.

But he had seen into the eyes of the men. He saw the woman and she was very attractive. He knew what would happen when the thugs tired of the looting. He could not bear the thought. In Manila, he had been a boy and been forced to watch an unknown girl raped and sodomized while he lay helplessly, a boot on his face, pressing him into the street. He could not shake the memories of that day. He was frankly lucky that the men had not raped him also, and he knew it. He could not let this happen. He could not set this example for his boys.

Carlos prayed the 91st psalm. He had memorized it in his youth from the Revised Standard Version, Catholic Edition of the Bible.

He who dwells in the shelter of the Most High,
who abides in the shadow of the Almighty,
will say to the Lord, "My refuge and my fortress;
my God, in whom I trust."
For he will deliver you from the snare of the fowler
and from the deadly pestilence;
he will cover you with his pinions,
and under his wings you will find refuge;
his faithfulness is a shield and buckler.
You will not fear the terror of the night,
nor the arrow that flies by day,
nor the pestilence that stalks in darkness,
nor the destruction that wastes at noonday.
A thousand may fall at your side,

ten thousand at your right hand;
but it will not come near you.
You will only look with your eyes
and see the recompense of the wicked.
Because you have made the Lord your refuge,
the Most High your habitation,
no evil shall befall you,
no scourge come near your tent.
For he will give his angels charge of you
to guard you in all your ways.
On their hands they will bear you up,
lest you dash your foot against a stone.
You will tread on the lion and the adder,
the young lion and the serpent you will trample under foot.
Because he cleaves to me in love, I will deliver him;
I will protect him, because he knows my name.
When he calls to me, I will answer him;
I will be with him in trouble,
I will rescue him and honor him.
With long life I will satisfy him,
and show him my salvation.

These words gave Carlos a great courage. He had always been a brave man, but he felt the very presence of the Lord on that spot. He knew what he must do. He was wearing full body armor, a helmet and carried the latest high tech carbine and pistol. He was an expert marksman and an outstanding fighter. He was now full of righteous indignation. He had had enough.

He reached over and whispered to his beautiful wife. Cecelia had already been praying for this. She could not stand to watch the inevitable assault. As a woman, she judged her man on his courage. If he could not defend the woman, he did not have a right to be a man. The man cowering on the grass there in front of them disgusted her. How could he let this happen to his family? She prayed for Carlos, prayed for the ministering angels of the Lord to defend him from all harm. She was no fool and she did not want him to die or suffer injury.

Carlos reached into his bag and pulled out his FN SLP Mk1 9 round 12 gauge autoloading shotgun. He quietly charged the weapon and slung it on his shoulder on a single point sling. He quietly instructed his boys to stay put and only fire if the men approached them. Roberto, 14, had the XD 9 Tactical, and Rafael, 16, had the Rock River 16" carbine and XD 40. Cecilia had her Ruger GP100 .357 loaded with .38 Special hollowpoints. The two boys nodded understanding, feeling simultaneous fear for and pride in their father.

Carlos slunk to the side, thirty feet from the family's hiding place. He shouldered his Rock River 20" carbine and centered the green illuminated Mildot Trijicon Accupoint scope on the shotgun wielding guard, the non-electronic fiber optic scope glowing brightly at 3 power. Carlos breathed and slowly pulled the trigger. The surprise break sent the 62 grain light armor piercing, steel tip round through the man's large head. It entered and exited the sides of the man's skull, exploding a three inch hole through his temple. He collapsed like a puppet whose strings had been cut.

Carlos sat and waited, the terrified family now splattered in blood. The man began screaming quite loudly, hyperventilating with each spasm of breath. The woman sat, stunned into silence. Yelling came from the interior of the house. Two men burst out onto the lawn. One had a large machete raised and the other had a Bowie knife. Both were screaming obscenities as they looked down and saw the body of their fellow looter dead in a pool of his own brains and blood, his arms and legs sprawled in impossible angles as he had died before his body had hit the ground.

Carlos sighted the Trijicon green dot rapidly on the chest of the machete wielder and sent three rounds through his unarmored chest. As the man began to fall, blood sprayed out of his chest and down his white shirt. His lungs had ruptured as the rounds penetrated and tumbled through the torso, sending deadly fragments shredding through his pulmonary arteries and aorta.

Before the first man had completed his fall, Carlos had already shifted the rifle onto the torso of the second man. Three more rounds slammed home, rupturing the man's lower heart, exploding the muscle's apex, sending blood pouring out into his mediastinum. The left lung burst as two of the rounds entered through his ribs, shattering the bone inward in a shower of shrapnel-like fragments, adding to the damage caused by the tumbling and disintegrating round. Pieces of copper, lead and hardened light armor piercing steel shredded the man's cardiopulmonary system. He staggered forward, blood now foaming from his mouth, a twisted grin of rage now forming.

The machete man lay crumpled. The Bowie knife wielding maniac charged forward, not seeing Carlos hiding in the bushes, but moving toward the general direction of the fire. Carlos switched to plan B. A rapid double tap rang from his rifle, the two bullets crashing through the calvarium and into the delicate brain matter, exploding outward out of the back of the man's head, yellow and red matter spraying out onto the lawn. The man's head jerked unnaturally back with the frontal impact of the two rounds. He collapsed, his fingers and legs still jerking, foamy saliva starting to emanate from the corners of his mouth.

Carlos had seen the saliva before. His patients in the hospital had this symptom sometimes. Why was this here? Was there infection in the community at large? Did it explain the violence? He had never gotten the definitive samples back from the CDC on the cause of this. The test results were due back this week. None of the initial testing had shown a cause for the plague that seemed to afflict more and more each day. Their hope for an answer lay in Atlanta. Now that the power was out, likely from Angus' solar event, they might never know the answer. Carlos had a horrible thought. Was there a connection between the recent crime wave and the infection?

No time to debate plague forensics now. Carlos set down the AR-15 and grabbed the FN SLP shotgun and raced towards the couple. He looked down at the man and woman. He checked their pulses while watching the front door of the house. The man was now moaning and babbling incoherently. The woman just stared off into space, glassy eyed. Emotional shock. They had both shut down mentally. It was useless to try and reason with them, and they would be totally unpredictable. They could try to attack him as easily as attacking the criminals.

He scampered past the helpless couple and ducked into the house, diving left as the shotgun raised to the right. The hallway was empty. He heard breathing upstairs. He reached onto his vest and snatched off a pepper spray grenade that he has purchased at a police supply warehouse. He pressed the actuator nozzle and held his breath, pointing the spray away from himself, and immediately hurled the canister into the house.

Still holding his breath, he dived back out of the house. Coughing and strangled curses came from the upstairs. A chair crashed out of a second story window, landing on the lawn. Smoke billowed out of the door and windows. A man leaped out, landing badly and twisting his ankle. He had what appeared to be a small hunting rifle, perhaps a .22 semi auto. Carlos swung the shotgun and fired into the man's upper torso, nine pellets of 00 buckshot penetrating and destroying the man's trachea, esophagus, aortic arch and exiting through the upper thoracic spine, transecting the spinal cord partially as the man fell backwards dropping the hunting gun. The man tried to breath and his chest seized in a spasm, fluttered and he gasped out his last breath, blood streaming out of his nose and mouth and the multiple holes in his sternum.

Another man reached out of the window with some type of cloth over his face. Pistol fire rang out as the man shot at Carlos in the lower abdomen. The 9mm hollowpoint round rammed into the lower margin on Carlos' level IV multihit plate and stopped harmlessly in the first 1/4 of ceramic aramid composite. White aluminum oxide powder dribbled out of the small hole in the plate's surface.

Carlos retuned fire, sending three rounds of buckshot into the man's body. The man jerked, cried out and fell out of the window, the pistol arcing out of his grasp. Carlos dived for cover as the pistol impacted the concrete front walkway and discharged the round in its chamber, sending the bullet wide, luckily in the opposite direction from the people on the lawn. The pistol was an older Spanish design, notable only for its cheap construction, lack of safety features and unreliability.

"Cecelia, everybody O.K.?" Carlos called. He worried about stray fire.

"O.K., all O.K." she replied.

Carlos walked over and looked through the house windows. He did not see or hear anything. The pepper spray was drifting out into the yard. The couple still sat there, the man sobbing now like a baby, the woman still in shock. She looked up at him and mouthed a "thank you," before looking back and holding the head of her man in her lap. He remained there, limp and useless in her arms. There was nothing more he could do here. He could not make them want to live. He suspected the same scene would play out a thousand different ways across the world, if this really was the big one as he suspected.

He nodded at the woman and jogged back to the bushes. He hugged Cecelia. His sons looked at him, a mixture of confusion, fear, awe and love on their young faces. They had never seen death before. Unfortunately, this would not be the last time they saw it in this brave new world. Carlos grabbed his pack, secured and stowed the shotgun and changed a fresh mag into the AR. He slung the weapon, grabbed his bike handle bars and set off. His family quickly followed, the gentle breeze lightly blowing the woman's hair as she hugged and rubbed the head of her boyfriend. The Corpuz family moved onward, their goal now almost in sight.

East Goodlettsville, TN
Suburban neighborhood near the Gunn house
July 3rd
2:31p.m.

Gwenn dropped off the store owner at her house. The neighborhood seemed very quiet, like all of the people had left. It was like a ghost town. Doors were open, articles of clothing and goods sprinkled on some yards, the owners clearly trying to escape with some of their belongings. There were no signs of graffiti and no smoke was coming from the houses. The woman waved as she entered the house. A man, presumably her spouse, ran and hugged her, waving his thanks. A hunting rifle was slung on his shoulder as he greeted her.

Gwenn turned out of the neighborhood and started to head up the street when two men jumped out of the bushes and blocked her way. She as going only five miles an hour and started to accelerate at the sign of the threat. The men did not appear to be armed or infected. They started waving her down and the one onto the driver's side jumped out of the way before being hit and the other one grabbed the side of the vehicle on the passenger side and pulled up the ramp.

"Hey, lady! Stop the truck, we need a ride!" The man was white, short with black curly hair and a mustache, about thirty. His forehead had a port wine stain and his breath stank through the window. His eyes were wild with fear and anger as the truck continued accelerating, the rear view mirror revealing the other man running after them, falling behind as the truck reached ten miles an hour.

He reached through the window and started scrabbling at the door catch when Margaret Dill produced her stainless steel Smith and Wesson snub-nosed .38 Special and cocked the hammer down with her left thumb, pointing the muzzle into the face of the man. He froze, arms still inside the cabin.

"Listen here mister! Let go of that door and hop off or I'll peel you off myself" Margaret yelled, her small voice raised in a thundering command, "understand?" her voice quiet and small now, decision etched into her features.

She raised the gun to the man's forehead and he looked into her deep brown eyes, the pupils narrowed the way they do when they see something they don't like. Her irises seemed like a deep well, memories of past pain and loss etched into their depths, steely determination clearly visible. Her finger began squeezing on the trigger, God help the one who ignored this woman's warning. The man jumped without looking, landing and rolling on the grass, the vehicle now at fifteen miles an hour and climbing.

Gwenn shifted gears and glanced over at Margaret. Their eyes met, years of understanding flowing between them in an instant. She reached over and squeezed the tip of Margaret's shoulder. "Thanks."

No reply was needed. Margaret smiled a thin smile and the family continued slowly east down the back road, heading towards the Mackenzie House, their progress slow but steady as they stopped to survey and push vehicles out of the way with the bumper, or veered off the edge of the road to go around abandoned cars. The sun continued blazing down, the Southern Summer heat relieved only by the breeze of the moving vehicle, its lumbering green and brown frame navigating the roadway, like a beetle crawling across the battlefield of some forgotten war.

But it proves more forcibly the necessity of obliging every citizen to be a soldier; this was the case with the Greeks and Romans, and must be that of every free State. Where there is no oppression there will be no pauper hirelings.
—Thomas Jefferson, letter to James Monroe, 1813

CHAPTER 21

Tulley Farm
Five miles north of Gallatin, TN
July 3
4:07p.m.

Lucien Tulley walked into the kitchen. Abigail was cooking dinner on the main kitchen propane stove and the smell was intoxicating. On the floor of the living room was all of the extra gear they had not yet prepped for evac. In case they had to get out of the compound immediately, Lucien had tasked his kids with organization of the gear. Clothes, food and medicine were stacked neatly as Evi and Donovan rapidly organized and stowed gear in Rubbermaid bins, labeling each bin with its contents.

The McKnights were helping in the kitchen and Sean and Sam were on patrol, now imitating bushes on the perimeter of the compound. Doug McKnight was scanning the perimeter with binoculars, checking each boy's position every three minutes, in case they needed to signal silently. Lucien walked back outside, past the small mountain of gear that the McKnights had brought. They easily had ten thousand rounds of ammunition. There were several guns in cases along with electronic equipment. Doug's huge Barrett M82A1 .50BMG rifle dwarfed the other guns. Doug McKnight had already outfitted each Tulley with an FRS or FamilyRadio Service radio. These clipped onto the ballistic carriers. They were settling in to the house well, the children quietly playing near the kitchen.

Lucien looked out over the one acre garden plot, smelling the dark earth and rich organic mulch. Tomatoes, squash, herbs, numerous species of peppers, and gourds dominated the plot at this time of year. Some canning had already been done. They augmented their stored dry beans, rice and wheat with fresh vegetables. Summer was usually a bountiful time on the Tulley Farm.

Lucien prayed his thanksgiving, a bittersweet prayer of love and sorrow. He knew in his heart of hearts that all of this would soon be gone. He did not have the heart to tell his family yet, but he knew that Abigail already had guessed. His screaming, sweating dream last week had awakened her. The children were old enough to understand that all things in life were temporary and that the only constant in the universe was the Creator, the Lord Jesus Christ. All things came and went. All things, good and evil passed away. Only the Lord remained. If you wanted to live forever, you had hope only in Him. His promise endured forever.

Lucien remembered the dream. It had felt so real. He and his family believed very strongly in dreams and visions. In the dream, the number seven kept appearing. Seven men, seven stars in the sky, seven mountains. This was the only reassurance that he had from the terrifying vision. Without that reassurance of God's presence with the holy and prime number, he might have thought that the Lord had abandoned him.

What would become of them? He did not know, for the vision had ceased before revealing his future. He had felt helpless to protect his people. He knew that regardless of whether he died defending his family or lived through the despair, he would be in the hand of the Lord at all times. He knew their very steps would be directed. Go here, move there. Do this, do that. He had always known it would be this way. He had put so much faith and trust in this piece of land. He had sunk roots so deep and accumulated so many preparations that he thought it fitting that the Lord would show him this way instead. Lean not unto my own understanding. He knew the Word. He knew that God made foolish the wisdom of man, and that the foolishness of God was wiser than the greatest wisdom of man.

Nevertheless, terror still abided in his heart, so real was the vision of loss. This beautiful land. Land into which he had poured blood and sweat and tears, would all soon fall to the unclean. He had seen a vision of wave upon wave of destruction. Unclean souls pouring through the fields, crushing the work of the season, defiling the vision of his family's future. He knew that the end of the Age was upon them. The old and the weak crushed under the weight of this biological force. All that he had hated about the corrupt society in which he had refused to participate had gone away, it simply did not know it yet.

The death of the innocents, the slaughter of the lambs was already commencing. The day the Enemy would cover the Earth with his power. He knew it must come; he grieved for the loss. He had faith that the Lord would prevail in the end of all things, that only He could bring about a new creation. His study of the Bible showed him, convinced him that this was not the ultimate end, and that society would yet reform again. What would emerge was unknown, the future cloudy, the mists of uncertainty hung upon the land in his dreams. The angel of death had returned to Earth, and he feared for his family. When the crops were trampled by the unclean, he would know that the time had come. Then he would know; they would all know. The Lord Jesus protect us all.

Farmland near Highway 109
7 miles north of Gallatin
July 3
4:10p.m.

Chloe walked on, trudging through the farmland near the road, trying to stay well away from the road as well as any farmhouses that were nearby. Sam and Pirelli were just a few feet behind her. They hunkered down in a creek bed and Sam took his pack off and filled a canteen, adding iodine tablets to the water. He carefully swirled the iodine water on the threads of the bottle and sealed the canteen. He would be able to drink it in thirty minutes; he would have to guesstimate the time. He pulled out a water bottle from the medical office and drank a huge gulp. He took an empty water bottle from each of the women and repeated the process. He warned them to wait thirty minutes as well.

Their feet hurt and they did not talk about anything else. They shared a small meal of expired single serving breakfast cereals from the clinic and beef jerky that Samuel had in his kit. Sam had already shared some of his gear. He had given each woman a small disposable lighter, good even after the fuel was gone, as the strikers could produce a spark hundreds of times to ignite dry tinder. He had given each a small pocket knife from his truck's tool box. They sat, weary and exhausted, their minds wandering unbidden to the horrific scene that they had witnessed earlier.

They had seen several more houses that were attacked either by the infected government emergency units or by infected plague victims, clearly both driven mad by the illness. They had run from each scene, unable to help as they were unarmed and had no training to fight, save Sam, whose first priority was to defend and protect the girls. He had made a promise to Dr. Gunn, and he planned on keeping it. They were about halfway to home, he figured. Things had cooled off since leaving the city limits, but they could still hear the distant screams of various farm houses suffering whatever form of violence had occurred. The population density was far lower here than in town and he prayed that they could make time, continuing to walk at night. Only time would tell if they had the stamina to continue. They had to reach home: three families depended on them. The fear of what could have befallen them nagged at the minds of the trio. Chloe stood up first. She had granddaughters to find and protect. Sam and Pirelli followed, up the long hill and ridges, steadily climbing closer to the unknown and the loved ones that they prayed would already be safe. The sun moved across the sky, its late afternoon angle casting longer and longer shadows. The dark patches of shadow spread imperceptibly slowly, covering the earth like waves of black void, building and growing, threatening to blot out its dominant species.

Mackenzie House
Hendersonville, TN
July 3
3:03p.m.

Carlos looked up the hill and scanned the perimeter. They had seen no further looting since intervening with the young couple earlier in the day. Carlos saw no activity here. The neighborhood seemed starkly empty in fact, as if all of the living souls had just left. There were signs here and there of burning, looting and violence. Abandoned cars littered the streets, their windshields cracked. Cracked windows could be seen on some houses. Others seemed totally untouched. The pattern seemed completely random.

But there were no people. Carlos wondered at this strange development. He remembered all of the infected patients that he had seen at the clinic and hospital, and he remembered violent episodes at the grocery store and gas station in the last few days. Where were all of the people? He wondered about this. Did they all evacuate or had they all died. Perhaps a combination of the two could explain. His family came rushing up at his hand signal. They had been hiding in the bushes with the bikes and gear. Cecelia pushed both of their bikes and he grabbed the handlebars of his, his two packs weighed evenly across the frame.

They pushed the bikes up the hill to the house. There were no signs of a fight here. Carlos hesitated and then simply knocked on the door. He paused when there was no answer. Carlos looked to the left and he saw a tiny flash of movement in the shadows of the hedges. A barrel shifted imperceptibly to the side and he froze. The barrel covered Carlos' chest. The door cracked open.

"Hopscotch," said a voice behind the door.

"Platinum," replied Carlos, completing the sign-countersign exchange

"All clear, Madison," said Beth Mackenzie, speaking to her daughter while opening the door for the Corpuz family to enter. Beth was 37, a year younger than her husband Matt. She was a local pediatrician and still practiced, despite her three kids. It was very hard to have kids during med school, but somehow she managed. A good Catholic, she followed the church's teachings on the primacy of life. Madison, 16, was still outside, covering the door from her vantage point. Kimberly, 12, was a little fireball, full of fun and love. Sean was 8 and a clone of his father, right down to the silent mode when encountering strangers.

Carlos ushered his family into the house after leaving the bikes and gear in the garage. They walked in to the spacious house and sat on the sofas. Carlos looked at the now useless plasma TV and wondered if things would ever be the same.

"Impressive security," he said, his face tight. He really was impressed. He just didn't like guns pointed at him. Still, for a girl of that age to be mature enough to not panic with strangers near was pretty amazing.

"Thanks, and sorry about that as well," said Beth. "We have been doing that for a few hours, since the neighborhood went nuts."

"Really?"

"Yes. People started wandering around when the power went out. Some really strange stuff. Some people were running down the street. Looked like looters maybe, when a couple of neighbors ran out and just attacked them. Pretty awful stuff. I can't be sure, but I thought one of them was biting another guy. Anyway, we locked up and loaded the guns and have been real low profile since that happened. A lot of people just seemed to walk away. I don't think the neighborhood's actually empty though. I think people are hiding like we are."

"Beth, God bless you for taking us in," Cecelia said, tears welling up in her eyes. She had not been the same since the attack in her home. All of the blood. Everywhere. It would never come out of the carpet. She felt sick at what Carlos had needed to do to keep them safe. Then she had felt even sicker when she thought of what could have happened if he had not been able to protect them. The thought sent shivers down her spine. The memory of seeing the attacker's body in the roadside ditch where Carlos had dragged it would flood back into her head without warning.

They set up a rotation for guarding the perimeter and Cecelia started helping in the kitchen. She planned on getting more of her goods later, if things cooled off some and they got access to working transportation. For now, they prepped some snacks, things that required no cooking as they did not want to give away their occupancy of the house with cooking smells.

Rafael took up a position under cover of some old burlap sacks and junk on the opposite side of the front yard, carefully concealing himself in the material. His position safely flanked Madison's without covering her with his muzzle. They would be able to engage any threat from the front in a three-way crossfire if shooters from the house joined in any skirmish. They could also both cover the rear flanks of the house as well. The center of the backyard was being scanned by Roberto, as he sat under the canopy of the back deck. The back yard was mostly wooded and backed up to more woods that ran for a couple of miles, should they have to egress under cover.

Carlos prayed silently that all of the group members would make it. It was going to be a long night ahead, he feared. The wind gently shifted, slightly easing the still stifling heat. The shadows of the lawn had just started to lengthen. The plants soaked up the sun, their slow, inexorable growth starting to reclaim the land that humans had once dominated, their green fingers reaching to worship the brilliant sun.

Unmarked railroad track
Somewhere in East Nashville
July 3
6:05p.m.

The girls walked slowly on, the heat of the early evening still emanating from the ground. The sun was sliding lower, heading towards the horizon. Smoke drifted from innumerable fires in the distance, in all directions now. They were passing some of the lowest income zones in town now, the region showed slow movement in the distance. All of the activity seemed to be focused on the roadways, out and away from the railroad tracks.

It was as if no one remembered that the tracks existed. They had seen several people nearby; all had their backs turned away from the tracks. Occasionally, gunshots and screams would echo from the distance, sometimes close. The girls had hidden dozens of times, finding cover where they could. There were trash cans, abandoned vehicles, ditches and hedges within the vicinity of the tracks, so they were never very far from potential cover. They moved on, cautious of the way. They wondered what their families were doing. They both worried about their loved ones. They had seen other murders, but all at a much greater distance than that of the events of the early morning. They continued their march north, the earlier gentle breezes giving way to a new calm.

Spence Creek State Park
10 miles Northeast of Gallatin, TN
Rees house
July 3
6:09p.m.

Scott Rees checked his bandage. The wound looked clean now that his wife Stephanie had scrubbed it out with a new toothbrush and iodine. That really hurt like hell, but they didn't have the luxury of gentility when it came to a potential wound infection. He seemed to be tolerating the antibiotic well with no adverse reactions so far with the second dose. He still could not believe that someone had actually bitten him. Seemed like some kind of zombie movie. If it had been a dog, he would really be worried.

He probably shouldn't have worried, though. When he was hired on in his current job, the boss had lost his prior rabies vaccination records. The man was such a jerk that Scott had considered quitting, but Stephanie had reasoned with him. He didn't like the fact that he had to repeat those damned rabies shots, but they had been condensed to only five shots in the arm at least. He did fine, and as usual, his wife had been right.

He replaced the bandage and set back to the gear. They were consolidating their gear in case they needed to bug out. With no communication to the outside, he was frankly concerned. The campsites were becoming less and less friendly as the day had progressed. Also, it looked like Gallatin might be on fire, or at least something was burning in a big way in that direction. If there were a forest fire, they had already set up fall back positions. He worried more about civil disorder, worried about the long term ramifications of a solar event. Damn it if the group hadn't been right. He still couldn't believe it.

At least his vehicle still turned over when he keyed the ignition earlier in the day. The sky blue 1974 International Harvester Scout II had a carbureted 345 V8, and seemed unaffected. At least they could move if they had too. He looked out, and Stephanie was loading the vehicle with gear and extra gas cans. She had her plate carrier vest on and her Colt 6920 carbine slung over her back. He worried what the future would bring. He prayed the violence would be over, even though he knew the request would be in vain. Oh well, he thought. Back to packing.

Unmarked roadway
50 miles or more East of Gallatin
Calvin Family Deuce and a half
July 3
6:10p.m.

The accelerator was pressed to the floor of the aging vehicle, its engine roaring in protest. The occupants holding on and praying, John Calvin braced himself on the wheel as his fourteen-year-old daughter Hailey leaned forward, the dashboard providing some cover as the hail of deafening 5.56mm rounds boomed from her M4 carbine. The vehicle shook and twisted, metal smashing against metal as the roadblock of abandoned vehicles spun sideways in each direction crushing the would be ambushers in its wake.

Hailey nearly dropped her rifle as the massive vehicle rocketed forward against the blockade. She rolled around to the right as she continued her assault on her family's would-be attackers. Round after round boomed until the thirty round magazine emptied. She pressed the magazine release with her right thumb and slammed a fresh mag home, the expended one clattering to the floor of the cab. She dropped the bolt release with her right index finger, as her father had taught her. You always had to be able to work every tool with either hand. She looked back and the assailants were out of sight, gunfire had erupted from the rear of the truck, her mom now engaging the enemy.

The shooting stopped as the fifty mile an hour speed rapidly put distance between them and the threat. Hailey engaged the safety and sat back in the seat. Sweat glistened from her brown skin, her breath coming in waves. She didn't know how many people she had shot, certainly several had gone down. She had been moving so fast that she did not have time to think. It had been either shoot or duck, and she couldn't leave her dad without covering fire. She did not have time to be sick or feel sorry for herself as the family raced towards the safety of their retreat. She felt sad. Very sad. Those assholes would have killed them or worse. She had seen the movies. She knew what happened to girls when things like that happened. I'd kill them all before I let that happen, she thought, tears coming to her eyes unbidden. She removed her glasses and wiped her eyes on her shirt.

Her dad's hand reached over and squeezed her shoulder, "I'm so sorry, baby. I'm so sorry."

Northern edge of downtown
Gallatin, TN
July 3
6:10p.m.

Smoke rose from the now burned out city. Ashes blew across the faces of the men and women gathered on the street. Antique vehicles rumbled quietly, their gas tanks filled by siphon from the now dead pumps of the city's service stations. Edward Douglass clenched his fists, the M1A slung on this shoulder, ready for deployment. He now wore his Multicam tactical shirt and pants, his Tactical Tailor plate carrier rigged with the heavy .308 twenty round magazines. He gritted his teeth, staring down at the sight at his feet.

Time and wisdom had not prepared him for the cosmic injustice that he witnessed now. Rage, anger, hatred, pure righteous indignation boiled beneath the surface of his exterior calm. His mind spun in circles of grief and shock. The horror of the scene challenged his grip on reality, threatening to overturn his sanity. He glanced around the gathered group. Several men and women wept openly. Some vomited. The crumpled, charred bodies lay in a pile, some appeared to still grasp for mercy, their arms held up against the tide of insanity that suffocated them. Their charred remains evoking classical images of the victims of an ancient, deadly volcano, whose victims were unearthed, persevered for eternity in the death throes of their unspeakable agony.

Horror and shock coursed through Edward's veins, sending cold waves of grief and hollow emptiness to the core of his battered soul. Why? He asked the question, knowing that God and nature would not answer. He already knew. The madness that men contained in their minds had been unleashed upon the world. The Earth had come under the spell of horror, its own offspring ravaged by disease, their minds lost to the insanity of the moment.

A great wave of change had begun, a change from order and decency to chaos and unspeakable horror. The spiral downward of humanity was complete. Those who had perpetrated these crimes had sunk to the bottom-most levels of the natural order. The devils that wreaked havoc laughed at the scene that they had created. The swirling turmoil that surrounded this group would overturn all order, all righteousness, if he did not act, and act now. The Republic must stand, it represented all that was good and right and holy about humanity. It represented the ideals of the founders, the very fabric of the society that they had sought to produce. If it fell, there would be nothing left to believe in, nothing left to live for. Nothing left to die for.

People swore at the Earth, kicked the ground, sobbed in agony and cursed God. Their tears mixed with the ashes of the pyre of destruction and their faces blackened with the rage of hopeless despair. Ed looked up to the sky. He prayed a silent prayer for strength. He knew that God was still there. He knew that He would not leave them. No matter what. And now he knew why he had been born.

He stood up, turned and walked down the street towards the salvaged vehicles. The crowd parted and Issac placed a hand on his shoulder. His men stood behind him, rifles slung at the ready. A current of energy thrummed through the crowd. No words were spoken.

Silence hung in the mouths and in the minds of those witnessing the scene. Issac reached his hand out and produced the contents of his pocket. A small, complete edition of the Constitution of the United States of America was in his hand, its worn black leather cover speaking volumes without words. Issac placed it solemnly into the hand of his leader. Edward took the vital document and closed his fingers upon it. Tears streamed from his eyes as he silently bore witness to the rebirth of the dream.

The dead bodies behind Edward lay where they had been slaughtered. Small framed skeletons of women and children still with their feet and legs spread apart, where the gruesome deeds had been committed before or after their murder. The larger bodies of men crumpled where they fell, crawling towards the smaller, weaker ones, clearly trying to save them from their agony, their arms reaching and clawing towards the innocent. The bodies bore witness to a horror unspeakable.

Ed looked up at the crowd, silent, his heart now filling his chest with a desperate hope. He looked over at a child, held by his mother and something in his mind snapped. Some invisible switch clicked on, his fear and despair gone. He stared into the sky and cried out, the black book in his right hand. He yelled at the top of his lungs.

"Lord! Hear us on this day!"

The crowd paused and stared, transfixed on the man in front of them. Their hearts and minds scrambling towards hope, they listened intently. The horror of the day had shocked most into a stupor of depression. Edward's cry seemed to blast away the fog of despair.

"Lord hear us and give us strength to love and serve you! We give you thanks for this day. And ask for your help in restoring this nation that you allowed to grow. We ask for your protection in this endeavor and as we seek to bring to justice all of those who are responsible for this horror at our feet. We thank you in the name of your Son, our Lord, Jesus Christ. Amen"

The amen rippled thought the crowd. Ed looked back at Issac. The bond was formed. The course set. The Document would rise again, rise to the heart of the society that it had been meant for. It had been born out of the ashes the first time, and it would be reborn this time out of the ashes again. This time, they would succeed. But for now, justice must be served, and the debt of horror must be repaid.

For night's swift dragons cut the clouds full fast,
And yonder shines Aurora's harbinger;
At whose approach, ghosts, wandering here and there,
Troop home to churchyards: damned spirits all,
That in crossways and floods have burial,
Already to their wormy beds are gone.
—William Shakespeare. <u>A Midsummer Night's Dream.</u> 3.2.379-384

CHAPTER 22

Mackenzie House
Hendersonville, TN
July 3
6:09p.m.

The large camouflaged vehicle came to a stop in front of the house. Gwenn jammed in the parking brake and dropped nimbly to the pavement, her rifle at her right hand. She was joined by the rest of the family who hopped out of the other side. The house looked empty. So did the neighborhood. Bizarre. She thought about the number of people that they had been forced to avoid on the way here. She didn't understand how the neighborhood could appear vacant.

She walked to the front door and paused. She looked to the left and right. She had good peripheral vision, though like her husband, she needed reading glasses. She saw the tiniest movement and paused, raising her left fist in the air. Margaret Gunn started to walk forward when Joshua pulled her arm violently.

"Grandmother! That means FREEZE!" he said, terror on his Asian face.

They both froze and Gwenn slowly clicked the emergency release buckle on her sling with the left hand and slowly lowered the rifle on the ground. She still had her pistol in a cross draw holster, but pulling it out to set on the ground would involve, well, pulling it out. That was out of the question. She had seen the muzzle tips move on the left and right.

Margaret Gunn followed suit and placed the revolver on the ground. She had kept it in her lap in a nylon padded belt holster. Since she wore no belt, it was what she had to keep in her purse. All three froze then. The front door opened. Beth Mackenzie peered out from the door edge, AR-15 in hand, muzzle just out of the door, pointed at the ground.

"All clear. I know them. They must not know the sign," she said to the guards. Both teenagers lowered their rifles, but remained concealed.

"Roger, all clear."

"Roger, all clear."

Both replies we're clear, but not very loud. Anyone out of the immediate vicinity would still not be aware of their presence, which was the idea. Beth opened the door and set the AR to the side.

"Gwenn, you scared the hell out of me. I thought you knew the password."

"Sorry, missed that one," said Gwenn, picking up the rifle and re-slinging it after connecting the release buckle. Margaret and Joshua followed. They walked into the house and Carlos and Cecelia greeted them all in turn. Cecelia offered cold snacks and the group took cold cuts and cheese slices greedily. There had been no lunch on this chaotic day. Gwenn trotted back to the truck and grabbed her pack and returned to the house.

"I want to try Angus on the Ham handitalkie," she said. "Can I go to an east facing upstairs room? I need to use my antenna." She produced a small folding high gain directional antenna just like the one Angus used.

"Sure, what is that thing?" asked Beth, looking over the radio.

"Ham radio, 2 meter handitalkie rig with a directional high gain antenna. It's used for longer range if you know where your contact is roughly located. It boosts the directionality of the signal within a given power range. Should get me 15 miles if we both use the rigs the same way, more if I can get higher up."

Beth led Gwenn to an upstairs bedroom and she tried the radio. There was no reply. She waited five minutes and tried again. She kept trying for twenty minutes, every five minutes.

Several miles from Mackenzie House
East edge of Hendersonville, TN
Roadside ditch
July 3
6:32p.m.

Angus and Matt took a breather, resting in the ditch. They drank from their Camelback hydration systems and snacked on granola bars from their packs. They had slipped off their packs and were truly exhausted from their escape and evasion so far. They seemed to have cleared out of the AO or area of operations of the crazed emergency services group, but they couldn't be sure. Angus took out his Yaesu handitalkie and consulted his map and the sky to get a rough west direction. He would have to aim the antenna at the general direction of the target to get a signal through. He didn't know where Gwenn might be, but everywhere from the Gunn house to the Mackenzie house was roughly west of their position. He turned on the radio, the station pre-programmed to the same frequency that they had used earlier.

"...ima, lima. Say again, lima, lima, lima. Over."

Angus waited for the break in the traffic, immediately recognizing the coded report. Normally, Ham radio operators could lose their license by using a code message. These were not normal times. Angus recognized his wife's voice and his heart leapt with hope, "Roger last. How copy?"

"Oh thank God! I mean, five by five! Are you O.K.? Where are you? Over," replied Gwenn, also recognizing Angus' voice as well.

"I'm fine, Matt is with me and we are just into Hendersonville, south of Long Hollow. Over."

"We are at Matt's house now. Joshua, Margaret and I. We ran into trouble, as well. Over."

"Roger that. We won't be to your location for a few hours. Over."

"We can't wait to get Kate," Gwenn said, emotion overcoming her voice. "Carlos is here with his family, I will have them come with us, over."

Angus thought about that. Carlos was one of the most capable members of the group. And he was loyal to a fault. He trusted his own life to Carlos, certainly he would trust his family's life to him.

"Roger that. Take Carlos and go. Go now, right now. Don't wait. You have the support you need. For God's sake, be careful. I love you. Over."

"Roger that." Gwenn felt a swirl of complex emotions. Fear over her daughter's and husband's safety. Fear of leaving Joshua. Fear of the whole world. Anger that this had all happened. Anger that society had done nothing to prepare. Sadness at what she had already seen in just one day. But that day was not over. Not by a long shot. "I love you too. Get here safely. We will be back at some point, I don't know when. Over."

"Talk to you soon. I love you. Out."

"Yes, soon. I love you!" Emotion choked her voice as she spoke. She controlled it. "Out."

Angus stared into space. His whole world had turned upside down in one day. He prayed for strength and safety. They would all need it. Matt slapped him on the back and they stood and surveyed the area through the cover of the bushes. It was clear. They walked carefully, rifles at the ready for the last stretch to the goal. The sun crept farther down. In the sky, clouds lazily drifted, oblivious to the turmoil and horror that lay below. The world of man was changing forever, and the Earth continued to turn, onward and onward.

Mackenzie House
Hendersonville, TN
July 3
6:45p.m.

The cantering horses neighed as they approached the house. Justin rode the first one in the group and his sunglasses glinted in the low angle of the light of the fading sun. He stopped at the front of the house near the street. Darryl pulled up behind slowly and quietly turned off the ignition of the diesel Ford truck. He hopped out and walked up to the horses and grabbed the reins of the lead horse and nodded at Justin, who dismounted and walked calmly to the front door. He knocked on the door, his rifle slung over his back on its two point sling.

The door opened a crack and Darryl could barely hear words exchanged. The door opened and arms came out to shake hands and hug him. There was a relaxing of tension that Darryl could feel, when he suddenly recognized the dim outline of part of two people flanking the house in the bushes. Damn, he thought. He didn't catch them at first. He wasn't thinking about guards, stupid of him. They had the drop on both him and Justin the whole time. Gotta pay attention! Glad Justin knew the password.

He looked up and two people came out and greeted him, a medium build Filipino woman and a young Filipino teen. They introduced themselves and took the horses by the leads and headed around the house to the back, presumably to toe them off. Apparently, doctors taught their families how to ride. He was impressed so far. He had met most of the group members, but not the family members. He was welcomed into the house and offered a cold MRE, which he gladly accepted, sitting down at the table to eat. The people in the house had been putting up black plastic sheeting on the windows, presumably to black out the windows. That made sense, given the smoking cars and signs of disturbance in the neighborhood.

It turned out that a group had just left to try and retrieve Tessa and Kate. Everyone seemed to think they had some chance of success. He mulled over the information. He wouldn't likely be able to catch up to them, it was getting near dark and if they did not return with his daughter, they would have to try in the morning. He would just have to accept it and move on. He silently said grace over the meal and tore open the Meal, Ready to Eat. He tore the pound cake pouch open and bit into the delicious foodstuff. The pasta primavera would make a great second course.

Bank parking lot
East end of Goodlettsville, TN
July 3
7:45p.m.

Rocket fire coursed through the sky in the distance, the heat of their explosions barely perceptible at this distance, the red plumes of their impact sprawling against the horizon. Automatic weapons fire chattered from the freeway ahead. The entire Long Hollow Pike exit of I-65 has dissolved into a war zone. Skittering rounds impacted vehicles, smashing glass and shredding metal. The blooping sounds of the 40mm M-203 grenade launchers from the north followed by explosions to the south. Somewhere, a large 50 BMG erupted, boom, boom, boom, boom.

From the south side of the freeway, a large group of perhaps two hundred people were holding the roadway, using the abandoned vehicles as cover, their own motorcycles and aging trucks and vans emblazoned with gang symbols. Automatic and semiautomatic fire erupted from their side as well. Another pair of 50 BMG rifles boomed northward from the biker's position.

The north side of the freeway was crawling with forest camo and desert tan military vehicles, mostly Humvees and utility trucks, some even the older Deuce and a half models. The turret gunner of a Humvee slumped behind his gun, blood spattering the men in the vehicle. Another man jumped up to take the dead soldier's place. They were too far away to hear the inevitable screams of agony and pain that would punctuate such a scene. They could clearly see the gunfire and smoke rising from more of the vehicles.

A black motorcycle exploded, the wheels and engine launching into the air, tearing apart the man hiding behind it, his limbs rocketing outward in several directions. Small arms fire crackled, sending an electrical intensity through the air. Suddenly a Humvee exploded from the bottom, the vehicle rocking upward and a bucking dance of death, it's hull cracked in half with the massive explosion. Clearly, someone had mined the roadway. More and more bikers drove up in their older Harley's and ancient trucks. The military contingent was outnumbered.

Gwenn saw movement from the back of one deuce and a half and the rear canvas flap opened and two men came out carrying a large shoulder fired rocket. She did not recognize the Dragon rocket system, but Carlos certainly did. It had enough range to reach well beyond their position here at the bank. He blinked once and looked at Gwenn. She understood the look, it conveyed all of the information she needed without words. They could not pass that way, and it had now become unsafe. Because Hickory Lake was south of their position and ran east to west for miles in each direction, there was no direct route south to the archery store. They would have to try another way, threading through the city of Madison, a network of suburban and urban neighborhoods between Goodlettsville and downtown Nashville.

The small team climbed back into the deuce and a half and Gwenn revved the engine and backed away behind the bank, where the large vehicle could not be seen. She really did not want that rocket in the tailpipe. It had all gone to hell. Tears now streamed down her cheeks as the three headed back, Carlos in the front and his teenage son Rafael in the back, watching their six. He had a clear view of the carnage as they sped as fast as the beast could lumber down the road, away from the newly formed combat zone. A huge contrail of rocket fire shot from north to south and a van exploded, sending streamers of flame in every direction. The fighting was still raging, as they veered over the hill, losing sight of the battle as the hills enveloped them, protecting them from errant fire. Gwenn prayed a silent prayer, as the diesel beast rumbled onward.

They worked their way back down the road and took a side road, veering south to try another way around the fighting. They drove through two neighborhoods and a golf course, taking short cuts that Gwen knew well. As they worked their way through the golf course, the team looked over to the right and saw several people walking slowly through the grass. Smoke billowed from several of the expensive houses lining the fairways. Car windows were smashed and many of the front doors of the homes were bashed in. Some bodies were sprawled out on the front lawns.

They turned onto another road and started back towards Madison, with the idea of navigating the neighborhoods and back roads that led to Nashville over ten to fifteen miles or so. This would be extremely dangerous as the population density only grew in that direction. The lower rent districts south of Madison into north Nashville were never the safest regions in normal times. Gwenn shuddered to think about them now, when even the exclusive golf course houses had seen such violence today. They rumbled on out of the neighborhood and into a commercial district, nearing a freeway underpass. The vehicle skidded to an abrupt stop.

Carlos looked ahead, his furrowed brow and steely eyes staring at the very face of chaos. Smoke drifted across a scene of complete disruption. The sun crawled low and was blocked by the freeway overpass, casting a dark shadow of gloom over the scene. Vehicles were jammed together in an impossible network of confusion. Windows shattered, hoods smashed, tires burning, the road block of dozens of vehicles was unnavigable. Stretching as far as the eye could see, the road and underpass of the freeway were completed jammed. There was no way around the network of abandoned vehicles.

Movement caught Gwenn's eye as she looked past the smoke and wrecked vehicles clogging the only other southern artery out of town. People were walking their way. The tattered clothes and ragged look of the group did nothing to calm her as she glanced at Carlos. He flicked the safety of his AR-15 off and slowed his breathing. Shit, thought Gwenn. She put the large truck in reverse and started backwards, looking for a place to turn around. The cars in the road and to the sides were blocking her way.

The noise from the big engine caused more people to look up from their rambling walking. Several people stopped rummaging through the broken car windows and stared at the large truck and its occupants, their glazed eyes and drool-covered chins sent waves of terror through Gwenn, as she slammed the large vehicle into a small white sedan, crushing the tiny two door car's hood, as she attempted to turn the beast around. The noise attracted more attention. Several people in front of the crowd started moving towards them.

Shit, shit, shit! Gwenn's mind raced as the scene started to unfold before her. Four men started an all-out run towards the truck as Gwen slammed on the gas, the truck retreating as fast as it could. She was trying to get the rear of the vehicle past the T junction, where she could go forward and right again to escape the scene. Carlos spoke softly in Tagalog, whispering a prayer to the Virgin for her help, and thanking the Lord Jesus for this life to which he had been witness. He prayed for Rafael's safety as well.

"Rafael, get ready!" he yelled loudly to his son in the back, "They are coming! Stay calm and shoot anyone that moves! They are all infected. You are strong!"

A pause and then Rafael answered, "Yes Sir! I won't let them past!"

"Do not get out or go near the back! Only shoot them if they come near, we cannot stop, understand?!"

"Yes, Father!"

Carlos cursed the bastards that made this disease or let it out. My son's innocence is robbed from him today. Lord help him. He thought to himself as he prayed on in his native tongue. The first of the wave of attackers were now fifty feet away. Carlos breathed in and out halfway. The optic was leveled. A steady squeeze. The rifle bucked and rang out, a headshot dropping the first. Another headshot dropped the second. He missed the third headshot and emptied four rounds into its upper torso. The fourth was ten feet away, preparing to leap onto the truck when three rounds tore its face and neck apart, sending it skittering to the pavement.

The truck rumbled backwards as ten more of the horde neared their position. Twenty to thirty more were only fifty feet behind them, all now breaking into a run. Rafael could not shoot that fast from the back. Carlos looked at Gwenn, now reaching the T junction, preparing to put the truck in forward gear and turn right to escape. They needed time.

"Don't stop, no matter what. I'll catch the back gate," Carlos said in his thick Filipino accent, grabbing the door handle as he prepared to jump.

"NO!" shouted Gwenn.

"DO IT!" Carlos yelled uncharacteristically.

He leaped from the cab as he dropped the half empty 30 round magazine from the gun, and slammed in a fresh mag, this time a 100 round Surefire high capacity. You could not go prone with this magazine, it was too long. But for standing and fighting, nothing beat it for reliable, high capacity fire.

Gwenn slammed on the brakes and jammed the truck into gear as Carlos rounded the side behind. Gwenn could not make out the words, but Carlos was shouting commands at Rafael, probably so his son would not shoot him in the confusion. Rapid fire rang out. Gwenn had never heard a semi auto rifle fire that fast. Three rounds per second rang out from the 20 inch barreled Rock River Designated Marksman Rifle. Carlos was taking full advantage of the Trijicon Accupoint 3-9 power green illuminated Mildot optic. He had set the power at 3x to transition rapidly at closer range. He was putting three rounds into each attacker's upper torso, sometimes having to use six shots for each. The bodies began to litter the ground twenty yards away, the oncoming infected tripping and stumbling over the fallen.

Rafael was returning fire as well, more slowly and missing more, but still connecting with several and helping halt the advance. Gwenn slammed on the gas and saw the wave of oncoming attackers falter. The truck was reaching five miles and hour as Carlos leaped back and placed the rifle on safe, clambering into the truck bed.

"Go! I'm in!" Carlos screamed out. "GO, GO, GO!"

Gwenn jammed the truck into second gear as the mass of infected still pursued but began to fall back. More shots rang out as a few of the faster runners fell to the well-aimed fire of father and son. They turned the corner back into the golf course, skidding a tire as Gwenn took the corner too fast. She slowed slightly. She did not want to turn this beast over on its side. Then she jammed the pedal back down again on the straightway. She breathed more slowly as the scene of the violence faded from view. They were silent as the distance went by, Gwenn threading her way back the way they had come. After a mile or so, Carlos yelled for her to stop and he climbed back up front as she did.

They did not talk as they headed back to the Mackenzie house. The reason for the neighbors' absence from their homes slowly began to dawn on both of them. This wandering mass of violent, irrational, infected humanity appeared to be composed of those infected who had vacated their houses when the power went out. They would have to warn everyone. If a group like that were to attack a house....

Foothills of the Cumberland Plateau
Private forested road
Group property
July 3
8:01p.m.

John Calvin crawled forward on his elbows, binoculars in hand. He had been scanning the area after they had hidden the Deuce. The tire tracks and cut lock on the gate indicated obviously that intruders had entered the compound. He was wearing a ghillie suit and appeared to be a small, slowly moving bush to anyone nearer than about fifty yards. Beyond that, he was utterly invisible. In the dying light, the effect was even more pronounced.

He peered through the optics at the two older model trucks that now sat in front of the group's private property. His blood boiled. The group had spent thousands of dollars purchasing the property in trust and thousands more equipping it with over a year's supply of food and water, medicine and ammunition for everyone and their extended families. And now, some assholes had decided to help themselves. Somebody had obviously gotten wind of the house and its contents. John wondered how much they actually knew about the compound.

The compound was equipped with state of the art intrusion defenses including a smoke fogging machine that could generate an enormous plume of instant fog that would fill the house on remote command, forcing all of the occupants out. If that failed, there was even a backup system, made by the same company that dispensed pepper spray into the house's duct work, fogging that compound with pepper gas in a matter of a minute or so. Unfortunately for John, they all would have been fried with the solar flare. He was stuck figuring this out without the high tech defense systems. This would be a tricky night, and a long one at that.

Over the course of an hour, he noted the number of intruders, their weaponry and habits, their locations and movement patterns, and then he slunk backwards towards his waiting family. This would be a hard thing to do, but the alternatives were starvation and death. It had to be done. And besides, he was really pissed off now. And it was a bad idea to get John Calvin pissed off.

Mackenzie House
Hendersonville, TN
July 3
8:32p.m.

Rafael grinned as Angus and Gwenn Gunn hugged and kissed each other as they headed out to the watch positions in front. Matt and Angus had arrived a few minutes ago and each man had been very glad to see his spouse alive and well. The lights were very dim, covers of thick plastic and cloth were on each window. Candles burned in lieu of brighter lights. The outside guards had been rotated and the teenagers sat quietly and ate cold MREs, looking somewhat shell-shocked after the events of the day. They had been in school and leading normal lives before today, and now everything had changed. Many of them had killed people today, something no one else in the group other than Matt had any prior experience with in the past.

Carlos frowned when he saw the Israeli bandage on Matt's upper shoulder. He gloved up, removed the bandage and surveyed the wound, as Matt sat silently on his kitchen stool. Beth grimaced and left the room, tears starting in her eyes when she saw the wound and the stony expression of fatalism in her husband's eyes. She knew it really had hit the fan now. He could have been killed and the look reinforced that message without words. Carlos spent the next thirty minutes debriding and cleaning the wound. It would be left open as there was really no tissue left to approximate together. The furrow had simply been gouged though the skin and upper muscle layer by the bullet. He applied a sterile alginate dressing to the wound that could be left on for 24 hours between changes. It was a waterproof moist wound healing technique now favored by the wound care specialists. Wounds treated this way healed twice as fast as prior dry techniques, with less risk of infection, basically sealing off the wound from the outside world and providing a moist environment to allow for cell growth and repair. With care, it would heal in two weeks and Matt would do physical therapy and exercise the arm to prevent muscle atrophy. Carlos started Matt on Keflex four times a day. They had thousands of capsules and had even planned for the contingency of eventually running out of them as a close substitute could be made from cheese mold in the future, if needed.

The group had been blessed to lead safe lives. They all trained with weapons, but they all prayed never to have to use them. Most had been lucky enough never to have had to kill before. This day had been a complete shock to most. Some, like the Gunns had been home when it all went down, as they were home schooled. The Corpuz children had had the day off as their father had taken them out to simply enjoy the day with them. He tried to do that every few months. He did not want them to feel that he didn't love them.

Madison Mackenzie had simply walked home when the lights went out. Her school was only three miles away and she got home in an hour, after the power went out. She and her mom had been able to set up the house to defend it, like her dad had showed them. At school, the teacher had tried to maintain order, but Madison knew it was hopeless, and just walked away right in front of her, while the teacher screamed at her. The others had stared in shock. Madison walked to her sister Kimberly's classroom and the two headed home. It was pure luck that Sean had felt a mild sore throat and had been home resting this morning.

No one else at the school seemed to grasp the reality that it was over. It was all over. She kept thinking about social media, and the utter futility of it all. She had been tired of it, even at fourteen. It had all seemed so stupid. She had always been a bookworm by habit, and she preferred the company of a good book to some of the idiots in class. Now she was eating military food, her AR-15 slung on her back, staring at the two Corpuz boys. She had overheard that Rafael had shot at some people, but he was not talking about it. He seemed to take it in stride for now.

Justin had set up a watch schedule, every two hours there was shift change, two at the front and one at the back. That way, no one was as likely to fall asleep. The crew settled in for the night. It had been decided to try and get Kate and Tessa out in the morning. Justin flung his sleeping bag out in the spare room, on the guest bed. The Gunns and Carlos had taken the first watch. They all had been too keyed-up to sleep anyway. The teenagers would take the next shift at 12:30 and then he, Darryl and Beth Mackenzie would take the next shift after that at 2:30. Then, Matt and Angus would cover the front from the emplacements, and Margaret Dill would cover the back from the porch seat from 4:30 to 8:00a.m., or longer, until the teenagers could start the day shifts of six hours each at 8:00a.m. The Gunns and Carlos or Beth could cover from 2:00 to 8:00p.m. And then the cycle could repeat, unless they evacuated, if the Gunns had not returned, or in the event of another emergency.

In the morning, Darryl and he would set out on horseback to get the girls. They would travel near the railroad track in hopes of avoiding the groups of looters and infected now apparently roaming the area. The Gunns would try another longer route by truck at the same time, hoping that the horde would have moved on to another location. He prayed for pleasant dreams. He prayed for safety. And he prayed for the families here, that their mission would succeed and that no more suffering would befall them. He lay down on top of the bag as it was very warm in the room, and he closed his eyes, thankful for his health and safety. Tomorrow would be its own day, with its own challenges, and he was glad that, for him, this day was over now.

I have seen the movement of the sinews of the sky, And the blood coursing in the veins of the moon.
—Allama Iqbal, "Secrets of the Self"

CHAPTER 23

Somewhere North of Old Hickory Boulevard
Northbound Rail Line
Madison, TN
July 3
9:07p.m.

The brush and wooded lot on the edge of the railroad track gave good cover for the pair of girls. They were exhausted after sneaking along all day escaping and evading. They had worked their way up the edge of the Cumberland River after witnessing the looting and murder earlier in the day. The horror of the event still haunted them. They had walked right though the edges of several people's yards in order to get to the train tracks. Tessa and Kate figured that the line would be mostly forgotten and abandoned. There were no trains on it that they had seen so far, and the people that they had seen were all looking towards the road, never at the tracks. It was the easiest way to cross through this dangerous area.

They had hidden several times as groups of people wandered by them. Sounds of violence and looting had filled the air and several of the places where roads came near the tracks had been very tense moments. They would sometimes just freeze and wait for the movement and noise to subside. A couple of times, they crawled or ran by open sections easily visible from the road. They usually just walked at a moderate pace, saving their energy should they have to suddenly run or fight.

They had seen several wooded areas and thought that they could bed down in one of them. When it grew dark an hour ago, they kept walking on for a while and this helped get them through some of the more open areas that lacked cover. They were bone tired now. They had set out a cold camp and had eaten some MRE meals from Kate's bug home bag. They still had plenty of water and could get more when they needed it. Kate had insisted that they fill their water bottles completely before they left the river's edge.

Kate had used a handkerchief as a pre-filter and used her Katadyn water purifier as the water could have been contaminated with industrial runoff and the activated carbon filter would help eliminate many of the toxic compounds that could harm them, in addition to filtering any harmful microbes in the water. Ten minutes of pumping filled their water bladders and another five minutes gave them an extra liter to drink each and they downed that and refilled on the spot again. They each still had over three liters of purified water, in addition to their full bellies. Keeping hydrated was important to Kate as she, like her father, got a headache if she became dehydrated. The summer heat lingered in the dark bower.

They did not speak, except in a low voice directly into each other's cupped ears. They did not want anyone else to hear them. When they had finished eating, it was past 9:30. They did not know the exact time, but they figured it was one to two hours after sunset. Tessa agreed when Kate suggested they bed down for the night when they could still see without flashlights. They went some yards away and cleaned themselves with Hoo Ahhs tactical large body sized wet wipes. They required no soap or water and were effective to prevent skin disease. Both of their fathers had used these in the Air Force and both girls understood that you had to keep a modicum of cleanliness to prevent disease.

They returned to their site and spread out their olive drab sleeping pads and sleeping bags, also in muted colors. It was too hot to sleep in them, but they used them as extra padding and slept on top of them. Kate pulled over the large two person ghillie blanket after dragging it a few feet through the nearby ground to collect dirt, leaf litter and twigs from the natural site. She pulled the mesh and burlap blanket over them, creating a highly effective concealment for their position. They both whispered near silent prayers and squeezed each other's hands and fell asleep. Tessa was a light sleeper, and frankly, they were both too tired to stand watch without falling asleep anyway. The ghillie blanket would have to suffice to conceal their position.

Foothills of the Cumberland Plateau
Private forested road
Group property
July 4
1:09a.m.

The sound of the pin being pulled out of the smoke grenade could have warned the trespassers had they not already drunk themselves into a stupor. The best John could tell, five of them in two older trucks had taken up residence in the house. He was crouched under a window, waiting to toss the canister into the dwelling. There were metal shutters on the windows, but the men that took the place over either did not know about them, or did not care. They had left all of the windows open as it was a hot day and the night only slightly less so. The combination of a hot day, likely dehydration, deconditioning and the beer and drugs had allowed the group to sink into a deep sleep. John peeked over the edge of the window.

Beer and liquor bottles littered the floor. Marijuana pipes and drug paraphernalia also were visible. Food wrappers were strewn about the place and pornographic magazines were stacked next to one of the beds. The porn. God, why did you have to show me that? John prayed silently for God to purge the memory from him as his mind brought the images unbidden into his thoughts. His hands shook and his brow beaded with sweat. He felt that he would vomit. He would have to destroy it before his family could see.

When he had begun recon for the night op, he had entered the trucks to disable the vehicles in case the men tried to use them. He had planned on simply disabling them and sending the interlopers away at gunpoint, alive but frightened enough never to return. What he found on the front seat would change his mind forever. He had been around the world with the military and had seen things that truly disturbed him. But he had never seen this.

The images of the photos in the crumpled brown paper bag were not those from a commercial magazine or other mass produced smut. No. These were personally produced, Polaroid images and color paper printouts from a home photo printer. John felt the bile in his throat and had to force the vomit back down before he lost control. The children, both boys and girls, were young, perhaps seven to ten. Rage filled John's mind, threatening to overwhelm his control. Their faces spoke of fear, pain, horror and shame. Ropes held them fast as the unspeakable was committed, the images forever frozen in time, their agony and grief crying out for vengeance. He had returned to his family to plan the op. He told Denise that they all must die. His look made her realize that she did not want to ask why.

He tossed the canister into the room. He raced to another window and tossed in a second canister. Smoke began to billow out from the house as coughs and tumbling movement could be heard. John tucked himself tightly against the wall, hidden under a small shrub. Yells and more noise now echoed from the house. A large, overweight pale figure bounded out of the house, cursing as he ran, wearing only shorts and one sock. His beer gut hung low over his pants and John could smell the body odor from twenty feet away. A pump shotgun was in his right hand.

He stopped and turned around, peering into the darkness, unable to see John. Another man burst out of the house and stopped where the first was standing. The second man wore a pair of blue jeans and a long sleeved shirt, with the arms rolled up. John could not tell the color in the dim light.

"Goddamned place is on fire!"

"Fuckin-A! Piece o' shit old house. I told you we shoulda picked somewhere nice. This old, shitty barn, fuckin-A man!"

The conversation went on for a few more seconds as the remaining three other men came out of the house. One of them yelled loudly, tossing the still smoking, burning hot smoke grenade out onto the yard.

"Dumbass mother fuckers! Somebody's out there you fucks!" the man said, a scowl crossing his sharp Latino features. The evil grin spoke volumes without a word. He must be the gang leader. Everyone else looked sheepish and began scanning around the yard. One had a Coleman lantern, its yellow glow now illuminating the scene.

"Look around, find the piece of shit that did this," the leader said."LISTEN HERE MOTHER FUCKER! YOU BETTER RUN, CAUSE WHEN WE FIND YOU, WE'RE GONNA FU.."

The man's speech stopped abruptly, his breath now gurgling out in spasms. A dark liquid poured from his mouth and a hole in the center of his chest. He collapsed. Another man started to yell and began screaming in raspy tones, unable to draw breath, this time the mild clap of the suppressed .308 round heard over the quiet. It had been fully masked by the leaders yelling beforehand.

The group stood there, still not understanding what had just happened. It began to dawn on the remaining three as the second man collapsed in a heap. They started to dive for cover when John fired his 12 gauge Mossberg at the closest one, the buckshot blowing the man's head into small pieces, his limp body dropping like a marionette with its strings cut. The last two men began screaming and running for the trucks, firing their guns wildly in every direction. John dived for cover, thankful that his family was over one hundred yards away, behind the embankment of the observation post.

When they bought the property in trust, the group had dug a trench high on an overlooking hill and roofed it with beams of pressure treated lumber before covering it with waterproofing layers of bentonite and plastic. Vegetation and sod were placed over it and the inside floor was lined with gravel and there was a long bench built in it. The front had a removable hatch and the inside was stocked with MREs, water, ammunition and a Savage model 10 FCP-SR, designated "silencer ready," as it had a factory threaded barrel. A Gemtech suppressor and Leupold Mk 4 scope rounded out the package. Denise and the children were inside what was effectively a military style shooting blind, protected by several feet of thick earth and which was totally invisible in the dark. The intruders on the ground would not even know from which direction Denise's shots had come.

The first man to reach the truck opened the driver's side door and was instantly shot through the abdomen by the tripwire shotgun that John had rigged in the seat. John had placed a sandbag mount with a simple double barrel shotgun and trip wire connecting the trigger to the door handle. The unbraced recoil had blown the gun back through the cabin of the vehicle and cracked the stock, ruining the gun. John had found the gun in the bed of the truck and had the idea when he found a large roll of tripwire in the other truck.

The man collapsed and began moaning loudly, his pitiful cries a stark contrast to the vulgar promise of violence that his gang leader had just uttered. The last man saw his friend go down and began to run down the road leading out of the compound, abandoning the other vehicle. John could not let him escape. He would likely bring more friends back to attack them in their sleep. The man had chosen this life of crime, and had stolen someone else's house and belongings. He had made his decision.

John swung the shotgun around on his back using its two point sling. He pulled his AR 15 out of its Eberlestock backpack scabbard. The Aimpoint optic was useless since the solar flare and he had since removed it from the gun. What still worked perfectly were the Trijicon green tritium night sights he had previously installed as backups to the red dot. As they said in the military, "two is one and one is none." He always had a backup to everything if possible.

The man was seventy five yards away and running all out straight away. He did not think to weave from side to side. John took a kneeling stance and prayed a prayer for forgiveness and shot the man through the back. The man tumbled forward and disappeared from sight in the grass. John would have to finish them. He stood quietly and signaled Denise to prevent the children from seeing what had to be done. Wails of agony were coming from the gutshot man by the truck.

John walked quietly, silent tears of anger, tears of shame running from his eyes. Eyes that had already seen enough horror, Lord why must they see more again? He walked to the man by the car. The obese white man spit on John's shoe and snarled an unintelligible word. The shot rang out, the bullet piercing his skull and mercifully ending his agony. The body slumped down, arms spread out to the sides. John walked along, grass crunching under his feet. It had been a dry summer so far. That must be why the fires in town had spread so fast. There had not been rain in three weeks, he absently thought as the approached the last man, who was now crawling forward, dark blood blossoming from the center of his back.

The man was young, Latino, maybe twenty years old. He wore blue jeans and a navy tee shirt and high top boots. He looked like many regular people in the area. How had he gotten mixed up with these guys? John wondered as he prepared to end the man's futile struggle. The shot was through the back, and it appeared to have hit a major artery. The man would be dead in minutes from blood loss. The man turned and looked at him.

Dark eyes full of fear and pain stared at John, piercing his heart with compassion. John paused. The man rolled over on his back. He had no weapon. John stood there for what seemed like an eternity stared at this young, handsome Latino man, peacefully awaiting his death. John knelt down and checked the man for weapons. He did not resist or cry out. John looked into his eyes and took the small Gideon's New Testament out of his cargo pocket and handed it to the young man.

The man took the small book and kissed it, squeezing it firmly in his hand, his fingers tremulous with the loss of blood. No words were spoken. John knelt at the man's side and prayed for both of their souls. The man looked up and smiled at John.

"I'm sorry," the young man softy spoke, his breathy words coming fast.

"It's going to be OK. I'll pray for you," John answered. "I'm sorry...I didn't understand" John didn't know that this was a good man, trapped in the company of bad men. His anguish and regret boiled inside of him.

Tears streamed down John's cheeks as he held the man's hand, the New Testament still clutched in his palm. The man smiled again, his breath coming in waves now. The man looked at John again, "you were just protecting your home," the man panted. "I'd have done the same. I forgive you."

John stared at the ground, hot tears of anguish flowing from him at the unfairness of this all. The man laid the tiny book on his chest, the blood from his wound seeping into the pages. He clutched John's hand tightly and looked into his eyes.

"I didn't mean to hurt anyone. My brother said we would be safe here," he gasped and choked. "He said nobody lived here." The man's face turned pale as he caught his breath again, "I didn't know."

The man looks into John's eyes again, desperation, fear, pain and regret all mixed in his expression, "Forgive me."

"I forgive you too. I'm sorry. I'm so sorry."

"Dios mio. Father forgive me, for I have sinned against you...."

The man stopped, the blood loss draining the life from him. His words ceased, his eyes still open, staring upward, the smallest smile still on his peaceful face. John wept.

Somewhere South of Portland, TN
Small stand of trees
Cold camp
July 4
12:31a.m.

Sam watched over the two women sleeping soundly. He had been up for an hour or so, awakened by bad dreams. He was haunted by images of destruction and death. He could not shake them. He felt terrible grief and shame in his inability to protect the victims he had seen attacked today. He would not let that happen to the girls. He would get them home, or die trying. That is, if there was a home left to go back to.

At least it was still quiet out here in the country. He had a feeling it wouldn't last, and he really wanted to get back to his family. They were near Chloe's place. Hopefully, her grandkids would already be there or at the neighbor's house. Pirelli lived near his farm, so that would be on the way. They would have to decide long term what was the safest option. He knew that getting the families together would increase their odds of survival against whatever might come. He made up his mind that he would invite the girls and their entire families to the farm. They could live there indefinitely, if they could defend it. There was a well, a creek and lots of arable acreage to farm. His neighbors were Mennonites and they had primitive farming techniques, but did quite well. Maybe they could work a trade. Three nurses had a lot to offer. Maybe this really would work. God help them if it didn't.

He saw the light of the fires coming from Portland. He knew that the situation must have been the same as Gallatin. He was just glad that he wasn't in Nashville now, with its high population density. He couldn't imagine.

Somewhere North of Old Hickory Boulevard
Northbound Rail Line
Madison, TN
July 4
1:32a.m.

A noise brought Tessa awake from her dream. She had been running through the field with her daddy, laughing. A younger memory of life, beautiful and innocent. She started, but remained quiet as she saw the netting above her face and smelled the burlap of the ghillie blanket. She remembered where they were. She touched Kate.

Kate blinked and held her breath. The girls remained absolutely motionless as they heard the distinct sounds of walking feet. Not just two feet. Many, many feet. Tessa looked over to the right and saw a shadow cross right over them, illuminated by the weak moon and starlight. Another crossed. They heard shuffling and breathing. They froze in terror.

Outside of their sleeping blind, dozens of people were slowly walking past, down the tracks and across the wooded lot. The people shuffled slowly, moving as one organism, slowly engulfing the terrain. Occasionally, a fight would break out amongst the people. Snarling and yelling followed by silence or in some cases screams of anger and then screams of pain. The amoeba of infected humanity inched past, its direction and ultimate goal unknown.

The girls had placed their site in a small stand of trees, fairly closed in, with the brush providing some of the cover. People seemed to have gathered in a huge group and were heading north and west. Many were crossing the railroad track at right angles, some were walking down the tracks themselves.

The number of people kept growing. Kate and Tessa remained frozen in horror as several of the creatures' feet landed within inches of the ghillie blanket. Kate had bought it thinking it could cover them up from distant observers. She never dreamed that it would be needed up close. Snarling and breathing got louder. Someone had stopped.

Panic rose in Tessa's throat. She wanted to run, she wanted to scream. She wanted to be anywhere but here. Her mind raced. Her pulse quickened. She felt that her brain would explode. Then a small, slightly callously hand tightly squeezed her hand. It seemed that she was not alone in her panic. A hand reached down towards the ghillie blanket. The stained fingers reached down and down, coming ever closer to the girls' faces. Terror blossomed in their minds. This would be the end. They could not survive this. There were too many. The hand came within six inches of Tessa's face.

A crinkle of plastic was easily heard. The hand had reached just to the side and came up with a piece of trash which it placed into its mouth and chewed, crunching what once must have been a food wrapper. The figure loomed over them and walked onward. They held their breath. It moved west, past the girls. The group of people must have numbered in the hundreds, the parade of humanity went on for what seemed like hours, eventually ending with occasional stragglers following for several more minutes.

Calm slowly returned to Tessa's mind. After an hour, there were no more people seen. What were they all doing, wandering around? Incredibly, the blind material had worked perfectly, in combination with the natural local debris and the darkness. Tessa thanked God for His grace. They would all need it. To get home they would need grace and strength and luck, she thought. She whispered to Kate and they decided to set a watch now, Tessa took the first shift. With no way to tell time, the sentry would just awaken the other when she became sleepy. They had already slept several hours. It would be a long night.

Mackenzie House
Hendersonville, TN
July 4
4:02a.m.

The clip clop of horses walking was greeted by the rumble of the deuce and a half's engine roaring to life. The teams were already setting off towards their common goal of finding the girls in Nashville and returning them safely. Darryl and Justin were on horseback and heading to the railway spur that would connect to the main line and south to Nashville. Angus and Gwenn together in their deuce would try to navigate back roads through Hendersonville and Madison. The team had failed last night due to the hordes of infected and traffic jams, but the worried parents would not sit and wait. They had to try. Each set out a different way, the horse team directly South for the rail line and the Gunns to the east to try other back roads, in hopes of avoiding the traffic jams.

Both teams had packed rifles and spares with over a thousand rounds of ammunition per team, preloaded into magazines in case of a firefight like the one yesterday. They were not going to go into a dangerous situation unprepared. They would have used their very last supplies if needed to try and save their families. Luckily, even if they used up all of their ammo, each family had thousands of rounds more stockpiled away. They even had reloading ability with components ready to assemble, reusing the old cartridge casings. They had chemical case cleaners even in the event of power outages. Their food supplies were huge, as well, and they stored enough medications and gear to stock a small hospital, so many of their group being medical professionals. The supplies were fairly evenly divided between their respective homes and the mutual property in the hills.

Waving a salute to the Gunns, Justin and Darryl whirled their mounts around, trailing the third riderless horse, ready for the moment they should reach the girls. Each group had an abiding faith that this two-pronged approach would succeed. While realists, and schooled in the toll that the evils of the world could take, they believed that God would help them find their children.

Back at the Mackenzie house, Carlos took over duty as the watch commander, sending his two sons Rafael and Roberto, as well as Madison Mackenzie, out to the watch stations. He put everyone else not sleeping to work preparing the gear for evacuation and magazine loading in case of a firefight. The day had already started in the dark predawn, the plastic screens covering their activities in case anyone was watching. It would prove to be a long day of hard work.

Around the world, governments were trying to control the panic and disorder that was becoming rampant. Certain cites such as Tokyo, Tai Pei and Munich, and many parts of Western Europe were doing well now, as they tended to pull together during emergencies. In Japan, where no looting had occurred even during the prior Tsunami, society was regrouping to deal with the solar disaster. Unfortunately, even those places which routinely kept order had been exposed to the rabies plague, and their social institutions would ultimately not be able to keep order in the face of the disease's ability to destroy its victim's control of their own negative emotions.

Armies were turning against their commanders and riots were breaking out as more of the infected weren't able to cope with the new stresses occurring from the loss of expected services. Companies were forced to shut down, sending their workers home. Goods could no longer be transported as all of the rail and trucking fleets were paralyzed.

The infected were now breaking out in record numbers from hospitals. Previously, the normal utilities enabled the staff to feed, medicate and care for the infected, even the dangerous ones. Now, the hospitals' staffs could not cope with the flood of infected patients pouring in and the exodus of the heavily infected out into the community. As in Gallatin, these mass escapes of patients proved to be extremely violent.

Military and police units had already engaged large crowds of people who angrily demanded that the power be restored. More often now, the groups did not speak, but simply charged and attacked. It seemed that the riots had been ongoing to a much greater degree that anyone in the government or media had revealed. Now, entire military units were abandoning their posts and rushing home to care for or try to protect their families.

Military units from Clarksville had been engaging civilian gangs at several checkpoints and were at a stalemate, unable to press forward to pacify the situation. More and more of the groups or "herds" of infected people were wandering around in search of food. Infected military personnel were acting erratically now and numerous suicides and murders had been occurring on bases throughout the world.

Governmental control had all but evaporated. Small military units around the country were still using hardened communication networks. Their aircraft, land vehicles and ships were still working. Were this a solar event alone, the US and other governments around the world would probably still be able to maintain some order. The combination of the plague and solar event, however, would prove to be the undoing of the world's governments. When the food delivery trucks didn't show up at grocery stores at three a.m. according to schedule, the existing food stocks would all be depleted within a day, three at the latest in the most remote, lightly populated areas.

Fires raged through major and minor cities throughout the globe. Every terrorist and antigovernment organization seized on the opportunity to claim victory for their causes. Civil unrest reached epic highs as people everywhere started to realize that the almighty government could not defend or feed them. In oppressive countries in which the people hated and feared the government, the rioting still occurred, perhaps with more fervent anger. But destroying property, looting and killing have the same effect, regardless of the reasons.

Fire fighters, emergency medical workers, police and public safety officials were unable to perform their duties. Many had already been calling in sick and more would be sick with the plague soon. Those that were still at work could not physically get to the sites in which they were needed. The spiral of chaos that had begun with the worldwide spread of the virus hit critical mass when the power went out around the globe. Communities were falling apart, long-held hatreds seethed to the surface as one group blamed the other for the collapse. At the end of the first day, looting, rioting, arson, murder and lawlessness consumed most of the United States and the world. The Nation's birthday would prove to be even worse. Dawn would occur shortly, the sun's beautiful new light shining upon the final collapse of the Republic.

It is infinitely better to have a few good men than many indifferent ones.
—George Washington, Letter to James McHenry, 1798

CHAPTER 24

North Gallatin
City Limits
Triple Creek Park
July 4
7:32a.m.

Edward Douglass wiped the sweat from his brow in the early morning light. Birds sang and chirped in the park under the cloudless beautiful blue sky. It was truly a marvelous morning, gorgeous to behold. His mind wandered back to life before this madness. He knew that everything had been changed forever. The world could never be the same. The dying time was upon them and the most difficult days were ahead.

His deputies called from the edge of the field, the firefight now finished. He walked over to the white truck, now riddled with bullet holes, and sighed. These would have been useful to have, EMP hardened new government trucks. What a waste. Blood ran down the driver's-side door, staining the clean white of the Ford truck. The bodies inside lay as they had been killed, their arms and heads slumped down, their bodies riddled with bullet holes. Hundreds of rounds had gone into this last truck, the fury and rage of the town now spent. These men represented the last of the Sumner County Emergency Management personnel. What Ed could never know was that these men were infected first because they had taken their role of community defense so seriously. After all, they had sent their own delegation to the very security convention in which the first attack occurred. They were all infected before anyone else in the county even realized what had happened. The very type of plague event that they had so long prepared for had come as a thief in the night and stolen their minds, leaving them at the mercy of their own infected rage. They could have been anyone.

The night had been a very long one. They had been fighting all night, and there were casualties in his group. The better training and weaponry had won the day, however. It seemed that the insane men were capable of murdering and raping the helpless, but that the infection had made them ineffective at attacking armed, trained men.

The remaining members of the Sheriff's department and Gallatin Police Department had been combined into one cohesive fighting unit. All of the ranking officers of both forces had been killed in the initial violence, and those who had survived the attacks and avoided the infection needed the mental stability of a joint command structure. During a disaster, this joint command was supposed to be under the auspices of Emergency Management. After witnessing the horrors of the day, no one would even consider this plan. Instead, the Gallatin Police Officers asked to be rolled into the Sheriff's Department, as the Sheriff's charter predated the incorporation of the town, and thus their own department. In this period of near total uncertainty, the historical provenance comforted the men and the units blended well, most having grown up together. All contact with the Gallatin Police Department personnel that had been dispatched to guard the evacuees heading to Hendersonville had been lost.

The new Sheriff's Department had caught up with the murderous crew around midnight and has been able to kill the last ones, just a few minutes earlier. Four of the volunteers lay dead. Also, Jack Sutherland, the overweight lawyer, had been shot in the left forearm and Nathan Ford, the Vanderbilt EMT, had been shot through the left calf. Both had been stabilized with Celox wound coagulant and Israeli bandages.

They were being seen now by a local surgeon who had been on duty at the hospital when it burned down. Charlie Blake was 38, a general surgeon in Gallatin with a successful private practice, before today. He and many other people had joined the Sheriff's crew once things had settled down some. Charlie was using what surgical gear had been salvaged out of the ER, before everything burned down. The Gallatin Fire Department had been extremely helpful when they had run from the nearest station to the hospital fire. They had pulled out dozens of people and had the foresight to remove equipment and supplies before it was all lost. The firefighters had set up an emergency tent in the center of the high school football stadium parking lot. It was centrally located and had not burned with most of the rest of the city. They were triaging the wounded and using the supplies salvaged from the hospital to perform minor surgeries.

Charlie cursed and asked for more light. He was working on Jack Sutherland's forearm. The ulna had been smashed and Charlie hated dealing with orthopedic wounds. He had flushed out the pistol wound and removed the debris and bone chips, he was now sewing the tissue back together and couldn't see well under the tent. A helper, a girl of about ten, leaned closer with her Coleman lantern, its warm glow now illuminating the sterile field that had been hastily prepared. Charlie apologized and thanked the young girl.

It had been a day. He had flushed and closed the younger man's calf and figured Nathan would be fine. That one had missed the bone and tendon. A week on crutches and some luck and couple of days on Bactrim, an inexpensive but powerful antibiotic ought to have him back to nearly new. He would have used a week's worth, but he was nervous with the limited supply he had on hand. The local, privately owned pharmacy had simply donated its entire stock of medications to the effort with no strings attached. A stunning gesture, but not one unexpected, as its owner was well known in the local charities as a dedicated Christian man.

Many of the town's doctors were either killed in the hospital fire or simply in another town when the event happened. Many of the specialists split their time between Gallatin and other towns. The rumors were that a large part of the population of Hendersonville was gone, just…gone. All of the people from Gallatin who had traveled there were also unaccounted for. Those damned crazies must have killed them. Stunning, to think about tens of thousands of people dead. Between the fires, looting and psychopaths, it had been a bad day. And what the hell was up with those guys, anyway? Charlie pondered this. Was this infection really a plague that made them crazy?

He wondered about all of this, not having any answers. He was just glad he wasn't in the hospital when it burned down. He had been coming in from the surgery center to his office. His car shut off outside of

Gallatin and he walked the rest of the way, literally with the clothes on his back. He was already in scrubs when he reached the burned out hulk of the hospital and saw the fire department stretchers. He had started to work on the injured and it just grew from there. His wife and infant son had joined them as she came to the hospital looking for him. It had taken them all day to find him here. The stories of murder and devastation which she told him were shocking. He hadn't seen it, but he believed her. He was just glad they were safe. One of the school administrators, a former kindergarten teacher herself, had set up a temporary daycare, right next to the hospital tent. The town was fighting to stay together.

Two of the four men who died in the night's firefights were not killed immediately, but had been shot in the chest. They had been taken back to the hospital tent and Charlie had not been able to save them. He had used more equipment than he should have, but he just didn't have the heart to give up without trying. Unless they found more supplies, his triage would take a whole new, and unwanted meaning. Those who could not be saved would not have supplies wasted on them. This was turning into a frustrating and difficult world for a surgeon to live in.

Corner of Main Street and New Shackle Road
Hendersonville, TN
July 4
8:07a.m.

Gunfire erupted from the store. Angus cursed under his breath, his palms sweaty with concern for his friends in the building. He had patronized the store for years and most of his firearms came from there or had been shipped directly to the store for transfer. He loved the honorable, customer-friendly policies of the family owned business and his heart grieved at the site in front of him now.

Cars littered the streets, completely blocking any hope of passing for days. There were over one hundred vehicles stranded in various postures, some in ditches, some right in the middle of the road. The wall of vehicles continued back in clusters as far as the eye could see, easily several hundred cars jammed onto this formerly busy road at the downtown junction. Wes Smith had purchased the property with an eye for business. He already had one store in a neighboring town and had truly grasped the potential of the region's market. He had sold thousands of firearms here to a broad swath of the local community, and the local police loved the man, as he offered discounts to anyone he felt needed them. Now, those very firearms were being used to defend the people of the area in this new and dangerous time.

Today, the few in town who had decided that it would be a good day to get a free gun were here to take them by force. A dozen or so scruffy looking men and a few women in biker leathers were engaged in a massive shoot out with the gun shop's staff. Rounds pinged off the pavement and hard surfaces and slammed through the parked cars' thin sheet metal. Angus and Gwenn were over 200 yards away. Once again, they could simply not close the distance. They had been trying all morning to find a route through the area. Blocked at every turn, every side road clogged, and his patience gone, Angus slammed the buttstock of his DPMS Mini SASS into the side of the truck. The tough Ergo F93 stock dented the thick steel sheet metal and both surfaces were lightly scratched.

"Sorry," Angus said, wishing he had controlled himself better. He did not normally abuse his gear.

"That's O.K., baby," Gwenn replied, squeezing her husband's left arm at the shoulder. "I'm pissed off too."

They both looked at the scene and saw the firefight. Gwenn thought back to the night before and shook her head. "Bastards will steal anything. They should've prepared themselves better. Now they are desperate. People will kill you for a meal if they are hungry enough. And then rationalize it later, claiming it was 'do or die,' and that somehow makes it OK. I mean, these guns were not that expensive, mostly. People wanted a new jet ski or sauna, and spent their money on crap. Look what they get. Shot in the head for trying to loot now. Those bastards are trying to kill them to steal their lawful property. Murderers!"

She looked at the scene, "We can't stand here and do nothing. We can't help Kate, but we can help Wes. I know Darryl and Justin will get through. I believe it. I just know it; I don't know how. We have to help Wes and his boys. See if you can get an angle on the looters. I couldn't stand it to find out Wes or his boys died and we could have stopped it."

Angus grunted and then, for the first time in over 24 hours, his mind paused. Stillness and silence entered his troubled conscience. Long ago, he had sobbed at the idea of killing. He had done so for the first time yesterday. It had really bothered him last night. Even though the men's minds were long gone. Even though they were infected and they were committing unspeakable atrocities. He remembered the face of the man he had shot through the chest. All night, he lay awake trying to sleep. Staring at the ceiling, he saw the scene, over and over again. The shock, the blinking lack of understanding. The surprise of the man's expression, even through the haze of the disease. He had been stunned at having been shot. Angus would drift off to sleep and be jolted back awake with cries of anguish and disgust at his actions. Even though he had saved Matt from a certain death, it didn't matter. He had killed a man.

But that was yesterday. Angus' mind snapped. The fury and rage he felt boiled up inside his head. He thought of all of tears, sweat and effort that he had put into keeping his family safe. All of the lost opportunity not pursued because he had training to do, or equipment to buy, or skill sets to hone. All of the honest dealings that he had experienced with the gun store's owner, the thousands of dollars that the honest entrepreneur had donated to Angus' charitable causes over the years came flooding into his mind. The faces of the children, who would have had no Christmas, save for Wes' generosity flashed across Angus' mind. The fact that Kate could be lost forever made his heart nearly stop, the grief of the thought was too overwhelming. A rage uncharacteristic for the humble man swirled through Angus, warming his limbs and steeling his mind. Today, these bastards were going to pay.

Angus swung down under the large Deuce and tossed his patrol Camelback backpack onto the pavement and steadied the weapon's front hand guard on the pack. The barrel was free floated and pressure along the hand guard did not affect the point of impact of the weapon. Gwenn slid under the truck next to him, both shielded by the shadow. The enemy would not be able to see where the fire was coming from due to the shade and highly effective flash hider of the rifle. Gwenn scanned the scene with her 10 power binoculars. She started pointing out aloud the available targets in the field of view. Several men and one very rough looking woman were firing on the gun store. The return fire from the store was intense, but apparently, the attackers had found effective cover, as the attackers were unharmed by the hail of bullets coming from the shop.

Gwenn recommended a left to right pattern of target engagement as the shooters on the right were ahead of the ones on the left and might not realize that they were being fired upon as their comrades were behind them. Gwenn used her Zeiss laser range finder to note and report to Angus the 227 yard to 239 yard ranges of the targets. Gwenn was glad Angus had insisted on keeping the gear in the Faraday cages. It would have been ruined and useless without the protection. Angus found the first man in the scope and placed the appropriate marking of the reticle on his head.

The rifle had been set up to make use of the heavier sniper round now used by the military, but could also use the lighter steel tipped rounds that the group had stored in bulk. The point of impact of the rounds was within one inch at 100 yards and Angus had preprinted ballistic tables for a number of common rounds that he kept with the rifle kit, in case he had to switch ammunition. This allowed him to know where any of the ammunition he used would hit without having to re-zero the scope. He knew that the lighter bullet hit just under one inch high at 100 yards and knew the point of impact for the varying rounds for each reticle marking on the scope. In this way, he could gauge the distance manually or by laser and then pick the closet reticular dot to the range, place that marking on the target and fire. The caliber was so flat shooting that the round would impact within only 1-2 inches of the marking in most every case. Both Angus and Gwenn were wearing ESS protective glasses and Peltor noise attenuating electronic hearing protection, extra earmuffs that Angus had stored in the bug out bags that fit easily under their helmets.

Angus wore the same clothing that he had worn yesterday, Beth Mackenzie having hand washed the clothes in the sink and hung them to dry. They had been slightly damp when he put them on, but he had sweated into them within minutes of wearing them under his body armor anyway. The shirts had standard sleeves and T shirt material torsos to make them more comfortable under body armor vests. He was grateful for the clean clothes. Gwenn wore a matching Multicam set as well. Both had removed their helmets when they went prone under the truck. It was very hard to see or shoot long distances while wearing a ballistic helmet.

Angus spoke, "Ready."

Gwenn spoke, "No wind value. Engage at will. Send it."

Angus prayed a silent prayer for accuracy and exhaled half of his breath. The JP fire control trigger group was factory set at just a hair under four pounds and the surprise break of the trigger pull was clean. Angus saw the pink mist of exploding brain matter fill the scopes field of view as the first man's head dropped out of view, his body falling limply and suddenly to the ground. He could not hear the noise of the SKS rifle clattering to the pavement, and he doubted that the others in the group did either considering the number of people firing and the complete lack of ear protection in the group.

The scope swung past barricades and vehicles to the next target. The burly, white haired woman wore a black leather vest and her naked arms were covered in tattoos. Her bolt action scoped rifle fell out of her hands as the match grade 77 grain Black Hills M 262 mod 1 cannelured bullet pierced her skull and sprayed her brain matter onto the side of the barricade. Angus rapidly swung the scope to the third target and started to squeeze the trigger and paused as the next man's head began to bob and turn from side to side.

"Target aware. Send it now," Gwenn calmly said, as the attacker frantically jerked his head around trying to see where the shooter was that had killed his two colleagues.

Angus shifted to a center mass hold and finished squeezing the trigger and the man fell, the bullet impacting and transecting the aorta, just above the heart. The bullet traveled through the great vessel and began to tumble head over heels, impacting and crushing the upper mid thoracic spine, the heavy round now shearing into a dozen pieces from the incredible torsion of suddenly hitting a liquid target and being forced sideways on impact by the hydrostatic shockwave its impact generated. The man was dead within seconds of the impact, his lifeblood staining the asphalt a bright arterial red as liters of the fluid poured from the wound channel.

The Gunns were on a slight rise above the scene, the top of their large truck visible to the attackers. The couple was engaging the enemy through a gap in the cars ahead of them, but the top of the vehicle had finally been noted by the assaulting force. They had been so focused on the gun store, that they had not even noticed the Gunns' arrival. Bullets began impacting the top of the vehicle as the attackers shifted their aim. The glass of the windshield popped as several bullets hit the upper margin of the glass.

Gwenn produced her AR-15 and slammed the trigger back several times, her shots smashing windshields and sending the attackers back in surprise. One man was struck in the leg and tumbled back, his mouth open, his screams of pain not audible over the erupting gunfire. Angus regained his view through the reticle and shot down two more men in the chest, their rifles firing into the air futilely as they went down, one now crawling away, dragging a limp arm and leg. The man smeared thick blood on the warm pavement as he crawled ten feet and then slumped and stopped moving. Fire from the gun shop's direction took out several more of the looting gang as the tide of battle turned. Angus and Gwenn scanned for targets and finding none waited for the sounds of gunfire to subside.

Five minutes later, all was quiet and several figures came in leaps and bounds from the gun store, their moves covering each other's advance. Angus yelled out from under the truck, the men stopped and took cover.

"It's me, Angus Gunn! DON'T SHOOT! My wife and I have been shooting at these looters with you!"

The gun store team lowered their guns to port arms and waved, yelling out as they did, "HEY DOC, THAT YOU?!"

"YEAH, IT'S ME, DOCTOR GUNN! I'M WALKING TOWARDS YOU! DON'T SHOOT!"

Angus walked out with his heavy rifle slung across his back, both hands up and out over his head. The lead man from the store met him halfway and several of his family and staff followed him. Handshakes and greetings were exchanged all around

"Thanks, Doc!"

"Hey Doc, how's it going?!"

"Glad you guys showed up. That was getting a little too close for comfort!"

Angus smiled and shook hands. He knew almost everyone in the small family owned business. Gwenn followed after Angus waved her forward. They exchanged information and prepared to head back their own way. Wes had called over one of his staff and he ran back to the store and returned with another man and two ammo boxes full of 62 grain M855 5.56mm ammo, a full 840 rounds. The other man had a sack full of twelve gauge military buckshot, spare AR parts and reloading powder and 175 grain .308 match grade bullets for reloading.

Angus looked down at the gift and shook his head. "I can't take this stuff from you man. We will always help you. You have never treated me wrong. I am ready for this stuff because of your fair treatment and good equipment you sold me. I can't take such a gift."

Wes grinned and turned his gray head to the side, the grin spreading his close cropped beard into a friendly smile. He winked at Gwenn and turned back to Angus and said, "Listen friend, I can't move all of this gear away from the store. You'd be helping make sure it doesn't fall into the wrong hands. And also, I do owe you now. Please don't refuse me."

"Of course. I just would help you no matter what. Thank you, all of this will be used. I really appreciate it."

"I know. You guys be safe now. We've got to get the gear back to the house now," he said referring to the family farm out in the county. They shook hands and parted ways. The Gunns headed back to the Mackenzie house, their emotions a mix of frustration and thankfulness for the ability to help out friends. Gwenn prayed a silent thanksgiving that they were not injured, and they headed out, the diesel smoke rumbling from the large truck's exhaust as they navigated back through the sea of broken automobiles, picking their way as carefully as they had before. Each was quiet on the return journey, silent prayers sent up to heaven.

Airstrip
Ft. Campbell, Ky
Just North of Tennessee Border
July 4
9:13a.m.

Equipment and personnel bustled across the busy airstrip as preparations were starting for the operation. The air crews were loading the helicopter gunships with massive stores of ammunition for the guns each carried. Smaller aircraft were being checked over as well. The op was a go. Word had come down after National Guard units were unable to quell the rioters.

Most of the 101st Airborne and its associated 5th Group units were overseas at the time of the solar event. Communication with them had not been effectively established. The military was fragmented, small units working within the framework of each unit's central command. Technicians were racing to fix systems taken down by the event. Small skeleton crews remained in the base and full air support was still available to the base commander. His commanding officer, LT General Beauregard T. Smith was at the base for an inspection of the 5th group.

Smith was a four star general, and the commander of all US Special Operations Forces. He was stationed at Ft Bragg, NC and had arrived three days earlier to personally inspect the 5th group, who were otherwise known as the "Green Berets" by uninitiated civilians. Under normal conditions, he was one of most high ranking officers in the Army and the US military. Due to the communications disruptions, Smith was now the highest ranking military officer in the US Military who had access to working long range communications. He had been infected last week and was already showing signs of aggression and paranoia in the face of the solar event. He had ordered a full recall to the base and the personnel had been arriving piecemeal over the last 24 hours. This further enraged him as he saw the low percentage as evidence of the need to escalate the situation. When the National Guard could not get through on I-65 North of Nashville, he flew into a rage and demanded action.

The infected could not be allowed to reach the Kentucky or Alabama borders. Personnel on the base either did not realize the truth or preferred to ignore any evidence that might suggest global spread of the contagion. Communications between bases in Alabama, the Midwest and units in Tennessee were all coordinated now. It had to be stopped. Smaller units would mop up any infected in the rest of the country, or so everyone on base had been told. They would draw the line. They did not need to know any further details. Word had come on high from command. Nashville would burn.

Nations die first in the big cities.
—Austin O'Malley, "Keystones of Thought"

CHAPTER 25

Southern Madison
North of Nashville and West of Hendersonville
Rail Line
July 4
10:47a.m.

The clip clop of the horses could clearly be heard on the gravel bank of the tracks. The morning air was already hot and heavy and the horses moved south at a steady pace. The riders never paused, but continually scanned ahead, their rifles at the ready. Motion to the left side of the tracks caught their attention. A flicker of movement in the brush was there and then gone.

Darryl stopped. Justin stopped also, hearing the noise as well. Both men flicked their rifles' safeties off, Justin with his thumb on his AR, Darryl with his index finger on his AK. They glanced at each other, ready for anything. The sun beat down on them as they remained steady on their mounts, the horse's tails swished away flies, and the tension of the scene could have been cut with a knife. The men had already dodged a half dozen "welcoming committees" with apparently uninfected survivors setting up roadblocks and traps. They had dodged several groups of infected people wandering the streets. They were very much on edge.

Darryl peered into the shadows of the brush and fixed his eyes on the area of movement. His heartbeat slowed as he strained to determine what it was that had made the movement. His muscles tensed, like a tiger ready to pounce. His left hand squeezed tighter and tighter on the front hand guard of the AK, his knuckles turning pale despite their dark pigment. Time slowed as he focused all of his will into discerning the cause of movement. His mind raced through the possibilities, ravening beasts and white, once human teeth grinning in his mind's eye, a leering caricature of the infected. His breathing steadied. This was almost unbearable, waiting to see what flashed from the brush, death perhaps, or madness incarnate. His arms tensed, he could feel the aura of intention flowing from his comrade just feet away. He prepared his mind, his pulse quickening now for the moment...

"Daddy!?"

A voice broke over the silence, the tension exploding in a wave of palpable relief. The men's mounts wavered to the side as their muscle tone decreased. Justin sighed and Darryl roared, "Tessa! Is that you?!"

The young figure of a thin, beautiful black woman appeared slowly from the brush, the ghillie blanket falling to the gravel below. The young woman smiled, her face lit in an expression of utter happiness and relief. She charged towards the horse, spooking it slightly.

"Easy baby," Darryl said to the horse as he pulled the reigns and dismounted to bear hug his lost daughter. Tears of joy filled his eyes and ran down the corners of his eyes, softening the usually granite-hard visage. Tessa also wept silently and then sobbed, her emotion coming in waves.

"It's all right!" she called.

Her companion dropped easily from the brushy area and walked calmly over, her pack on and compound bow in her hand, broad-headed arrow still nocked at the ready. She smiled softly and grinned. Darryl released Tessa and then hugged both girls tightly, Kate holding her bow out to the side to protect them from the broadhead's razors. She giggled and then Tessa grabbed her pack and bow and they waved a shy hello to Justin, who tipped his head and smiled back.

"Man, are we glad to see you guys!" said Kate. "We thought we'd never get back home. How did you guys know to come down the railroad tracks?"

Darryl smiled, "My Tessa would have figured it out and I knew you were both smart girls. Are you both OK?"

"Yeah."

"Yes sir."

"How did you get out? I see you have your bows."

Tessa paused and looked at the ground. Big tears welled in her eyes again. She stopped, unable to speak, the horror of death and fighting too fresh in her memory. The shame of having to kill, even though only in self-defense, overwhelmed her for a moment. Kate stood stock still, emotion buried deep under her thick layer of self-control.

"Oh baby. No, baby. Don't cry," Darryl said, hugging his daughter. "It's not your fault. You had to protect yourself. I'm so proud of you. We thought you were dead."

Tessa looked into her father's eyes. "It was awful. They...they... killed a man...and came towards us...we ...we had our bows...it's all we could do...they just wouldn't stop...they were killing him!!" She broke down into sobs, grief welling up and heaving its way out of her, the tears cleansing her of the anguish. She paused and regained control of her breathing.

"Mr. Washington, Tessa did really well. She was very smart and very brave. I would, we both would be dead if she hadn't been. We had to shoot several people that tried to attack us." Her speech increased in speed, "Mr. Washington, there are thousands of them. Thousands. We almost got caught, while we were sleeping. Their like a 'herd,' or something. It's like a damned zombie movie, except we're in it! Sorry! But really, it is. They don't stop. You can't threaten them. You have to shoot them over and over. It was horrible."

Darryl looked at Kate and nodded, "I know, we have seen them too. I hate to tell you this, but we are going to have to go right through them to get home."

Shock drained the color from Kate's face. Tessa looked up and stared at her daddy. She nodded, "We'll make it, 'cause you guys will be with us!". She smiled at Justin.

"We need to roll, Darryl," Justin said.

"Saddle up girls, I'm afraid we've only got one horse, and no remounts. But it's only six miles from here to a safer area and only a mile past that to the house. At least it was safe when we were there this morning. With these damned infected people wandering around, who knows. We've got spare rifles in the saddle bags. You'll need them if we are unlucky. Swap out your gear."

The girls stowed their packs on the back of the men's horses. Their horse would be strained with two riders and they could not add the extra weight. They removed two generic M-4s, each with a group standard Aimpoint comp M2 red dot optics in repeatable Larue lower third co-witness cantilevered mounts and Daniel Defense DD A1.5 fixed rear backup sights and standard pinned front sight posts with Meprolight tritium green front backup sights. The Aimpoint optics actually worked as they had been stored in Faraday cages by the Mackenzies prior to the solar event as backup sights. The mounts allowed them to be placed on and off the rifle with no change in mechanical zero. They had bought several extra rifles with full kits when Matt had a large bonus from work a few years ago. They had stored them for "the rainy decade" and it did appear that description fit the bill for their current circumstances.

The carbines were DS Arms ZM4s and were fully milspec and had adjustable two point slings mounted to the receiver and front sling mount. They had analog Surfire G2 Nitrolon flashlights that were for all intents and purposes EMP proof due to their lack of IC chips in their construction. Tessa slipped on her coyote brown SKD plate carrier that her father had brought along, a low profile, lightweight carrier with multihit level IV plates and jammed four extra mags into the carrier's mag pouches. The girls slung their rifles and loaded a mag each and slung a shoulder bag with six extra thirty round mags each over their shoulders. Kate had no body armor and would have to get her vest when they got back to the house.

Tessa mounted the horse first. Her armor would protect them both if fire came from the front. Kate mounted behind Tessa and they turned about and then chambered rounds in their rifles, keeping the selectors on safe and their muzzles away from the others and their horse. Justin radioed in the contact. They started north, Darryl briefing them before they left the stopping place. They would try to sneak, and fight only if needed. They would walk to save to horses' strength. If it came to a run, their lives would depend on their horses being fresh. They moved slowly along the track edge, all eyes and ears focused ahead, scanning for potential threats.

Mackenzie House
Hendersonville, TN
July 4
10:55a.m.

Gwenn set the handitalkie down and sighed. They would be O.K. The guys had found them. The morning had been spent getting the Deuce back to the house and they had used up some water, precious diesel fuel, and ammunition in the failed attempt. They needed their regular supplies. Angus walked over.

"Thank God they are O.K."

"I know. I am still worried about them getting out, but we need our gear, and we need as much as the old belle can carry," she replied, referring to the deuce and a half, so named because it could carry two and a half tons, or five thousand pounds, off road. It could carry ten thousand pounds on road. They needed their gear, and she was frankly worried about looters. There was nothing that they could do at this time with the Deuce.

"I agree, Baby. I'll go get the gear, and Carlos can come with me. I don't want Matt lifting anything heavy with that arm yet. Darryl left his keys. You and Matt meet them as far as the F-250 can reach them.

That should at least cover the last few miles of the rescue op. That's where the most resistance was anyway. That's where the infected were congregating. I hate asking you to go, but you aren't strong enough to quickly move the thousand-plus pounds of gear we need from the house, and I know I couldn't keep you here anyway if I tried, with your baby girl out there. I don't want to lose you getting Kate back. Please, Dear God, please be careful."

"I will. I love you," Gwenn said and nodded, her face bright for the first time since this started.

He called Matt and Carlos over and briefed them on his suggested plan. They would leave in an hour, minimal staff could defend the house. Basically, the teenagers and their moms could hold down the fort. It was an all or nothing suggestion. Angus would get more gear, now, before their house was looted or burned down.

He turned back to Gwenn, "I love you Baby, don't get killed, O.K. Please be careful!"

"You too! I love you!" Gwenn replied, eagerness to save her daughter warring with fear and uncertainty.

The teams geared up and used some of Matt's extra supplies. They took smoke grenades, extra ammo, spare rifles and armor to throw over the doors of the F-250. They said their goodbyes as Beth assigned the watch to the Corpuz boys and her daughter Madison. They would just have to do double shifts, since the younger Mackenzies were not yet combat trained, and Margaret Gunn was sleeping after her longer shift. The rumble of engines caught the attention of some neighbors poking their heads out of the windows. Several people had materialized out on their lawns to watch the scene. It made Matt and Angus nervous, but they waved at the families. The local non-prepper's families would not run out of water or food for some time; most had at least a week of food and some far more. The water pressure was still working, and likely would for some time. As they rolled down the street behind the Ford, Angus worried what he would find upon his return to his house.

I-24
South of Pleasantville, TN
July 4
11:00a.m.

Cars littered the freeway, their hulks covering every lane in each direction. Traffic cones blocked one lane in each direction, the prior roadwork now forever uncompleted, the desperate drivers long since fled from their useless vehicles. Smoke rose from many of the metal forms, before spreading across this no man's land of smoldering metal and asphalt. Small farmhouses in the nearby countryside lay empty, their occupants having fled in the face of the chaos and death that had approached from the roadside. Flies buzzed over the half-eaten livestock, the oval rows of orthodontically spaced teeth marks still visible in the midday sun, the animals' agony still etched on the faces of the fallen cattle. Blood soaked into the grass, the horror of the events that had occurred only a day before still visible, the stench of recent death hung in the air.

A young girl in a stained white cotton sun dress and rubber galoshes hunched over a carcass, the recently dead animal lay still in the quiet of the rural day. Crunching, rending and tearing sounds emanated from the scene, small fingers blackened with maroon blood partially dried in the heat. The breeze was stubbornly absent, the stillness punctuated by the ripping sounds. A wind chime lay motionless on the front porch of the small farm house. The overweight body of an elderly woman lay in the front doorway, the screen door resting against her arms and lifeless face. Flies buzzed across her skin. A cat darted out from the kitchen, chasing a squirrel that had wandered inside.

The body was sprawled out, dark stains soaked into the hardwood floor of the porch, part of the head missing. Inside the doorway, halfway down the hallway, a second body lay slumped against the wall, chin resting on the chest, the upper portion of the head gone, the .45 Colt revolver still in the hand, the arthritic fingers still clutching the weapon.

Riverfront Park
Downtown Nashville
July 4
11:30a.m.

The small boy squatted under the bush, frozen, his fear rooting him to the spot. Gunfire rang out nearby. The rat tat tat of rapid semi-auto fire and the sounds of smashing windows punctuated the air. Hollow screams and echoing sobs rolled in from the close packed downtown streets, just one block over. Running feet shot past his position. He remained frozen, terror overwhelming his mind, replaying the events of the past day. His hunger and thirst were overridden by his survival instinct. He knew, automatically. He must hide. He must stay here, and never move again. Mommy didn't mean it. Mommy didn't mean it.

Small motel parking lot
Georgetown, VA
Western outskirts of Washington D.C.
July 4
12:17p.m.EST

Siraj sat in the back of the rental van, sweating. This was the moment he had been created for. He prayed his thanks to Allah. His very name, Siraj Al Din, meant "Light of the Faith." All things would come together now. The power outage and the destruction that followed had been a sign from Allah that it was time. The plan would work; he knew it was noon, by the position of sun in the sky. The backup plan was still in place, and even though he could not communicate with his colleagues, they would know. Allah would guide their hands.

The large device had been removed from its lead-lined case. They had not been able to get any closer to the viper's nest, to Satan's stronghold. There were radiation detectors along the beltway that precluded any closer attempt at locating the bomb in the downtown area. This was close enough. The Russian made device was very powerful, and the fallout would travel westward, even if the buildings on the east side of town remained. No one could live here for decades. They would crush the Great Satan today. Today, on its birthday, the Beast would die. It had sent its troops and pornography, money and corruption around the world. Now Allah had shown the way. The decade of planning had only been reinforced as the plague had spread around the world. It was a sign from Heaven that they were justified in their plan.

The hardest part had been keeping the van safe from looters and those, those things that ran past. They looked like men and women, but he knew the djinn when he saw them. His amulet would protect him. He had been in the motel, looking out of the window for the entire day, awaiting time for their backup plan. They were set to simultaneously detonate at noon today. The power went out yesterday and he had sat tight in the motel. He had seen the madness start and grow as people killed each other. This would not matter. He knew his destiny.

He had waited with no food or water for the entire day. It would not matter. He made his way to the van and avoided the djinn, by sneaking out to the van at night. They had not seen his movement, and now, he knew, the time was upon him. He knelt towards Mecca and prayed, a last time before entering paradise. He turned to the device. A motion outside caught his eye. Three figures raced up on the van and slammed themselves into the window, teeth bared, screams of furious agony accompanying the onslaught. Hands smashed at the glass and shattered it, cutting the wrists and fingers to ribbons. Slavering wails of victory and pain pierced the parking lot. The djinn had found him. He closed his eyes and said aloud, "Allahu Akbar!"

The fire of heaven ignited. Solar plasma was created in the parking lot as every piece of matter within several hundred yards disintegrated into vapor. The superheated plasma and vapor spread outwards at an unbelievable pace, smashing down buildings in an unstoppable wave of purifying destruction. Victims about to be slaughtered and the infected cannibals were together turned to ash, their particles blasted outward at several hundred miles an hour. An initial burst of light blinded anyone within 50 miles who was unlucky enough to be looking in that direction. The shock wave obliterated Georgetown and the Western half of D.C. The mushroom cloud began rising upward into the sky, its signature of despair etched into the clouds. Within 30 minutes, New York City was destroyed with an identical device, located in Queens. Other than the military and citizens near enough to the blasts to see or feels the effects, no one else in the world even knew that the cities had been destroyed.

Ft Campbell
Command Center
July 4
1:49p.m.

Command and Control had been lost. When the detonations in Washington and NYC had wiped out the two cities, all communication between the civillian government and the military command structure had been lost. The President and Vice President were both unaccounted for. They had been in D.C. when the solar event occurred for a large partisan fund raiser that was supposed to be held on the 4th of July. They had communicated to the Pentagon that they would stay in the D.C to "give a show of strength and support to the people during this terrible natural disaster."

Not that anyone could see them, as all of the radios and TVs in North America and the world for that matter had been fried by the solar wave front. Only military and some HAM radio operators with shielded equipment were still broadcasting. And none of them gave a damn about politicking. The chain of civilian command had been utterly destroyed. The sitting president was no friend of the military and never listened to their advice about protecting the government, anyway. It now fell completely to the military to run the country, until order could be restored.

These were the thoughts that ran through the clouded mind of the only remaining LT General in the US Armed Forces. He had been touring the Army facilities at Ft Campbell and inspecting the "Special" units housed there. In the media, they were referred to as "unit name withheld," but the world knew them as the Fifth group or Green Berets. They ran missions with Rangers and the 101st Airborne Assault and were conveniently housed there in Tennessee, just a few miles from the Kentucky border.

Calls for help had been coming in from several major cites over the past day. Military units in Atlanta, Dallas, Houston, Indianapolis and Nashville had all requested air support and more ground troops to quell the rioting and infection. So far the General had not responded, except to Nashville. He had received word from the local commander about the firefights, looting and quagmire in which the National Guard units were bogged down. They had come south on I-24 and could not get past a massive thousand car traffic jam brought about by commuters trapped in a construction zone and had rerouted their forces to I-65 and had been stopped cold by what appeared to be anarchist gangs that had advanced weaponry, likely stolen from armories in the area.

The general had also been infected by the virus. His staff had attended the original convention and had infected him shortly thereafter. His judgment, along with that of the base commander, was slipping away. He was infuriated at the idea that troops were being attacked by civilians. When the Pentagon was lost, he began to believe that there was a connection between the plague, the bombing, anarchist roadblocks and a terrorist takeover of the country. He ordered bombers from Barksdale to "perform a saturation investment of the enemy position." In plain English, he had ordered the destruction of an American city by conventional means.

The chaos that covered the area had prevented many of the fliers from reporting for duty. Those who did report were clinging to anything that could hold life together. Moral altruism went right out of the window. They accepted the orders and focused all of their attention to carrying them out. Many of the crews were already badly infected and their judgement was impaired. Some had attacked others and had been shot on sight. The chaos spurred the remaining flight crews into high gear. The bombers would arrive within the hour.

Gunn House
Goodlettsville, TN
July 4
2:15p.m.

Carlos froze as a shadow darkened the garage doorway. He pulled his CZ 9mm out and automatically flicked off the safety. He paused inside the garage as the shadow moved closer.

"Hello? Anybody in there?" A voice called out from the driveway.

Carlos sliced the pie around the corner, pistol at low ready. Angus was inside getting gear. They had parked the deuce backside near the garage door of Angus' house to get the load of gear. They had been at it now for some time and the vehicle was about half full. It was devastating to Carlos, thinking that he would likely be the next to have to decide what to bring, thinking of all of the family mementos that simply would not make the cut.

Room in the truck had to be for food, medicine, clothing and anything that could help them survive. Luckily, all of the group members had already taken photos or scanned every important or sentimental document or image and had saved them onto DVDs,CDs, SD cards and USB drives, all kept in small Faraday cages. They did not know what format would be usable in an uncertain future, Doug McKnight had suggested the idea, and as he was their computer expert, everyone had readily adopted the advice.

Carlos swung quickly into view and the woman standing in the driveway screamed and clamped her hand over her mouth. She stared, terrified at the small, wiry Asian man who held his gun pointed below her feet. She froze and they both heard an upstairs window slide open.

"Carlos, it's just my neighbor. Ginny, sorry, this is Carlos, one of my best friends. He's helping me move some things."

"Roger that," Carlos replied, making safe and holstering his firearm. "Sorry Ma'am."

"Angus, what's going on?" The neighbor asked.

"Long story, we're moving away for a while. Things are really bad in town. I suggest you guys do the same. It's not safe around here. Listen, don't get near anyone acting odd. There are some really sick people walking around and they are contagious."

The neighbor just stared at Angus, his head partly out of his window. She nodded at Carlos, who had gone back to loading gear into the trunk. He nodded back and resumed his work. They had loaded all of the family's ammunition, over twenty thousand rounds, half in .22 long rifle. Carlos returned to the reloading bench and used a ratchet to remove the equipment and place it gently into a 25mm ammo box of carbon polymer. The powder and bullets followed into the truck, another ten thousand bullets and far more than enough powder and primers for the purpose. The supplies were mostly 5.56mm and 9mm, though the Gunns had reloading dies and supplies for every caliber they owned save the .22, and they just kept lots of that ammo.

Angus had loaded all of the firearms and archery equipment first, then food and tools, now the ammunition. Soon he would have to stop and perform the worst job. Carlos could continue with the loading of the clothing and cookware. Angus gathered up a load and walked down the stairs and out of the garage. He patted Carlos on the shoulder and muttered a thanks. He walked up to Ginny, a 50 something small framed woman who lived across the street. They hugged and Angus pointed to the city.

"See that smoke rising? It's fire from looting and people attacking each other. You've got to get out. Where's John?," he said, referring to her husband.

"He's inside, doing the same thing you are. How did you get your truck to run?"

"It's old. It just runs. That's why I bought it in the first place, in case something like this happened. Do you guys have anywhere to go?" Angus had a concerned look on his face as he furrowed his brow.

"John's dad has a place in the country we can go to. I don't know how we are going to get there. It's just north of here, but our cars don't work."

Carlos looked at Angus, a stern expression in his eyes. Carlos knew what Angus was thinking before Angus even spoke. He relaxed his brow and smiled. He knew it was the right thing, even though he didn't like it. They couldn't abandon these people. Angus knew them and had been neighbors, he understood. Carlos, pulled out his Yaesu handitalkie and grabbed a large fox hunting antenna and hopped up onto the bed of the truck to get elevation. He pointed it in the direction of the Mackenzie house.

"Mike 1, Charlie 1."

Static rang from the handset.

"Mike 1, Charlie 1."

The handset spoke, "Charlie 1, Mike 2. Read you 5 by 5, over," Beth Mackenzie spoke into the radio, using the groups convention of numbering in which the spouses were 1 and 2 and the children were 3,4,5 and so on down the line. The first letter was usually the first letter of the family name. For certain ops, the scheme would change, especially if they thought an enemy might be listening.

"Detouring from original plan. Making run north of current position to assist evac in progress, over."

"Roger that, what is ETA?"

Carlos looked at Angus. Angus turned to his frankly confused looking neighbor. She stared at him, understanding slowly dawning on her face.

"How long will it take for you to get ready to go. We are very, very short on time. We can take you and a very small supply of your stuff, if we leave soon."

Tears started in the corners of her eyes and she snuffled out a reply of "one hour," and nodding and wiping her nose, she raced back to her house, tearing through the door, yelling for her husband.

"Unsure of exact ETA, estimate one to two hour delay. Will notify once commencing, over," Carlos spoke into the mike.

"Roger that, report back with new transit location once able, over."

"Roger that, Charlie 1 out."

"Mike 2, out."

Carlos hopped down and put up the radio and antenna into his pack and returned to loading the gear. He did not second guess his friend. Angus slapped him on the shoulder and grabbed his work gloves and a shovel. He had waited as long as he could. The gear was almost all in the truck and Carlos could finish. He walked into the backyard. The smell was obvious, but not overwhelming. The bags had done their job, and Gwenn's efforts at keeping the body from scavengers had worked. He knelt down beside Penelope's body bag and placed his hand on the now swelling bag. He prayed a silent thanks, tears now starting at the corners of his eyes. He collapsed onto the grass, face down, sobbing uncontrollably. His body shook with the rigors of grief. Pain and anguish flowed out of him like a tsunami, wave after shaking wave racking his tired body.

He lay there for five minutes and then abruptly stood and placed the shovel into the sod and kicked the blade into the good earth, the smell of freshness and life rising from the spade cut as he turned the sod over. Silent tears flowed from his eyes, his muscles thankful for the hard labor, his mind thankful for the activity to crowd out the grief. An hour later, he was done, a four foot deep hole now holding his beloved dog. He tamped the earth down and pulled the Book of Common Prayer from his BDU pocket and read the service for Last Rites, culminating with a private prayer of thanksgiving to the Lord Jesus for giving them such a faithful dog, and for her bravery, here at the end of all things.

He wiped off the spade and tossed it into the bed of the deuce. He moved up the trailer and hitched it to the back of the large truck, and began loading the last of the gear. There was enough space to hold some extra gear and he looked across the yard to the neighbor's house. They had a pile of things on their driveway, ready to load. He motioned to Carlos and they went room to room to make sure nothing critical had been missed. They had a year's supply of food for four, two years' worth of meds, a full complement of batteries and rechargers, solar panels and radios, all in Faraday cages, a year's supply of dog food, cooking pots, clothing for all family members, 45 gallons of gasoline in 5 gallon cans and ninety gallons of water. In addition, a full set of tools, gardening implements, seeds and a 5000 kilowatt generator went into the truck bed, completely filling its ten foot length. Some gear went onto the trailer

Angus checked the breaker box, water and gas line and assured that they were all turned off. Gwenn had already done it when she left. They locked up the house and Angus silently prayed that they could make another trip later to get more gear. He doubted very seriously that it would be possible. He wondered what would happen to his beloved house and the personal things left inside. Would looters steal them, or would a fire consume them? Would archeologists find a time capsule later? He doubted that, also. They fired up the deuce and drove a few yards to the neighbor's house where they were greeted with hugs and handshakes. After loading the neighbors gear, they pulled out of the neighborhood, several other neighbors staring blankly at them as they moved past. They headed north and Carlos connected with Beth and relayed their new location.

The night has been unruly: where we lay,
Our chimneys were blown down; and, as they say,
Lamentings heard i' the air; strange screams of death,
And prophesying with accents terrible
Of dire combustion and confused events
New hatch'd to the woeful time: the obscure bird
Clamour'd the livelong night: some say, the earth
Was feverous and did shake.
—William Shakespeare. Macbeth. 2.3.54-61

CHAPTER 26

Southern part of town
Hendersonville, TN
July 4
2:33p.m.

Booms and echoing crashes in multiple waves met the group's ears. The horses turned and whinnied, cantering nervously, the staccato percussive blasts frightening the animals. The sky to the south was lit by flame and smoke. The low droning of the aircraft was audible, even at this distance. The ground that they had been on this morning was alight, shattering blasts punctuating the previously calm air.

The horses had crossed Madison creek well enough. They seemed to remember the way, though they had only crossed it once before. They had to leave the tracks and veer off to the side a ways to find safe crossing. Everyone got a little wet, some very wet. But everyone made it safely across. The girls simply had to dismount, their combined weight too much for the horse. They had climbed to the top of the hill and back to the rail line. This was where they had been when the destruction of Nashville had commenced. Large aircraft, at least two dozen had flown in and released thousands of munitions, each containing sub-munitions. What the lay press called "cluster bombs" had been released and the combination of explosive and incendiary forces was smashing the city into oblivion. Many structures remained, but anyone unlucky enough to be in the blast radius was likely to have been killed. It was a death zone. The craft left almost as quickly as they had arrived, their payloads exhausted in the futile effort to stem the spread of the plague that had already circled the globe. The governmental response was typical: too much of the wrong thing, too late to help.

Darryl shook his head in disgust. He did not know the details, but having been in the Air Force, he got the gist. He turned his horse around and continued for home, the others falling in line. Stealthy movement a mile or so ahead near the tracks escaped the group's notice. Blurred shapes lumbered through the shade of the brushy trees adjoining the rail line, their herd-like patterns of motion familiar, yet terrifying.

Southern outskirts of Portland
Chloe Pearl's house
July 4
2:37p.m.

The three figures darted along the edge of the house towards the noise. Sam led the way as the girls ran behind. Chloe was breathing heavily, trying not to panic at the sounds. Screeches of pain and terror emanated from the house. She tried not to imagine what was happening, but after all that she had seen, her mind raced ahead.

"Grrwoooahhllgghhhh!!!!" The gurgling screech echoed from the building, sending shock waves of terror through the weary travelers' minds.

Sam reached into his pocket and flipped open his Gerber Gator pocket knife, its large wide blade usually reserved for skinning deer. Now it would be the difference between life and death. Sam strode up the back steps and into the kitchen. Chloe and Pirelli followed steps behind. They entered the darkened kitchen and the smell hit them like a boot to the face. Death. Death lived here. It walked the Earth naked, and hid here in the dark.

Sweat poured from the three nurses, their breath coming rapidly, their eyes wide open for movement, yet wanting desperately not to see what must be inside.

"Sccrrrooooggghhhllllllll!!! Schunnnffffhhh. Schunnnffffhhhh." The creature screamed and then breathed heavily through its nose. In and out, the tortured breath sounded. Thumping steps thudded on the floor, the metallic grinding, sliding of metal scrabbling across the wooden floorboards. A shadow of a tall figure appeared around a corner into the living room, now just visible in the hallway to the kitchen.

Chloe suppressed an urge to scream and thought as rapidly as her fear-wracked brain could manage. She turned to the side and snatched out a long wickedly sharp French chef knife out of the drawer and handed it to Pirelli, grabbing a thinner butcher knife for herself. Her Ruger P95 9mm pistol was in the bedroom, in a punch code safe, its computer chip obviously long since fried. The thing was in between them and the room.

On the floor a large lump. No, two lumps appeared, darker blobs on the floor in a sea of darkness. Chloe always kept her blinds closed to keep out the heat in the Summer. The house was sweltering, over eighty degrees now, the closed windows and doors holding in the stench of death. The thing turned, its face a smear of dark, thick fluid, claw marks from fingernails having raked across one now useless eye. The dark stains ran from its lower chin and covered its neck. Wild hair stuck to the stains and matted across the face. The man must have been handsome, in a rugged eighties rocker way, his chiseled features and wavy hair now distorted in a rictus of infected agony. In its right hand was an axe, covered in black stains, dragging across the living room floor.

The eyes, well-adjusted to the dark saw the movement in the kitchen. The pupils narrowed and the thing hunched and screamed, "Gaaaaarrrrggggghhh!!" Spittle flew from the mouth, revealing teeth covered in black stains. It lunged down the hallway, the single bladed axe raised high, now in both hands.

Sam charged low and thrust upward, catching the creature under the ribcage, the four inch blade tearing into the epigastrium and chest cavity, piercing the upper stomach and nicking the lower apex of the heart. Blood erupted from the beast, flooding out onto its chest and Sam's right arm.

The creature did not howl. It was as if it had no response at all to pain. In fact, this was exactly what had occurred. The reason the infected had to be shot multiple times or with large caliber weapons, was their complete lack of pain response. Normal people experienced extreme pain when shot, slashed or stabbed and the pain response overwhelmed their ability to continue fighting in most cases. The infected had no such reaction. They fought until blood loss or tissue damage stopped their ability to attack. Sam realized this all in an instant, just as he realized that he would have to scrub himself to prevent infection, as he was now covered in the deadly infected blood of the thing.

It stumbled forward and turned on Pirelli. She held the knife in front of her and Chloe slammed her butcher knife into the thing's right rib cage. Air fluttered out of the eight inch deep puncture wound, and then sucked back in as the now sucking chest wound robbed the creature of half of its oxygen supply. The axe came down right towards Pirelli, just an instant after she rolled to the side. The blade bit deeply into to cabinet where her head had been a moment before.

As the beast wrenched the axe out of the cabinet, Sam lunged towards its back. He couldn't risk grabbing it around the neck as he knew it might bite him and infect him with the same plague. He raised the thick bladed knife in a hammer grip, flipping the blade down. Just as the axe came free, the Gator's blade slammed home, right into the base of the thing's spinal cord. The tough, high carbon stainless steel had a very high Rockwell hardness that, while too brittle for a sword blade, acted like a super hard ceramic when it contacted the bone of the spine. It punched right through under the force of Sam's considerable upper body strength, crunching into the thick lower cervical spinous pedicles and sliced clean through the things upper spine, completely transecting the cord. The thing's head jerked back instantly and it fell to the ground, snapping the blade off the knife handle that Sam still clutched in a white knuckle grip.

The body lay limp, the creature's eyes and mouth still working. It had been paralyzed, but was not dead. Sam pried the axe out of the things roughened hands and slammed the bade deep into the fallen creature's skull. Pirelli vomited and wiped her mouth. Chloe stood stock still, blood dripping from the butcher knife still in her hands. She walked inexorably slowly towards the lumps on the floor. As she stood over the brutally murdered bodies of her son and daughter, she wept. Streams of anguish flowed from her eyes as she screamed aloud, sobbing and crying out to God for help. Her children must have come to check on her and regroup when the power went out. But where were her grandchildren, her two baby girls? She sobbed uncontrollably. Just as she thought her lungs would break, a soft sound under her feet rustled beneath the floorboards.

**Fort Campbell
Command Center
July 4
2:40p.m.**

The general stared in disbelief out of the window of the office compound. The large rotorcraft was approaching at the wrong vector. The Apache twisted at an impossible angle, its rotors corkscrewing out of control as the multimillion dollar aircraft drew at almost 200 miles an hour towards the building. The general sighed. No point.

The vehicle filled the window before it smashed into the small building, rupturing fuel lines and starting several small fires. Its segmented fuel tanks did not ignite. The entire command staff was instantly killed. Dust floated across the tarmac as the dead and dying lay sprawled out under the rubble. Three 5th Group operators jogged past, gunning down everyone in their path with casual ease. They sprinted past the crushed office and onto base housing. They started going door to door, killing the helpless occupants. Fires spread through the base and the combat control facility as the military lost control. Several other US military installations had already become combat ineffective due to loss of personnel or similar violence within the past hour.

Hendersonville, TN
Rockland Road
Rail line overpass
July 4
2:42p.m.

Gwenn stared through her binoculars at the three horses. Her heart leapt as she saw her baby girl riding behind a tall thin dark skinned girl. Tessa also looked OK. She felt relief course through her and was about to wave and call when movement on the edge of her vision caught her eye. It had been tricky getting this far ahead with the truck. She had driven. You always put the better shot riding shotgun and if anything, Matt was a very good shot. They had gotten about as far as they could go, worming their way around the abandoned cars and so far had avoided all contact with the infected or the looters of the previous day. They were near and to the South of the gun store's location.

"Shit," she heard Matt call out softly. He was staring through the ten power SS10x42 scope of his Sage EBR Springfield M1A, an accurized civilian M14 clone in semi auto. It was capable of keeping 10 rounds of match grade .308 in a 10 inch target at 800 meters. It was semi auto, and was much faster to shoot than a bolt gun. While not so accurate at extreme range as a bolt gun, it was far faster to shoot. Unfortunately, that feature of the weapon system would now be put to the test.

Gwenn's attention shifted back to the binoculars and horror flooded through her. As the horses were moving up the rail line, several figures appeared, at a dead run, heading directly towards them. The distance made exact details hard to make out, but the people appeared disheveled and dirty, several rolling their heads back in what appeared to be howls of animal rage. The sounds began to become audible. The hoarse croaking of the infected sent chills through Gwenn's spine. The horses began galloping at full tilt as the riders were firing with one hand on their rifles, the others on the reins.

Gwenn shouldered her M4 and looked through the red dot optic. It was unmagnified and simply did not provide enough detail to safely shoot at this distance. She glanced over at Matt who had a laser rangefinder in his hand, peering through the optic.

"470 yards and closing!" He yelled out, stowing the tiny device and settling in behind the fifteen pound gun. Gwenn silently prayed and began scanning around their position. She could not help, the distance was too far for a safe shot with her rifle. She could easily kill the very people she was trying to help. The fact that Matt was about to fire directly into her daughter's position did not escape her, but she had seen the results of the Navy man's extended range sessions. She prayed for The Lord to guide his hands and eyes.

Matt relaxed his breath and established his natural point of aim, eyes closed. He opened them, exhaled and squeezed the trigger. The .308 caliber 175 grain Black Hills Match bullet tore from the barrel and rocketed towards the target. Milliseconds later the round impacted the torso of a running infected man, ten feet from the girls' horse. It spun the thing around and the horse passed by, the thing up and running after them too late to catch them. The thing would probably die several hours from now, but it did not matter to him, Matt did not have time to think. The next wave of creatures was upon them, Darryl and Justin fired rapidly, sending several down as the horses ran right over them, crushing the infected foes.

Matt kept up a steady rate of fire, emptying the 20 round magazine and speedily rocking another home and releasing the bolt. More shots echoed down the tracks as shot after shot hit home, sending the infected spirally over and clearing the path for the horses. The group was now only about 200 yards from the overpass. A noise caused Gwenn to turn to the right.

Her blood froze.

"Matt, look out!" She cried as three infected ran up the road towards them. Her carbine cracked ten times sending center mass hits into each body. The first two tripped and sprawled onto the roadway, now crawling slowly, hands forward like some kind of obscene dance, their faces rubbing into the pavement. One stopped, a large pool of blood spreading in a halo around the body. The third, a woman, was bleeding from her abdomen and screaming, mouth open in a leering grin of horrific intent. Ten feet away, her head exploded as the 62grain M855 round ruptured her cranium. Her inertia, carried her body forward missing Gwenn by inches.

Gwenn gasped and scanned the area. Several more infected were running at them from one hundred yards away. Gwenn carefully settled and triple tapped two more on the chest, the creatures falling away. Matt's rifle spoke and the other two fell to head and neck shots from fifty yards. The horses were now upon them.

"Sweetie! Up here!" Gwenn cried out, motioning with her left hand, the rifle still held in the right, her two point adjustable sling over the neck and arm. The horses leaped up the embankment without hesitation. Matt fired another magazine dry and Gwenn finished off the remaining three infected on the tracks as he reloaded.

"Mom! You're alive!" Kate cried out

"I love you baby! But come on, jump in the truck, looks like Tessa's horse needs a break!" Gwenn said glancing at the foam on the animal's neck. "We've gotta go now! More of those things are coming!" Gwenn said, looking to the horizon where more infected people could be seen walking towards their position.

Kate leaped from the horse and hugged Gwenn's neck and kissed her. She yelled "thanks!" to Tessa and tossed her backpack into the backseat of the truck and climbed in the seat. Matt nodded at the men.

"We'll ride, you drive the women," Darryl said, nodding back.

"Roger that! But Gwenn's driving, I'm riding shotgun!" Matt said, scooping up his rifle, and leaping around the truck and into the passenger seat. He slammed the door and Gwenn climbed in, gunned the engine, backed up, turned the truck around and headed home, the horses at a fast canter behind her.

They kept up the pace for several miles and stopped when they reached Matt's neighborhood. From there, they slowed to let the horses walk. The neighbors were outside now, doing varied work, cooking on grills, nailing boards on windows and talking. They stopped as the parade of truck and animals moved past. Several waved, the group waved back. Gwenn was glad when they got out of the truck and were greeted by the sentries. When they entered the house, the two dogs jumped for joy. Kate fell to the floor and sobbed when Gwenn recounted the tale of Penelope's death saving the family.

Angus and Carlos arrived at dusk and the family reunion was bittersweet. Angus hugged Kate so tightly that she thought he would squeeze her to death. They both cried. Carlos announced that they should start prepping for the retreat. He recommended that they leave as soon as possible tomorrow. The neighbors made him nervous. It would be a long night of packing up gear.

Northern Louisiana
Northwest of Barksdale AFB
July 4
3:29p.m.

The massive aircraft abruptly jogged to the left and then to the right. The lead bomber called for status. The infected crew members of the unstable aircraft were beyond understanding the words spoken over the radio. Suddenly the craft veered sideways and slammed its left wingtip into the opposing wing of another B-52 in formation. Both aircraft lost control and began to pirouette towards the ground, flames and smoke billowing outward as the macabre dance of slow motion death played out. The altitude was high enough that the trajectory carried the craft onto the base. The flaming hulks smashed into the airstrip and the control tower and the massive explosions destroyed the majority of the base, a firestorm of destruction fanning outward as the other aircraft now had nowhere to land, the runway covered in burning debris.

The other pilots would eventually put down on secondary airstrips, but the military's ability to maintain air control over the Southern U.S. was effectively eliminated in a day. Infected personnel at this and other bases attacked their colleagues, or simply went AWOL, leaving the leadership without any effective response. This same type of event played out across the globe as the remainder of combat effective forces lost the ability to function. The combination of the solar event and plague proved to be a one two punch, sending military planners back fifty years at one fell swoop. Smaller units were still functioning autonomously. This left units at the whim of the lower ranking commanders. Some integrated themselves into their local communities, protecting them, while others would destroy everything in their paths, raping, looting and pillaging. The time of global conflict was over for years to come. The battles of the immediate future would be fought over neighborhoods and towns, food sources and supply caches. It was a brave new world.

Nashville, TN
Downtown
July 4
3:39p.m.

Fires raged through the demolished city. Rubble was strewn across dozens of city blocks, the once famous city now a crumbling heap of blackened earth, its citizens crushed under the weight of metric tons of debris. Fires spread to the river's edge and beyond, gouts of orange and red slipping in amongst the dead, the charred remains of city and people co-mingled in an orgy of destruction. Parts of limbs and torsos were scattered to the four winds, heads lay askance, some still attached to their bodies, others ripped off and crushed beyond recognition.

The last desperate act of a government losing control had played out here. A citizenry that trusted and relied on its master government for all guidance, all prosperity, and all sustenance had died this day, its own master crushing it beneath the heel of its boot, uncaring to the last. A sudden event, but not a surprising one. The drama had played out countless times before. Stalin, Hitler, Feudal England, Rome, the list was endless. Corrupt rulers who took their power from the people and then when the people needed them most, destroyed the very citizenry that had placed them in office.

Wind created by the superheated fires carried the dust of the bodies of one hundred thousand souls across the plains and hills. The cry of injustice would never come. The battle had already been lost before it had even begun. The plague had signaled the end, the death throes of a kingdom, dying for the past one hundred years, its glory long spent.

Alexis de Tocqueville got it right when he said that democracy couldn't last because the majority would realize that they could vote themselves money and that the system would collapse when this occurred. His writings were prophetic, his vision correct. Any good student of history could clearly see the path. The plague and the solar events were only harbingers of what would ultimately come regardless of nature's whims. Mankind had created his own hell, now he would have to find a way to live in it.

Southern outskirts of Portland
Chloe Pearl's house
July 4
3:40p.m.

Chloe washed the girls' hair with the backyard scrub bucket and soap. She scrubbed and scrubbed, saying her prayers of thanks while cleaning the days grime away, washing away as much of the horror as possible. They had already used the Clorox bottle in the laundry room to rinse off the blood from themselves. The shock of the events of the day slowly subsided as the suds worked deeply into the girls' matted hair.

The two grandchildren, Mattie Smith, age 9, and Rebecca Smith, age 12, had hidden under the crawl space of the house when they heard the commotion inside. Chloe and the group had found them when she had heard noises under the floor. They had raced outside and under the house, not knowing what to expect. Now, a bittersweet reunion followed. The girls had been hiding in terror all night and day under the house since yesterday when the grisly murders had been committed. Chloe could only get a partial story of what exactly had happened. The girls were quietly staring at the grass now, still obviously in shock at what they had witnessed.

The best Chloe could tell, the madman had simply wandered into the house and killed the children's father and aunt and simply remained in the darkened house afterward, wandering around with the axe. The girls had fled under the house when the intruder came. They had to be coaxed out afterward, so great was their fear. Once they came out, they were given water and then everyone scrubbed down with the Clorox and some cleaning brushes.

Sam buried the dead in a shallow grave in the garden plot where the soil was loose and soft and dragged the infected man's body out to the edge of the property by the road. He then rewashed himself. The work seemed to be therapeutic to him. He was a tough man and had the job done in forty-five minutes. Sam said grace and Chloe and Pirelli prayed aloud and placed cut flowers on the makeshift grave. Chloe wanted to leave this place forever and never come back. She knew if they survived, someone could come back and deal with gathering supplies and cleaning out the house. Chloe had some men's clothes from her ex-husband that fit Sam and Pirelli was petite enough to fit into her older granddaughter's clothes. Chloe had changed as well and then set to scrubbing the girls' hair, which had been matted badly from the experience.

She rinsed the soap out with the fresh water that they had drawn from the water heater reservoir. The tap did not work, as Chloe's place was on a well that had a digital pump, which of course was useless now. Chloe thought that they could really use a hand pump. Sam suggested that they eat and then immediately travel to Pirelli's place now, before sundown. After the horror seen here, Chloe agreed. They gathered fresh gear and weapons. Chloe used the manual backup key lock on the punch code safe to retrieve her handgun.

She had fifty rounds of 9mm hollow point and another fifty rounds of full metal jacket or FMJ ball ammo for target practice. Sam loaded the gun and its extra 15 round magazine and gave it to Chloe who attached it to her belt with the inexpensive Uncle Mikes nylon holster she kept for it. Everyone had good footwear on and Chloe dressed the kids. Sam found a good thirty dollar machete with a nylon sheath in the garage and gave Pirelli a four-foot pruning hook to carry. He took an eighteen-inch long Fiskars camp axe, a hatchet or tomahawk-sized tool that had a good balance. He slipped the sheath of the machete onto his belt and slid the axe through his belt along his back.

They organized book bags with clothing, tools, food, water, medicine, bandages, and ponchos that could be used as tarps for shelter if needed. The bugs were out so they all sprayed insect repellent onto themselves. The DEET stung some on their freshly clean skin. Chloe gave Sam a small pair of binoculars and took a box of strike anywhere matches and candles from the kitchen. They ate a small meal of cold canned goods, chili and mixed veggies and headed out.

The trip to Pirelli's house took a few hours, and they were tired when they arrived. Chloe and the grandkids rested on the front porch while Sam and Pirelli started setting up for the night. Pirelli's husband Steve was very glad to see his wife and they embraced for some time, tears of joy flowing from the couple. Sam thought about his wife and family and was eager to get back home, but knew they simply had to stop for the night. He was exhausted.

I set out on this ground which I suppose to be self evident, "that the earth belongs... to the living;" that the dead have neither powers nor rights over it.
—Thomas Jefferson, letter to James Madison, 1789

CHAPTER 27

Mackenzie House
Hendersonville, TN
July 5
1:25p.m.

The crew had returned from the Corpuz house and was gathering up all of the remaining gear. Beth could not actually believe that they were leaving, maybe forever. This was her house; her kids had grown up in it and she had lived her life here. But it was not enough to keep her from doing what had to be done. The other families had left their homesteads, and now she must do the same.

Beth hopped into the passenger seat of the Deuce and signaled to Matt. It was time to go. The siblings were ready in the back with Madison guarding the rear. The Mackenzies were financially successful. They actually had two reserve vehicles, unique amongst the group. This deuce and a half was their main unit, but they also had an older model International Harvester scout, just like the one the Rees family had. The Corpuzes were using that today, which was a real blessing, as they did not yet have their own EMP-proof vehicle. The Gunns headed up the rear in their deuce with the Washingtons in lead in their F 250. The two deuces had extra trailers in the back, loaded with the Corpuz family's extra gear.

There would be food and water and lots of pre-cached equipment at the retreat. John Calvin had made radio contact and told them of the events of the first day. The neighbors here had already started asking for food and medicine; some were angry when they were turned away. Beth worried about the theft and looting that would likely occur after they evacuated. But that was a trouble for another day: God help the neighbors if they resorted to theft. All of the really important stuff was either waiting on them at the compound in the hills, or with them in the trucks. The engines gunned to life and the convoy set off. Beth stared out of the window, tears of regret falling gently from her cheeks, regret for the state of things, the loss of all gentility and grace, the loss of her home, the loss of innocence. She prayed to God for guidance in these dark days.

The convoy rolled out of the neighborhood, in close interval formation. The radio chattered with comm between the units. All was well, so far. The neighbors looked on, some smirking, some staring with mouths agape. Life would never return to normal. Beth was just glad that they had set up their own section in the compound. Privacy would be at a minimum in the next months. Having an area that they could call their own was psychologically important. They crossed town heading for the rendezvous with the other group members. All hands were on deck, so to speak. All eyes scanned for roadblocks and signs of danger.

Bledsoe house
Portland, Tn
July 5
1:30p.m.

Sam smiled, as Thomas Bledsoe hugged his stepdaughter Sophie. Thomas, now 43, had married his wife Pirelli, now 28, after her first marriage had ended in divorce. Pirelli's two kids were never wanted by their biological father. Thomas worked in construction and had no kids of his own and had never wanted any before meeting Pirelli, having had a vasectomy performed in the years before they met. When he met her kids, he fell in love with them and was one of the best fathers in town. He was well-known to leave work early to attend ball games and was always carrying one or the other on his strong, wide shoulders.

Sophie was 10 and her brother James was 7. They both adored Thomas and considered him their only real father. They had no memory of their biological father as they were very young when their mom was remarried. Sophie ran out of the kitchen into the backyard, squealing in delight. Chloe and her grandkids sat on the front porch, sipping lemonade. Sam hesitated and then allowed himself a small smile. He was too paranoid. Everything seemed all right. Finally, Sam had a moment of peaceful reflection.

"Eeeeeeeeeeeeee!" A terrible cry echoed from the back yard. The shriek sent shock waves through the house.

"Mommaaaa! Mommaaaaa!" The young girl's voice cried out in desperate fear.

Sam snatched up his camp axe and machete and raced out of the screen door and burst onto the scene in the backyard. His blood chilled as he stared upon the scene. He flung the sheath off of the machete in his left hand and raised the axe in his right hand and tore through the yard, the door behind him slamming open as others raced into the yard.

The scene was chilling. Sophie was ten feet up a small tree in the yard with four infected around her climbing up after her, snarling like animals. Their disheveled clothes hung on their frames, leaves and twigs covering their clothing. It looked as if they had walked through a bramble patch, and they may very well have as the back of the property backed up on just such a patch. They did not seem to notice Sam as he bore down on the ones nearest him.

A shotgun slide racked behind Sam as he reached the first one, a woman in a tattered dress, wild brown hair flailing about as she struggled on the tree. The axe slammed into the back of her torso, crushing several ribs, blood spurting out of the back right side of her body. She turned and leaped backwards, catching Sam by the hair, her lips curled in a leering grin.

Her teeth flashed as she prepared to sink them into his face, rearing her head back in triumph as Sam toppled onto his back. The boom of the shotgun made Sam's ears ring as the 12 gauge triple ought buckshot load ruptured the woman's head, spraying debris in all directions. Sam rolled to the right side and flung the lifeless corpse away, wiping his face with his sleeve; bloody gray gunk covered his shirt and face. He spit reflexively, terrified of contact with the diseased flesh. Turning quickly, he prayed for safety, as he set upon the next infected people.

Pistol fire rang out multiple times, as Chloe fired ten rounds into the torso of a man who had turned towards the noise and away from the tree. The man collapsed under the withering fire. Sam hurled his axe into the face of another, the blade slamming into the nasal bridge and cleaving the nose and left front cheek off. The creature turned and gurgled a hideous roar through the bloody facial defect, its voice strangled, nasal sounding from the sudden loss of sinus resonance, and then it set upon Sam.

The machete swung easily to the midline, Sam's palm up as the blade slammed into the thing's neck and transected its right side, burying its edge tip into the lateral cervical spine. Blood vomited from its mouth and poured out of its neck as grasping hands reached for him, a visage of horror slowly loosing strength as its steps shortened and it collapsed before reaching him, the thing's dark lifeblood rippling out of its body and pouring across the grass of the lawn. Rifle fire cracked through the yard as Thomas Bledsoe's Winchester model 70 .30-30 spoke, several rounds hitting the last man in the torso and head, silencing his blood-curdling screams of rage. Sam reached towards the terrified girl and pulled her towards him. She shook with the tremor of unfathomable fear, her childhood shattered in an instant. Blood soaked into the thirsty soil of the dry backyard as the prostrate forms presented a testament of a world gone mad, a puppet show of insanity. The marionettes' strings were now cut by the brave defense, launched by these friends, these survivors of this deadly, terrifying, brave new world.

Spence Creek State Park
10 miles Northeast of Gallatin, TN
Rees house
July 5
2:35p.m.

Scott Rees and his wife Stephanie loaded up the last of their goods into the all-terrain trailer, hitched behind their International Harvester 1974 Scout II. The faded sky blue paint was still pretty on the classic vehicle. Stephanie cried quietly as they prepared to leave their house. She glanced at Beth Mackenzie, sighed and halfheartedly waved. She smiled at Gwenn Gunn and then hopped into the SUV as Scott started the engine. Its carbureted 345 V8 made no fuss as it was designed before the advent of the computer chip.

They headed next towards Bethpage. Scott absent-mindedly scratched at the bandage on his arm as Stephanie smacked him on the elbow to make him stop.

"Sorry," he said, eyes never leaving the road. The wound itched some, which he thought was a good sign as he knew this likely meant that it was starting to heal. It was clean and did not have any odor, and the bloody drainage had stopped quickly with pressure. Stephanie had thoroughly cleaned it and the antibiotics seemed to be working. He glanced at Stephanie for an instant and could practically read her mind. She was deliberately not looking at the wound. She looked at and spoke of everything else on the trip to Bethpage. It was clearly obvious that she was worried. He was too. After all of the zombie movies that he and the guys had seen, he couldn't help but worry.

Bethpage, TN
5 miles East of Gallatin
Washington House
July 5
3:01p.m.

The trucks lumbered to a halt in the long drive. Nervous eyes looked out from the small homestead, rifle barrels pointing their way. Sudden squeals of delight echoed from the front hall as Susanne saw her father step from his truck. Tessa dismounted from the passenger side and her mother Simone sank to the ground, rifle still cradled in her arms as the sight of her baby girl walking uninjured into the drive overwhelmed her. She sobbed uncontrollably, her chest heaving with emotion, bottled up since the start of this mad event, now bubbling forth in an exultant outpouring of thanksgiving. The rifle slid into her lap as she raised her hands in prayer, eyes closed, tears streaming down, her silent thanks to Jesus readily seen on her lips as she repeated the mantra over and over again. Her breathing slowed as His love flowed through her and she regained control. She stood and Tessa grabbed the AK and held it to the side as she fiercely hugged and tried to kiss her mother through her N95 mask.

The group had taken to wearing black nitrile gloves and the charcoal gray tactical N95 masks used by police officers when dealing with potentially infectious suspects. This recent precaution would hopefully prevent any further spread were any group members infected. Everyone prayed that it was unnecessary. Simone laughed and motioned to Darryl. He nodded and Simone grabbed a handful of the masks and placed them on everyone in her family group. They used some hand gel from a large pump dispenser on the counter. The Gunn family and Scott Rees stood in the doorway, the other group members setting up a security perimeter and monitoring the vehicles, their actions as automatic as if they did this sort of stuff every day. Their previous monthly tactical training was really kicking in now.

Jesse Washington, his wife Samantha and 11-month-old daughter Julia were present, as well as his best friend Cleo Stanfield. They all packed into the living room as Tessa told an abbreviated version of her escape and travel home. Simone sat and stared at the floor in stunned silence. They had experienced none of the horrors so far. They had seen some odd people walk by, down the road, but had not stopped them or investigated them at all. A shudder of fear ran through her. These infected. That's what they were. They all staggered and shifted about. For whatever reason, they had not noticed the small homestead. But how long would that last, and how many more were there?

Simone was, if anything, a highly intelligent and logical person. She thought through her concerns, and she did so now, the group quietly watching her response, interested in what she would say. Listening to the tale, it seemed that there were two types of infected. One type was without intellect, but could run, attack and bite. The other seemed to retain their intelligence, but committed such acts of atrocity that their very humanity was called into question. Whatever this disease was, the infected seemed to be in a state of permanent paranoia and psychosis and they seemed utterly immune to pain. How else to explain the multiple wounds required to dispatch them.

The Washington's family preparedness plan was, as was everyone's, always a work in progress. They were ready for storms, earthquake, small scale terrorist attacks, even minor government meddling. But this event, this was on a massive scale. They had never considered pooling their resources with other families. Darryl and Simone were fiercely independent. They planned on relying on the few members they had in the house to defend it from attack. They simply didn't have enough men or ammunition to cope with this level of threat. She stared at Darryl. Understanding dawned on the man as he nodded. She fixed her gaze on Angus.

Angus glanced back, "Been waiting on you to figure that out. You know we saved you an empty bunk."

"I think we just did," she said, relief spreading a grin on her face, clearly visible around the edges of the mask. The families had known each other for years, and there were few thoughts that escaped the friends' understanding.

"Sweetie, we need to get our gear," she said to Darryl, smiling still.

"Yes ma'am," he replied

Tessa looked rapidly from one parent to the other and back again, understanding dawning on her. "You mean we get to live with Kate?!"

"Yes Sweetie, as long as they'll have us." She looked back at Gwenn, who was now smiling ear to ear. Tessa and Kate were literally jumping up and down holding hands, talking in teenage girl rapid fire, occasional words understandable to the older adults in the room. The Washingtons spent the evening packing up their gear, as the larger group made an expedient cold camp with rigid light discipline, so to avoid any unnecessary attention.

Bledsoe house
Portland, Tn
July 5
7:25p.m.

Sam smiled as the girls hugged his neck. Thomas winked as Pirelli turned her head back to her husband while still hugging Sam. The girls hugged him again and now the grandkids and children ran over, mobbing Sam as well, hugging any part of him they could find. He had changed clothes, after meticulously scrubbing himself with soap and a lukewarm bucket of water, using another bottle of Clorox to clean himself. He remained terrified of infection. They would have to get some type of protective gear in the future.

The mob of smiling people relented and Sam caught his breath again and smiled at Thomas. His offer for everyone to move to his farm had obviously been well received. He had promised Dr. Gunn and felt that this would be the best way to protect everyone. Also, the extra hands and eyes would frankly be needed on the farm as well, now that the world had changed. They would need to come together to work the fields and defend themselves from these crazed infected plague victims.

He had made it clear that, since it was his house, he would have the last say on anything and had spoken with Thomas privately after he cleaned and changed clothes. This time he had put on a pair of Thomas' jeans and one of his shirts. This was getting old, but it sure beat the hell out of turning into one of those things. He just prayed that his Clorox and soap were enough protection.

They began packing up their worldly possessions. They could always come back for another load as it was only a few miles to the Wallace farm, but they needed food, shelter and supplies now. And weapons. Lots and lots of weapons. Sam and Thomas went throughout the house and pulled out every knife, machete, axe, shovel, baseball bat and tool that looked potentially lethal. They grabbed a large stack of hickory axe handles as well. Those could be used to repair axes, make clubs or even make really good takedown recurve bows. Sam grinned at the remembered knowledge from his time woodworking.

They loaded up as many blankets, canned goods, Clorox, soap and clothes that they could, trying to think of what would be most important. They took the first aid kit, sewing supplies, nails, duct tape, glue, ratchet sets, fence wire, candles, matches and an extra metal gas can with five gallons of unleaded, used for the lawn mower.

They took all of Thomas' hand tools, as well as his extensive gun collection. It was a practical assortment of hunting rifles and shotguns, twenty nine guns in all, from .22 bolt actions with inexpensive scopes, to seven round .30-30s, shotguns and revolvers in .357 and .45 Long Colt. Sam took, with Thomas' permission, a five and a half-inch barreled Ruger Blackhawk single action in .45 Long Colt. It had a .45 ACP cylinder that he stowed in his small backpack. He loaded it and put the two boxes of shells in the pack, sliding the leather holster onto the belt he also borrowed from Thomas. Each took a .30-30, Thomas his original pre-1964 Winchester model 94 and Sam a more recent Marlin model 336, both with six round tubes. They slung black nylon bandoliers of twenty cartridges each over their chests. Each girl took a shotgun: Pirelli her Mossberg 12 gauge 935 hunting gun with a 28 inch barrel, and Chloe an older Remington 870 in .410. Each grabbed a box of slugs and buckshot and loaded their purses with shells, after filling the shotgun's tubes.

Thomas took his own Ruger KGP-141 stainless steel .357 magnum four inch barreled revolver and stowed it in a leather Galco holster on his right side. He had never been so fast with the single actions as Sam, since he didn't do the historical reenactments that Sam did. Sam's skills with the less sophisticated technologies were now coming in handy. They began loading up the fishing boat with gear and attached it to the ancient Ford pickup that Thomas kept as a fishing truck. Thomas, Pirelli and Sophie sat in the cab, while Sam, Chloe, and the rest of the kids sat in the truck bed, next to boxed gear.

The truck started up after Thomas sprayed starter fluid in the carburetor and revved the engine. The sound was music to Chloe's ears. She never thought the idea of an old clunker like this could ever make her happy. They moved slowly down the road, rifles and shotguns pointed outward in every direction, eyes alert for movement.

Wallace Farm
Outskirts of Portland, TN
10 miles Northeast of Gallatin
July 5
8:15p.m.

    The truck pulled up into the yard, dogs bristling and barking as the vehicle approached. Sam leaped out and called to the dogs to prevent them from attacking. The last thing they needed was dealing with a dog bite. They immediately started tail wagging and stopped barking, happy to see their master. Sam's wife, Carolyn, came to the front porch, shotgun in hand and sighed in relief. She set the gun against the railing and opened her arms for her man. Big tears welled in her eyes as he vaulted the stairs to the porch in a bound. He picked her up and spun her around, laughing with joy. They hugged and then he set her down and introduced everyone in the new group.

    Sam's kids were there, and also armed. Trey Wallace, 31, stepped out onto the deck and 27-year-old Jessica poked her head out as well. The real surprise was Jessica's ex-husband, Jim Summers. The kids had been visiting him and he had made it around town through the countryside on foot with the kids over the past days since the power went out.

Jim was 30 years old and a recovering alcoholic. He had been an architect and now worked with a local construction crew. They had divorced when his drinking had destroyed their marriage. After the divorce, he hit rock bottom and had turned his life over to the Lord Jesus at church one morning. He had never been the same since. Jessica had kept her distance, fearing a relapse, but he had remained clean for these last two years.

Sam shook hands and hugged his daughter and the grandkids, Sarah and Becky, aged six and seven respectively. They all appeared none the worse for wear. Sam looked at Jim.

"You are always welcome here, Jim," said Sam, peering with his icy blue eyes at the man who did not wither with the gaze.

"Just wanted the kids safe, didn't expect anything for myself," Jim replied.

"Children need their father. You should stay here, I insist. Most everybody will have to sleep in the barn, but we'll work it out."

Sam spoke very quietly to Carolyn and she squeezed his hand and nodded. He walked back to the deck and spoke to the gathering group.

"We've all got work to do. This won't be easy, but if we all pull together, I know The Lord will help us get through this. I have been blessed with this farm, and with my friends. Now it's time to return the favor. You all can sleep on the deck or barn. We don't have many bedrooms or much space. We'll all have to pull our weight and I know this is a scary time. But I know we are tough enough. Now let's get some chow!"

Everybody squeezed into the kitchen and a large soup kettle was there, full to the brim with vegetable beef stew, cooked on the propane range. The aroma was heavenly and it comforted all present. Fresh cornbread baked over the backyard campfire was steaming on the table as well. Glasses of well water and sun brewed tea were passed around, an odd assortment of styles, given the number of guests. Everyone ate heartily, some sitting at the table, others standing or crouching on the deck. It had been a long day, but the men were already planning the day's work for tomorrow. There would be much to do in this strange, terrifying new land that was their home.

Tulley Farm
Five miles north of Gallatin, TN
July 5
11:37p.m.

Smoke drifted across the battle plain, crops lay smoking, the ruin of their stalks foreboding the ill to come. No harvest, no food. Desperation. Bodies lay in twisted heaps, agony etched upon their faces, both the infected and clean alike. The sun beat down on the scene, uncaring in her endless revolutions, an astronomical regularity of divine clockwork. A child, now orphaned, knelt at the foot of one of the bodies. Her wails of piercing sadness echoed through the devastated landscape, a keening of that which was lost forever.

Time and earth shifted. Darkness covered the scene, a more familiar place, a homely place. Goats shifted in their pens, wind drifted lazily on the hot night, scents of earthy goodness wafted through the pastoral scene. All was right with the world. Slowly, a foul wind ebbed across the pasture. Footfalls stealthily approached, the smell of blood drawing the hungry. The goats shifted, brayed nervously, an evil presence now holding them in thrall.

The land recoiled at the touch of the boots and shoes. Unclean. Unholy. The swarms of moving bodies now emboldened by the sight of the barn and the rich animal smell of bounty. Sentries gave the alert, radios crackled at the recognition of the advancing horde. The limitless swath of the unclean defied imagining. Endless wave upon wave of lost souls pouring through the countryside, drawn by the promise of a meal, their animal instincts unblinded by the travesty that corrupted their minds. Movement along the ridge line. Feet running to man the stations. Not enough men. Not enough ammunition.

Desperate bravery. Fire echoing through the valley, the gentle, pristine pasture stained with the blood of the horde. Unstopping weight of numbers bore down upon the glade. On and on and on the flood tide of lost humanity wandered forward, faster now, aware with deadly intent of the new bounty that they smelled. Hunger for the new arrivals, the sweat scent of fear mixing with the animal scent of the pasture. A new hunger arising. More for all to consume. Refocusing of the wave now pressing forward to both the ridge line and the barn now. No. No. God do not let it be! No. No!

Engines revving. Desperate flight. Cries of animal pain and agony from the barn. No! No! So gentle. Undeserving of such a fate. Wave upon wave of lost souls pouring forth. Unclean feet upon the blessed land. Too late, vehicles stall under the weight of the onslaught. Metal unmoving under the pressing weight of the tide of unclean humanity. Fear, terror, agony. Incredible valor. Too late to stem the flow. Too late to stop the tide of insanity from purging life from the land.

Teeth ripping, rending, fingernails tearing, clawing. Inhuman agony. Leering evil. Weight of pulling limbs tearing life's heart out. Bodies kicking and screaming, pulled from the vehicles. Desperate slashes, jabs and punches. Final shots fired at the mass of roiling destruction. The tide of onrushing death smothers all. No hope. All is lost. No. No! NO!

Lucien sat bolt upright in bed, sweat soaking the sheets, his breath coming in waves. His family was at his side, bursting through the doorway, his wife holding his arm, all awakened by the screams and the shouting. His heart still bursting in his chest, the weight of despair and agony slowly passed into the oblivion of the night. He regained his control. He turned and looked at his children, standing in nightshirts and shorts in the doorway, worry etched into their faces. He turned and looked at his wife, worry creasing her brow, as well.

The McKnights stood behind on the top of the stairwell, awakened, but not wanting to intrude. He stood, walked to the window and stared out to the pasture land. Not this way. It would not be this way. He prayed a silent prayer of thanks to his Lord and Master for the warning. He turned from the window to his family and friends.

"We have work to do."

It is a far, far better thing that I do, than I have ever done; it is a far, far better rest that I go to, than I have ever known.
—Charles Dickens, "A Tale of Two Cities"

CHAPTER 28

Gallatin, Tn
One block from Courthouse complex
Western side
July 5
11:59p.m.

Isaac looked out into the thick dark night. He could not shake the feeling that something was out there, something terrible and without remorse. Ever since the fight with the Emergency Management people, he had been on edge. The city dwellers in Gallatin had converged on this compound and the public library a couple of blocks over. Tents had been set up in the parking lots of both buildings and their numbers had swelled to about five hundred so far. It had been a terrible loss. Thousands had lived here. Between the fire, the plague and the attacks, only these few survived the initial collapse. People still could be sheltering in place in houses all over the county, but in Gallatin, so many places had burned down, that the death toll would be hard to estimate.

Everyone was taking contact precautions to avoid spreading any diseases, especially whatever this plague was that turned men into animals. Social distancing and basic hygiene seemed to be working. No one got closer than five feet and there was no hand shaking. Food prep was an exception, but they had managed well so far, with no one showing any erratic behavior. Hopefully, the plague had stopped spreading through this community.

A noise drew his attention. A trash can lid fell off of its can onto the pavement. Issac quickly keyed his mike twice, a silent alarm that something was up. Movement at the perimeter of his vision caught his eye. Shit. He saw several people walking through the dim night, looking into trash cans and rummaging through litter and debris, bringing morsels to their mouths. They walked forward, not stumbling. They could not see Issac from his position, behind the shrubbery. Well, OK, he thought, we can take those dozen or so easily. Just need to aim for the...

His thought abruptly stopped. A hundred or so shambling figures appeared at the edge of his vision, disappearing into the black, with more behind. His ear piece chirped twice and then twice and then twice more as three other perimeter guards reported enemy contact. Mother of all that is good and holy, he thought. If four of them saw the same thing, the number of people coming must be massive, as the guards were spread out far amongst the town.

Rapid footfalls sounded behind as more guards came up from the back. Issac turned and spoke to the young teenager who had come to get word on the contact. Issac looked the terrified pimply-faced boy in the eye.

"Tell them we all have to leave now. There are hundreds of them."

"Yessir," the boy whispered and raced back to the compound.

Issac clicked off the safety off of his Daniel Defense M4 carbine and prayed for strength. The line of advancing infected was now one hundred yards away and closing. They had not seen him yet, but the lights of the courthouse behind him caught their attention. They moved faster, hunger driving them onward. Issac thought of the families huddled in the buildings. Children and the elderly, and men and women of all ages trying to stay safe, huddled together in family groups in the hallways, lobbies and offices, most sleeping soundly now. The group of infected poured forward, sniffing at the air, a new hunger in their eyes. They had been subsisting on what they could find in trash cans and amongst the debris of the destroyed towns. They had grouped themselves into herds apparently. Issac shuddered.

The line of infected closed to fifty yards. Damn it, he would have to act, even without orders if they came any closer. Issac sighted in on the head of a large man wearing rumpled and stained mechanics overalls. He inhaled and exhaled half of the breath. Now would be a good time, Ed, he thought of his friend, who was now in charge. Now would be a good time.

"Engage." The earpiece rang as the command to attack was given, Edward's voice clear and distinct. The shot rang out, but all Isaac heard was a thud as the round impacted the infected man's brainpan, rupturing his head like a ripe melon. Issac wore Peltor Comtac active ear protection. The muffs fit easily under his ACH helmet and blocked the noise of the shot and amplified his regular hearing twenty decibels over the normal. His radio earpiece was taped to the front of the left microphone where its tiny signal would be amplified easily. He would not lose his hearing tonight.

Rounds cascaded from his position as infected after infected fell to the well-aimed fire. Issac could hear other sentries engaging the infected. The sky lit up from the muzzle blasts of a dozen sentries attempting to keep the wall of advancing death at bay. Behind him, Issac heard movement and he glanced to see dozens of people running and regrouping. The wall of infected humans closed to twenty five yards as he slammed in a fresh magazine. Sweat poured from his brow as he continued to engage the threat. He was not going to be able to stop them.

They closed in another five yards just as Issac's magazine ran dry. As he changed mags and caught the old one into a dump pouch, he thought of all that life had brought him. The Lord had been good to him. He had a beautiful family, a wonderful woman, a job he had loved, truly a blessed life. Now, it was time to go. He pressed the bolt release on the third magazine and just as the horde fell within ten yards, a dozen flaming bottles sailed overhead, slamming into the crowd and smashing onto the pavement. Flames erupted as each Molotov cocktail broke, sending gasoline gelled with laundry detergent spraying out onto the crowd.

Screams of fury sounded, as the loud chatter of small arms echoed through the rubble field. Fire sailed to the left and right of Issac's position. Bodies fell and the advance was halted as each oncoming infected was cut down where he stood. A much louder booming rolled through the former churchyard as a 50 BMG let loose in rapid semi-auto fire. Someone had dragged a Barrett M82A1 out of the rubble of one of the local gun shops that had burned down. It had been very dusty, but had appeared to be in good order. It seemed to be working just fine with the scavenged 50 BMG ball ammo that they liberated from another shop that had been looted incompletely, but had not burned down.

As each 670 grain bullet impacted the crowd, several infected went down. Two or three would collapse with each shot, their bodies savaged by the awesome power of the munitions. As the rounds blasted through the first row, they continued to travel through the crowd impacting with reduced velocity the rows behind. The advance slowed to a crawl.

"Fall back and provide covering fire." Ed's voice came over the radio, "Marines, we are leaving!"

"Alpha 1, Roger last," Issac replied, laughing to himself at the movie reference. These infected were like a swarm of aliens.

"Alpha 2, copy," Jack Sutherland, the 57-year-old corporate lawyer, replied

"Charlie 9er, roger that," Clay Masterson, the 41-year-old, steely blue-eyed air conditioner repair man, said.

"Bravo 3, roger that. Let's get the hell out of here!" an exuberant Nathan Ford said, his Vanderbilt EMT training warning him of danger. The louder boom, boom, boom of his M-240 semi-auto .308 registering in Issac's left ear.

Issac backed away, as his colleagues laid down suppressing fire holding the line. He ran and ducked behind an older pickup. Jack Sutherland was talking to two volunteers from the town. The young men had hunting rifles and shotguns slung over their shoulders with pistols on their hips.

"We've got to stall them for long enough to evacuate the group!" Jack said, sweat pouring from his forehead. He wore a Multicam ball cap in lieu of a helmet now.

"We can't let our families die like this, Don!" one volunteer named Sean said.

"No, we can't," replied Don, the other volunteer.

"We're taking the truck, clear us a path! If we don't make it, tell our families we love them!" Don said to Issac and Jack.

Issac looked at Jack. Jack grinned, a demonic gleam lighting his face.

"It's been a good run!" Jack said, "We'll both give 'em Hell! Two chances are better than one. Issac, you guys grab those propane tanks and throw them in the 59' Chevy pickup there," he said pulling out a large bundle of dynamite from his patrol pack. He had saved the bundle from his work on his property, when they were blasting the ground to add on to the house. His friend had been the contractor and had looked the other way when Jackie had liberated the bundle those years ago.

"Looks like we need this now, not later. I was saving it for later, but if we don't use it now, there won't be a later."

Issac looked at his lifelong friend, "Are you sure, Jackie boy?"

Jack Sutherland rose to his full and considerable height. He stared at his brother in arms, his maniacal smile softened now. Jack thought back to his last appointment with the urologist. He thought about the biopsy results and he thought about the radiation, surgery and chemo that he would have been destined for, had the power not gone out. He thought about his beautiful wife in her coffin, dead from the drunk driver. He wondered about his kids and grandkids living in Florida. He prayed for their safety. He pulled Issac into a bear hug.

"Never more sure in my life," he said, staring seriously at his friend. "Now get me that propane before time runs out!"

Issac looked at his friend again, his steely eyes peering deep into the man's soul, and he saw the truth. He nodded and then raced with three other volunteers to the Sheriff's office where the fuel had been stashed. The constant sound of gunfire echoed through the ruined town as dozens of men fought desperately to hold the infected horde at bay. The battle line stretched through three hundred yards of blackened city blocks. The wall of fighters was slowly falling back, as desperate townspeople were hurriedly evacuating in every vehicle that they could use.

A wealthy local concrete magnate had donated the entire contents of his auto barn to the city. He had a collection of eighty antique autos that would have made Jay Leno proud. The town was using these, plus the others they had scavenged earlier to make their escape. The town had spent the better part of the day fueling each and collecting all available supplies in the area. They had thought to make the downtown their home again. While that contingency was not working out, the planning already done was enabling hundreds to escape. The exodus had already begun. Cars and trucks were rumbling away to the east, towards the airport, where the town had agreed to meet, if an evacuation were required.

The Sheriff's office was lighted by Coleman lanterns set on low, a dim light through which staff members were hurriedly packing up gear for the evacuation in progress. Against the flow of people and goods outward, Issac and the volunteers moved into the main hall and into the office to the right. There, on the floor, were fifteen twenty-pound propane tanks salvaged from yards all over town. Most were full, summer grilling season having started in earnest, before the disaster struck. In addition, the volunteers loaded nine five-gallon plastic gasoline cans into the truck bed. Many of the tanks had already been taken and loaded away, but what was left would do the job.

Moments later the tanks were loaded into the truck bed. Jack grabbed the duct tape in his left hand and began strapping the tanks together. He ignored the short arm cast on his left arm, though Issac could see the pain on his friend's face as he worked. He added the bundle of dynamite and taped it to the center. Jack paused and stared at a young family loading their daughter into a waiting truck. It would work. It had to work. All depended on it.

Life was hard. Experience had taught him that what happened to you was almost never fair. You had choices in this life, and those choices defined you, defined who you really were. He had never been a religious man, but he had always believed in God, and he had tried to live up to the standard his father had set for him: do for others what you wanted them to do for you, and don't make a fuss about it. He shook hands, hugged Issac and leaped into the truck, before he could change his mind. He revved the engine and tore out of the parking lot, roaring towards the waiting mass of the infected. The creatures were now bursting through the battle lines at intervals, charging the shooters, screaming in fury at being denied their prize.

The two other citizen volunteers sped away to the North, waving and yelling at the crowd of the infected. A large, dark-skinned man leaped from the line and landed on top of a defender, sinking his massive jaws onto the man's face, stifling the defender's cry of agony before it began. It reared its head back, blood streaming from its teeth down its neck and roared in victory, just as a .308 round ruptured its head like an overripe watermelon.

Issac waved at Luke Dodson, the 26-year-old ex-army sniper, who had just reloaded the Barrett M82 A1. Luke waved back and began concentrating fire ahead of Jack's truck, punching a hole into the wall of the infected. The handsome Clay Masterson was standing near the line and saw the action and must have understood the plan as he began pouring withering blasts from his Rock River .458 SOCOM into the same area, the massive slugs crushing the heads and torsos of the infected, while the old truck slammed into the line, barreling forward one hundred feet, before rocking to a stop as the bodies piled up under its transmission case. The engine revved again and then stalled.

Bodies flung themselves onto the top of the truck, slamming hands and feet into the sheet metal and glass, smashing their way down, down the wave of depraved humanity intent on its prize. Jack Sutherland's big Saiga 12 gauge boomed twenty times, his drum magazine going dry as the attackers collapsed, faces and chests full of buckshot. New waves of attackers piled on top of the truck again, pulling at the glass and metal, fingers scrabbling towards their meal of flesh. Issac knew what would be next as the time slipped by. The realization of the close distance of only one hundred yards dawned on him.

"All units. RETREAT! RETREAT! RETREAT!" Issac screamed into the mike, until he was hoarse with the effort. Defenders turned and ran, legs pumping hard as the wave of infected broke and pursued them with the horrible speed of the criminally insane. Time seemed to slow to a crawl. Volunteers on the roofs of the buildings were still shooting their hunting rifles into the crowd, covering the ground defenders' exit. The defenders were running for their lives, keeping ahead of the mass of insanity behind them. One stumbled and fell, the beasts upon him in seconds, before he could stand again.

Issac ducked into a doorway of the Sheriff's office and the time was up. The blast wave rocketed past him, hurling bodies outward like rag dolls, the plume of flame racing outwards and upward five hundred yards in diameter. Window glass shattered in a half mile radius. Issac's Peltors completely shut off for five seconds afterwards, but his ear drums remained intact. He ducked back around the doorway and looked onto a scene from a war movie. Bodies were piled in all directions, charred beyond recognition. It was impossible to tell the infected from the defenders. He looked up and the nearest of the infected horde appeared to be more than five hundred yards away. The glow of the explosion had turned the night into day and now the mushroom cloud of smoke and flame drifted upwards to the heavens.

Issac did a mental check and it appeared that most of the defenders had made it past the blast zone. They had turned back on the infected and were now gunning them down. The nearby infected still ran at them as if nothing had happened. Issac pulled out his Keltec KSG 12 gauge shotgun from his shotgun case on his backpack and fired ten rounds into a cluster of the running infected, knocking them down before they could reach him. He fired five more rounds and dropped the shotgun pulling out his Wilson Combat 1911 .45 ACP, sending six more rounds into the last of the horde on this side of the blast.

He snatched up the shotgun, slung it and transitioned back to his M4, which still hung on its two-point sling. He slammed in a new magazine and raced to the waiting trucks. He looked back over the scene. The two volunteers in their truck were running north, parallel to the front of the oncoming horde. They were screaming insults and waving their arms at the infected, drawing them northward and away for the evacuees. He prayed that God would be with them, and then boarded the bed of an old pickup truck. His unit sounded off on their radios. All accounted for. All except Jack.

Gallatin regional airport
Eastern border of Gallatin, TN
July 6
6:37a.m.

Dawn broke over the ragtag group of survivors, their vehicles circled on the airstrip, ready for immediate travel, if needed. The huddled citizens of Gallatin awakened to the new reality, a reality of bitter loss and defeat. Smoke still rose and the land was dusted in the ash from the night's fires, brought on by the massive explosion that allowed them to escape the ravenous horde of infected attackers. Their town had been lost. They had no supplies, save what they had carried with them, and they had used a huge quantity of their munitions, simply surviving the night. All of their plans lay in ruins, trampled under the feet of the horde.

Had it not been for the sacrifice of Jack Sutherland and the successful diversion of the brave volunteers, all would have been lost. The volunteers had been able to get in front of the horde and lead them into the countryside and escape to the group. Ed paced across the tarmac, his thoughts laser focused on their next course of action. He had sent scouts out to determine where they should go next. Cottontown, the coal plant, Spence Creek, he was not sure, but he knew they needed a defensible perimeter, and they needed it now.

Thousands lay dead in the town. First the plague victims had attacked and then the fires killed many. Next, the looting and rioting killed even more. More people had wandered off sick, only to return in the infected horde, bloodthirsty unholy beasts, driven purely by animal lusts. Of the thirty-thousand-plus inhabitants of the town, only five hundred had gathered together after the disaster. Many had died in their homes, infected and paralyzed by the plague. Others were too afraid to come out and burned up in the fires. Sill more had been killed by the infected directly. But most had become part of the infected horde itself, their minds long gone from the ravages of this new disease. It defied understanding. Of the five hundred, only 402 made it out alive last night. Ed silently thanked The Lord that he and his family had escaped unharmed.

Foothills of the Cumberland Plateau
Private forested road
Group property
July 6
8:03a.m.

Breakfast dishes were clanking in the kitchen as the group members finished cleaning up after the meal. They had eaten a combination of simple cold cereals and powdered milk, with coffee and hot tea. MRE bread made for fairly good toast as well. The Calvins had been hard at work cleaning out the refuse left by the thieves who had moved in the day of the event. The walls and floor were sparkling and the burn marks from the large bonfire John had used to dispose of the bodies and trash had been covered over. John Calvin had buried the bones and ashes in a mass grave on public land far from the compound. He had made quick work of it to avoid getting waylaid or attacked, but felt that even criminals deserved a proper burial. He could not bring himself to bury them on the compound property for legal and personal reasons. He already remembered the fight too well, having awakened at night in a cold sweat every night since the shootings. He marked the grave with a wooden sign that read, "looters and child rapists, may God have mercy on them."

Angus' mother, Margaret Gunn, was examining the stores of goods that had been brought above ground from the group's underground storage unit. She peered over her glasses and winked at little Joshua who was chewing his last piece of toast and jam. She looked forward to cooking a real meal this weekend. She worried about her other sons and their families, her sister and her family and even about her ex-husband, but she prayed and turned it over to The Lord. There was nothing she could do about it. She was thankful that she had been here; what a miracle! If she had been home…well enough of that talk. She began perusing the labels on the food supplies again, thinking about what she could make for dinner. She might not be a gun-toting patriot, but even those types needed to eat! And she planned on providing what they needed, in deference to their generosity. Also, some of these folks would need a haircut and thank The Lord, Gwenn had her spare foot treadle Singer sewing machine. Taking exercise at the same time as sewing! Life would be tolerable here.

The compound was actually several buildings and storage facilities compactly arranged in a tight knit central complex, situated on one hundred acres, surrounded by forested land. The main house was an old farmhouse and had five bedrooms, all small, but functional. A family with ten kids could live here. It had a large kitchen that took up most of the first floor, save a small area for a living and large dining room directly attached to the kitchen. The two tables could seat fourteen each and the back screen porch could handle at least as many more. Adding in extra chairs, T.V. dinner trays and couches, about fifty people could eat at once in the house. There was a large cast iron restaurant stove that Margaret had donated years ago in the form of a birthday gift to Gwenn. It was six feet long, ran on propane or natural gas and had a regular oven and another large enough to fit an entire hog in, over four-feet wide. The right side was a standard four burner arrangement and the entire left sixty percent of the stove top was a flattop cooking surface. You could literally run a breakfast cafe on just the one stove. It was connected to a series of three huge propane tanks located one hundred yards from the house, a tactically wise decision on their placement.

The out-buildings included a large new barn with an office and a separate four-stall stable that included a guest room, complete with sleeping quarters for one or two people. The property also had a mother-in-law cottage with two rooms that could sleep four people, or a large family if cots were used, in addition to the paired queen sized beds. Also, there was a workshop, with a field dressing station on the back side away from the house, a generator shed with both diesel and wood burning generators, a very large woodshed and several underground units. The compound was very large and the addition of the extra outbuildings had driven up the cost, requiring that the group members share the expense of funding through a LLC, or limited liability corporation. Everyone contributed equally, and all had the same plan for preparedness.

Other features made this property different, as well. There were no stock animals in the barn. Instead, it was practically full of raw building materials. Everything that could be purchased on clearance, as overruns, or at a bulk discount was loaded unceremoniously into the barn over the years. The barn had a new roof and kept things very dry. Huge pallets of concrete mix, pressure treated pine, thousands of buckets of nails, glue, adhesive, caulk, tape, and industrial chemicals filled the space. Posts, barbed wire spools, vehicle parts, pipes, plumbing equipment, and more filled the space almost to the rafters. Over one hundred thousand dollars' worth of supplies were contained in the space. The doors had double locks and the contents had been insured against loss with a group policy. They had planned on building a bigger home eventually, and had been saving up over time to reduce the building cost. Now all of that gear would really come in handy.

In addition to the other buildings, a small two room metal building was set up to use as a field hospital, complete with sterile equipment and tables that could be used for surgery, if needed. None of the doctors was a surgeon, but Matt and Angus had been trained by the military to first-assist a surgeon in a disaster. Also, Carlos was an expert with critical care and ICU procedures. The group prayed that they would never need the facility.

The underground systems were divided into storage and living space. They were located into a hill near the side of the compound. It had taken five years to set up the complex, with significant cost for the shelters. Two thirty-foot-long by ten-foot-high culvert pipes were used, with wooden floors added that were used for storage space underneath. This left eight-foot-tall ceilings and the sides were divided into bunks three high and three long on each side for a total of 18 bunks in the living space unit and potentially 36 if the second unit were used. This would allow up to 36 people to weather a tornado in comfort, or a slightly longer event, for a few days.

A nuclear attack on nearby Nashville would result in high radiation levels that would dissipate rapidly. While the group had 29 people so far, others such as the Washingtons could be added. Plans included eventually double the underground system's size to allow for longer contingencies. As it was configured now, the second unit was used as a high tech root cellar, storing food, meds, weapons, electronics and ammunition. Water was stored in a 10,000 gallon underground tank that was refilled by rain catchment and well water via a solar pump. There was a second tank of equal quantity connected to the main house, operated on a separate solar powered well system.

Fuel was stored in multiple tanks for heating, cooking and vehicles. There were 5,000 gallons of diesel and also gasoline, 1000 gallons of fuel oil and three 500-pound propane tanks, all located between one and two hundred yards away from the compound in case of fire or explosion. They were arranged in three locations so that one accident or attack would not take them all out. Governmental regulations and environmental lawsuits had made use of the much safer in-ground tanks impossibly expensive and risky. One mistake and the EPA would destroy the owner. Regulatory pressure had effectively wiped out the market for the in-ground tanks in the years prior to the event.

The Calvins had made very effective use of the LP/OP, or listening post/observation post which was cut into the military crest of the tallest hill overlooking the property. There was a private road that led from the public county road to the compound. It was a landlocked 100 acres of mixed field and forest. There were two small ponds and a creek that ran though the eastern portion. The property was adjoined by five other lots, all of similar size, mostly owned by local farmers who planted corn, sorghum, soybeans, and cut hay and hunted the land.

The group kept underground caches of weapons, ammunition and electronics. These were buried in hidden locations around the property. Metal debris was buried all over the property, on purpose, to foil any would be prospectors or government agents by inducing a high false positive rate from any metal detection search. A six month supply of dry canned goods for each group member was kept in two fully concrete lined root cellars near the house. More food was inside the house. A small vegetable garden was planned, but had not been started yet. Plans to build a second house with the materials in the barn were in the works, when the collapse occurred.

With the number of group members at its max and the Washingtons at the compound as well, it would be close quarters for the foreseeable future. Sanitation and infection prevention would be paramount. It would be a difficult transition, even for these close friends who had planned for such contingencies. As the group packed up gear for the day's work of logistics and security sweeps of the area, the sun began to heat up the morning air, its energy intensifying the already muggy stillness that blanketed the valley. The teams divided and headed out to complete the tasks of the day, determination etched on their faces as they faced the uncertainty of this new reality.

A great people may be killed, but they cannot be intimidated.
—Napoleon Bonaparte, "Political Aphorisms, Moral and Philosophical Thoughts"

CHAPTER 29

Gallatin Coal Plant
Southeastern border of city limits
6.8 miles from city center
July 7
9:07a.m.

The team huddled under the hedge, sweat beading on the brows of the men as the peered through binoculars and spotting scopes at the compound before them. They had driven to the boat ramp and stowed the truck behind some bushes, where they could easily escape, but couldn't be seen by a casual inspection. They had then crept unseen into position above the plant, using trees and brush to cover their movement. Below them, several armed men sat on the hoods of their white government security trucks. Occasionally, one of them would bellow a harsh sound and pound on the hood. In response to this violent display, several of the others would scamper away, like chimpanzees fleeing an angry dominant alpha male. After a few moments, they would slink back into place and cower under the vehicles, their courage slowly returning.

Drool ran onto the shirts and down the chins of the men, their hands clawing into near fists, holding their pistols and AR rifles. Several of them scanned the area, looking oddly vacant as saliva ran from their open mouths. Their breathing came in waves, as the drool coated their faces and dried in great crusty clumps against the skin. One suddenly grabbed another and began to beat down viciously on the victim's head with the butt of his pistol. Brains splattered out of the infected man's skull as bone split and matter and blood flew out. The attacking creature unzipped its pants and urinated on the dead man's body.

The team held still in the shadows, monitoring the scene without reacting to the utter horror that they felt. Here, in front of them, was the human condition devolved to its base form: a primate hierarchy, its animal form naked in its simplicity and ferocity. These infected had not lost all power of thought. Just as several of the Emergency Management officers had been infected and maintained some semblance of intelligence, this group had also maintained partial memory and understanding. Their animal lusts and rages were totally ungoverned, and the sight of such inhumanity was shocking to behold.

The teams signaled each other that they were in position by chirping once on the radio. They used two meter handi talkies on a simplex frequency for close range communications. Issac's team was divided amongst the units sent out to scout the area. They acted as trainers, radio officers and commanders in the various units and this coordination was possible because of their diligence with maintaining their equipment in Faraday cages. They still kept a portion of their gear in the cages in case of recurrence of solar or man-made events even now.

The .308 175 grain Sierra Match King bullet traveled at 2600 feet per second from the muzzle of the Sage M1A as it rocketed towards the target. The bullet impacted the leader's head and pink mist sprayed out onto his nearest followers. As the thing went down, its head exploded outward, as it slumped on the hood of the vehicle. Before the other creatures could react, a hail of incoming fire from two dozen rifles in three different directions cascaded down upon the group. Bodies collapsed in heaving agony as the targets tried to crawl away, their lifeblood pouring onto the pavement of the parking lot. Windshields burst, shards of glass spraying outward in dramatic testimony to the overwhelming force brought to bear on this group of infected guards.

These things' prior lives had been of service protecting the power plant, their diligence and energy spent defending a vital industry. The plague had robbed their minds of all reason, all compassion, all humanity. The atrocities that had been committed here upon the helpless staff trapped after the collapse would never be fully known, the evidence having been partly consumed by fire and ravenous hunger. The power plant compound would have to be cleansed of their actions before children and mothers could live here. It would be a terrible work, but one worth the very real cost in the nightmares of those who would see the evidence firsthand before scrubbing the walls clean of their shame. By the evening, a large bonfire would send its smoke to heaven, a last small dignity afforded the bodies of the slain.

Radio calls went out as the Charlie unit began mopping up, walking calmly through the parking lot shooting an occasional survivor in the head, a mercy stroke that would not have been reciprocated. Alpha unit remained in over watch, monitoring for any incoming forces, while the eight men in Bravo unit moved in to sweep the physical plant. Alpha would join them after five minutes. The first men into the plant ran back out and vomited upon the sidewalk. Heaving and wiping their mouths, they would calmly return and begin the sterilization of the building. They would find enough cleaning chemicals in the janitorial closets to complete the all-day job, once more reinforcements came to assist. In all, one hundred men and women would work for eight hours scrubbing the walls and floor. Some ceiling tiles would be discarded, the workers unable to remove the stains from the porous surfaces.

The main building was massive and would be able to house the entire contingent from Gallatin, all 402 survivors. The next step of reconnoitering the outbuildings was completed by Charlie unit, once they were relieved on overwatch. There were no horrors here to report, thank God. The main compound had a huge supply of fuel in three containers each larger than community swimming pools. They had been used to power generators to provide power for the town, coal having not been the favored mode of generating despite is massive potential and cheap cost. The prior presidential administration's blind obsession to "green energy" defied logic and reason. The plant was capable of producing huge amounts of power with small environmental impact, but this was lost on a government whose powers of reasoning could not even produce a balanced budget for its own use.

Here, the stockpiles of coal were truly massive, as well. There must have been millions of pounds of the clean burning fuel ready to be used. The quite literal mountain of the available resource present on site meant that, God willing, no one would freeze to death this winter. And it also meant that the local forests would not need to be denuded to keep up the supply of fuel. Yes, there were some issues related to the coal plant. A fly ash heap had built up over the decades of use and there was a nearby lake which was used to store waste water and had heavy metals contained within it, including cadmium and mercury. Growing crops would have to be done well away from this region. However, the benefits of the location vastly outweighed its drawbacks. There was literally a lifetime's worth of fuel here for the stoves and fireplaces of these survivors. It was an incredible blessing, and the townspeople understood it well, many of them having ancestors who had lived in the town since the Civil War, and earlier, and who had seen hard times and famine in the past. The abundance was shocking, but very welcome.

Gallatin Coal Plant
Southeastern border of city limits
6.8 miles from city center
July 7
6:23p.m.

From all of the possible locations, Edward Douglass, the newly appointed Sheriff, had selected this one because it was a defensible position, its back to the river bend and the front narrowed to two passages by road. There was enough equipment here to rebuild their shattered lives, and the infrastructure seemed largely undamaged by the collapse. God was great, indeed. He had blessed the town beyond all hope. The area would have to be built up, walls would have to be built and manned if they were to survive the coming months. There was no telling what other threats lingered in the new landscape. The herd of infected could still come at any time. They must work fast and secure the new compound. Now, if they could only find enough food, they would be set for the winter.

Ed thought these things as he paced the halls of the plant, his staff walking behind him, sending children and teenagers as runners to relay messages to the working teams. It would be a challenge, but with a little luck and the Good Lord's help, they just might make it through. Ed grinned with his usual smirk, catching Issac's eye, as he walked past the impromptu tactical operations command center that they had set up in one of the offices. Maps covered the walls and tables and runners ran in and out of the area. Issac grinned back. It had been a long day, and now as dinner time came, the tired group settled down around in circles with whatever food that they still had, eating quickly, for there was still work to be done.

Wallace Farm
Portland, Tn
July 7
7:01p.m.

Sam grimaced as he stood next to the old truck, his hand resting on the .30-30, his mind dull with fatigue. Before him lay the cow's body, on its side, desperate with pain. It was partly chewed up, still kicking and panting. Sam cycled the lever gun's action and pulled his bandana over his mouth and slipped his safety glasses and ear muffs on. No point in going deaf. The crack of the 170 grain round was a dull thud through the passive muffs, its copper jacketed bullet rupturing the writhing animal's brainpan, ending its struggle. Sam had gone to check on the neighbor that owned the adjoining cattle ranch and found the man dead in his bed. The rancher clutched a will, ceding the entire 2000 acre property and cattle herd to Sam and his family. It was an astounding gift. Sam could not tell if the man had killed himself with poison or died naturally, but they buried the body and had a funeral that day, thanking the Good Lord for his graces.

This was the third cow today that had been partially eaten. The first two had been dead, at least. Same thing, though. The infected were sneaking onto the land and eating the cattle. Three more had been bitten, but had not been eaten. They had all been shot because no one would risk eating the meat due to the possibility of infection. Nobody knew what it was. It seemed to come out of nowhere, although there had certainly been signs. Crime, really violent crime had come before, as well as this summer flu. Sam started to think they were the same thing. They would have to post guards now, to prevent future attacks.

The palisade that Sam had planned was coming along slowly. It would protect the house and grounds. It would take a month, with everyone working on it nonstop; more as they lacked enough tools, and the ground was hard without any recent rain. They were using nearby forested land adjoining the farm along with some walnut, locust and hickory trees that were on the farm itself. Sam would never condone taking anything that was not his, but times were different now, and he knew that he must change or they could all suffer death. Sam promised himself that he would pay for each tree that he took if anyone ever came with a legitimate claim against him. They had at least dug in foxholes near the road and put a rotating guard in the two positions, everyone spent four hours a day there. Each guard had a duck call. Three calls meant an intruder. Another guard with binoculars stayed back on the porch and scanned the area, listening for the calls. If contact were made, that guard would alert the group.

They had gone to check on their neighbors on each side and across the way. All were dead, their bodies either in their homes or on their property. All seemed to be victims of violent attacks. Limbs and faces had been torn off, some meat missing from most, with unmistakable human teeth marks. Sam personally knew most of them and was filled with anger at what he had seen. They looked around for any family coming to retrieve their belongings, but none had come, so they began to move any usable items over to the farm. They kept the items separate, in case any family of the neighbors came to claim them. Sam personally left a note that did not give the address, but only his name that the things were waiting. That way, if looters came through, they would not know where to come to steal the goods.

Two young people from the community had already wandered onto the farm and were well received by Sam's kids, who had apparently been to high school with them and vouched for the young couple. They had seen some other people drift by, but no one else had stopped. Some clearly looked infected, perhaps recently, as they did not yet display the typical violent behavior seen in the other victims. Luckily, no one else seemed to be sick, so far. Sam counted his blessings as he tied a rope to the animal's legs to drag off with the truck to the burn pit. The bodies would have to be disposed of carefully. The remaining 490 head of cattle would feed them for a long time if their luck held. Sam tied off the rope to the trailer hitch, revved the old engine and set off for the pit.

North of Gallatin Coal Plant
Southeastern border of city limits
3 miles from city center
July 8
1:03p.m.

Issac jogged along the railroad track, the muffled footfalls behind him almost silent as the team approached the train. Movement up ahead caused him to duck into bushes along the side. This would need to be quiet. They were too close to the town center to risk unsuppressed gunfire. Luckily, Issac and his group had prepared long ago for just such an eventuality. They needed to see what was in the train. The large number of survivors had already half depleted their food supply. Due to their rapid flight during the previous onslaught, the townspeople had been very limited in what they could carry, and now all of that food left behind was likely contaminated by the infected.

Issac said a quick prayer and gave thanks to The Lord that the train was even there in the first place. Regardless of what they found, He had already carried the group through the fire. Issac believed that they would not be abandoned now. They needed food, most of all. Issac knew that this rail line carried corn and wheat, as well as industrial chemicals. This train had a number of those cylindrical ammonia cars. But it also had mostly what appeared to be grain cars. It would be a blessing beyond all hope if any of them had edible grains on them.

Much had already been accomplished in very short order by a town wanting desperately to work together. Other teams had scavenged restaurant cooking gear and had been cooking over outdoor fire pits, hastily made on the coal plant compound. A group of doctors from the local hospital had set up a miniature medical clinic and were treating various illnesses, as they were able. They were extremely limited with their gear. Medical supplies were a third priority, after ammunition and weaponry. Some teams were busy blockading the road using metal scavenged from the nearby industrial complex. They had managed to push some beautiful, brand new government trucks in place to use as rolling roadblocks on the roads that approached the coal plant. The trucks were otherwise utterly useless now that their computer control circuitry had been fried by the solar event.

The team stopped and ducked for cover behind Issac. Sounds of muffled grumbling and gurgling unintelligible speech sounded from ahead. Issac peered through his Steiner binoculars. Twenty or so infected wandered along the side of the tracks, occasionally smashing their fists into the unyielding metal of the rail cars in impotent rage. They must smell food, but have forgotten how to open the doors or valves on the cars. They showed no sign of leaving the area, and after five minutes, Issac motioned to his team without looking back. Two runners came up, following the command signal.

The hand signals conveyed the plan and the team spread out and Issac and Jonathan Burke, the 38-year-old truck driver, jogged down the railroad track, the team fanning out behind them. Each had a Ruger Mark II .22 long rifle pistol fitted with a small eight inch long suppressor. As they neared the infected, one slavering woman looked up and started to growl when a .22 caliber slug pierced her forehead. The shot was so quiet, that Issac could hear the bolt on his friend's gun move back and forth to cycle the action. Issac's pistol clicked out three rounds as three more heads came into view, just as an arm shot out from the space past the nearest rail car. The fingers grabbed Jonathan's neck and started to pull, screams of ecstasy echoing from the infected man's throat, his victim being pulled inexorably towards the grinning teeth.

Jonathan's left palm slammed up against the wrist of his attacker, breaking the forearm bones, but the creature would not let go. Jonathan shoved the muzzle of the gun into the waiting mouth and fired three rounds. The creature slumped, its fingers letting go suddenly. The other infected turned and screamed and began charging down onto the men. The pistols emptied their ten round magazines and the men turned and raced back the way that they had come.

As they sprinted past, the rest of the team began firing their .22 rifles fitted with improvised suppressors. The empty 20 ounce water bottles were duct taped onto the barrels of the rifles. The makeshift devices were far less efficient than the purpose built devices on the pistols, but were effective enough nonetheless, their reports sounding like palms clapping hard together. Infected after infected fell to the barrage of fire, but still more were on Issac's and Jonathan's heels.

Just as they were about to be run down, two men leaped up from the side and swung wooden handled axes directly into the chests of the first two creatures. The infecteds' screams were cut off as abruptly as they started, the axe heads burying themselves into the things' rib cages. The men dropped the axe handles, the steel heads still imbedded in the attacker's chests as the infected collapsed backwards, legs and arms still working as their lifeblood surged forth from their wounds. More infected ran up as Issac and Jonathan turned, having reloaded their pistols while running. Ten rounds each from the two pistols ended the threat, dropping the last five infected as they ran up the tracks.

The men stood stock still, having emptied their pistols, eyes darting to the left and right. Jonathan reached for another magazine and prepared to reload his pistol. Suddenly, a shape darted from the left towards the group. The volunteers from town were also slowly trying to reload their .22 rifles, mostly bolt actions and some semi auto small game hunting guns. The men fumbled with the tiny rounds as they looked up, terror in their eyes as the shape lurched into view. The creature moved with impossible speed, claws and teeth out, a howl on its lips. The red polo shirt it wore was stained with black gummy liquid. Blood dried on its lips mixed with saliva running in gutters down its chin. The leering face of death descended upon its victim, the closest volunteer, who scattered rounds of the diminutive caliber onto the ground in a desperate, trembling attempt to load the older bolt action rifle.

Jonathan's fresh magazine jammed and hung up as he botched the speed load, the Ruger's angled grip not having been designed for rapid reloading. He cursed as the thing bore down on the quaking volunteer. Movement as fast as the monster itself flashed from the right, the greenish brown fatigues blurring with speed of execution. Issac's katana swung out from his back scabbard, even as he moved to meet the deadly threat. The kesa cut angled downwards, a 45 degree arc of death, striking the still-moving beast with astonishing speed. The Paul Chen blade impacted the thing's left collarbone, its differentially hardened blade simultaneously cleaving into the bone and muscle with its hardened edge and flexing behind the sword's hamon to absorb the tremendous impact velocity with its flexible and toughened core. The blade cleaved the monster's body into two pieces, the edge traveling through the left collarbone, ribcage, spine, sternum, heart, lungs and liver edge in a textbook kesa cut. Issac stood stock still, his shoulders squared, the sword held down low and to his left, the blade dripping runnels of the creature's blood. Blood spattered Issac's face and uniform and the ground beneath his feet as he stood, breath heaving in and out, unimaginable exertion focused in so many seconds. The thing's body had tumbled past Issac, each half diverted to the side, its blood gushing out in a second onto the ground, as if open paint cans had been kicked over, the dry soil soaking up the infected fluid. The volunteer cowered behind Issac, shaken to his core.

Issac surveyed the area and his men and the volunteers from town quietly sounded off. Everyone was accounted for and no one was injured. Issac nodded to the volunteer and pulled off his patrol pack, unsnapping it with his left hand. The pack dropped onto the ground behind him as the ditch snaps released. He laid the sword down gently and pulled out a pack of Clorox countertop wipes and scrubbed his hands, face and neck, the cleaner stinging his skin. He then religiously cleaned the katana. He had thought to prepare before the mission in case of contamination. Jonathan snatched a wipe and scrubbed his own neck where the infected man had touched him earlier.

Issac walked calmly over to the first car. He held his breath as he reached his hand for the release lever on the grain car. He paused. The group walked up behind him and he could almost hear the silent prayers. All depended on this. He turned the handle and dry corn kernels poured onto the railroad ties on the center of the track. As the precious grain fell like manna from heaven, quiet tears trickled down Issac's cheeks. Jack had died for this; it was not in vain.

Therefore, since we are surrounded by such a great cloud of witnesses, let us throw off everything that hinders and the sin that so easily entangles. And let us run with perseverance the race marked out for us
—Hebrews 12:1 NIV

CHAPTER 30

Gallatin Coal Plant
Southeastern border of city limits
6.8 miles from city center
July 9th
9:37a.m.

Adrian Johnson was a tall Black man with a beard and smile that even Santa Claus could not best. He was a Baptist preacher and had been trapped in downtown Gallatin when all of the power went out. His small congregation had all died when they were praying in their country church and the building caught on fire. All twenty parishioners had died that terrible day. He had learned of the tragedy from one of the teenagers who hadn't gone to church that day and found the smoking ruin, when the boy went looking for his mom, after she had not returned.

It was a devastating loss and now, with all of the chaos that had taken place since then, he wondered what The Lord had in store for their group of survivors. He knew the Bible. He knew that hard times were more common than good times. He knew what the end of a world looked like. It had happened countless times in the ancient past, with the loss of an empire here, or a natural disaster there. But never, never had he thought that it would really happen now. Those parishioners who wanted the end of the world to come soon were all fools: he saw that now. There was no rapture, no painless entry into the afterlife of Heaven. It was all a lie.

But he had to go on; he had to put on the show. Even if it was only for himself. He looked around. How could these people just be working, building, planning? It was all over! Didn't they see? The Lord's wrath was upon them, there would be no escape. He hung his head and sobbed, grief overcoming him.

"Preacher, you O.K.?" asked a man that walked by him, stopped upon seeing the man's distress.

Adrian couldn't speak. His head hung down, limp, as the stool near the wall held his weight. His feet would have already given way, so great was his distress. The man placed his hands on Adrian's shoulders and squeezed them tightly.

"I don't know much about religion or God and all. But I do know we are alive, and if there's somebody up there, He means for us to keep trying. Why else would we still be here. Let me get you something to drink."

The man walked off towards the makeshift kitchen and returned with a bottle of boiled river water. Adrian took it and looked at the man, Tears wetting his thick salt and pepper beard. The man smiled at him, his nondescript white, clean shaven face such a contrast to Adrian's powerful, rough, weathered visage. Adrian remembered segregation as a child, he remembered racism. It was not found here, not in years, not now. Maybe if God could cure that ill, He could find them hope, as well. Still not able to speak, Adrian smiled at the anonymous man and raised the bottle, taking a swig.

The Good Samaritan winked and walked back to the electronic units he was working to fix. Maybe, just maybe. Hope. They could surely use it. Right now, they could use a sign, a message from Heaven that they had not been forgotten. He swallowed the water and prayed silently. The heat of the day began building as work continued in desperate haste, the uncertainty of the immediate danger drawing them onward, onward towards an uncertain future.

Wallace Farm
Portland, TN
July 9
12:30p.m.

Lunch was finished now as the expanding group of people set back to the tasks of the day. Many friends and family members of those already at the farm had been added to the list of survivors taking refuge at the Wallace Farm. A dentist, a veterinarian, several local craftsmen and one of the local Baptist preachers had joined the ranks of this new family. The barn was filling to the brim with new people. Hammocks and new triple high bunk beds were being added for sleeping space. Full latrines were dug to accommodate the new people. Basically, these were modernized outhouses. They were dug on a hill far away from the well and farmland. No point in everyone getting sick: the compound was expanding. The palisade was taking longer than expected, but it was coming along. Manual labor was slower than this modern generation was accustomed to seeing.

Portland itself was now a ghost town. No one had been seen in it for several days, and that thought frightened the inhabitants of the farm. It was just spooky. Where did everyone go? There would be long days ahead. At least the town hadn't burned, unlike Gallatin, and they would be able to scrounge for food, medicine and gear. Sam looked out under the shade of the oak tree and smiled. His daughter Jessica and Jim Summers, her recovered alcoholic ex-husband were talking and smiling.

"How's it going?" Jim asked, smiling at the woman he had never stopped loving.

"Pretty good, considering," replied Jessica.

"Considering what?"

"Considering that the world just ended and I am talking to my ex!" she replied, giving a coy grin, her beautiful cheeks blushing against her will.

"Well, it could be worse, I suppose," Jim nodded, winking at her.

"How's that?"

"Well, for starters, you could still be stuck married to a jerk like me!" Jim said, his laughter and self-effacing humor genuine.

Jessica laughed and smiled at the handsome man. She paused and a serious look crossed her face. "It's been a long time. I was worried about the kids, but I was worried about you too." She faced the ground, her hands in her pockets, shoulders shrugged up.

His hand came out and touched her elbow. She relaxed at the touch and turned towards the house. She smiled, seeing her daddy looking on, smiling at them. Jim turned and nodded at Sam. Sam grinned and walked back into the house.

Jim was really coming into his own during the crisis. He had grown into the kind and caring man that Jessica had once remembered during their dating, the man she had originally fallen in love with, before the whiskey had almost destroyed him. He was hard working, kind, always quick with a kind word, and she wondered what the future could hold for them. Her heart still ached with remembrances of nights spent sobbing into her pillow, while he slowly tried to kill himself, on the couch at three a.m., bottle in hand, his mind inexorably succumbing to the effects of the demon spirit. Only his faith in the Lord Jesus had saved him from the oblivion found at the bottom of the bottle. Time would tell if he had really changed, but now, at least, she was open to hope.

Gallatin Coal Plant
Southeastern border of city limits
6.8 miles from city center
July 9
4:31p.m.

Bicycles raced towards the makeshift barrier on the roadway. Security along the northern entrances to the compound had been beefed up, since the townspeople had arrived. Abandoned and non-working vehicles made up a crude roadblock now, manned with sentries pulled from the general population. The barricade consisted of cars and trucks stacked two high by a working diesel forklift that they had found on the property. The barricade covered the road and the ditch beside it. In the center, there was a portion made of two sedans stacked on top of each other that could be rolled from side to side to allow traffic through. This section was inset behind the other main sections. It represented a weak point, but guards on either side could shoot down from a raised platform onto any attacker trying to cross the section.

Anyone who had basic firearms experience was asked to rotate on shift. This gave everyone a break from the sometimes backbreaking work going on inside the compound. Most people had previous firearms experience, either hunting, plinking on private property, or at one of the several popular indoor shooting ranges in the area. Gallatin was a town of the gun culture, and its citizenry prided themselves on their knowledge and understanding of what they considered a fundamental human right and skill set.

Sentries armed with an assortment of hunting rifles, shotguns, pistols and various optical devices including binoculars and spotting scopes, viewed the oncoming bicyclists with growing alarm. The ten sentries called out challenges to the dozen or so people, but to no avail. They simply kept coming, riding as hard as they could, as if the Devil himself were chasing them.

"Stop! Stop right there or we'll be forced to shoot!" The head sentry, Trey Nellis, called out. Trey had assumed the role of chief mechanic for the town, as he had been a very good car mechanic, before everything fell apart. Unlike the others, he did not like sentry duty. The long days were boring to him and he would rather be working on fixing something.

The bicycles finally stopped, some at the back crashing into the ones at the front. The faces of the survivors were blank slates of war-weary fear and exhaustion. The fact that ten gun barrels were pointed at them from thirty feet away did nothing to calm them. The front bicyclist, a middle aged brown haired man, raised his hands, trembling in fear. Sweat ran into his eyes, his hair a tangled mass, his clothes tattered. Bruises covered his cheeks, his left eye swollen shut as though someone had beaten him nearly to death.

"Please! Please! For the love of God, let us in! They are almost here!" the man spoke in an urgent plea, his voice tremulous with fear, his eyes glancing nervously over his back. He was terrified.

"Hold it right there, mister," said Trey as he shifted his grip on the Remington 700 .30-06 hunting gun that had been salvaged from one of Gallatin's many gun shops during the fires. "Who are you, and what do you mean, 'they're almost here'?"

The man shook with terror; every second spent standing still worsening the tremor. "The police! The police are almost here!!" His voice broke in anguish, sobs of grief choking out his voice. "Please God, please God, let us in!! Let us in! Oh God, you don't understand, they're here!!! Oh God no they're here! You've killed us! You've killed us! Oh God no!" He sobbed uncontrollably and placed his feet on the pedals and hands on the handlebars, taking a deep breath and preparing to ride forward into the waiting guns along the barricade. He would rather be shot here than turn back towards whoever 'the police' were.

Trey looked in disbelief at the scene. The bicyclists all began to scatter, some headed for the barricade, others sideways into the ditches on the sides of the road. Whatever they were running from terrified them so much, that they had lost all reason and were prepared to fling themselves towards a certain death rather than turn back. Screams of terrified fear erupted from the survivors as four older model pickup trucks rumbled into view, heading south along the roadway, coming directly at the roadblock.

"Contact, contact, contact! North point barrier! Repeat, contact at North point barrier!" Trey screamed into the FRS radio, lent to the sentries by Eli Smith, the 35 year old history professor member of Issac's crew that had spent time training the volunteers in basic radio communication over the past several days. He had stockpiled dozens of electronic devices in Faraday cages long before the event occurred and now was loaning them out to everyone he could find.

"We need help now! Four trucks coming down the road! Regular people on bicycles, as well!" Trey looked around at the scene and yelled out to the sentries, "don't shoot these people! That's an order!"

To the terrified bicyclists he yelled out, "You on the bikes, get over here now!" He motioned towards the side of the barricade where there was a small opening large enough for one person at a time to cross. The barricade could be moved aside partly, to allow for movement of vehicles through the barrier, but Trey was not about to move that now, with four unknown vehicles approaching.

The bicyclists began yelling "thank you!," and "God bless you!" In hoarse and exasperated tones as they poured towards the opening, some completely abandoning the bikes just to get behind cover. The radio crackled in reply, the entire scene taking only one to two seconds to unfold.

"Sentry North, roger that. Reinforcements en route. Hold position, do not allow ingress of civilians."

"Roger that, holding position, civilians being secured." Trey replied.

"Dick, Justin, get off the line and guard these people now," Trey ordered two men from the barrier to the side to secure the civilians.

The two men raised their weapons high and leaped from the barricade and trained their hunting rifles on the survivors. The bicycle riders huddled in a group behind the cover of the barricade with hands high, some breathing heavy, others saying prayers, others quiet and motionless. The guards looked grim and none of the strangers felt like testing the waters.

The trucks slowed down and stopped about fifty yards from the barricade. No motion came from the unidentified vehicles for several seconds. Then a door opened slowly and a man got out of the passenger's seat of the first vehicle, a faded brown, rusted 1970s Ford truck. The man was wearing a jet black uniform with a navy blue police tactical vest loaded with a rack of what appeared to be at least ten 30-round Magpul AR-15 magazines, two to a pouch, with five pouches loaded and the sixth pouch replaced with what appeared to be a combat medical kit. Three Glock 22 .40 Smith and Wesson magazines were located to the upper left side of the vest. The stiff outlines of rifle plates were visible beneath the PALS webbing of the vest. A single point wolf hook was present on the right upper shoulder of the vest. He must have removed the rifle before exiting the vehicle. A Safariland tactical drop leg holster housed the full sized Glock 22 on his right leg. A Multicam baseball cap completed his outfit. The words "Hendersonville Police Department" were emblazoned on the patch on the left shoulder of his uniform shirt.

The man had grey hair and appeared to be in his early fifties or late forties perhaps. He had his hands raised in the universal "I surrender" pose. He smiled, but his eyes remained steely grey and cold, remorseless and without emotion. Trey aimed his rifle directly at the man's face, knowing that the chest plates would easily stop its high powered round. The man walked around to the side of the truck, five feet laterally and spoke.

"Hello there!"

"Stop right there," Trey replied, "That's close enough."

"We come peacefully, but we have a warrant for the arrest of those suspects that you just let in." The officer replied.

"Who are you?" asked Trey, knowing he would not like the answer.

"Hendersonville Police Department. I'm Lieutenant Sullivan and we are going to proceed with our warrant. Now just move aside and we'll be on our way." The man's eyes never waved from scanning the defender's positions.

"I don't think your navigation is correct, Sir. This is Gallatin and you are well outside of your jurisdiction," Trey replied, his heart beating hard in his throat. He always respected authority, had since his childhood. Now here before him was a police officer and he was refusing his instructions. But deep down inside, he knew something was wrong. The bicyclists behind him were pleading with him, all at once, begging for him not to send them with the Lieutenant. Why would they do that? These people, four men, eight women and three kids did not seem like criminals. Trey looked at the other vehicles. In the truck beds and cabs, there must have been twenty heavily armed men. Their weapons were all military style, AR-15s and police shotguns. Each wore some type of body armor. Some even had PASGT and ACH helmets on. All had radios and none looked nervous. These were hardened men and they outgunned the defenders significantly.

"Son, I'm only going to say this once. We have a warrant and are coming through. Move aside and no one will get hurt."

"I'm not going back, you can't make me!"

"Bastards!"

"Oh please God, don't make us go back!"

The cries from the strangers, obviously refugees, strengthened the defenders' resolve. Trey looked at the men beside him and they all nodded. No two-bit cop from out of town was going to order them around. After all that had happened, life was just not the same anymore. One of the defenders cycled a round into his Marlin lever gun. Another pumped the action of his 12 gauge Winchester hunting gun, cycling a slug into the barrel. Trey rapidly cycled a 150 grain Remington Power point round into the bolt gun, keeping the Nikon Buckmaster reticle fixed on the officer's face.

The officer looked at the men, scanning back and forth, eight gun barrels pointed around at different windshields, vehicles and at him directly. He nodded, smiled and eased back towards the truck.

"O.K., O.K., no reason to get hasty. Why don't we talk this out? Let's be reasonable. I hear what you are saying..."

As he was speaking calmly, he glanced at the driver of the truck who keyed his shoulder mounted radio mic. Suddenly, he dived into the truck, as full auto fire erupted from the convoy, shattering glass in the windshields of the new, but useless vehicles of the barricade. Luckily for the defenders, cinder blocks and sand filled the passenger spaces of the vehicles, stopping the rounds cold. The defenders began firing rapidly into the convoy, their hunting rifles unable to keep up with the rate of fire of the attackers. Shotguns boomed and screams went out from each group and men went down, clutching their injuries.

The man with the lever gun next to Trey fired a round that smashed through the windshield of the front truck. The driver collapsed, the back of his head blown out onto the rear windshield which simultaneously cracked as the .30-30 round passed through the driver's head and lodged in the upper thigh of another officer standing up in the cab. The officer in the cab screamed out and squeezed the trigger of his select fire police Bushmaster 10 inch barreled AR-15 carbine and the magazine emptied, bullets spraying wildly in every direction. The man in the cab next to him, took several rounds in the torso and left arm and collapsed, falling out of the truck cab onto the pavement, dead before he hit the ground.

Trey looked over to his side and the lever gun clattered forward onto the pavement in front of the barricade. The man slumped down, blood pouring from his chest. Trey brought his rifle up and aimed for the head of another cop who had jumped out and run into the ditch on the side of the road. The scope was set to 3 power, which made target acquisition easier. The man was raising his AR-15 as Trey centered the crosshairs on the man's head and squeezed the trigger. The round impacted the attacker's face and his head snapped back and he slumped to the ground, face down in the ditch. Searing pain rocketed through Trey's shoulder as blood splattered out from above his collarbone. Trey screamed out and fell backwards onto the wooden platform behind the barricade.

More fell next to him. There were only three defenders left on the wall. He turned and looked back towards the Coal Plant. It seemed like every available vehicle near the gate was racing towards the barricade. Motorbikes led the charge and men leaped off of them, dropping them sideways where they stopped, feet from the wall. Trucks slammed on brakes just behind and men and women raced up to the platform, rifles and shotguns in hand, grim determination etched on their faces. Fury and anger at the attack swept though the community.

How dare they! How dare anyone attack them. After all that they had been through, what right did anyone have to hurt them?

Two women who had been on the motorbikes began engaging the attackers with semiautomatic AR-15s salvaged from the local gun shops. Different people had different firearms that they either owned or had taken from the site of the ruined town. There had been no order to the distribution of these found weapons. More defenders piled onto the platform and the rate of fire accelerated. A gas tank exploded in one of the attacker's trucks. Trey turned back and peered through a crack in the barricade.

The attacking police officers had fanned out and were apparently pressing the attack when the reinforcements arrived. Man after man was gunned down as they were caught away from cover. Luke Dodson, the 26-year-old ex-army sniper defended the position. His 338 Lapua Magnum bolt gun thundered as he engaged the vehicle's occupants. Nathan Ford, the 29-year-old Vanderbilt EMT leaned his huge black frame into the barricade. His huge Ohio Ordinance M240SLR boomed again and again, its surplus .308 ball rounds powering through the vehicle's sheet metal. A thunderous boom sounded next to Trey, deafening him momentarily.

One of the defenders flashed an evil grin and cycled the bolt of a huge bolt action rifle. The man was a retired dentist who collected guns, and this one was his baby, a Winchester model 70 in .458 Winchester Magnum. He fired again. The 500 grain solid bronze projectile rocketed out of the barrel at over 2000 feet per second delivering well over 5,000 foot pounds of energy to the target, only fifty yards away. The engine block of the third truck cracked, as the round easily penetrated the grill and radiator, lodging several inches into the cast iron assembly. Steam erupted from under the hood, as the driver vainly attempted to crank the engine. He leaped from the vehicle and dived into the back of the fourth truck, which was already speeding backwards in reverse.

Bullets sank into the fenders of the vehicles and skipped on the pavement next to the assaulting force, pinning them down. They attempted to retreat and were shot as they ran, bullets hitting in the plate armor stopped, but those hitting the pelvis, lumbar region and limbs slammed home. Three of the attackers were crawling away as the last truck rounded the corner, still in reverse, tires squealing, white smoke wafting from under its chassis. About ten men had clambered into the vehicle and the remaining lay dead or dying on the roadway or in the three smoking hulks sitting in the roadway.

One of the cops who was crawling away turned on his back and started screaming for his mother. He appeared to be a young man, in his early twenties. A helmet covered his blonde hair. Blood covered his legs where several rounds had ruptured the bones and arteries. His left thumb was missing where a shotgun slug had torn it from his hand. His lifeblood poured onto the pavement from the severed pelvic and thigh vessels. His cries ceased abruptly.

Two other cops were still crawling away, M4 rifles still in hand. One turned and began firing at the barricade. Ten bullets stopped his progress. The last one kept crawling.

"Throw down your weapons and we will give you medical help!" Jonathan Burke, the tall, truck-driving member of Issac's band called out. The 38-year-old man had genuine concern in his eyes and really meant to help the man. The cop kept crawling and refused to comply. He made it about fifty yards down the road and collapsed. The

26-year-old Luke Dodson kept the man fixed in the reticle of his SS 16x42 MRAD scope, the Savage M-110 BA had two rounds left in the magazine, having expended three so far and another entire five round magazine, before the fight had ended.

Luke looked at Jonathan and they both nodded. Jonathan leaped over the barricade and ran from man to man checking pulses. Eli Smith, the 35-year-old history professor of the group, kept his M39EMR M1A moving between other downed men in case they tried to attack. Luke kept covering the last cop while Nathan asked everyone else to aim their weapons down at the ground in case anyone got nervous. The band of fighters did not trust the civilians' restraint, yet.

None of the remaining attackers had survived. Edward Douglass surveyed the scene as medical crews tended to the wounded Gallatinites. Dr. Blake, their surgeon, would be busy well into the wee hours of the morning. By the end of the night, seven defenders would lay dead, and four more would survive their wounds. It would be a month before Trey could use his left arm, and his shoulder and collarbone would forever ache when the barometric pressure changed.

Eleven of the attackers were dead and about half of their equipment was salvageable. Some radios and rifles were shot to pieces, but others worked well. None of the radios ever gave a signal, though. The escaping cops were no fools. They knew that once the radios fell into their enemies' hands, they would be monitored. Ed wondered what kind of communications they were now using, the bastards. Four working Bushmaster 10 inch barreled carbines and two Remington 870 combat shotguns, four Glock 22s and one Glock 23 survived intact. About 700 rounds of assorted ammo and 23 AR-15 30 round magazines were salvaged. The rest of the gear, about the same amount, was heavily damaged, but still spare parts were pulled from the units to cannibalize, when needed. About two thousand empty cases littered the scene. Five helmets were saved. One had a tiny, long scratch, where a round had glanced off of it during the shoot-out and two more were shot through with rifle rounds. Some of the men did not have a helmet on before the fight. The trucks were a total loss and were moved and dumped in the lake after any salvageable parts had been removed. The guard was redoubled and the heaviest weapons were reallocated to the guards at all of the perimeter sites. The mistakes of the past would not be repeated.

The bodies were buried along a strip of farmland north of the site. No marker was provided. The stories of the survivors were chilling. They were all quarantined for a week and two of them were shot in the head, two days into the week, after they began to try and attack the others. Luckily for the rest of the group, they were kept separately and none of the others appeared to be infected.

During the week, twenty six Gallatinites showed signs of infection. Most locked themselves up in the makeshift jail converted from the security guard shack, though eight did not report symptoms and, when confronted, fled into the river and the woods. The rest begged to be shot, and lots were drawn for a firing squad. Of the twenty men and women selected for the firing squad, six refused and one was removed, as she was related to one of the infected. Another two vomited and dropped their rifles at the moment of execution and the remaining eleven quietly carried out the shooting. By the time they were brought out, several of the infected tried to attack the guards and had to be restrained. In all, sixteen family members, friends and neighbors had to be shot. It devastated the community, but the remaining

381 survivors held together, Adrian Johnson preaching to the group of God's grace and love.

Several days after the shoot-out, Wes Smith, the local gun shop owner that the Gunns had assisted, and his family escaped Hendersonville and entered the compound, unarmed, with only the clothes on their backs. Their tales along with the tales of the first group of refugees made it clear that Hendersonville had become effectively a dictatorship. The mayor and the chief of police had been at an emergency meeting with most of the city council and high ranking police, EMS, and fire fighters when a group of mid-ranking police came in and killed everyone in the room. They installed one of the city councilmen as mayor and began a campaign of terror to force their will upon the town. The entire event appeared to have been well rehearsed and it seemed that the lower ranking councilmen and police had planned the coup for some time. Several units of firefighters, about a third of the Hendersonville police personnel and all of the Gallatin police who had relocated to Hendersonville earlier in the week fought a brief series of shoot outs with the controlling faction. All of those resisting were killed in the fighting, or summarily executed, afterwards.

Citizens were rounded up by the police in the middle of the night and taken to work camps set up by the city. Forced labor rebuilding the city was started and violators were shot on sight. All private possessions of anyone resisting the police were seized and anyone resisting was also summarily executed. Families watched in horror as their fathers and husbands were shot in the back of the head, while kneeling before their rulers. The police state that ensued was complete.

The refugees from Gallatin and other cities were treated even worse. They were effectively classified as second class citizens and while some citizens of Hendersonville retained minimal authority, none of the outsiders had any rights. They were all forced into hard labor. Anyone trying to escape was hunted down. This was what occurred with the first refugees.

Apparently, Wes Smith had enough clout in the local government that he had fooled the new mayor, now acting dictator, into believing that he supported the plan. He had enough sense to know where things were going and he was able to simply walk out in the middle of the night. No one expected him to leave, and the police never realized that they had escaped. The returning police had recommended against attacking Gallatin again and the loss of so many police officers in one day had convinced the mayor not to try. Gallatin would be safe from their immediate neighbors for now. Food and supplies from the train cars and city were pouring in to the compound. Rebuilding of the infrastructure continued, as the people came together, around their leader.

Our dead brothers still live for us and bid us think of life, not death / of life to which in their youth they lent the passion and glory of Spring. As I listen, the great chorus of life and joy begins again, and amid the awful orchestra of seen and unseen powers and destinies of good and evil, our trumpets, sound once more a note of daring, hope, and will.

—Oliver Wendell Holmes, at Keene, NH, before John Sedgwick Post No. 4, Grand Army of the Republic, Address delivered for Memorial Day, May 30, 1884

CHAPTER 31

Foothills of the Cumberland Plateau
Private forested road
Group property
July 10
10:35a.m.

Beth Mackenzie coughed slightly as she carried lumber to the waiting deuce. She had not been feeling well at the start of the day and last night, she had experienced several awful nightmares. The doctor in her was screaming at the top of her lungs, but the mom in her refused to acknowledge the facts, and so she kept working. She had begged off kitchen duty, knowing what was happening, and refusing to risk infecting anyone else. This outside work, with gloves, and open air, and distance to the next person was ideal, she thought. Last night, she had refused to snuggle with her husband, Matt. She blamed a migraine and it was really true, she still had the headache now. For the week before, she had been on her period and never really liked close physical contact during that time anyway, so she had not really had close contact with anyone for the past eight days. She was a germaphobe in the kitchen and washed her hands ten to twenty times an hour while cooking. She prayed it would be enough.

She paused as she wiped the drool running from her mouth. Gwenn Gunn was staring at her, eyes fixed on her mouth, pupils narrowing, an expression of controlled horror building within her lifelong friend.

"No. No, don't let it be. Tell me..." Gwenn said, still fighting for control of her emotions.

"What? Let what be?" said John Calvin, pausing with his load of wood cradled in his arms.

The group had already begun the compound build out. They were starting with a fence of barbed wire at the perimeter of the compound and had finished plans last night for a formal wall inside the barbed wire perimeter. There would be shooting positions, observation posts and the entire thing would be reinforced with sandbags and soil filled HESCO type embankments. The HESCO was a simple, easy to use square sided tall container that was to be filled with soil or gravel to form a very quick but very effective ballistic barrier.

The group had made their own out of landscaping materials using hog wire and landscaping fabric. The resulting 3-foot thick, 9-foot long, 4-foot high box was made of three subsections each 3x3x4 feet in dimension. These were lined up and then interlaced with the neighboring units and filled with dirt, gravel, sand or rock, or any combination of soil type. The resulting wall would withstand RPG direct fire as well as any lesser ballistic threat. Nothing could stop overhead threats lobbed over the wall, but this would still be a huge survival advantage.

The first step in the use of the homemade HESCO "concertainers" was to complete a simple wall around the compound. Later on, a second layer would be added to the base and ultimately, a third layer would be placed atop the two base layers, creating an incredibly effective eight foot tall wall that was effectively immune to all but the most massive direct blast. The top would be covered with barbed wire in a coiled spiral. Not the actual "concertina" razor wire, but certainly, the next best thing. Broken glass would be set up high as well on the wall to add additional deterrent for any uninvited guests. Foxholes and new LP/OPs were being dug as well to provide better security.

But for now, all work had ceased as those present stared on in shock and horror. John set down his load and walked up, concern in his eyes. His wife Denise Calvin held her hand to her mouth, tears streaming from her eyes as she turned away, shaking her head in grief. Matt put his post hole digger down by the fence row and walked over to the scene.

"What's wrong, sweetie?" he asked, wiping the early morning sweat from his brow.

Beth looked up, the remaining drool still on her lip. She had fear in her eyes, as her emotions swirled across her face. Matt paused and swayed, his feet losing grip. He collapsed and sat down hard on the grass, his breath coming in waves. The reality of his life crushed him, as all of his dreams of a better future were snuffed out in a black instant, waves of emptiness and alternating rage echoing through his tortured mind. His daughter Madison came running over to him, seeing him fall.

"Daddy! Are you O.K.?" she said as she crossed the yard in a few seconds, her long legs pumping hard, worry in her expression. "Mom, what's wrong with Daddy?"

"Stop! Don't come over here!" Beth said, emotion thickening her voice, making her usual lilting speech husky and deep.

Madison stopped and looked at the scene. Her eyes flitted back and forth from one parent to the other. New drool ran from the corner of her mother's lips and the sudden furious truth exploded in her mind.

"NOOOOOOOOO!!!!!" She sobbed, "Mama!!! NOOOOOOOOO!!!! Oh God no! No! No! No! Oh God make it stop! No! No!No! Oh God help me!" She screamed as she collapsed on the ground, her lungs heaving in sobs.

She pulled out her Springfield XD9 from her hip holster and tried to move the quivering barrel towards her head, her hand shaking in agony, the emotion completely overwhelming her. The pistol fell out of her hand and clattered onto the rocky patch of soil, its triple safeties preventing a discharge. Gwenn was already racing towards the teenager and kicked the gun away as she also removed her Kabar knife from its sheath and tossed it away, holding the girl's shaking form as she collapsed in sobbing agony. Wails of grief flooded from the young girl's frame as sorrow unequaled poured out of her tortured soul.

The rest of the group, save the two Corpuz boys on LP/OP duty and Tessa Washington, who was caring for her sister Susane, had gathered around the scene. Scott Rees, the park ranger, helped Matt to his feet, their strong arms locked in a forearm embrace. Matt's fingers clutched at his friend's arm, drawing strength from the older man's courage. Beth looked up at him and smiled... a quiet smile. She looked over at her daughter, Madison, and exhaled slowly.

"I didn't want to tell you, I wasn't sure yet. I love you very much. You can't let it happen to me. You all must promise me. I won't turn into one of those things." She stared at her friends, her eyes grave and her brow furrowed. "You can't let it happen."

The summer breeze drifted across the meadow, sweet scents of clover and grass mingling with the gentle buzz of insects and the call of songbirds. This was a beautiful place, that was one of the reasons that it had been chosen. The clouds drifted lazily by, the concerns of the humans in the yard unnoticed by the natural world around them, and yet there was hope. Somehow, despite all of this agony and emotional wreckage, the group members had not lost faith. In the center of this terrible storm, they came together. Despite all of their different backgrounds, the group members found commonality in this grief. They held together, where others would have surely fallen apart. Somehow, the Holy Spirit provided comfort, even in the midst of this horrible truth.

Gwenn, still holding the teen girl, began softly singing the words to "Spirit of the Living God, fall afresh on me." As the group took up the refrain, the soft music echoed through the valley as, one by one, each took a knee and bowed his head, some using their rifle butts on the ground to support their weight as they knelt in the presence of the Lord. It would be a long time before they moved from the spot.

Tulley Farm
Five miles north of Gallatin, TN
July 10
11:47p.m.

Movement was heard through the trees, pattering feet, unsteady in their gait. The smells of farm life drifted across the valley. Fresh hay, animal fur, growing crops all combined into an intoxicating scent. The powerful cocktail of life drifted well down into the valley and onward towards the town, its siren song promised goodness. It's wafting bouquet enticed the unclean, their hunger ravenous now, as their ranks increased.

The good earth recoiled at the touch of the unclean feet and shoes. The unholy swarm of infected humanity pressed onward, now emboldened by the sight of the barn ahead, the smells of its animal bounty driving the unclean wild with hunger. Sentries on the hillside noted their advance into the valley of the blackberries. Radios crackled at the recognition of the advancing horde. The limitless swath of the unclean defied imagining. Endless wave upon wave of lost souls poured through the countryside, drawn by the promise of a meal, their animal instincts unblinded by the travesty that corrupted their minds. Movement was seen along the ridge line. Feet ran to man the stations. So many infected, so many unclean flooded forth into the valley.

Fallback positions were manned as the units gave ground ahead of the onslaught, their numbers tiny in comparison to the vast horde. Their hearts beat faster, terror surging through them as the horror approached. Lights in the house clicked on as the family awakened to the murderous horror that threatened them. The sound of goats braying echoed from the barn. Figures clad in woodland ghillie suits popped out of foxholes and ran full tilt towards the house, panic threatening to overtake their minds.

The infected bore down upon the barn, lust for flesh and blood driving them onward, the animal smells wafting past infected nostrils. They clambered forward, stumbling and clawing their way towards the feast. The barn doors were barred, the increasingly loud sound of bleating animals echoing inside. The lights in the barn were on, showing through the cracks. The meal before them, they smashed and tore at the doors until they gave way. Pouring inside, dozens stumbled onto the hay and were swept forward as hundreds more behind pressed forth, crushing the infected humans up against the walls of the pens, snapping gates and bones amid the onrush of crazed humanity pressing forward in terrible bloodlust and hunger.

The ones at the front looked around in confusion. Fur and hay and straw covered the ground, a megaphone blared the bleating noises of sheep and goat. Fans blew, oscillating behind huge wads of collected dog hair and animal droppings, sending the warm earthy smells into the night, their simple motors made in the fifties, long before the advent of integrated circuits. The megaphone from the same era wired up to a smartphone dutifully kept in a faraday cage by Doug McKnight, the car battery and protected inverter running the system plus one 150 watt standard light bulb found in a closet.

More pressed into and started around the barn, the rest of the flood tide of humanity now moving towards the house. Sitting on his front porch, Lucien Tulley looked behind him at his wife and family and nodded at the McKnights who were already sitting on the back of the truck bed of the Tulley's 1970s Ford truck. Lucien's oldest son, 21-year-old Samuel Tulley and his girlfriend 20-year-old Grace Winifred were in the front of the truck with Lucien's wife Abigail in the center. Grace's brother Josh sat on a dirt bike next to the truck. The Winifreds had watched their parents get attacked and eaten by a group of infected several days ago and had only just escaped to the Tulley Farm with their lives. Next to the truck were several dirt bikes and four wheelers and an old 1960 Land Rover. Both the Land Rover and the Ford had flatbed trailers mounted filled with supplies. The truck had about twice as large a load as the Rover.

Lucien looked over at his youngest son, 17-year-old Sean Liam, and nodded. The men both held RC remote controls in their hands. Sean nodded back and everyone held their breath, some covering their ears. Both men pressed their keys simultaneously.

The detonators sent radio signals across the valley, taking only milliseconds to reach their receivers. The detonators were set double on each charge, one set from each remote, in case of a failure of one. The model rocket ignition wires heated instantly detonating the charges of fireworks explosives carefully harvested from the stash of M80 firecrackers found in a nearby fireworks stand. The half empty gasoline cans spaced around the barn instantly exploded and sent fireballs though the barn, engulfing the infected with flame. The straw and dry wood of the barn lit up like a bonfire. The infected inside were instantly killed and the hundred or so pressed around the barn caught on fire and went running in every direction.

The men simultaneously flipped their next switches and a line of flame erupted from the other side of the road as more model rocket fuses ignited gasoline and paraffin soaked rags and brush piles, dried out in the month's blistering heat. A one hundred yard wall of flame erupted in between the house and the barn. The infected screamed and ran in every direction, some right into the fire. They stumbled as they tried to reach the families on the other side, caught in a web of loose barbed wire strung across the grass near the road. Their flaming bodies thrashed about as more hurled themselves into the waiting death.

Lucien nodded and they all trotted to their respective vehicles and headed down the road away from the carnage, the truck and Rover leading the way, cargo in tow. Doug McKnight stood over the cab, his DPMS LRT-SASS .308 ready in hand, Grace Winifred riding shotgun with Sam's AR-15 pointed out of the window. Lucien and Sean were last on twin four wheelers. Radio checks confirmed everyone was out. Even the four family goats rode peacefully in crates on the back of the Rover's trailer. Their milk would be sweet indeed during the coming days. Lucien looked back at the house, all of his irreplaceable heirlooms buried deep on the property, well away from unclean hands or prying eyes. The food stores were mostly on the trucks. He hated the loss of the rest and the barn, but the house might survive until a future time. Even if it all were destroyed, his family was safe, so far. He thanked The Lord for the warning and prayed for safe passage to the compound.

They drove down back roads and cut around large towns as they went, trying hard to avoid roadblocks. Midnight passage was dangerous at best, but their plan seemed to pay off. They met little resistance. They had to shoot several infected at one point who ran out onto the road. Most of the infected seemed to be congregating near towns or farms, clustering together like some kinds of beast herds. They did not know about the roadblock John Calvin had encountered, but by the time they reached it, the only remnants of it were bloodstains and claw marks on the fender wells of some of the vehicles. Bones scraped and chewed nearly clean lay in a heap near one of the abandoned vehicles. The tires of the Rover crushed one of the half eaten skulls as they passed on, the McKnights covering the children's eyes as they passed, now approaching friendly territory.

They arrived close to dawn and were challenged at the gate. Tears of joy on both sides were exchanged followed by shock as the news of Beth's infection was told. The families were ushered into the main house and cots were laid out for their use. Detailed infection prevention rules had been in place since the morning in the hopes that the infection would not spread. Each Tulley and McKnight washed outside with buckets of soapy cold water and hand gel and thumbs up signs and nods soon replaced handshakes on the property. While the Tulleys hated the concept, being closer to the very earth itself as farmers, they abided by the law of the land and were grateful for the lodging, promising hard work for their keep, which no one doubted for an instant. The fact that they had 2,000 pounds of dried food, milk goats, sheep and goat-herding guard dogs and their own ammunition depot with them didn't hurt their welcome, as able bodies were needed always to defend and man the compound. It was a solemn morning followed by a quiet day.

The next several days would be filled with intense work on the compound. Stored goods in the barn would be used to finish most of the HESCO barriers and log huts built to store equipment would be framed out roughly, foundations poured with the concrete bags from the storehouse. The barn could be completely cleaned out and converted into temporary housing eventually, though that would take months to be sure. New animal pens were put up near the barn. Eventually, more houses could be built on the land. There was plenty of acreage to go around. The place could eventually resemble a small medieval village with a common green and small houses, if they survived the coming time. They had always planned on building out. Now, with the momentous changes that had occurred across the land, it was finally being done. The work helped with the grief, while improving their chances of survival. Beth was kept quarantined in the workshop outbuilding, well away from the group, her daughter bringing her food and keeping watch. The rest of the group watched the teenager as well, as she had been tight-lipped after the events that had transpired.

North Portland, TN
Redeemer Church of the Faithful
July 11
11:30p.m.

Fire burned in the hearth, its evil flames crackling as the wood of the pews was consumed upon the altar. The sink torn from the wall and dragged into the sanctuary served as fire pit. The smoke hung in the air like drifting sheets of darkness, outlined against the white walls of the formerly beautiful church. Stirring figures slunk across the background, their hooded shapes dark as if out of a medieval carving.

Sounds of eating and breathing echoed through the empty hall of the church, its windows long since smashed in the death throes of the town. Slobbering and whining noises were low and contained as if fearful of retribution. A lone figure knelt in front of the fire, hands out in front of him, the flames dancing along his shadow, cast upon the ceiling and wall of the building, a huge hulking shape, doom in its visage. A hollow face, a gaunt man.

Grey hair swirled across the forehead, unwashed since the days of recent turmoil. Its mind was now clearing of the agony. The disease was but a portal, a path to true understanding for those with the strength to endure. The rebirth. The cleansing. His mind focused briefly on the memory of the crushing agony of destruction of the will, the self, but he knew the future lay past that now. He had been given his senses back. Days as an animal were but a foggy dream now, a dream of release and terror, of lust and thirst. But no matter now. The New Master had given him sight. He knew now that the old master was a myth, meaningless now. He knew what would be to come. He knew what The New Master wanted.

Wallace Farm
Portland, TN
July 12
10:01a.m.

Work progressed slowly with the palisade and compound, everyone suffering in the summer heat. New people kept coming to the farm every day. An effective quarantine zone was established at the edge of the farm. No one wanted to say it, but everyone was worried about the risk of infection. Some tarps and wooden boards were rigged up for shelter as the new people came in. The plan was to have them wait three days before entering the rest of the group. One new group that had walked in yesterday began to show erratic behavior and when one of the middle aged women tried to attack a guard, she was shot and killed and the other four people from the group had run screaming into the woods and off of the farm.

The rest of the time was very peaceful and a veritable herd of tents and lean-to shelters began springing up around the farm. People were nervous about the infection risk and were starting to move out of the barn for fear of catching the dread disease. The social distancing seemed to stop any spread of infection. One scouting party had found cleaning supplies in a nearby paint store. The chemicals were stockpiled to clean cooking utensils and pots and pans and the toilets. Several outhouses were dug on the property and building supplies from nearby houses and businesses were pouring in now. They began planning what would amount to a small row of houses with a common lawn like a pioneer village. The plans were to expand the palisade around the entire compound, using old forts from the area built in the 1820s as a guideline.

Jessica walked along the arc of the partially finished palisade, water jug and plastic cups in hand to provide a welcome drink for the workers. Jim Summers was using a post hole digger, his shirt off, tied to his waist in the sweltering heat. Mud caked his pants, where dirt and sweat had mixed. Around his neck was a string with a large man's gold wedding band hanging across his heart. Jessica paused and looked at the golden ring and hesitated.

"I never stopped wearing it, just hung it around my neck when it was final," he said, referring to their divorce.

She looked down at the ground and then back up at him. The morning light brightened his face, which seemed to glow with a vibrancy that she had not seen since she had dated the man, those many years ago. Shame and frustration warred with the memory of his addiction. Her ring had been sold long ago to pay the rent after the divorce.

"Mine's long gone. Sold it to make a way for the children," she said, honesty flowing from her mouth. Things needed to be said.

"And you'd be right for doing that. I never deserved you in the first place," he replied, no shock or anger in his handsome eyes. "I was blessed with you and then threw it all away. I, I...."

"You don't need to say anything. It is what it is," Jessica replied, sorrow of things long lost in her voice.

"I know, but I want to. I'm sorry I ruined our lives. I'm sorry I ruined your life. It's all my fault, and for nothing. Can you ever forgive me?"

The hot air and sun beat down upon them, sweat dripping from their brows. The still, sweltering closeness of heat and atmosphere seemed to compress time and space, the workers next to them seemed to disappear from view and reality as this outpouring of honest, needed truth was spilling forth. Jessica brushed a sweaty lock of her beautiful hair from her face and breathed out, looking at the man she once loved, honest regret washing over her face. This was the one person in the world that she had loved the most, and yet he was not the same. Something, Someone had changed him. If The Lord could love her and every other sinner, then maybe she could love him again.

Fear and hope warred in her mind, the tumult broken when his hand reached out and gently grasped hers. Her mind snapped back to the here and now, the man she had loved and could love again looking intently into her eyes, the question still on his lips, "Can you find it in your heart simply to forgive me? I don't deserve it, never have."

A surge of emotion flooded through her heart, hope and thought mixed into one overriding desire. A desire to clear out the malice and anger, a desire to set things right. She looked into his eyes and for the first time saw the shadow of the One who had forgiven her so many times.

"Yes."

This is my commandment, that you love one another as I have loved you. Greater love has no man than this, that a man lay down his life for his friends.

—John 15:12-13 RSV

CHAPTER 32

Wallace Farm
Portland, TN
July 13
10:01p.m.

Ten-year-old Sophie Bledsoe sat still on her sleeping bag, the rustling sounds of movement freezing her with fear. Her breath came in short gasps, her muscles held rigid, fear rippling through her small frame. Outside the small tent, leaves rustled and twigs snapped as the shadows of movement away from the house could be seen through the thin tent walls. Her brother, seven-year-old James sat up, rubbing his eyes, he started to speak and then looked as Sophie, her eyes wide in terror and froze in his place.

Outside, figures clad in hunting garb moved forward out towards the fields. Their father, Thomas Bledsoe, Pirelli's husband, crept along, ahead of a small group of similarly clad men and women. Their movements were echoed by three other groups, spaced a dozen yards apart. A hand reached toward the tent zipper and pulled down rapidly. The children froze in terror, too frightened to wet the sleeping bags or cry out.

A face poked into the tent. It was their mother, Pirelli. She looked rapidly at the two and motioned a finger to her mouth, in the universal sign for quiet. She motioned with her left hand for them to come quickly. The children obeyed, slipping on tennis shoes and moving rapidly out of the tent, behind their mother and into the main house.

As they passed into the building, the lights were all off and there were no candles lit. A dozen women and children were crowded into the kitchen, all looking out the window into the night. The light of the moon shone brightly onto the fields, the silhouettes of people moving away from the house. A dark stain of movement was barely visible on the edge of the field, a roiling, chaotic mass, with no discernible order appeared under the trees, heading for the compound.

Women quickly began pushing furniture against the doors and windows, moving as silently as they could. The dining room table was turned on its side and pushed up to cover the picture window. Drapes and curtains were pulled and stacks of books were stuffed with drapes and sheets and towels into the gaps, anything to protect them from the oncoming horde.

Shots rang out in the distance. Now that the quiet was broken, hammers and nails came out, plywood and bed slats were nailed across the windows and doors. The families cowered in fear, kitchen knives, bats and some pistols and shotguns in the hands of the women. A baby cried out and was shushed and soothed by the mother. None of the older kids spoke. Several toddlers slept, blissfully unaware of the impending terror.

Outside in the field, Sam and fifty men and women crouched, shooting as they picked out targets as the mass of infected humanity approached. Luckily, the cattle were on the other side of the property already, their instincts ahead of the humans. Thomas took aim with his .30-30 and fired a round into the chest of a large man lumbering forward at the front of the group. The round impacted and the man simply kept coming forward, showing no sign of pain, only a slight reduction in his speed of movement.

"Damn it!" Thomas said, cycling another round into the Winchester, this time aiming for the head. The 170 grain soft point impacted the man's jaw and took the left half of his head off above the neck. The man stumbled and collapsed, three more infected taking his place. Perhaps two hundred to three hundred infected swarmed across the field, far fewer than had swarmed across the Tulley Farm, but with no evacuation plan here, even a small number could do terrible damage. More rounds went off and some of the infected fell, others kept going forward. Sam swore under his breath.

"Aim for the head, dammit! Shootin' them in the chest don't work!" Sam yelled out, "Everybody retreat a hundred yards fast and then start shootin' again!" Sam's accent was coming out thick in the heat of the moment.

The defenders ran full tilt and dropped behind a ditch at the edge of the main field. Sam could hear bolts and levers cycling new rounds into the guns of his people. He began to worry even more. There was only a limited amount of ammunition for these weapons, mostly hunting rifles, a few pistols and some shotguns. Many of the shooters were inexperienced and would hit about one out of five times. Head shooting a moving target was not easy, even for the most experienced hunters in the group. He did not know how many infected had been downed, as the mass of inhumanity simply walked right over the bodies of the fallen.

The mass of infected were now only fifty yards away and they were only a hundred yards from the house. Sam's lever gun spoke again and again, each round carefully aimed and dropping another infected. He reached into his pocket and pulled out a handful of rounds and slipped them one at a time into the loading port of the rifle. Six more went down to his careful, aimed fire. He reached again and pulled out the last three rounds and reloaded. The infected were twenty yards away. Some people were already running away towards the barn.

"Retreat to the barn!" Sam called out.

The line of defenders ran as fast as Sam had ever seen men and women run. They tore through the field and yard, beside the house and regrouped inside the barn. The infected followed inexorably. Some turned off towards the house and the defenders who still had ammo fired at them, stopping some and drawing the attention of the rest. The bodies of the infected littered the yard and field. Perhaps half had fallen, so far. The moans of the infected could now clearly be heard, snarling wails of agony, stopping the hearts of the Portlanders with an icy chill.

"Get some tool and axes, we're runnin' out of ammo!" Thomas yelled out, fear speeding his speech. Men raced into the barn and grabbed what they could find. Sam grabbed an axe and threw a cane knife to Thomas who caught the sheath and drew the 22 inch machete, slinging the sheath to the ground. Sam glanced over and saw his ex-son in law, Jim Summers running away towards the tents. Coward, he thought. God damned coward.

Several men were still shooting. Sam had given his pistol to his wife and told her to stay in the house. Both his and Thomas' other guns had been distributed amongst the group. Sam figured if everyone had a gun, their chances would be better. He was not sure now that he was right, given the poor accuracy of the volunteers. If they got out of this, training was in order if they ever got any ammo. He never expected to have to go in hand to hand combat again with these things. Only a handful of the people here had any hand weapon other than a pocketknife. Sam had his tomahawk hanging from his belt, a replica of a frontiersman model from the late 1770s, truly a thing of beauty. With perfect balance, it would be needed today. He also had the machete that he had picked up along the way.

The infected closed in, screaming with bloodlust now. Inside the house, the women shielded the eyes of the children. They would be next, once those outside were dead. A large man raced forwards, his face twisted in a rage unequalled, as the virus chewed at his brain, neurons succumbing to the onslaught of destruction. Another ten feet and Sam would swing the tomahawk. The last rounds of the defenders were fired. A pistol flew through the air and bounced off of the shoulder of an infected woman. Men and women turned their guns around, held by the barrels, ready to swing at their foes, like some mad frontier epic, reborn from the ashes of the lost past.

The man was feet away, Sam's blade rose back preparing to slash down and suddenly, from the left, a tomahawk stuck the infected man in the skull. It had been flung accurately through the air and imbedded itself into the creatures head. Blood and brain matter sprayed out and the thing went limp, collapsing and tripping the three of those behind. Sam glanced to the side. There, at the edge of the field of battle, Jim Summers raced into the fray, Revolutionary War officer's saber in one hand, throwing a swag roll to the beleaguered defenders from the other, shouting instructions as the men hastily unrolled the blessed gift, pulling out a dozen stout weapons: sabers, Bowie knives, and tomahawks from the swag bag's fabric protective covering.

Jim shrieked a battle cry, "The Republic!" at the top of his lungs and instantly the head of an infected flew into the air, toppling onto the turf, eyes still wide in shock. Another and another went down as the man waded into the midst of the fray. Jim must have spent the week sharpening the swords, Sam thought as the battle raged. The re-enactors always used blunted swords that were made of the same steel as a sharpened sword, and could take a tough hit directly onto another blade without breaking, but were much safer to use, as they could only cause blunt trauma in a stage fight. Sam also had several of the dulled blades for reenactment. Of his own kit, the only fully functional items were his Bowie knife, black powder Pennsylvania long rifle and the tomahawk. All of the other gear was for show.

Others in the group were charging forward into the fray, emboldened by Jim's desperate bravery. Blades slashed as the mass of infected pressed forward. Two men at the front lost their footing and went down screaming as the horde tore into them, blood spraying in a horrifying orgy of death. The momentary gap in the wall afforded those behind to regroup for an instant before the bloodstained demons turned back towards the survivors. In that instant, rage swept through the community, rage against the onslaught, rage against the horror and injustice, rage against the world gone mad.

Jim slashed again and again, heads and arms of the infected horde flying in every direction. Others pressed the fight forward, screaming similar battles cries or just yelling to push their courage to the sticking point. Sam swung his axe at another and another, rending limbs and crushing torsos. Blood covered his arms, his brow set in a visage of undaunted courage. Jim's face echoed the look. He swung and pirouetted like a dancer, flashing steel contacting every foe, his ballet of death not yet complete. He fought like a man possessed; bodies sprawled at his feet, righteous fury boiling forth from him like a volcano of emotion. Tears streamed from his eyes as he sung out, his beautiful baritone voice echoing across the valley. Others fought on next to him, stunned by the vision in front of them.

He sang to the glory of the Most High God. He sang the hymn that changed his life, the song that saved his soul from the fires of damnation. The words flowed from him, a testimony of salvation. He, the man who had once ruined his own life, and nearly the life of the woman he loved, sang out the hymn of praise, the hymn of ultimate grace and forgiveness. As the words flowed from him, the infected crowded around him, his arm tiring for but an instant too long. The things swarmed around him, leaping forward like ants trying to topple a grasshopper, teeth slashing out, fingernails reaching. A bite raked across his sword arm, another onto his calf. The heads crumpled under the weight of the pommel of the sword as he fought on more desperately.

Still the song poured forth, the statement of thanks to his Creator for rescuing him from the darkness. More infected swarmed forth, his left shoulder viscously clawed by rough fingernails, another creature slashed open as blood and gore flowed forth from the bowels newly cut open. The defenders pressed forward, another falling under the weight of the attack, Sam's axe head buried in the chest of its last victim, his tomahawk and machete slashing back and forth now with unstoppable speed. Sam fought with every last, desperate ounce of his strength and courage to reach Jim. Tears now streamed from the eyes of the defenders as well, Sam's vision blurred slightly as hot tears flowed, the battle raging on before him.

The words flowed on, shakily now as Jim's injuries and blood loss accelerated. Others in the group took up the stanzas and added their voices, the infected unable to comprehend the sound. The survivors pushed forward, the line of defenders turning the tide of the advance. The bodies piled up, the numbers now even on each side. The beautiful words drove them forward.

Jim thought to himself of his life and the life he should have had, and now, God willing, would have in Paradise. He thought of the undeserved grace given to him by God, the forgiveness. It truly was an amazing thing, truly an Amazing Grace. He sang the hymn on and on, having memorized the stanzas, during his recovery from the demon in the bottle. His thigh ripped open as another infected bore down upon him. He smashed down again with the pommel and again stabbed and slashed outward, the bodies piling up around him. He could feel his lifeblood ebbing, the pain of his wounds receding as the world around him grew dim. He was aware of his body moving on its own, killing, crushing, defeating the monstrosities that threatened his family.

The ballet of death was at an end, the music ceasing from his lips as the last stanza was reached. A light of unbearable beauty opened in front of him and the world grew dim. Here, he saw The Lord of All Creation. He was truly the Way, the Truth, and the Life. He was the Door that Jim would walk through now. Jim's sword fell from his grasp as he collapsed onto the pile of the dead beneath him. He lay still, a small smile fixed on his handsome face, covered in blood and sweat. Here, there had never been a coward. Here, there had been the one who gave it all, just like his Lord had done for him, those two thousand years ago.

The group looked around at the scene. Those standing over the body of the hero wept openly, still holding their weapons, many from Jim's own kit. Their very lives had depended on this man before him. Fully half of the infected host had met their end at his feet, their bodies splayed out in a widened oval around the man. Ten people lay dead or dying from the group. Seven were quiet and three were in obvious agony. Sam looked out and realized that he did not know any of these victims before the world had ended. Screams of pain and anguish and shuddering breathing came from the field. Sam wanted to run into the woods and never come back.

After asking men to give whiskey to the dying and praying with the three men who lay mortally wounded, Sam walked over to two people seated off to the side and squatted down. Tears still stained his cheeks. He hated this entire thing. He wanted to scream and tear his hair out, but he knew he could not give in to his emotion. He had to be strong for what was left of this community. He asked some of the men to form a perimeter and spread out to watch in case anymore infected came. The attack had come from the opposite side from where the palisade was being built. They only had a fraction of it up now and it would be some time before it was fully ready. He wished it had already been finished. This all would have gone very differently, indeed, if it had.

Both of the bite victims were holding cloth bandages torn from their own shirts. They were two newcomers from town and had been bitten, one on the shoulder and the other on the hand. The injuries were not life threatening on their own. One, a young woman, was hyperventilating and the other, a young man, was staring at the ground, unable to speak.

"You can't let us turn into those...those monstrous things!" the woman shrieked, sobbing, still breathing fast. The man next to her squeezed her hand and looked her in the eyes. They were obviously a couple.

What would he do? Would he have them commit suicide? Would he execute them? Would he keep them locked up until they killed someone else trying to feed them, or until they killed each other? And how could he keep them safe from others trying to kill them? What did God want him to do? He couldn't believe this was the choice. He silently prayed for help.

"I don't know what to do," he said to the couple.

He looked at them. His honesty seemed to take them aback. They relaxed some and the woman smiled a thin smile at him. She patted her man's shoulder and he looked up, deep emotional pain etched into his eyes, the events of the last few days having been seared into his mind. He smiled also.

"Look, I am not asking for anything. We are just scared and we won't end up like that. I know suicide is wrong, but what other alternative do we have? I won't hurt anyone. I just... won't let that happen...." His voice drifted of, his gaze wandered off to the distance, the thousand yard stare taking him into the deep memory of recent horrors, horrors so profound that life would forever be divided into the time before and the time after the change.

"Just give us a proper burial after this is done. We've already been killed. Worse than killed. Changed into a killing thing. Can't be. Just can't be. I won't let it happen again..." the man spoke as he again drifted off into the living memory of the recent past.

What horrors did he see and partake in that so changed him? Sam didn't need to know. He understood well enough, and the thought was right. This wouldn't be a question of a vote. This would be done as they wished. The man hugged his woman and they pulled out their pocket knives. They looked at each other and smiled and nodded. They drew the small, sharp blades across each other's wrists at the same time. A woman from the group walked up and Sam's glare sent her back, herding everyone else away from the scene.

Sam knelt and prayed with them, new tears of loss and horror flooding from his cheeks. He cried out to The Lord. He sobbed as the couples faces turned pale in the moonlight, the black blood pouring from their wrists. He held their shoulders and said the twenty third psalm. As his voice broke from the emotion, the couple slumped down and leaned into each other. He had completed the prayer and they lay dead.

They had refused to hurt another or even risk another's peril at their expense. The universe had fundamentally changed and the shockwaves of grief that flooded though Sam's heart overwhelmed him. He sat for a long time, sobbing with his face in his rough, work scarred hands, his large frame wracked with grief. Grief at the loss, grief at his failure, grief at the horror. Just when he thought he could not go on, a hand touched his shoulder.

He looked up and saw in the bright moonlight his wife Carolyn, her strong, small hand squeezing his shoulder, love flowing from her into him, strengthening him, giving him hope. She smiled and he stood up. It had been an hour or so since he had sat with the couple. The group had been busy moving the infected across the field, well away from the livestock. There would be more work to do in the daylight. Sam's son, Trey Wallace, the 31-year-old near clone of his father, was busily moving infected with a wheel barrow. His daughter, Jessica, was holding Jim Summer's lifeless hand. The man had finally redeemed himself, and now he lay fallen on the field of battle. The crew had carefully left his body where it had fallen and had removed the roughly one hundred infected bodies from the scene.

Sam walked over to her and she jumped up and hugged him, knocking him back a few inches. She sobbed and screamed and wailed and then went limp in his powerful arms. He carried her to the house, her limp form exhausted with the night of grief, fear, pain and sorrow.

Sam ordered everyone to scrub themselves with the new batch of lye soap he had just made late last month. It was not fully cured, as that usually took six weeks, but he hoped that the caustic alkali in the mixture would do a good job killing whatever the infection was that they had all been potentially exposed to, during the fighting. No one argued and the water tank by the barn was discernibly less full, after all of the washing had been done.

It was now well past midnight as Sam figured, and he took his family to their rooms and asked the guard to be rotated. Sam asked that some more women take the shifts, given most of the men's exhaustion with the fighting, and every woman in the group volunteered, even those that had fought. Sam then asked everyone who had fought not do a guard shift and the rest reluctantly agreed. They hit their bunks hard, most sleeping as soon as their heads hit the pillows, but some, unfortunately, were unable to sleep. Occasional screams rang out that night as the inevitable post-traumatic stress began to manifest itself on the group. Sam only hoped that his Bible was right when it said that the weeping shall endure the night but joy would come in the morning. It would be a long night for many.

Once more unto the breach, dear friends, once more;
Or close the wall up with our English dead!
In peace there's nothing so becomes a man
As modest stillness and humility:
But when the blast of war blows in our ears,
Then imitate the action of the tiger;
Stiffen the sinews, summon up the blood,
Disguise fair nature with hard-favoured rage;
Then lend the eye a terrible aspect.
—William Shakespeare. Henry V. 3.1.1-9

CHAPTER 33

2 miles North of Gallatin Coal Plant
Coal plant main road
South of the Airport
July 14
7:41a.m.

The rumble of truck and motorcycle engines drew nearer, the sound echoing from the abandoned buildings north of the compound. This advance team of attackers was already in place, waiting on their signal. Intelligence gathering into or out of this region was hampered by the impassable downtown of the city of Gallatin, as this was in between the coal plant and the westerly cities of Hendersonville and the rest of Nashville to the west and south. It was impossible to send scouts safely through the area due to the heavy concentrations of infected in the area.

The engines continued forward, Josh just couldn't understand how they had gotten around the infected. They must have pushed far north, around Cottontown, before entering this area from the North. There was only one way that anyone could know about the survivors rebuilding the coal plant: the attackers from Hendersonville. What did that mean about Hendersonville? Had they already fallen to this gang? Regardless, they were here and they were Gallatin's problem now.

"Papa 1, Charlie 1, We have movement of vehicles at checkpoint. Request backup, over." Josh spoke quietly into the small radio. A pause followed. Josh could hear his heart beating in his ears. The young man had never been the military type, and frankly, this terrified him. It was bad enough to have zombie-like people trying to eat you and tear you to shreds, now these assholes had to come in and try to kill everybody.

He always hated bikers, and biker gangs were even worse. The Harleys and vehicles seemed quite a bit older than the typical style, but that made sense, given the solar event's destruction of anything new that had not been shielded, like his small radio, donated by those army types who answered to the Sheriff. He thought back over the last few days, of the frenetic work, the sermons from that really nice black preacher, the homemade cornbread. The defenders had been at it nonstop, since the Sheriff was really worried about this kind of attack. They had significantly improved their defenses, adding fences and shooting positions all along the roads leading into the coal plant compound. Although it would probably take months, they were even trying to restore the power, and only a handful of workers were spared to work in the power plant. The rest slogged through, day after day, moving, hammering and digging.

Finding the train and its store of food had been a godsend. The river water was being purified with boiling. They had an effectively unlimited supply of coal, literally a mountain of it on the premises. They had rigged up ovens to cook the meals and heat the water. Hot showers were not yet allowed, they had too much to do before constructing baths yet, but it was possible to get a bucket of the hot water and use a wash rag or shirt for a good scrub. It was next to heaven, given that life had changed so dramatically since the event. They didn't have any soap: the bars that they found were saved for the surgery room.

They had converted one of the offices into a surgical suite, with boiled water, clean towels and soap salvaged from the site's bathrooms. The next room had been converted into a pharmacy with a sterilization unit outside, made from a small toaster oven. Coal was burned in an old fuel drum turned on its side, with the bottom of the unit attached directly to the drum, allowing the unit's heat to pass into the oven by direct conduction. The thermometer would reach over seven hundred degrees. The assorted surgical tools scavenged from town before the arrival of the infected horde had been brought to the compound.

Minor surgery had been done several times on cuts and even to set a broken bone sticking out of a guy's finger, but yesterday a man had died from a gallstone attack. The doctors had operated on him using morphine and Versed from the pharmacy stock, but he lost too much blood and they had not yet established a way to donate the lifesaving fluid. The surgeon, Charlie, had thrown down his tools and stormed out of the building, walking by himself, a mile out into the woods on the compound.

Ed had waved off the guards who had tried to follow him. They didn't want to lose their only surgeon, but Ed had known better than to pressure him and had sent a team around north to watch the perimeter while Charlie got the anger and sadness out of his system. He had come back after a couple of hours and no one had said a thing about it. Several more had succumbed to the infection and had either slit their wrists or run off screaming into the river, swept away in the current, in their approaching madness. The handshake prohibition and monitoring seemed to be working to stop the spread of the illness. Josh wished that this day was not happening as the radio squawked back.

"Charlie 1, this is Papa 1, Roger last, awaiting guidance. Hold position. Repeat, hold position. Do not fall back."

Shit. The military guys had called this type of order a D.I.P. or "die in place" order. The men around him sighed and readied their rifles. The first motorcycles could now be seen, low slung black shapes rumbling slowly ahead, their riders like some hellish advance guard of an unholy army. The hogs had rifle holsters in various positions, some on the front, some on the back. Each appeared to have some form of long gun. The riders wore a variety of clothing from blue jeans stained with dark splotches to full leathers and spiked helmets. Some had beards halfway down their chests, while others appeared to be more clean-cut. It seemed as though they were as cobbled together as were the citizens of Gallatin.

The place in which they hid was on the side of the main road, about one mile north of the compound gate. They were the scouts for the town, each having volunteered for the duty. Most had lost all of their loved ones. Some sought revenge, others oblivion. Regardless, they all knew they were likely to get killed eventually. Josh wasn't sure he felt like getting killed today, though. Before the power had gone out and everything had gone to hell, he had a beautiful wife and he loved his home here in Tennessee. About a week before it all had hit the fan, his wife had become infected with this plague. He had watched his wife of two years turn into a monster over a period of a few days. She had been on the police reserve force and seemed to be one of the first wave of people that swamped the hospital.

Before it had burned to the ground, he had gone to visit her in the hospital and on the day before the power went out, she had tried to bite him and had to be restrained and sedated by the nursing staff. She had managed to bite one of the technicians sent in to draw her blood. Her eyes. They were like...like hollow vacuums of emptiness. It was as though there were nothing inside. That is, until some came within biting range. Then she would turn. Turn into the monster, snarling, slashing with her teeth. Anything to spread the infection it seemed. They didn't know what it was, but he had a childhood memory of a dog in his neighborhood with the same look. He remembered that the dog had been rabid, and had been shot, after attacking a man on the corner. The eyes were the same, hollow until someone came into focus, then full of rage.

The motorcycles came ever closer as they awaited contact. The rumbling now terribly loud, he could barely hear his own breathing.

"Roger last, engaging enemy now," he said, his voice elevated over the din now.

He pulled up his Remington 30-06 700 BDL and settled the scopes crosshairs on the fourth biker. The other men near him settled their rifles on the fifth and sixth, according to their training. They tapped each other with their left hands, the ready signal. Josh drew a deep breath.

"Ready...aim...fire," Josh yelled, just over the noise.

The three bikes went careening across the pavement, as their riders collapsed, the high powered hunting rifles making their marks. The men rapidly cycled another round and proceeded to hit the next three bikers in a row. Each of these also fell off of his hog and collapsed. One lay alive on the road, crawling forward, as the bike behind him ran over his legs, causing the bike to spin out of control and smash in the ditch. By now, the first three had stopped and were trying to turn their heavy, unwieldy bikes around in the limited space of the service road.

They would not make it that far. While the hunting rifles that the scouts were armed with were not true "scout rifles," or lightweight rifles with forward mounted optics designed for rapid target acquisition, the three scouts had spent years taking running shots at deer and other game. This was the reason that they had been selected for the mission. They were well able to hit a moving target. Using the tools that they knew the best, they felled the three bikers before they could escape the field of fire.

As the men cycled their bolts again, several of the attackers had lined up and were firing into the brush near their position. Josh prayed that they had not been seen. The advance was in broad daylight and their position was well into the shade of a cluster of trees to the side of the road. Rounds impacted above his head and his heart sank. Their location had been spotted. Josh began to order his fellows to retreat despite the orders from the Sheriff, but before he could speak, he looked down the road and his heart stopped. A van had pulled over in the first of a wave of attacking vehicles. A short, white bearded man wearing leather and a bandana do-rag leaned over the hood of the van. Men scattered away from him as the AT-4 antitank rocket settled onto his shoulder, the tube pointed directly at the scouts.

As Josh started to scream instructions, the rocket shrieked across the one hundred yard distance and slammed into the tree to their side, the explosion instantly killing the three men where they crouched. Josh's hands still clutched the smoking, charred frame of the Remington rifle as his last breath exhaled through tattered ribs and destroyed lungs, his chest wall crushed by the explosion. The men's charred and torn bodies were strewn across the road, the stolen National Guard hardware clearing the way for the enemy advance.

Northwest access road
3 miles North of Gallatin Coal Plant
Along power line corridor
July 14
7:44a.m.

The gunfire to the east could be faintly heard. The guard post members shifted nervously in their foxholes. Their position was south of the Sheriff Department's shooting range and had a view of the power line corridor, which was an unpaved grass strip about a mile long, leading north into farmland and then to town. They had a view of the waterway and could see anyone walking or trying to drive up the corridor. They clearly overheard the radio chatter that had been occurring between the easterly scouts and the compound. They were waiting for similar die in place orders and didn't look very happy.

One man motioned with his hand, looking through binoculars. Near the edge of the road that led to the shooting range and training center, there was movement. The range had long since been cleaned of anything of value. Most of the ammunition and salvageable equipment had been secured in the compound. During the collapse, some looters had come by and two deputies had scared them off thankfully, as the range had been well stocked.

The glint of metal shone from the roadway, about a half mile away. The rifles the defenders had could not reach a fraction of the distance and they felt very safe given the distance. The unit boss keyed his radio mike.

"Papa 1, this is November 1, come in over."

"November 1, go ahead."

"Thanks Gracie," said the unit leader, violating a key tenet of radio discipline, or COMSEC, communications security, in that one is never to name anyone directly due to risk of interception of the signal by an enemy. "There are vehicles stopping along the road north of our position now," the man continued, violating another tenet of COMSEC, in that he just revealed his position relative to the enemy forces. If they were listening...

"Damn it, November 1, keep communications security. Roger last, hold position for now, over," the compound dispatcher replied.

"Sorry, roger that," replied the sheepish unit leader.

The movement of vehicles stopped and people could be seen walking around what appeared to be several old trucks and motorcycles. An older 1970s van pulled up and some men got out of the back and pulled something heavy and large out of the back of the van. The long, black thing was set on the hood of truck and two men settled down near it. Seconds passed and nothing happened. Muzzle flash came from the end of the long tube and the sound of a loud boom followed.

The men looked on bemused, the distance was over 700 yards and they almost began to laugh. Their world had always revolved around hunting and everyone knew that you couldn't hit a deer at more than 300 yards, maybe a touch further. The idea of hitting a man at distances over double that was laughable to them. Sure, they had heard of sniper in the military doing it, but that was overseas, in the desert, not here.

A skipping and pinging sound was heard over their heads to the left. The man holding the binoculars cursed and turned to look at the team leader when a second flash and boom came from the enemy position. An instant later the man's left arm exploded. Bloody cloth and shreds of the upper arm tissue held what remained of his lower arm dangling at his side. The man stood in his foxhole, in shock as his lifeblood gushed from the socket, stunned disbelief on his face. He collapsed and disappeared from view as another flash and boom came from the vehicles.

The unit leader screamed, "Get down!" as another round slammed into the dirt in front of his position, sending debris into his unshielded face. He screamed as dirt and tiny rock chips crashed into his eyes, blinding him, as he wore no safety glasses. The stolen Barrett M110 SASR or special application sniper rifle continued to rain fire on the remaining two men, now cowering in their foxholes. The unit leader fumbled and dropped his radio and stepped on it, crushing the antenna, rendering the priceless device useless.

The third man cowered, sobbing into his hands, his mind full of the shock and horror of just witnessing his best friend's murder and bloody death. He was totally unaware of the approach of the vehicles down the grassy corridor under the power lines. As the vehicles came within fifty yards, the leader popped out of his hole and fired in the direction of the sound. Blindly cycling his bolt, he did not hear the ping of the M67 grenade tossed out that landed two feet from their foxholes. The intense explosive pressure wave and shrapnel instantly killed both men.

The enemy vehicles poured down over the destroyed outpost, slowly rumbling forward. Fully thirty trucks and two dozen motorcycles passed the foxholes, rumbling south towards the compound. To the west another ten vans and trucks headed down the main road with another two dozen motorcycles, rolling south, with no resistance, towards the citizens of Gallatin, now finishing breakfast dishes and preparing for the day's work.

Gallatin Coal Plant
Southeast border of city limits
July 14
7:48a.m.

Whistles blew all over the compound as word of the lost communications with the Northern watch emplacements spread. Edward was in the radio room after the first scouts called in their report. By the time he heard the second unit call in, he had already ordered a mass alert. Children and the elderly were being herded deeper into the power plant. They did not yet have any method of evacuation. It was stand or die, in this case. There was nowhere to run.

Issac had mobilized his men into two reaction squads to lead the townspeople against the incoming forces. Assumption was the mother of screw up: Issac knew this and he assumed nothing. He had prepared both teams to be fully mobile and able to shift positions as needed.

North of the compound, wire fences with intermittent embankments made of tires, dirt, sand and abandoned cars, had been installed halfway across the parking lots, giving long fields of fire into the woods north of the plant. Issac sent his teams out past these to meet the enemy head on, before they reached the compound. The reaction forces had roughly twenty men each. Each man was as heavily armed as possible, no extra weight was carried save extra ammunition. One medic went with each team, two volunteers from the local pharmacy. The surviving nurses and doctors were kept deep in the compound to await casualties as they could not be easily replaced if they were killed or wounded.

Edward Douglass, the Sheriff, sent every able-bodied man and woman to the fences, armed with everything they had left. Several teenagers were asked to serve as runners to carry equipment and messages. The salvaged guns from the town and the local gun shops along with what ammunition they had, went with the citizens. There was very little stockpile left, and no 50BMG cartridges, after the first encounter with the infected, as so many rounds had been used in the flight from danger. Everyone had a least some type of firearm. Most had long guns, rifles and the less common shotguns, and some had only pistols.

Some citizens had their own personal firearms, others had only what had been salvaged. The weaponry, with the exception of Issac's units, was completely unstandardized. Most of the people had no truly effective way of carrying the firearms or ammunition, and rifle protective body armor was exclusively seen on Issac's units and the remaining police personnel. Binoculars were spread out throughout the group, as were whistles. The surgeon, Charlie Blake had made sure every person had a combat bandage in his pocket. He had recruited a group of older schoolchildren to make the items out of salvaged bed sheets and towels. Each one was a copy of the highly effective Israeli bandage and could mean the difference between life and death in a severe injury, such as a gunshot or other bleeding injury. The mass of absorptive cotton was attached to rolls of fabric that could act as a tourniquet to stop bleeding. While he wished they all had the Quickclot and Celox blood coagulating products that Issac's team carried as a matter of course, he still felt better having distributed the low-tech life saving devices.

The people lacked equipment, certainly, but they had a fire in their belly. They were well fed, well rested, had a unified belief system, as most were churchgoers and the town had always stuck together through thick and thin, all the way back to the 1820s. Unlike the nearby towns that contained more outsiders, Gallatin was a cohesive group when it came to countering disasters. They had come together during civil war, famine, economic downturns, storms and tornados and they were coming together now. Furious anger boiled up inside the townspeople, as they thought of the injustice of the attack and the brave young men who had certainly died, when their positions were overrun.

The men and women ran full tilt to any position that they could find along the fence. Ed had to call some back and send them along the river to monitor it for any sneak attacks along their flank. Runners had notebooks and paper scraps and pens and pencils ready to take and deliver commands to the fighting positions. Ed told the secretaries to escort the children and elderly into the plant and barricade themselves in with whatever they could find. He ran out into the parking lot and took position behind a fighting embankment that they had made from sand filled tires that used river sand still wet, after only two days.

Two runners came up to his position and readied their notebooks to receive orders. The two teenaged boys were literally shaking in their shoes. Ed smiled at them and nodded, his M1A and 1911 at the ready. Ed wore body armor and a helmet just like Issac's crews. He had been a prepper long before any of the current disaster had occurred. Luckily for Gallatin, many of the citizens had been like-minded and had their own weapons and ammunition. A few even had soft body armor that had been handed out by the police, though that was not useful against rifle fire, only pistols and shotguns.

Those who had experience had spent some time each day from the beginning teaching what they knew to those around them. As almost everyone had grown up around guns, they all had some knowledge, though, as with the western scouts, many lacked a true understanding of the military arms and capabilities. Several Sheriff's deputies jogged around and spread themselves out, so that each fighting position would have at least one officer. Ed had stressed this when readying the compound. He figured that the officers could better motivate and direct the defenses that way as they were all trained in weapons and knew small unit tactics well.

Nervous eyes glanced over the embankments, perhaps ten fighting positions in all. Ed wanted a continuous wall eventually, but there had only been time to slap together an intermittent defense so far.

Wire, both barbed and smooth ran loosely between stands placed on the concrete and asphalt of the parking lot about twenty-five yards ahead of the embankments. Their sole purpose was to slow down anyone attacking to allow time to shoot them. There were still large gaps in the fence as it was not nearly complete. The section by the river was wide open as Ed had been more worried, correctly as he now knew, about attack from the North, from the direction of the town center.

North of the Coal plant
Western flank
July 14
7:51a.m.

    Issac leaned deeply onto the roof of the old Ford truck holding his Daniel Defense M4 on target, now visible coming over the hill, the bed of the truck shaking violently under his feet as he braced himself for the fight. Clay was next to him, M4 in hand and ready. The powerfully built 29-year-old Nathan Ford pressed the gas pedal to the floorboard of the truck, his dark black skin glistening with sweat, eyes peering through ESS bronze tinted eye shields, focused on the oncoming threat. Three hundred yards separated them from the oncoming attackers, their old vans and previously retired hogs churning earth on the dirt road.

    Behind Issac, three more trucks sped along at the same sixty miles an hour, breakneck speed on this dangerous dirt track. Somewhere to the East flank, another identical team rocketed towards their destiny, as well. The roar of the old engine drowned out all sound as the two men leaned into the rooftop. Another gun barrel pointed out of the passenger side, a young man, Jason Finley, behind the DPMS AR-15 stock. He was the captain of the local football team and had witnessed the murder of his mother by his own plague-mad father's hand before he and his sister escaped. He did not know whether his father was alive or dead, or where he could be now.

Jason's agility and drive to defend the city were immediately evident to Issac and he was selected for the reaction team. His father had obviously taught him to shoot. He had hit a four-inch target at one-hundred yards immediately after running a mile in under seven minutes and doing fifty push-ups and sit-ups, Issac's new standard test for membership on a reaction unit. This was primarily to save ammunition and to weed out the less fit without wasting precious resources. He could refine the process later, but so far it had worked well and had yielded three dozen new recruits right off the bat from the four hundred survivors.

The booms of incoming fire were drowned out by the engine, rounds impacting the truck's sheet metal. Issac flipped off the safety and slapped the roof with his palm twice. All three men drew down on the lead van and began pouring effective fire onto the target. About twenty rounds of the first ninety fired by the three men slammed into the windshield and engine compartment within ten seconds, killing the driver and front seat gunner, destroying the engine's manifold, carburetor and radiator, sending the vehicle into a sideways spin.

The van turned and rolled onto its side as the nose tucked under to the left and hit a pothole, the driver's bloody and lifeless hands still gripping the wheel in a rictus of mortal oblivion. The van tumbled three times and the hubcaps and sheet metal from the fenders flew violently from the vehicle. It landed sideways in a ditch to the side of the road, allowing the enemy vehicles to go around it to the left.

Issac cursed under his breath. He had hoped the van would block the road and stop the advance. The next vehicle, an older 1950s truck with a rusty finish of unknown original color sped past the fallen van, passenger firing a rifle towards the Gallatinites. Rounds pinged across the hood and smashed the windshield. Issac motioned the trucks behind him by waving his arms in a circle. They had worked out a plan before leaving the fence line and the trucks in back slowed down and formed a wide, three vehicle roadblock as Issac's truck sped up to meet the threat head on.

The 41-year-old Clay Masterson gave a grim look at his friend, as Issac slapped the roof three times. Seat belts came off of the two men in the cab and the doors cracked open, the distance between the oncoming vehicles was now one hundred yards. Issac slapped the roof three more times in rapid succession and Jason Finley leaped from the cab into the grass, the borrowed police level IV rifle plates in the thick nylon carrier vest and Sumner County Emergency Response Team level IIIA helmet saving his life during the tumbled roll. He came up and immediately sank to a belly crawl to cover behind a tree.

Clay and Issac leaped simultaneously off of the opposite sides of the truck, landing and rolling in the dirt and grass on the side of the narrow road. Both stayed down when they hit, Clay badly spraining his ankle and Issac breaking a lower left lateral rib, not covered by his plate carrier. He gasped for air as the wind had been knocked out of him. The world spun for a moment and he saw, from the corner of his vision, Nathan leap from the driver's seat as the car continued on, a cinder block on the gas pedal.

One second later the truck smashed head-on directly into the oncoming enemy vehicle, the fronts of the vehicles smashing into each other and crumpling as the back axles both lifted into the air. Whether the biker driving thought he could play chicken and win or if he was just too stupid to stop, the result was the same. The unrestrained passenger flew through the windshield and smashed into the Gallatin truck's windshield, the lifeless body halfway through the glass, as the driver was impaled onto the antiquated steering column of the old truck. The vehicle behind the lead slammed on the brakes and caused a pileup on the road, the motorcycles unlucky enough to be in between the automobiles were crushed, as the pileup blocked the road. Gunfire erupted from both sides, as the attackers, now on foot, pressed their larger numbers forward and South.

And when the servant of the man of God had risen early and gone forth, behold, a host compassed the city both with horses and chariots. And his servant said unto him, "Alas, my master! What shall we do?"
And he answered, "Fear not, for they that are with us are more than they that are with them."
And Elisha prayed and said, "Lord, I pray thee, open his eyes, that he may see." And the Lord opened the eyes of the young man, and he saw; and behold, the mountain was full of horses and chariots of fire round about Elisha.
—2 Kings 6:15-17 KJ21

CHAPTER 34

North of Gallatin Coal Plant
Main Access Road, Eastern Flank
One quarter mile north of the compound
July 14
7:53a.m.

The 52-year-old Harold Simpson ducked under the cover of the makeshift barricade, bullets slamming into the sheet metal of the abandoned vehicle. They were badly outnumbered and he knew it was only a matter of time before they would have to fall back. Another round of those heavy weapons and they would be finished. Already six Gallatin men lay dead, while the gang's stolen National Guard grenade launchers and rockets blasting past their cover and demoralizing the advance force. Their assault continued unabated, rounds slamming into the barricade and pinging off the top and edges, rattling the already shredded nerves of the defenders. Harold looked up at the 35-year-old Eli Smith, his six-foot three-inch frame hunched down behind cover, his Sage M1A gripped tightly in his hands, fear and frustration on his handsome face.

Harold called out on the radio, holding his left ear closed against the torrent of noise coming from the gang firing at them, "Papa 1, Tango 1."

"Tango 1, go ahead, over" replied the compound radio dispatcher.

"Bravo, bravo, bravo, how copy?" replied Harold, giving the code words for evacuation plan bravo, or as Ed's favorite science fiction movie explained the plan "Marines, we are leaving!"

"Roger last, 5 by 5," said the dispatcher using the correct Ham radio and military communications term describing the signal strength and clarity of the communication as 5/5 and 5/5.

Harold nodded to Eli as the two men motioned with their arms for everyone to prepare to fall back to the trucks. Someone would have to stay and buy them time. Before Harold could decide to sacrifice himself, the 38-year-old Jonathan Burke came running over with two gas cans and two men behind him carrying two tires each. One man was a Gallatin volunteer whom Harold hadn't met before.

"Harold, just light the damned tires! I see that look in your eyes, we've already had enough die today, goddammit!" screamed the unapologetic Jonathan, motioning frenetically at the tires he was now soaking in gasoline.

Harold sighed and nodded, the tires would give cover for the retreat, emitting a huge cloud of black smoke, which hopefully would allow for their escape. Jonathan used his Zippo lighter to light a stick that he had wrapped in cloth on the tip, forming a crude torch. The men had placed the tires at eight foot intervals behind the barricade. Jonathan lit each in series, grabbed his rifle and started firing over the barricade, as Harold motioned the rest of the team to step up their covering fire. Luke Dodson, the 26-year-old former Army sniper, settled back into the stock of his Savage M-110 BA 338 Lapua Magnum. He was nestled into an embankment well behind the front line and had a clear view and excellent cover. He nodded and sent a barrage of rounds down range, one every three seconds or so, shattering the windshields and bodies unlucky enough to be within his sight line. Others started shooting frenetically as well, expending ammunition at an alarming rate.

Ducking the incoming fire, the men ran back to the evacuation trucks, once the smoke became thicker. Eli and Harold came last, ducking the entire way. The trucks had been peppered with bullet holes and the windshields and windows had been shot out. Pain seared through Jonathan's forearm as a rifle round penetrated his left radius, shattering the bone. Blood erupted from the wound and blossomed onto the rolled up sleeve of his Multicam uniform. He screamed and let go of his M4 and pulled out a CAT or combat application tourniquet and applied it to the forearm just below the elbow, deploying it with his good hand. He screamed again as the truck lurched around at the moment he pulled tight on the Velcro straps, almost passing out from the pain. He was in the front seat of the cab of the ancient truck and the driver, a volunteer from Gallatin looked over with wide, terror filled eyes at the injury.

"Keep driving! Shit!" yelled Jonathan, the profanity keeping him focused and awake. "Fuck, fuck, fuck! Goddammit all to Hell!" he screamed as tears of pain ran unbidden from his eyes.

Rounds kept slamming into the truck as the driver recovered and floored the pedal, slamming everyone sideways, as the vehicle lurched onto the pavement and away from the carnage. Jonathan lay sideways, the bleeding stopped by the tourniquet, staring at the ceiling, his mouth moving slowly, no sound coming out. The pain was so intense that he lay in near shock, momentarily unable to move. For several moments he drifted into and out of consciousness, rounds still slamming into the vehicle. Screams of terrible sadness came from the truck bed.

"No, no, no! No God! Not Ricky!"

"Aghhhhhhh! Help me! Aaaaggghhhhhh! He..help...hee..help..."

Gurgling froth came from the mouth of the young man, his breath heaving in sobs of unrelenting pain and anguish. Anguish at the loss of his teenaged life, anguish at the loss of his potential. He was going to be a doctor. Before this.... Hands pressed rolled up cloth torn from his shirt onto the hole in his chest, sending bright blood foaming out of his mouth, like a volcano of red froth. He buckled and twisted and heaved a rattling sigh, his breath stopping and his chest wall settling slowly down as the last of the air left his destroyed lungs. His eyes wide, he stared up at the painfully blue sky and lay still. Sobbing men held on to the truck bed rails as the vehicle raced towards the compound.

The other trucks followed, racing behind the lead, their injured bleeding and screaming as well, some blessed with unconsciousness, others writhing in agony. Eli Smith was in the last truck, leaning over the truck bed as he took careful aim and fired at the gang bangers as they were removing the barricade. Several went down before the truck rounded the corner and he lost sight of the attackers. He knew that it was only a matter of time before they cleared the wreckage and pursued them. He only prayed that they could make their stand at the compound. Maybe if the defenders could make them pay enough, they would move on and leave them. If not.... He thought of all of the children and women. The idea of the bikers touching them made his blood boil. As a history professor, he knew what barbarians like this did to their conquered. It would be better to die to the last person.

Main compound
Gallatin Coal Plant
July 14
8:01a.m.

As the trucks from the eastern flank crossed the wire barricade, volunteers from the medical clinic raced out to meet them with improvised stretchers made from sections of metal pipe with thick web straps sewn crudely across in a simple pattern to hold the injured. Like most of the improvised tools used here, they were crude, but effective and highly efficient in that they did not take very many man hours to construct.

Guards checked the men exiting from the trucks to make sure that no unfamiliar faces were seen. They did not want any enemy to infiltrate their ranks. Ed had warned them all to check for this, as a hostage type situation could have easily ensued at the checkpoints, much as he would like to think that his men would all die to defend them, his study of history warned him otherwise.

The wounded were carried to the surgery room and mothers and wives ran to their fallen, despite Ed asking them not to leave their posts. Waves of grief flooded though the community when the dead and wounded were unloaded. Many of the bodies and been left at the checkpoints, the situation far too dangerous to risk the living to honor the dead. Many who did not see their loved ones return, sank their heads and sobbed in grief, with this grim understanding. Order was beginning to break down as Ed turned from his guard station to rally his people. A shot rang out from the road to the north and Ed stumbled, searing pain shooting though his left leg. People in the compound screamed as they looked out to see the oncoming vans, trucks and motorcycles of the gang appear around the corner of the road.

Both groups began exchanging fire and the Gallatinites surged back to the defensive positions that they had abandoned when the injured had arrived. Ed looked down at his leg and saw a blossoming red patch surrounding a neat hole in his pants. Another much larger hole on the opposite side was oozing blood and thick marrow from the smashed lower tibia. His lower leg had been almost completely destroyed by the rifle round. The pain was intense, but Edward Douglass had experienced pain before. He calmly pulled out his own CAT tourniquet and used the two handed method to apply the device above his calf and staunch the flow of blood. He knew that he had about an hour before the lack of blood flow and oxygen deprivation would kill the leg, he knew that it would likely die anyway from the damage it had received. He also knew that without either the tourniquet or immediate surgery, he would die. He knew there would not be time for surgery. His mind raced for an instant through these possibilities, his Aikido training allowing calm despite the intensity of the pain, and his fear of the attackers.

He stood up, another man helping him limp back to the defensive position. He pulled his radio and ordered all citizens back to their defensive positions. His voice remained calm, despite the sweat on his brow. He had to hold it together. They had not seen the members of the team on the Western flank. Ed worried about Issac, the best friend that he had ever had. The vehicles moved up and an M72 LAW or light anti-tank weapon streaked across the parking lot, just missing a defensive embankment and slamming into the power plant itself. Ed's mind screamed out in fear for the children inside. The hit was high, about twenty feet up and he knew the kids were supposed to be on the ground floor. It was truly a huge building and he hoped that they would be OK.

Automatic gunfire erupted from the gang members, the stolen M249s cutting down people in the open. Bloops from the M203 grenade launcher tubes sounded.

"Take cover!" Ed screamed into his radio mike desperately. The men near him ducked, trembling. While there were some ex-military in the group of survivors, most simply had never seen military weapons used. The rounds impacted one of the fighting emplacements; the concussion of the blast could be felt through the ground as all of the defenders on that post were instantly killed.

The trucks moved forward towards the hole in the defenses. It was all coming apart. Ed silently prayed, thanking God for his Glory and for his forgiveness. Several people fled from their posts, dropping their guns and screaming as they fled to the river. Most were cut down by the bikers as they left cover. Some made it to the river and dived into the gentle current. None were ever seen again. Curses of "coward!" and "bastard!" could be heard from the defenders still manning their posts. More bloops and Ed didn't have to yell as everyone took cover, the rounds missing this time, but splashing shattered asphalt onto the parking lot, craters testifying to the horrible power that had been unleashed on them.

Ed leaned over the wrecked car that he was using for cover and took careful aim with his Springfield M1A and sent a 150 grain .308 round through the torso of one of the grenadiers. The man spun backwards and squeezed the trigger of the older M16A4/M203 and cut down several men behind him with fully automatic fire before collapsing from the heart shot. There seemed to be no regularity with the armaments used by the gang bangers. Ed knew that the newest Army weapons platform included separate M320 grenade launchers and M4 carbines. It seemed that these gang bangers must have stolen from a National Guard armory, as this would account for the variance in equipment.

The bikers poured fire into the compound. Bullets tore into cars, fighting positions, and hit the exposed defenders. The body count was rising.

Improvised Operating Theater
Gallatin Coal Plant
July 14
8:05a.m.

Deep in the center of the power plant, nurses and medical volunteers raced from stretcher to stretcher trying to stop bleeding, administer meds and help the suffering. The improvised O.R. was the scene of frenetic activity as Charlie raced through suturing a bleeding femoral artery. The man bucked and moved under the light anesthesia that they had used, as they did not have enough meds to go around. His mind had shut out all emotion. This was a mass casualty event, the worst case scenario for any medical professional.

He finished suturing the artery, yelling at the nurse, "Have Mitchell close this!"

Charlie was referring to Mitchell O'Shaughnessy, the 6"5', 300 pound Irish-American podiatrist who had walked out of the collapsing downtown on foot after the evacuation had already taken place. He had apparently just sauntered right down Main Street and crushed the skulls of three or four infected who had tried to attack him. He had been on the outskirts of town, heading to his apartment when the battle occurred and he just grabbed a lead pipe he found and walked all night following the direction the vehicles had gone. He had been a few blocks over from the main path and by the time he reached the airport, the town was preparing to head to the coal plant, so he hitched a ride and joined up, his apartment having already burned down. His retired parents had died in the fire, and he was never the same after that.

"Got it Charlie!" yelled Mitchell as the nurses looked up at the huge man who had stopped his bandaging of a leg amputation and ducked into the O.R. at the sound of his name.

Charlie tore off his gloves and donned a new pair. There were not enough gowns to go around, so he left his on, very little blood covered it as he had always been cautious and had a sixth sense about when a bleeder was about to spray. He knew not to get sloppy and touch his hands to his chest or arms like some surgeons did. He looked down at the sucking chest wound patient on table two who had just been brought in and took a deep breath.

"Light, suction, somebody get me a chest tube, stat!"

Main compound
Gallatin Coal Plant
July 14
8:07a.m.

Luke Dodson cursed as he pulled the last magazine out and stared at the empty magazine pouch on his Eberlestock rifle pack that he had been using as a rifle rest. The Savage was out of the Lapua .338 ammunition that been such a decisive tactical advantage in the past. He pulled out his Daniel Defense M4 from the pack, loaded a Pmag from his vest and began engaging the enemy. He scored several hits before the bloop of an M203 made him duck and cover. The round sailed over his head and smashed into one of the trucks that they had used to evacuate the checkpoint. It exploded in a fireball, the gas tank rupturing on impact. He could feel the heat on the back of his neck, despite the 80-degree morning temperature.

Men ran to and fro behind the barricades, firing back at the force that was steadily overwhelming them. They simply could not stand up to such firepower. Luke had killed over twenty men this morning and the gang showed no sign of stopping their advance. He pulled out the crucifix under his plate carrier and prayed for help, sweat pouring from his brow. *My help shall come from the hills, Lord.* He kept mentally repeating the psalmist's refrain.

Men poured from around the trucks, firing everything they had at the compound, the defenders ducking for cover under the onslaught. Loud rocket sounds and explosions sounded, but not in the immediate vicinity. Continued automatic fire from the west and north echoed across the parking lot. Both the defenders and gang members slowed their fire, confused by the sounds. The gang bangers started cheering and raising their rifles in a victory chant. Some gyrated and thrust their hips, licking their lips and wagging their tongues at the beleaguered Gallatinites. One bearded bald man licked his lips and grabbed his crotch while pointing his rifle one-handed at two women behind one of the barricades. The booms and crashes of explosions came closer, the automatic fire louder.

One Gallatin man reached over the barricade to fire his rifle and a gang banger shot him in the head, laughing. Voices and yelling could be heard now from the direction of the northwestern checkpoint, amidst the crackle and boom of fire. A rocket streaked out, missing the target and slammed into the river, exploding and spraying a fountain of water into the air. The movement of engines could be heard, as the gang members were whipped into a frenzy of exultation.

Ed peered over the embankment towards the north and his heart sank, thinking of Issac and his team. He had just breathed out a prayer for death with honor, when his heart soared. As he looked to the North, the bearded man continued his revolting display while the shooting from the gang bangers intensified. The desert tan M1117 ASV or Armored Security Vehicle pulled into the parking lot flanked by three woodland colored M1114 Humvees. The main M2 gunner of the ASV fired into the gang members, the .50 BMG rounds blowing holes into the torsos, exploding the heads and shredding the limbs of the attackers.

The bearded man collapsed as one round pierced his lower abdomen, exploding his intestines and shattering his lower spine. His upper torso flew back from the explosive force, over 15,000 foot pounds of force, over three times that of an average elephant gun. He gasped and tried to breath. Unable to scream due to the loss of diaphragmatic counter pressure, he died from the massive shock and blood loss, his lips curled in a silent scream of stunned agony and disbelief.

The Mk 19 grenadier on the ASV fired several bursts of 40mm grenades into the crowd, killing two dozen men in an instant. The vans and bikes exploded, their gas tanks igniting. The remaining vehicles and men tried to escape as the Humvees gunned their engines in pursuit. Two National Guardsmen were positioned over a dragon rocket launcher and fired on the lead van, as it headed northeast. The rocket screamed across the parking lot and the van exploded into a flaming ball, rolling over into the ditch. His body on fire, the driver exited the vehicle and ran a hundred feet, collapsing in the roadway, flames still engulfing him.

Ed looked up and saw Issac and Nathan standing shoulder to shoulder with the Guardsmen firing on the enemy. He looked over the compound and the people were cheering, firing into the escaping gang members, cutting them down, as they fled. The Humvee's turret gunners sent 50 BMG rounds into the crowd of escaping gang bangers, stopping them in their tracks. Within moments, it was finished. Dismounted National Guardsmen walked calmly through the field of battle, dispatching any attackers that fought back. A chaplain walked with them, trying to offer comfort even to the fallen gang bangers. One spit on him, several refused to talk, but one held out a hand and the chaplain gave last rights to the dying man.

Ed and Issac hugged and cried on each other's shoulders, the emotion of the moment and the relief washing through them overwhelming them. Ed looked at Issac with fear in his eyes. What if the Guard was planning on taking over? Did they just want the town as their slaves? Issac could see the questions before Ed spoke them.

"My friend, I would like you to meet someone," Issac spoke, leading Ed to the back of the convoy, his leg now a dull ache under the tourniquet, each step sending paroxysms of pain up the calf.

Main compound
Gallatin Coal Plant
July 14
7:39p.m.

The group surrounded them, National Guard on one side, Gallatinites on the other. A Major from the National Guard stood in the center. The once crisp uniform, now stained with blood, sweat and grime did nothing to hide the dignity of the man wearing it. Major Bradley Stockton of the Tennessee National Guard, a lean man, of medium height, with light brown hair, stood in front of the Bible, his chaplain holding it out for the crowd to see. Ed was on an improvised gurney, volunteers helping to prop him up to see the crowd. He was pale and haggard, his skin sallow and bleached-looking. His hair was disheveled and bedsheets covered his body from the waist down, tucked into the gurney. The place where the left lower leg should be was flat and vacant. The surgical anesthesia had worn off and the pain pills had left Ed groggy, but well awake.

The men looked at each other, serious intent carved into their rugged features. Ed nodded. The Major turned to the crowd and spoke, "I, Major Bradley Stockton, Detachment 1, 1st Squadron, 278th Armored Cavalry Regiment, Tennessee Army National Guard, hereby relinquish command of my forces to civilian rule, under the authority granted to me by my rank and privilege."

He placed his hand on the Bible and continued. "I give my oath to defend this City of Gallatin and pledge my forces serve the common good, under civilian rule."

Ed turned and faced the Major, who removed his hand from the Bible. Ed placed his hand on the Bible and spoke. "I, Edward Douglass, acting Sheriff of Sumner County accept your pledge of service. Major Stockton, you stand relieved."

The crowd roared its approval, hands waving, hugs between the civilians and guardsmen. The crowd surged forward to shake the hands of the two men. The chaplain was lifted onto several of the guardsmen's shoulders and carried around the crowd. The cavalry truly had come and saved the day. Certainly, there would be challenges ahead, and the legality of the proceedings was questionable, at best. But the two groups had come together to provide each one what the other needed.

The town of Gallatin needed an army to defend and protect it, to train it to fight, to survive this new horrific, chaotic world. And the Guard unit needed something to fight for, something to believe in that was worth dying for. Each benefited with the union; each gained strength from the other. The medical units combined. Gallatin offered an excellent surgeon, a pediatrician, two internists, a psychologist, a cardiologist, a family nurse practitioner, a podiatrist, several nurses and physical therapists, along with a host of volunteers, while the Cavalry unit offered several outstanding battlefield medics with extensive combat experience honed on the desert battlefields found in so many overseas wars. The combination would prove to be a lifesaving one.

The security teams offered hope of defense against this new madness, while the structure and engineering prowess of the Guard unit immediately began improving the security perimeter and physical plant. The organizational skills and discipline rubbed off on the civilians. The storehouse of food and domestic supplies and medicines found at the compound was impressive, while the munitions, weapons and vehicles offered by the Guard were desperately needed. Weapons training and allotment began immediately as the ranks of skilled shooters and vehicle drivers doubled almost overnight as the Gallatinites were already well skilled with basic firearms and vehicles. The townspeople offered hearth and home, skilled labor and technical ability not found in the Guard. Each group benefited greatly by the merging. A truly strong force had been formed by the alliance.

The story told to Ed and the others was a chilling one and boded ill for the surrounding region. The guard units had been mobilized to pacify Nashville and when the gang forces held them at bay in Goodlettsville, and forced a retreat, the carpet bombing of downtown Nashville had begun. After word of this horrific act spread, unit cohesion split the camps into two main factions, both supporting and reviling the action. When communication from the main HQ in Knoxville had stopped, the bickering reached actual fighting. The commanding

Lt. Colonel tried to regain order and was shot in the head by a Captain who appeared to have gone mad.

This was when Major Stockton had ordered what was left of his home unit to quietly disengage. The order went out smoothly and the unit left in the middle of the night during an argument between other units in the group. They had been moving cautiously from town to town trying to find a place to join when they reached Hendersonville. Most of the men in the unit were from Gallatin and they figured everything would be OK. They were wrong and nearly got into a huge pitched battle with the police force there.

After they left, they came North through Cottontown and got bogged down fighting herds of infected and finally reached Gallatin, only to find more infected. When scouts reported a firefight at the Power plant, they responded and figured out pretty quickly what was going on. They attacked the Northwestern flank of the gang members' fighting force, that had been divided into two units. When they reached the reaction force, Issac surrendered his unit to their command, hoping for the best, as he recognized some Gallatin boys in the unit. His trust paved the way for the rout of the enemy and the integration of the units.

When Ed and the Major met, they knew what had to be done immediately, each sensing the other's intent. A plan was hatched quickly and Ed was taken to the O.R., but it was too late, the risk of infection too great, and the damage was far too extensive to salvage his lower leg. Despite his surgery, the handover of power was done dramatically in a public forum to cement the bond and ease the tensions. Cleanup of the battlefield and medical care proceeded as before, and at the end of the day, fifty-seven Gallainites and three Guardsmen lay dead. Many more were injured. Issac's unit and the volunteers suffered the most injuries and more dead per capita than the rest, as they had engaged a far superior force, despite the odds. They were dubbed Davis' Rangers for their leader's undaunted courage. They were offered honorary rank and they all declined, preferring the status of sovereign citizen.

After the dead were buried, an honorary reading of the Bill of Rights was held in front of the main compound. An American flag was pulled out of one of the offices and unfurled and flown on the compound's flagpole. Everyone, even the civilians saluted it as it was displayed. There was not a dry eye in the house. The three hundred and fifty survivors and ninety three Guardsmen joined ranks into one whole unit, a living, breathing testament to the Republic that they would try to carry on, but this time remaining true to its original intent. Elections would be held and Edward Douglass would win the office of Sheriff. It would be a long late summer and fall and the year to come would be fraught with peril, but the seeds of hope would survive. The remnant would endure.

I do not fear the soldiers, for my road is made open to me; and if the soldiers come, I have God, my Lord, who will know how to clear the route...It was for this that I was born!

—Joan of Arc, at Vaucouleurs, 1429

CHAPTER 35

Outskirts of town
Dickie's Gun Emporium
Portland, TN
July 15
10:02a.m.

Chloe Pearl dug through the rubble and pulled out several dusty black guns. She looked up at Pirelli Bledsoe and her husband Thomas, who both grinned ear to ear.

"Assault Rifles!" Pirelli squealed, her voice artificially high and nasal.

"They are 'Modern Sporting Rifles' dear, don't you know!" Thomas replied, a goofy grin on his face. They were making fun of the media's obsession with anything practical, like guns in this case. They always seemed to vilify things that you needed. Things like a spanking from your parents when you were a kid, guns to defend yourself, religion, hard work, and the death penalty for murderers. They were all gone now, probably all dead or wandering around somewhere trying to bite everything in sight, defecating in their pants and generally lower than a cockroach.

They needed the outlet. It had been a terrible week. The losses at the farm had been almost overwhelming. No one would be the same, and they knew that it could happen again at any time. They had to be prepared. Several of them had gone on a supply retrieval operation. Some to the gun store and others were going house to house looking for the re-enactor's equipment. The list of mostly men was not that long and most lived fairly close. They had need of every weapon that they could find: swords, rifles, knives, axes, tomahawks, and ammunition. They had done a fairly good job so far of collecting food, but the near defeat at the farm had taught them all the importance of tactical operations. They were literally the difference between life and death.

Thomas looked down at the firearms that Chloe had pulled out. Two Rock River Coyote hunting carbines with flattop uppers, ready for scopes. These would come in handy for sure. They found three Mossberg combat shotguns in 12 gauge, seven hunting shotguns in an assortment of chamberings, including Remingtons, Winchesters and Mossbergs. Three snub nose revolvers from Taurus in 38 special and an assortment of 9mm, 40S&W, and .45ACP semi autos. There were a few .22 rifles, mostly kid's starter rifles and a few oddballs such as a .270 and .243 Browning A Bolt and a single shot Thompson Contender .44 Magnum ten inch barreled pistol.

All of these guns were scratched and damaged slightly. They left several guns that looked beyond repair. It looked like the store had suffered some kind of blast that had basically destroyed it. The store was fairly large and Thomas knew that they had far more guns for sale than they were finding here. They could not find the owner. His house was next door, but a search had revealed no sign of him, not even a note. Thomas hated the idea of just taking the things, so he left an IOU under a rock in case anyone found it. He was careful to only use the name of the Farm, not the location. That way, unless anyone finding it knew the owner, they wouldn't know where to look. The Farm was not nearly considered large in this area, even with five hundred head of cattle nearby.

They found a moderate quantity of ammunition in most of the calibers and some spare parts that Thomas knew would be helpful. He had taken some gun smithing classes and thought he could make some improvements. The real treasure was found under the bottom of the rubble, after some digging. An AAC 5.56mm suppressor with matching AAC Blackout flash hider mount. This was what the uninitiated referred to as a silencer. Far from silencing the shot, it simply quieted it. But that reduction in noise meant that from 100 yard away, they were quiet enough to be hard to detect. Close in, they were still loud enough to hurt the ears. If they could find a 9mm or .22 long rifle, now that really would be quiet. Those were so quiet that you could hear the parts in the gun move during the shot.

He wondered absentmindedly if he could make one. After all, the problem with obtaining them was the government restrictions, not the complexity of the devices themselves. They should be really simple. He would have to take this one apart when they got back to the farm. They loaded the gear into the old truck bed and got in, Pirelli sitting in the back, with Thomas driving and Chloe riding shotgun. Noise behind them drew Pirelli's attention. As they slowly pulled out of the parking lot, two people staggered out of the woods about thirty five yards away.

"Infected! Gun it Thomas!" Pirelli shouted.

Thomas looked in the rearview mirror and his heart skipped a beat. Two and then about twenty-five infected came racing towards the truck. He slammed his foot down on the gas and then immediately realized his mistake. The ancient carburetor stalled as Thomas let off of the gas and the vehicle slowed.

"What the hell are you doing!?" yelled Pirelli, chambering a buckshot round into her Mossberg 935 camouflaged waterfowl 12 gauge.

"Trying not to kill us by flooding the carburetor!" Thomas yelled back.

The truck crept forward at five miles an hour, as the gasoline slowly cleared from the partially flooded carburetor. The first two infected were ten feet away when Pirelli fired at the first one, a young, thin woman with long, stringy blonde hair and pale blue eyes, mouth curled up in a sneer, her pale skin and hair covered in leaf litter, her dress an undeterminable gray-black color. Her chest exploded and she stumbled but kept coming until the second round blew the right side of her head off and she collapsed like a marionette whose strings had been cut.

Thomas slowly eased up on the gas and the truck approached seven miles an hour, as Pirelli fired another round and missed. The second infected was reaching for the gate of the truck bed and grabbed on just as Pirelli got a bead on him. The creature looked up with savage bloodlust in its eyes. The young man would have been about thirty, trim and fashionable clothes now tattered and ripped clung to his frame. He wailed a moan and his head exploded as the 1300 foot per second 00 buckshot pellets slammed into his cranial vault rupturing his skull. Matter sprayed everywhere onto the truck as Pirelli kicked the still clinging hand from the lift gate, her heart racing as the herd of two dozen or so infected started to catch up. The distance closed to ten yards as the things were gaining. Slowly, the truck got up to speed and the things fell farther and farther behind.

The creatures never stopped running. They just kept coming. No pain, no exhaustion, just lust for flesh. The truck finally rounded a corner and the reached fifty-five miles an hour, as Pirelli sat in the back of the truck bed, exhausted from the moment's terror. Miles went by and they finally reached the Farm. Later that evening, the other teams arrived with a good load of bladed weapons, mostly reproduction revolutionary war cavalry swords, Bowie knives and tomahawks. All appeared to be "battle ready," a term used for swords and weapons that would not fall apart when used. "Wallhangers" were not safe at any speed as they would catastrophically fail and sometimes kill the users.

All in all, it was a good day; everyone made it back without injury. Rain clouds came up on the horizon and the sky darkened, as the earth trembled in static anticipation of the blessed moisture. Weeks without rain had dried out the cracked earth and scorched much of the vegetation. The heavy drops sank deep into the soil, as the dry spell finally broke. Cattle twisted their tails and headed for cover, the dust finally washing away from their dry hides.

Across the land, the silent backdrop welcomed the blessing from heaven. Rain cleansed the land, the bloodstained asphalt and concrete slowly coming clean as wave after wave of warm water cascaded down for several hours. The lack of modern noises intensified the experience, isolated the focus of those who experienced it through new ears. The trauma that the land had seen was not over, the desperate fights were far from finished, yet this momentary change in the landscape was a welcome respite from things to come.

Crops writhed in their imperceptibly slow dance, soaking up the bounty, sending its molecules coursing through their veins, growing, spreading, slowly covering the land. The inevitable cleansing of the Earth had begun. Wherever there were no people left to tend the settlements, grass and tree, vine and shrub would begin to cover the planet, to wipe the blight of mankind from much of the land. Like a body healing from the pox that had scarred it, the land would slowly, over the generation, heal. Those left would carve a new place amid the ruins of the old. It would never be the same, not for many generations. As the death knell of the old had sounded, so the quiet heraldry of the new began, its new tapestry starting to form as if the drought had been an interlude, a respite for the players to await the next act.

Foothills of the Cumberland Plateau
Private forested road
Group property
July 15
1:37p.m.

The rain finally stopped as the team continued scanning the perimeter. Twenty one-year-old Samuel Tulley, or Sam, as he was called, stared through the Leupold Mk4 scope and slowly squeezed the trigger of the Remington PSP. At 200 yards, the head of the infected snapped back, the report of the rifle echoing though the valley. He slowly cycled the bolt and scanned for a new target.

Doug McKnight sat next to him, his DPMS SASS-LRT braced on a tactical pack in front of him. He breathed out and slowly squeezed the match grade trigger and at 375 yards an infected lurched sideways, the 175 grain Sierra Match King that they were using slamming through the chest wall. Doug peered through his scope and saw the blood spreading slowly on the target's shirt. There would not need to be another shot, as the creature would eventually bleed out within minutes from the shot and would never get close enough for concern.

It had been a long day, sitting in the rain on over watch, but it was good to get out of the compound for a while, and this was a good place to clear your head. The foxhole was lined with sandbags and was miserable when wet and muddy, but at least they were away from the sorrow of the group. Beth had been sequestered from the rest of the group, kept in one of the outbuildings usually used for butchering meat. It was well away from the rest of the group and she would sit alone, with a guard nearby to watch her and keep her company.

She had already started to hallucinate and would sometimes talk to herself, a habit that she had never had. She would not let this go on much longer before she either insisted on an execution or simply tried to commit suicide. She had never changed her mind on this, and the group did not know what to do. Matt had retreated into himself. His grief was unimaginable and he lashed out at anyone who tried to pry him out of his shell.

Madison was worse. She required constant monitoring now. The younger siblings cried constantly, but would hug the other adults and their dad and at least accept some comforting. The Corpuz boys were alternating during the day and the adult women were taking turns sleeping next to her at night. They did not want a repeat of the events that nearly resulted in her suicide. She was off weapons details and guard duty till further notice. She had been working in the kitchen mostly and spending some time outside digging the embankments.

It had been a miserable week for everyone else as well. Social distancing went into overdrive. No handshakes initially; now no contact at all. But it seemed to be working as no one else showed any signs of the plague. Angus had been working on a plan for durable biological protection. All of their Tyvec suits were white, which was tactically unacceptable. He had not completed his design, but he felt that there must be a solution within reach. The first step was using the 3M half face mask respirators and the black tactical nitrile gloves that he had stockpiled for the group.

Angus felt that they had been very lucky so far with only one member contracting the plague. No one had any idea what to do about Beth, either. They were all, more or less, deeply religious. From Catholic to several varieties of Protestant, the group uniformly did not believe in suicide. But what part of serving God's plan could involve turning into a monster that would attack and kill or infect everyone in the vicinity? They had prayed and prayed for days, with no answer in sight. The Lord appeared silent on this issue. No one seemed to have an answer to prayer. As a result, the group members became more and more gloomy and difficult to be around. Doug felt better out here, where at least he could do something productive.

He spotted another infected and exhaled and squeezed the trigger, sending the Sierra Match King bullet at 2500 feet per second towards the target, though his barrel was only 18 inches, it did very well out to 600 yards. The round once again slammed into the torso and the infected seemed to be oblivious, but the wound would prove fatal within a half an hour or less, Doug knew from experience. He had been at this all week and had already killed several hundred infected.

He spent the nighttime hours reloading the match grade brass that he kept for his rifles. He used an ultrasonic tumbler with a fifteen minute cycle using one of the house inverters and a charged car battery to run. The cycle was very short and drained little current. For now, they had cases of ultrasonic cleaner. Later on, they might have to improvise. It would not have been possible with a vibratory case cleaner, as the cycle was too long to justify the power usage, and the noise would be a tactical mistake. The Faraday cages that he had constructed to protect the gear were proving to be invaluable. They had an abundance of ammunition, but he wanted to be topped off at all times in case of a real fight. So he used these cases multiple times and saved the surplus ammunition and several boxes of match grade factory ammunition for a stand up fight, preferring to use reloads where he could, as they theoretically might be less reliable, though he so far had not had any issues.

Sam was quiet and thoughtful. The entire idea of shooting people was so utterly alien to his existence before the collapse that he did not relish this duty. While Doug could rationalize it with his longer experience, Sam simply did it the way one would handle garbage duty or cleaning a toilet. It was revolting to him, but it had to be done. Both men cared deeply for their friends and family and each had his own way of coping with the new reality.

"What the hell? Call in now, Sam!" Doug softly yelled, tugging his friends arm and pointing at the two Humvees that just came into sight.

"Oh my God," said Sam, not calling on The Lord in vain, but truly for help now. "Sierra 1, Whiskey 1, incoming bogeys. Repeat, incoming bogeys."

Inside the compound kitchen, the radio blared the message, and Denise raced to the handset and keyed the mike, "Whiskey 1, confirm. How many bogeys?"

The house exploded into movement, kitchen tools dropped on counters or in the sink, vests and helmets slung on and rifles snatched up as five people raced out the door. Outside the house, everyone else was racing from their work to their posts, dropping shovels, axes and wheelbarrows, dirt flying everywhere as the group raced against time to present an effective defense against the unknown threat. Their radio discipline was exemplary. Everyone desperately wanted to know what kind of "bogey" had been sighted, but none clogged the channel with signals.

"Two Humvees, deliberate," replied Sam, sweat pouring from his brow, his young voice quavering slightly with fear. His message gave away nothing to the enemy about their location, should they be listening. It gave away no other information that could be used, and allowed the group to prep for their arrival. The term "deliberate" meant that the enemy was moving at a moderate rate of speed and not racing towards the compound.

Each of the group members reached his or her pre-appointed shooting position. There were foxholes and sandbagged shooting blinds all over the property and these were being expanded every day. Every shooting position had an ammo box buried in the front that contained six fully loaded Magpul M16 30 round PMAGs, a polymer magazine that could be left loaded long term due to the polymer dust cover that could be snapped into place over the top of the magazine and compressed the loaded rounds down away from the feed lips, preventing the strain that caused early failure of some standard magazines. The box could be easily dug out, but would not be visible to any enemy using the position, unless he knew about its existence.

Ghillie blankets were used to cover the blinds and the group members began quietly disappearing into their fighting positions. Each person put on their hearing protection and attached their radio ear buds to the outside microphones of the headsets and then put their helmets on and snapped the chin straps. This was a terrifying exercise and several of the members fumbled rapidly with the chore, hyperventilating until it was completed. Then they waited.

Back at the out building, Beth stood up, the Corpuz brothers both on guard duty for her and as a fallback if the compound was overrun. They both looked at each other quizzically and then back at Beth. Beth had a gleam in her eye as she stared down the road at the Humvees coming into view. Her eyes flashed and glittered and her concentration seemed to waver as if she were jumping back and forth between thoughts. She walked towards the boys, who slowly backed up. They had no desire to be infected, but did not want to shoot the woman that they thought of as an aunt. They stumbled back and called out on the radio for help.

Angus and Matt both leaped out of their foxholes and ran like hell to the shed. Both men reached the building at the same time. The boys were backing slowly away from Beth when they arrived. Beth looked crazed one minute and sane the next instant.

"Baby?" Matt said, big tears in his eyes.

"I love you Matt. I need the charges. I know you made them. He says I need them now," Beth replied, her hands held out. "And tell

Madison to get my best dress. You know, the red one. And a pair of heels."

"What? What the hell are you talking about!? We're about to be attacked most likely!" Matt extolled his wife, frustration, sadness and anger welling up in his voice.

"MATT." The voice that Beth used rooted all of the men to the spot. It was as if the Earth had spoken. Matt inhaled deeply, Angus held his breath, and the boys trembled.

"Do as I said. Now. My time is at an end and I have one more thing to do," Beth said as her concentration began to waver again and flutter back and forth between reality and whatever else was going on in her infected mind.

"My God Beth, what the hell are you going to do, walk down the road and hand them a bomb..." Matt stopped, understanding dawning on him in an instant. He lurched forward toward his wife, tears streaming down his cheeks as Angus and the boys held him back.

"NOOOO! God no! Please God no..." He broke down into sobs.

The focused intensity of the moment seemed to snap Beth back to the here and now. She knelt down towards her grieving husband and held her hand out towards him, stopped a foot from his face. She caressed the air near his cheek and he collapsed, the agony of the past few days flooding out through him. Madison was now next to him, her arm supporting him. She had come just behind the men when they arrived, but had stayed back. She now spoke to her father.

"Dad, she's right. We can't help her now, and she won't turn. She asked it of us and we would have to do it. God knows we can't, knows we don't have the strength to stop her from changing. So He's made the only way. This is the only way."

Her father kept sobbing and she turned to Rafael. "Run and tell Mrs. Gunn. She'll know where the dress is, and the shoes," she said, referring to Margaret Gunn, Angus' mom.

She turned to Angus, "Mr. Gunn, go get the charges, I'll stay with my parents. It's O.K. Please. Let this be."

Rafael ran without blinking to the house. The Humvees had stopped near the front gate and were examining the front of the property. They had not yet approached the front gate. Five heavily armed men got out and started walking around, some forward, others back to form a security perimeter. Something in the way that they walked seemed wrong. They seemed far too casual, like the way a thief scopes out his mark, or the feigned calmness of an attacker, just before a mugging. The team remained hidden, breath and pulse coming quicker every moment.

Angus moved rapidly to the back of the shed. This was the farthest shed from the house and it made an ideal place to store dangerous things. This was why Beth had been housed here when she had shown signs of the infection. He pulled out a padded ammo can marked, "charges," and walked back to Beth. He had a small box with detonators made from simple switches and model rocket fuses. Normally, there would be hundreds of feet of cable between the switch and the charge, but in this case Angus cut a two foot wire. He attached the fuse to the negative lead wire and left the positive lead disconnected. Beth could do that herself when she was ready. The charges were simple lead pipes filled with gunpowder from the reloading supplies. The model rocket fuse went into each one. There were five three-inch diameter pipe bombs in all, Beth took all of them as Angus set them on the ground.

"Do you know what to do?" Angus asked, looking at Beth.

"Yes. I'll need duct tape and the dress. And have Margaret or Abigail bring me an apple pie from yesterday. And a bottle of cheap whiskey. That ought to get their attention." She paused, her attention flittering elsewhere, whatever delusions flashing past were gone just as quickly. "And Angus, be ready on the trigger, there's only going to be the one shot at this."

Foothills of the Cumberland Plateau
Private forested road
Group property
Front gate
July 15
1:53p.m.

The men of the 278th who had killed their commander during the mobilization had decided that it was their turn to get what they needed. After all, the citizenry existed to support the military, right? These thoughts flowed through Sgt. Patron's mind as he waited by the gate. He was in no hurry. It was midday and they had already eaten a good lunch.

His crotch itched after doing that last little bitch this morning. Young pussy was always the best. The little bitch didn't even scream this time. The Lieutenant had saved that one for his private staff, and SSgt Smith gave him time with the girl this morning in exchange for a bottle of vodka that Patron had "liberated" from one of the civilians. The bitch may have had crabs. Preteen and had crabs! What the hell was the world coming to? Patron watched carefully as Simmons patrolled their six. He smiled a big boy scout grin towards the gate. You never knew if anyone were watching.

There was no point rushing this. Catch more flies with honey than vinegar, that's what his grandmother had taught him. This always went down the same way. Jones seeing the plague-heads being shot was an indication of survivors somewhere along here. The well-built gate screamed survivor group. All they had to do was be patient. Wait a few minutes, pretend to be helpful, offer advice and "official statements" from the "State Senate." Get invited in for dinner. Then kill the men and take the women. Maybe a boy or two as well, you know, for those guys in the unit. Now that it was open for the fags, you couldn't discriminate, now could you? Still, he couldn't see what they saw in them though, nuts and cocks, just not his thing. Oh well, to each his own, he thought as he glanced up the drive past the gate.

"Holy shit," Patron whistled under his breath at the sight before his eyes. In front of him, down the road walked a beautiful long haired woman in a tight red dress. She had tan high heels and was that an apple pie, and a bottle of scotch? Oh my God! This is even better! Pussy, pie and booze, delivered through the front gate! The men turned and chuckled. Patron turned away from the gate and gave a warning glare, then back to the gate and smiled a big cheesy grin.

"Hello Ma'am, can we be of any service? Do you have any medical needs?" Patron lied through his grinning teeth. His unit began to crowd closer to the Sergeant, the thoughts of the pie, the whiskey and the woman herself intoxicating them in the heat of the afternoon.

"Sure thing, sugar. I saw you from the cabin, thought I'd come chat a while. You boys look tired. Why don't we have us a picnic on the hood over here? Been mighty lonely. I prayed for a man, looks like I got a dozen, all for little old me!" Beth cooed, reaching the gate in sauntering strides.

The men salivated at the sight. Sure, she was a little think around the middle, but that dress covered her heavy tummy well, and it had been a while for the privates in the unit. Patron liked the game, liked letting them feel in control till it was too late. This was gonna be great.

"Yes ma'am, come on around with that." Patron looked around. Four men would remain on alert; that was enough. Hell, they had a hostage here anyway if it went south. "Is that apple pie for us?" Patron asked coyly, sliding his m4 along his back, hands out in mock surprise. "And is that a bottle of liquor? Now you know ma'am, we can't drink on duty!" he said, playing the good cop part to a T.

"Sure thing, honey. Come over here and let's put this on the hood and we can have some sweets, if that's all right, sugar?" Beth said, her accent as thick as the humidity that lay upon the land. Her mind was focused like laser on the role. She struggled with every ounce of her mental faculties to control the hallucinations, to keep her mind in the here and now. Her reality had been shattered with the infection. She could see another world now, and world of confusion, and sorrow, and world that she would be lost in forever. But not now, not yet. The flashes of reality came and went, and the longer she went, the worse it got. She focused all of her mental power to force the hallucinations at bay for just a minute longer. Everything was riding on it now.

Angus had shown her the trigger, but he really didn't need to, she had built the damned things herself. As she had not been allowed out of the shed, she thought she could be productive. He had shown her to make sure she wasn't hallucinating when he handed them over to her. She had strapped them on and run all of the charges to a single switch that she could press through her dress on the back. She had duct taped the charges around her midriff over a T-shirt and stuffed foam padding in a thin layer over the cylinders. When she was done in five minutes, she just looked overweight in a dress that was too tight, not exactly a rare fashion statement these days.

As she stared out at the men that now surrounded her, the hallucinations began again in earnest, her mind flashing back and forth between reality and the visions. She felt her control over her mind start to slip and then a fluttering slide show of horror began around her. One instant was calm and the men appeared normal, the next instant was indescribably horrific. Where smiling men had stood, large wings of black and grey sprouted from their plate carriers. Horns protruded from their heads through their helmets. Lustful foaming of their breath dripped from their mouths and noses, the foul steam covering the day.

Demons walked the earth in human form. The infection stripped the ability to perceive reality away and left a more basic construct in her mind. It was as if she could see into the souls of the damned and this was the image it produced to make sense of the sensory input. She could not tell where reality and hallucination intersected. The chief demon winked at her, his black and blue mottled face rapidly changing from human to demon as the alternation in her mind sped up to several times a second.

The light of the day flashed and the darkness of night blacked out the sun. Back and forth the vision proceeded, accelerating out of control. The effect was like a strobe light flashing, reality collapsing into a singularity of undying agony. All thought was tumbling down as the heavily armed men and their demonic avatars fluttered back and forth in her mind's eye. It was all that she could do to smile and not fall down. She could feel the heat of their desire, the lustful cravings in their loins. She drove herself one final step forward.

"Like what you see, baby?" she said, coyness and desire dripping from her voice in an unadulterated heady mix, her hips swaying as she lifted the edge of the skirt slightly. The men heaved and came forward, the Sergeant grabbing her hip as the rest of the men crowded in.

She smiled and Patron paused, feeling oddly that something was wrong, not certain of the moment. His grin wavered as hers intensified. He stopped and held his breath and she laughed a hearty laugh, echoing through her small frame. Still holding the apple pie with her right hand, she dropped the whiskey bottle from her left hand and reached for her back. The bottle smashed as the soldier let go of her leg and started to back away. God give me strength.

The vision of the demons fully took over, blocking out the light of day, their wings flapping frenetically to try to gain altitude and distance as they screeched in horror at the full realization that the hour of their destruction was at hand. Her hand reached the control just as the creature in front of her pulled a foot back. She fought with all of her might to make her hand work, whirlwinds of echoing fear, terror, regret, loss and sorrow tearing at her like clawing needles of wind-blown debris. She stood upon the edge of the abyss and felt the courage needed to drop forward. Her hand pressed the control switch on the small of her back and light poured forth crushing the demons in its wake. Sweet freedom.

The group members on perimeter guard duty had watched in horror and shock as the men had surrounded her, not yet knowing the plan. Matt and Angus shared a foxhole further back, out of the sight line. The bombs blew the woman and two of the five men into pieces instantly, the concussive blast and shock wave destroying the first Humvee, killing the turret gunner and blowing the hood off of the second vehicle.

The blast signaled the defender's offensive and the closest group members shook off horror and took advantage of the situation on their own, as there had been no way to brief them. Carlos immediately shot the second turret gunner though the helmet with his Rock River AR-15. Lucien Tulley shot the gunner through the chest at the same time with Doug's M82A1 Barrett, kept near the fighting positions for just such an event. The rounds easily and simultaneously passed through the helmet and chest plate armor, their matrices not designed for the respective rounds. The gunner died instantly.

Darryl Washington and Justin Clearwater shot the remaining men dead, taking head and pelvic shots until all of the men had been killed. The shockwave of the explosion made everyone's ears ring. Matt and Angus stayed in the more distant foxhole as Matt sobbed for what seemed like an hour. He buried his head into Angus' shoulder and wept for his lost love, his wife, the mother of his child. Back at the house, a similar event took place as Madison hugged Rafael, weeping quietly onto his strong shoulders. Despite their youth, the two young teens were very strong and quiet. It had become a new world, a dangerous world, one that did not suffer fools or the weak.

The mop-up commenced and a trove of equipment was gleaned from the vehicles, mostly from the second humvee, as the first had suffered heavy damage. A small crater was left in the ground and small pieces of charred flesh were found all over the area. Lucien, Donovan and Sean Tulley, along with Darryl and Simone Washington cleaned up the body parts. It was impossible to determine the identity of the pieces and a quick mass grave was dug off of the property near the road.

Everyone rotated digging the holes. The Mackenzies were hardest hit and in complete shock and simply could not function to help with the cleanup. Lucien and Darryl reassured them and helped hold the group together, strengthening the families' bonds. Kate and Madison drew closer together and Tessa Washington helped lighten their spirits. The three became like sisters. By the end of the day, the grave was dug and on the next morning, each said his or her peace at the funeral. Matt and Madison and the younger children couldn't speak and would never, ever be the same, but they all seemed to appreciate everyone's kind words. The group came together under the cloud of sorrow, their lives inexorably bound by the heartache and sadness. The future was even more uncertain, but hope somehow prevailed despite the terrible loss in their midst.

Victory at all costs, victory in spite of all terror, victory however long and hard the road may be; for without victory, there is no survival.
—Winston Churchill, speech to the House of Commons, May 13, 1940

CHAPTER 36

Wallace Farm
Portland, TN
July 16
3:45p.m.

Sam looked down the row of people. Each person had a deadly serious expression on his or her face. The .22 target rifles were out in front, each member focusing all of his intention on hitting the targets. Others were slashing with wooden practice swords, or wasters, at cardboard targets. Some joker actually found a stash of "zombie targets," popular fictional paper targets that people used for target practice. It kind of gave an entirely new vision of the "zombie apocalypse" to see teenagers whacking wooden swords at fake paper zombies. The real infected were so much more frightening than anything he had ever seen in film, that all of those movies and books seemed like child's play, compared to the reality that walked the earth.

Since the events of the last few days, the group of survivors had been taking combat training deadly seriously. Over the property, under the edge of the barn, a makeshift blacksmithery had started up, as one of the group had some skill with metal. Saber blanks were being turned out. Soon everyone would have his own copy of the Revolutionary War officer's cavalry saber, wielded so effectively by the fallen hero, Jim Summers, during the last attack by the infected. Never again would the group be unprepared. Forever, from now on, there would be training and skill. The people of Portland were taking their training very seriously as their lives really did depend on each other, more now than ever.

Foothills of the Cumberland Plateau
Abandoned farmland near highway
Three miles from Group property
July 17
1:20p.m.

Motion blurred past Matt's view through the binoculars. He swiveled his head and tracked the object. The Humvee was moving very rapidly, several men shooting backwards as the creature tore through the canvas back of the vehicle and lunged inside. Suddenly, the vehicle slammed head-on into a tree on the roadside. The violence of the impact made Matt loose the image momentarily. He refocused and saw several of the infected tearing into the vehicle, car doors being ripped open as the soldiers inside were pulled out and set upon by the infected horde. More and more infected wandered up and joined the attack.

Several more vehicles sped past. This was clearly a large contingent of what appeared to be National Guard, as their vehicle markings were identical to those of the unit that had attacked them yesterday. Several Humvees and two Bradley fighting vehicles approached the group of infected and began shooting. A large herd of the creatures was forming around one of the groups. The road was covered with the infected, swarming across the opposite field. Their bodies littered the roadway as more and more clambered up towards the vehicles. Machine gun fire from the National Guard units rang out, the M4 and M16 bursts combining with the M240s deeper growls and the M2 50BMG's booming sounds. Grenade launchers blooped their explosive rounds out into the creatures. Bodies flew back from the rounds' impacts, but the inexorable horde pressed in on the guardsmen.

The mass of infected humanity overwhelmed the first Humvees and the men inside were torn to pieces by the insane mob. The first Bradley driver panicked and tried to back up, his commander yelling at him from the turret. The vehicle backed into a ditch and was momentarily stuck. The main gunner fired several rounds of 25mm cannon fire into and then over the crowd of onrushing infected, as the APC skidded backwards into the ditch. The first two blasts killed several dozen as the rounds cleared a momentary swath into the group. Then the tide of infected swarmed over the vehicle, the machine gun and small arms fire hitting several in the chest, arms and legs. Unfortunately, this Bradley unit had not yet determined that head shots were more efficient in putting down the infected. It wasn't that the infected wouldn't die if shot in the torso, it just took longer and they did not respond to the pain that would have incapacitated an uninfected human.

The commander, stunned momentarily by the unexpected dive into the ditch, tried to pull the hatch closed on the Bradley but he was too late and one of the infected leaped onto the turret and crawled inside. Thankfully the group could not hear the sounds coming from the doomed crew. The erratic movements of the fighting vehicle suggested the carnage that was occurring inside the tomb-like interior of the metal cabin. The vehicle stopped moving and no one got out.

Scott Rees and Angus shifted position behind Matt and motioned low to the group behind them. They were two hundred yards from the fight ahead but the number of infected seemed to be increasing to a dangerous point, even from their hiding place. Before this battle had begun, the team had been monitoring the National Guard unit. From their sniper's hide, they had watched the National Guard unit attack and kill two men and rape two women that they had pulled from a small farmhouse. Angus and Matt had wanted to engage them at that moment, but Darryl, John and Scott had convinced them that they were too outnumbered to be of any help and would have only gotten themselves and the others killed. This seemed to be a much larger contingent of the same group that they had fought yesterday. It looked as though Beth's instincts had been dead on about this group of guardsmen. They were heading directly towards the compound and had to be stopped. If those Bradleys got anywhere near the property, there would be nothing left.

They had to stop them here; not one of these threats must pass onto the property. The group members would have to stand and fight. Whether the destruction came from the guardsmen or the infected, the result would be the same if they failed. Angus looked over at his men and nodded. The plan now was to wait and watch the two groups attack each other. They would then attack whoever was left.

A noise in the distance echoed across the land, the sound that had once been so familiar now stunned the survivors as the rotors of the helicopter beat against the air, its green frame black against the sky. The OH-58D Kiowah Warrior shot past them at over 160 miles and hour, its rotor wash raking across them, as they held their breath. The craft did not appear to see them and they had prepared a good hide under the trees. Still, the terror and shock had not even sunk in when the craft slowed and lined up over the roadway, like a bird covering its hatchlings with its wings, its reassuring shadow resting on the troops it protected.

Two of the vehicle's seven Hydra 70 rockets blazed forth from the launcher tube, blasting the crowd of infected to pieces, flames shooting out as a massive chunk of the wall of infected humanity instantly collapsed. The second Bradley unleashed a terrifying volley from its Bushmaster 25mm chain gun, the automatic canon sending bursts of armor piercing explosive death into the onrushing infected. Small arms fire from the remaining Humvees and men stopped the wall of infected. The Kiowah turned its M296 50BMG machine gun pod onto the infected horde, cutting down row after row, the pilot expertly weaving the machine gun fire, annihilating the infected ball of humanity.

Angus stared with grim intent as the casualties mounted. Still, some men were killed and another humvee was overrun, but the tide was turning and the mass of infected was stopped and destroyed. The helicopter started wide circles of the area, presumably looking for more threats on the ground. The men in the hide sat speechless at the carnage. Three Humvees and one Bradley remained, with the Kiowah circling overhead.

Angus looked over at Matt and grimaced. They both were ex-military and knew what carnage this large group of guardsmen could do with their hardware. The thought of the helicopter stunned them both. It was the first flying vehicle that they had seen since the event had occurred. They had no idea that anyone had recovered so fully as to have the ability to field such a complicated system. It alone could destroy everything that they had worked so hard to achieve, snuffing out all hope. Here it was. If they could not stop the advance, then there would be no home to return to at all.

Angus shuddered, thinking of the thermal imaging and complex cameras on the helicopter. They would certainly have already spotted the farm. Angus forced a calm onto his mind. They would have heard distant explosions if the compound had already been hit. And at any rate, there was nothing that he could do. They could not key their radios, as the guardsmen would surely detect the frequency and triangulate their location with the helicopter. They might even be actively jamming the area. While the scout Humvees that they had captured were not equipped with radio frequency jamming gear, Angus could see the trademark ITT antennas on the Humvees; there was no way to safely determine if they were active or had even survived the solar event. He only hoped that the group was seeing the same thing and preparing.

The 278th was well equipped to say the least. Yesterday's haul of weapons and gear from the two Humvees had been impressive. Slung to Angus' back was the greatest find, an AT-4 anti-armor weapon, an 84mm recoilless disposable munition designed to defeat tank armor. Darryl and John Calvin each had an M72 LAW, or light antitank weapon, a smaller, disposable Vietnam War era rocket, which was capable of destroying a moderately armored vehicle or building. These versions had recently been updated with larger payloads than the original and had longer tubes. Back at the farm, the group had kept three Claymore mines and two M4/M203 rifle/grenade launchers and large ammunition boxes, along with another launcher type known as a SMAW, and several dozen grenades of various forms. Matt held an M240B pulled from the wreckage, its 100 round ammunition chain in place at the ready.

"We've got to go now, that bird has a thermal imaging pod. Our heat signatures will give us away from the front. The only reason it didn't see us on the first pass was that it came from the back and our earth roof kept the heat down," said Darryl quietly, looking intently at the enemy.

"Fall back to the secondary positions. Go, before they recover and scan the area. They're fixed on the infected now, go!" whispered Angus to his team. "I'll take out the Bradley once I clear the hide, the back blast is lethal, get one hundred yards out. Cover me once I fire, my position will immediately be compromised. Have the LAW rockets ready in case I miss. Go!"

The men poured out of the sniper's hide and tore through the field behind them, their movements shielded by the small hill that had masked their approach to the hide. When Angus fired the rocket, he would have only a second to clear the area before he was cut down by return fire. The others would have to fire on the rest of the convoy to provide distraction. The men set themselves up in a hasty ambush, each spread out over a one hundred yard section of road. Angus waited in the hide until he thought that they were ready. They could not use their radios to coordinate their attack, so he had to guess at the timing. If he miscalculated and they were not ready....

Darryl dived into the ditch and prepped the M72A6 LAW rocket to fire by pulling the safety pin and quickly snapping the tube out to length. He lay prone in the grass, his body positioned steeply to the left side, to avoid the back blast, as he had been taught in the Air Force. John prepped his rocket and adopted the same posture, fifty yards away along the road, closer to the farm. The high roadside grass hid them well.

Another fifty yards along the roadway, Matt and Scott waited in the opposite roadside ditch, behind some trees. They had raced to the far position, past a bend in the road. Their part was crucial in the success of the mission. Panting heavily, the men struggled to set up the machine gun on its bipod. Scott carried another 400 rounds of ammunition in 2 ammo cans. They sat in the ditch, catching their breath slowly in the summer heat, their plate carriers and helmets baking them slowly under the intense sun.

Angus looked up just as the convoy started driving towards the farm again. They must have been in a hurry to reach the farm, as they left the Bradley where it lay in the ditch. He crawled through the thick grass out of the hide and prayed silently as he went. He prayed for strength to do what must be done, for protection for him and his family, for accuracy for his team. The Bradley was at the back now, the Humvees ahead. The guardsmen must be planning on a straightforward assault. He guessed that when the two Humvee team did not respond after the attack yesterday, their commander ordered a patrol to investigate the last known position. These guardsmen sickened Angus. After all of the heartache, all of the grief and suffering that the world had endured, they wanted to take even more away. The images that he had seen this morning of the screaming and sobbing women, shot while they tried to pull their clothes back on after their horrific rapes cemented Angus' wrath and intention. This would end here, one way or another.

The convoy rounded the corner and would now be in view of all of the team. Angus pulled the AT-4 weapon from his back and prepared it to fire, deactivating all three safeties. He adopted the sitting position in the tall grass, his head and the barrel tube just over the top of the vegetation. He was now fully exposed to the enemy, and worried, especially about the helicopter. No time to think, he took aim at the middle of the Bradley's treads, leading a few feet as the vehicle was moving. He exhaled half of his breath and actuated the fire control, his body frozen in place by muscle tension.

A powerful explosion blasted from the back of the weapon as the pressure equalized in the tube, sending the payload of explosive charge forward, offering no recoil to Angus as it streaked away towards the heavily armored vehicle. The round slammed into the upper tread assembly, just at the level of the top of the secondary armor skirt, two thirds towards the rear of the vehicle, under the turret assembly. The high explosive round detonated and tore a hole into the vehicle body, incapacitating the vehicle and instantly killing the entire crew.

The vehicle shuddered to a stop and the Humvees raced forwards, trying to get away from the smoking hulk. Army doctrine called for an immediate counter assault when a unit was hit by an ambush. Small arms fire slapped around Angus' position as he dropped the empty fiberglass reinforced tube and started crawling through the grass to the hill. He belly crawled away as fast as he could and just as he was almost over the hill a terrific pain seared through his low back. He collapsed and almost fainted from the pain. He lay in the grass, unable to move and heard the sound of rockets again. He felt warm liquid run onto the skin of his low back and buttock, soaking into his clothing. He fumbled at the clasp of his combat first aid or "blow out" kit, on the lower right side of his plate carrier, desperately reaching for the Quickclot stored there.

Darryl almost cheered as the Bradley erupted with smoke, the powerful munition destroying its ability to fight in an instant. He aimed at the first Humvee and fired, the rocket missing and sailing over the hood, slamming into a tree at the other side of the road, felling it as it shattered, sending huge wood splinters the size of men in every direction. His cheering turned to cursing at the older weapon. As Darryl threw his down, John Calvin's LAW rocket shot from its tube and smashed into the engine housing, exploding the vehicle and throwing it onto its side.

Men in the remaining two Humvees leaped from the vehicles and tried to get behind cover on the opposite side of the road from their attackers. The bloops of grenade tubes and the crack of small arms fire came from the guardsmen as they fired towards the rocketeers. Matt's M240 .308 bursts sailed down the length of the ditch, the guardsmen now directly in his line of fire. A simple dog-legged hasty two point ambush had been sprung and the enemy fell to the staccato blasts of the powerful gun.

Cockpit
OH-58D Kiowah Warrior
Treetop level one mile from compound
July 17
1:31p.m.

All of this had transpired in about five seconds, and the Kiowa Warrior helicopter came in fast to scan the area. They had been scouting over the nearby area and had flown directly over the farm, noting the outbuildings and horses. There weren't any heat signatures from any people, interestingly. They were preparing to radio the main contingent when the channel erupted with the reports of the ambush. They immediately turned back to the main group, two miles away, heading low, just over the treetops.

They passed over a hill and scanned the region past another ridge, clearly seeing the group members, their heat signatures visible even in the grass and foliage despite the heat of the day. The pilot lined up his gun pod and prepared to make a run, slipping over the final ridge. They would fix this one real quick. The gun lined up, the pilot slowed slightly to make a strafing run. At one mile out, he was ready and closing fast, just now passing the last ridge between them and the targets, no other enemy in sight. Their technology was so superior, it was a wonder that anyone believed that they could fight back, thought the pilot, a smirk on his face as he sighted first on a prone man crawling sideways slowly through the grass, holding his back, a hot spent rocket tube just behind him.

Vacant ridge line
One mile from compound
July 17
1:31p.m.

As the helicopter passed overhead, the foliage covered plexiglass roof of the hidden blind opened and Doug McKnight stood up, exposed from the waist up, holding the SMAW shoulder launched, multipurpose assault weapon, the 83mm tube aimed squarely at the rear of the helicopter. Though designed as a bunker buster and tank killer, the HEDP, or high explosive dual purpose round would suffice at such close range on a target of opportunity. The group had been worried about securing the road long before the first incident with the National Guard. As part of their efforts, they had dug a series of foxholes on surrounding ridges and hastily covered them with available materials. The Plexiglas and foliage covered blind, backed by four layers of foam insulation board prevented the heat signature from passing through, making the occupant effectively invisible to the advanced optical system. While other, more advanced optics were coming into use that might have seen through the shielding, none was readily available at the time.

The munition streaked from the tube, its powerful rocket blasting past the helicopter's downward rotor wash, and slammed into the lower rear fuselage of the craft, exploding the fuel tanks and engine, sending the Kiowah hurtling to the ground in a fiery ball of ruin. The helicopter veered to the left and slammed into a field several hundred yards from the ambush site, debris scattering and causing small fires to spring up where the flaming wreckage landed. The ground and foliage were still green with the recent heavy rain and the fires would soon smolder to a stop.

Foothills of the Cumberland Plateau
Abandoned farmland
Between group property and ambush site
July 17
1:32p.m.

On the ground, the guardsmen put up a brave defense and the drivers of the two intact Humvees managed to get their vehicles past the first wrecked truck, many of the men lying dead in the ditch. They fired in the direction that the LAW rocket had come from. The bloops of grenade tubes terrified the group members. An instant later Darryl cried out as tiny shrapnel imbedded itself into his muscular forearm, the explosion still some eighty feet away. He pulled out the hot triangular shard and tore an Israeli bandage from his blow out kit. John kept up covering fire with his AR-15 while he moved towards Darryl. A small piece of shrapnel had partially penetrated the brown tinted lens of his Revision Sawfly combat eye shields. The polycarbonate protective lenses had saved his right eye.

The attackers gunned their Humvee's engines and sped away from Darryl's position and raced past Matt and Scott who dived behind a large oak tree to avoid getting shot by the fleeing men. Matt felt a smack across his lower back and prayed, asking Scott to examine the site. Scott paused and looked over the area and saw a fine, white powder pouring from a tiny hole in Matt's back plate carrier, about one inch from the lower edge of the plate, its aluminum oxide ceramic powder pouring gently from the tiny hole, the bullet safely trapped in the matrix of Kevlar and ceramic. If the round had impacted one inch lower or he had neglected wearing the thirty pound vest, he would be dead or dying by now.

The Humvees headed directly for the farm. As they cleared the ambush site, the six men in the two vehicles scanned for threats. Their convoy had been crushed. This was not how it was supposed to go down. They had been on top. They ruled the day and the night. Anyone that got in the way was dealt with, just like their former commander. They didn't understand the events of the last few minutes. As they raced for the helpless farm, a figure in the shadows of some brush waited for the moment.

When the first Humvee hit the line on the pavement, she squeezed the detonator firmly and prayed. The signal reached the Claymore mine in milliseconds and the device exploded, sending its 700 fragments out at almost 4,000 feet per second, slamming into the first unarmored vehicle, killing the driver and front seat passenger and destroying the engine. The vehicle careened into the roadside ditch and the second one slammed into its rear, wrecking both vehicles.

The second Humvee's occupants were stunned as steam rose from the engine bay. Movement in the trees followed from the direction of the farmhouse. A distinctive bloop was heard as the first high explosive grenade sailed from an M203. The round went long and exploded into a tree, sending bark and leaf fragments in every direction. Another bloop followed within seconds and the round landed squarely on the top of the Humvee, its rear passengers already scrambling out of the truck. The explosion hammered the helpless unit and killed all but one of the men. He crawled into the ditch and ran out into the woods, his M4 still in hand. As he paused behind a tree, he turned and a pale, soot covered face leered at him through the shadows of the forest glade. Two feet away, the infected lunged forward, teeth sinking into the neck of the guardsman, his cry cut off before it started. Several more infected lunged out and held the man down as they slaked their unholy hunger and thirst.

Shots rang out from the distance and the infected paused and turned, bullets ripping through them from two hundred yards away. Head shots stopped two and three more, who came running towards the gunfire. Under the cover of the dense woods, Gwenn set down the clacker detonator that she had just used for the mine, pulled up her M4 and waited for the infected to get closer. To her right, her daughter Kate and her friend Tessa Washington fired from a kneeling position and to her left, Simone Washington also waited for the headshot. The infected reached fifty yards away and started climbing up the hill, slowing down and crawling up the hillside, taking hits to their bodies from the girls' assault.

Just as Gwenn was taking aim, a small mixed breed dog leaped out of the bushes in front of the creatures. One of the infected seized it and bit deeply into its back, the helpless dog yelping and clawing its way out of the monster's grasp. It raced down the hill and out of sight, its brown fur stained with maroon blood seeping from its wound. It disappeared out of sight just as two rounds slammed home into the infected's head. Several more shots finished the fight, the unkempt bodies reeking of sweat, blood, rot and feces.

Foothills of the Cumberland Plateau
Abandoned farmland near highway
Three miles from Group property
July 17
1:38p.m.

Back at the ambush site, the group keyed their radio mikes for the first time that day. John Calvin spoke into his radio, "Uniform 1, status check, units report in, over."

"Kilo 1 and 2, AOK, over," Matt reported for Scott and himself.

"Sierra 1, AOK, over," Darryl replied.

"Lima 1, AOK," Doug McKnight reported.

"Tango 1... hit...." Static filled the air as Angus still held the key of his mike down for several seconds, a spasm of pain seizing him at the moment of the call. "Need...medical assistance, over," his hoarse voice croaked out over the airwaves.

Foothills of the Cumberland Plateau
Private forested road
Group property
July 17
1:40p.m.

The entire group had heard the radio traffic. Gwenn's knees buckled and she sat down and wept, too far to help, and still watching for infected. The group back at the compound was coming out of the underground storm shelter and heard the call. They had been hiding from the helicopter as soon as Margaret Gunn had heard it in the distance several minutes before the fight. They all bent their knees and began praying.

Big tears streamed unbidden from Margaret's eyes. She was back in the car again, the crushed metal pinning her to the floor of the Volvo. Her blank face washed over with a pale white pallor, her soul empty, her sorrow too great to bear. Her son lay in a field bleeding, and she could not help. She prayed for intercession. She prayed that The Lord would have mercy, as he had for her on that fateful day when the world shook and her life turned upside down. Her golden retriever had survived in the back seat and had licked the glass shards from her face and had tried to guard her from the approaching rescue workers. She had calmed the loyal animal and remembered singing the hymn, "I am the Bread of Life," as the paramedics cut her from the cocoon of metal that had at once pinned and crushed her and also had saved her life. The burly men wept openly as they sang with her on that day. She would repeat it all again, if it could prevent her son's suffering.

Foothills of the Cumberland Plateau
Abandoned farmland near highway
Three miles from Group property
July 17
1:42p.m.

John and Darryl were the closest and raced to their comrade, rapidly assessing his wound. He had tried to bandage it himself and had not been successful due to the location and difficulty of using the blowout kit on his own back. He had lain in the field, in too much pain to move and refusing to use the radio during the attack, since too much was at stake.

"Angus! Shit, man. Are you O.K.?" asked John, seeing the blood on his friend's uniform.

Angus groaned, still in too much pain to speak well. "Hurts really bad. Can't get the damned Quickclot on it," he huffed out, pain sucking the breath out of him. Angus had never been shot before, and the stunning level of pain associated with the event simply sucked the air right out of Angus as he tried to speak. He frankly was amazed at Matt's resolve days earlier, when he had been shot. This hurt like hell. Tears from the pain had dried on his cheeks as he had been lying on the grass weeping quietly during the last moments of the fight, praying that his comrades succeeded in their mission.

The wound was not fatal, and Angus would recover, but the lessons learned on this day would remind the group of the value of life and the terrible importance of their equipment and training. Equipment had allowed them to defeat a powerful enemy and saved Matt's life. Training had gotten Angus almost out of the line of fire before he had been hit. If he had not cleared the area, he surely would have been hit multiple times and would not have survived.

As Angus was evacuated to the house with Matt by truck bed for surgery, Carlos prepped the kitchen table for the repair. He and Matt had the most experience with trauma and could easily fix the shallow but debilitating wound. The rest of the team met on the roadway and regrouped with the Tulleys, who had been on an overwatch on the opposite side of the roadway on the other side of the compound. They were able to safely secure a truckload of usable gear. The real prize was the undamaged Bradley.

The infected was still inside, asleep after eating a large portion of the dead crewmen's bodies. Lucien Tulley dispatched the creature with his pistol and the group piled up all of the bodies on the road and lit a fire to consume the dead, for there were far too many to bury. As much as the Tulleys despised such a pagan-like display, there simply was no other option available to them short of leaving the bodies to rot. The rest of the day was spent locking down, treating Angus' injury and setting up, in case of another attack. The captured gear was brought onto the compound in a staging area as it would all have to be sterilized and organized, before use. They all thanked The Lord in their own ways, to have made it through the day.

From this day to the ending of the world,
But we in it shall be rememberèd;
We few, we happy few, we band of brothers;
For he to-day that sheds his blood with me
Shall be my brother; be he ne'er so vile
This day shall gentle his condition:
And gentlemen in England, now a-bed
Shall think themselves accursed they were not here,
And hold their manhoods cheap whiles any speaks
That fought with us upon Saint Crispin's day.
—William Shakespeare. Henry V. 4.3.60-69

CHAPTER 37

Wallace Farm
Portland, TN
July 21st
8:31a.m.

Carolyn Wallace looked out of the window of the farmhouse and saw activity on the perimeter of the property. She reflexively reached onto the counter without looking and her hand rested on the handle of the Ruger 45 Long Colt single action revolver. During the attack of the infected, all of the women and older kids in the house had been given the handguns from the group. Her husband Sam had thought that this would be best and that they could defend themselves with the handguns in the tight confines of the house.

It turned out that all of the men and the few women who had ventured out on the patrol would have benefitted more from the extra firearms, as they had run out of ammunition, resulting in several casualties, including her ex son-in-law Jim Summers. Her daughter's grief had been hard to witness. Since then, the "support staff" or "noncombatants" in her son Trey's ex-military vocabulary were "issued" simpler weapons. This single action revolver was an excellent example of the concept. It was slower to shoot, but still worked well.

She fully understood the need, although the number of noncombatants had been reduced with the recent weapons training. She understood that also and agreed with the idea. But someone had to work the kitchen. And she knew enough about shooting to hold her own. She had just finished breakfast dishes in a sink of cold water and homemade soap, when the first sounds were heard. Engines blared against the quiet, homely noises of hand tools, saws and hammers working.

A flood of people tore through the yard to man the newly installed fighting posts. Foxholes and several elevated shooting positions had been constructed over the last few days. The time since the attack of the infected had been quiet. Work had gone on as before, after the funerals had been held. A preacher from town had joined the ranks and the Protestant service was actually very sweet and comforting. The palisade was about half built and work was progressing nicely.

They had butchered several cows and had been working to make jerky from them. The flies and lack of salt had been a problem. Smoking the meat seemed like a good solution, but the smell drew more infected. Sam had figured out how to catch the smoke in a water pan covering the smoker and this kept the smell and smoke down and also yielded homemade liquid smoke. This was the first homemade product that they had created and it put a sense of normalcy back into the days recently. Now, if they could only get more salt: they really needed a truckload of the vital crystal. They might be able to find some in town. They couldn't use road salt as the anti-caking agents used in it were potentially toxic. She wished they had seen fit to store more of the precious substance. They would eventually have to make a run into downtown.

Gunfire erupted along the road. She could see several motorcycles swing into view, firing rifles across their handlebars. She ducked and ran back to check on the children. She started praying for Sam and the others out on the lawn. God help them, God help us all!

Out on the lawn, Sam and Trey ran forward, unslinging their rifles. They always kept them ready and had hand sewn shoulder rigs with extra ammunition ready at all times. Sam swung his .30-30 around and yelled out instructions.

"Everybody to the stations! Everybody run!"

Chaos erupted as the men and women scrambled to their places. This was not going to be like the last time. Sam had made sure everyone was ready, guns in hand, ammo at the ready. Nobody complained about lugging the heavy equipment around, not after the last attack. Sam ducked behind a set of logs that they had placed out on the lawn for cover and looked around. From the left and right, fully 80 percent of the farm was either running forward or dropping into a foxhole or climbing a stand. He worried about those in the stands. They had put sheet metal around the floors and walls to protect against incoming fire, but getting up was still exposed. Once the snipers were up, though, they could rain fire down onto the threat. The snipers had the hunting AR-15s and the two stations were now manned. Inside of each position, extra magazines were positioned. Ten in each, most of what they had, and almost all of the .223 ammo that they had found. He prayed it would be enough.

One hundred yards out, running up to the gate with a toolbox, a biker was cut down by fire. His blood ran from his mouth as he tried to scream. He shuddered as more bullets slammed into his prostrate body. Another ran forward and Sam took aim, leading him as he ran. The .30-30 cracked and the 170 grain Federal soft point slug slammed into the man's sternum. As in so many deer hunts before, this type of shot was second nature to Sam, and his skill was proven effective. The man collapsed and folded up, his body crumpling and not moving after hitting the ground face first.

Two bikers revved their engines and rammed the metal pole gate. The bikes caught in the chain and did not break through. They put the bikes in reverse and Sam dropped one off onto the ground, the bike slamming into a tree near the ditch. Bearded men came running around the flanks of the roadway, shooting what appeared to be AR15s as well. A hail of gunfire erupted from all of the fighting positions, driving them back, one staggering as rounds hit his leg.

A van came at the gate full speed, snapping the chain as it drove right at Sam's position. He fired three rounds into the windshield as the snipers peppered the vehicle with fire. Blood sprayed onto the shattered windshield and the van careened sideways and slammed into the log barricade as Sam leaped back with Trey a foot behind. Debris caught Trey on the ankle. He screamed out and continued to run, dropping into the nearest foxhole, as his father ran to an adjoining hole.

Four men poured out of the back of the van and started firing on the farmhouse and foxholes, using the van for cover. Sam yelled for help, but could not be heard over the gunfire. He had never heard noise that loud before. Fully fifty people were defending the farm. Even the women from the house were firing from the windows of the second floor. It was all or nothing now. The attackers looked like outlaw bikers. They had beards, mustaches, and do-rags on their heads. Some were bald or had shaved their heads. Some had necklaces of what looked like ears, possibly from the infected they had killed.

More motorcycles sped onto the lawn; the bikers got off and used trees for cover. This was not going well and they had a limited amount of ammunition. The tide was shifting to the attackers' favor, as perhaps twenty more bikers poured onto the property. They looked like they were making an all-out attempt to take over the farm. The van must be their support vehicle, and it was being shot to hell. This terrified Sam. Why would they risk so much to take over the farm? All he knew was the time was now or never. He motioned to the men behind him and to Trey. He called out to Thomas Bledsoe who was firing his .30-30 from the next foxhole.

"Thomas, were going right around the van on three, load up now! Got it?"

"Yessir, let's kill these bastards!" Thomas yelled out, righteous fury in his deep voice.

His wife, Pirelli was back at the house, shooting a scoped deer rifle for all she was worth from the second floor window. Bullets skipped through the thin siding, but she never wavered, killing and wounding several of the attackers she could make out in the Nikon Buckmaster's reticle. The .30-06 slammed into her shoulder with each shot, but she was used to the heavy recoil of her Mossberg 12 gauge. She cursed like a sailor as she shot.

"God damned bastards try to come in here! I'll kill 'em all!"

Back on the front line, everyone had reloaded their rifles and shotguns, and checked their pistols. Each man had a least one backup weapon, some had two pistols. The mistakes of the first attack would not be repeated.

"Everybody, ready to go to the right?" Sam yelled out to the nearest foxholes.

"Ready"

"Ready boss!"

"We're ready here, Sam"

"Let's go kill those bastards!"

The Portlanders were angry as hell and ready for a fight. The bikers did not really know what they had done, by attacking here. They could not know the emotional bonds that now tied the people to the land, this land that they had already fought, bled and died to protect. Their families, their friends were buried on this soil. The very voice of the earth cried out for vengeance. As it had been in the beginning, when The Lord had heard the blood of Abel cry out from the dirt for vengeance, so it was the same now. The people of Portland were united, united against this foe today. Live or die, they would not allow this land to be lost. Even if it took every man, woman and child to die to defend it, these interlopers would not prevail. These bikers had picked the wrong farm.

"Go!" Sam yelled out as the small group of men leaped out of their foxholes and raced around to the right of the van.

The snipers realized what was happening from their vantage point and redoubled their fire into the attacker's positions, pinning them down as the hail of gunfire heated up. Sam and the others careened around the van, shooting as they went. Bikers behind the van did not see them coming. While running forward, Sam fired a round into the back of a fat man holding an AR15. The round tore a four inch hole through the front of his chest and the attacker collapsed, his rifle clattering to the ground. Thomas paused on his run and blew the head off of another man. The defenders next to him paused, knelt and shot the other two attackers multiple times, 12 gauge buckshot and deer rifle rounds bursting through their chests and abdomens. As the last bikers behind the van fell, rounds came from the enemy still on the road.

One man named Scott, next to Thomas, collapsed, several rounds blasting through his torso. The group had eliminated the nearest threat, but now was exposed to fire from the roadway. Sam ducked behind the van and motioned with his arm for more men to come forth from the fighting positions. Men and women both answered the call of this man who had taken them in and offered them everything, at a time when they had had nothing. The citizens to whom they had given shelter, and fed and clothed were very grateful and they honored that gift with their very lives, jumping up from the foxholes and racing to their leader's side.

Twenty Portlanders now at his side, Sam raced from the van to a live oak tree, the rest finding cover as they could. Sam motioned for them to hit the deck and lie flat. They dropped and kept firing, smoke now pouring from many of the barrels as they heated up from the intense shooting. Sam and Thomas looked at each other and nodded. Trey squinted in the morning light and looked on as the fighters pressed forward. It would be a good day to die, but a better day to live, he thought.

Sam yelled instructions and picked up an AR15 covered in a biker's blood and handed it to Trey. Trey had been in the military and was well experienced with the modern armament. He pulled two extra mags from the vest pocket of a dead biker and tossed them to his son as well. Trey nodded, breathing deeply, preparing for the assault.

Sam placed Trey and ten of his men and women behind trees and assigned fields of fire for each. Fifteen or so bikers had taken up positions along the road and were spraying an incredible amount of fire into the defender's positions. Trey and the stationary fighters would lay down a covering fire and Sam and Thomas and their team would run up the ditch and take out the bikers. Sam prayed a quick prayer, made his peace with his maker and nodded at the men.

"Charge!" Sam yelled, leaping up and swinging wide to the left, Thomas and eight other men behind him. The ten men and women left behind rapidly began pouring fire into the attacker's positions, making them duck and cover to avoid being hit. Sam ran as fast as his old feet could carry him, everyone right behind him. He reached the edge of the ditch and ducked into it, still racing along. Thomas and five more leaped over the ditch and ran along with him. Behind him three more men ran, rifles up to keep from pointing at their leader. Ahead, the attackers did not yet see them.

The one nearest them glanced over and his jaw dropped at the sight of the men racing hard, their work clothes smeared with blood and sweat and grime, burning hate in their eyes, cold faces set like flint. He turned to fire his rifle just as the slug from Sam's rifle caught him in the neck and tore a massive hole, blood splattering onto the men behind him. As the body fell, Sam levered and fired another and another round, the rifle going dry. Sam pulled his old Colt 1911 government model from his well-worn strong side leather holster and swung the rifle onto his back on its sling in one fluid motion. The hand cannon boomed, the 230 grain hollow point slamming into the chest of another attacker, the bullet flattening the man into the ditch.

The men behind Sam swung out to the right to fire and from the sides, the men rained bullets onto the attacking force. Thomas' .30-30 boomed again and again, striking biker after biker, before it went dry. He held the rifle in his left hand and, using his right hand, pulled out his .357 Magnum Ruger KGP-141 stainless steel revolver and blasted a huge hole in the head of a biker who had just turned to aim his rifle at Sam. The biker folded up and collapsed, his rifle firing once straight into the air as his finger spasmed onto the trigger in his death throws. Trey's ankle throbbed, but he kept shooting despite the pain. Biker after biker went down in the fusillade of death. Lives hung in the balance and no one here would call it quits, until the threat was annihilated.

Between the oncoming fire from the house, the sniping platforms, the advance force and the flanking teams, the bikers could not stand. They began to flee their positions. Sam let his men give chase, sending Thomas to make sure they didn't go too far in case of an ambush. The men shot every one of the attackers multiple times in the backs as they ran away, fury and pain and hatred expending themselves on these evil-doers. Not one of the attackers survived the attempted raid. Three of the defenders died and ten more were wounded, including Trey, his ankle injury minor.

Miraculously, Sam and Thomas were totally uninjured, though the three that died were all on the advancing teams of defenders. Sam set a guard to protect their position and had Trey and his men comb the wreckage and enemy positions for gear. They were careful in case of any booby traps, but there were none. The bikers seemed to need a place to take over and hole up, and were willing to do anything to get it. Perhaps the cattle, or the lure of the women drew them. They would never know. Burials and cleanup followed the attack. The bikers were burned off the property in a mass pyre.

Grief and joy at repelling the invaders combined together in a heady mix of powerful emotion. The survivors had come together and protected what was theirs and the group would never be the same. Sam worried about the next threat and began planning an even more effective perimeter, while his son Trey stared to plan even more military training for the group. It was clear that surviving in this brave new world involved knowing your way around a gun as well as a plow. Sam hugged Carolyn in the kitchen that night and they just stood there, tears of grief and relief quietly falling from their eyes. Tomorrow would surely bring more challenges, but the day was complete, and Sam was grateful that his family had survived another day.

Foothills of the Cumberland Plateau
Private forested road
Group property
July 23
4:31p.m.

Angus lay in the bed on his stomach, the bandages being changed by his wife, Gwenn. He hated this entire thing and it was taking forever to heal because of his eczema. The wound was from a gunshot that grazed over his buttocks and low back, leaving a long, jagged furrow as if a rusty plough had torn through the unprotected flesh below his Interceptor Body Armor. He was struck when crawling away during the fight, after he had launched one of their rockets and destroyed the Bradley fighting vehicle in the guardsmen's convoy. Had his team not stopped their advance, none of them would be here now, and certainly most would be dead, held prisoner or worse.

The ham radio waves were full now of tales of rogue military units killing men and stealing women and young boys as sex slaves. Many units had come down on the side of their local municipalities and were helping rebuild, but others were out for their own benefit. Angus was just glad that they had survived the events of the past few weeks. It was truly a miracle that more were not killed or maimed.

Scott and Matt had both been saved by their armor. Matt felt the bullet that would have killed him, but Scott did not even realize until he sat down on the back porch and took his plate carrier off for inspection that evening, that he had been hit two times in the back and once in the chest. The level IV multi-hit plates had saved his life three different times. Had the rounds been a few inches up or down, or to the sides, the soft armor under layer would have been of no benefit, as it could only stop pistol, shotgun and fragmentation threats. The shock and terror of battle had been summed up as "the fog of war," and the saying fit. No battle plan ever did survive first contact with the enemy. Scott had been stunned by the realization and sat on the porch of the house for an hour after the fight, helmet in hand, plate carrier at his feet, blank expression on his face. No one could talk to him during that time; he simply was not there.

His arm wound had healed completely and he thanked The Lord for his mercies. He still did not understand why he had not become infected. Clearly, they did not comprehend what this plague really was or how if behaved. So many unanswered questions lingered in that relatively quiet time after the attack. The days had been quiet except for a few small groups of infected that were rapidly dispatched by the overwatch teams. The military and police training of the group prior to the disaster had literally meant the difference between life and death.

Darryl and John had suffered minor injuries in the fight, several scratches and some small shrapnel wounds on John's hand and Darryl's leg and neck, likely from the M320 and M203 grenade launchers that had been used by the soldiers. Some of the rounds had come within 100 feet, too close for comfort with such deadly munitions. But the shrapnel wounds were only skin deep and Matt had sutured them up easily after the fight. Angus' wound was more complex and due to the nature of the injury shape, it had to heal by "secondary intention." In other words, his skin would have to grow in from the sides as there was no way to re-approximate the wounds edges. The process would take weeks and he would be on his stomach for most of it, as Carlos had forbidden him to lie or sleep on his wound.

Gwenn cleaned the wound while Angus fussed about the discomfort. "Ow, that hurts," he said, grimacing at the wall as she carefully removed the packing. Their extensive store of Kerlex was being used for this wound and the sterile gauze was laid first in a wet layer and next as a dry layer. The capillary action of the water movement automatically cleaned the wound. Matt had recommended the use of honey to cover the wound at night as several good studies had shown increased wound healing rates and so Gwenn applied this now and covered the wound with more sterile Kerlex. Eventually, they would have to make their own bandages out of fabric, but for the time being, and maybe the next several months, depending on how many more injuries needed treatment, they had an ample supply of medical gear.

Most doctors made terrible patients and Angus was no exception. The only good thing about the situation was that he did not require any more pain meds, as they truly were limited in their supply of narcotics. After the first thee days, he got along well enough with Tylenol and the evening's ounce of Scotch. Angus, being of Scottish heritage, had laid up quite a supply of the single malt beverage. Kept in the earth in a special cache, it would never go bad, and when consumed at a leisurely one ounce per day, it would last for years to come. It also would make an excellent wound sterilant, but they had gallons of rubbing alcohol to use up before that eventuality.

Gwenn finished up and Angus grinned at her and apologized for his fussiness, as he always did, and then pinched her on the buttocks gently as she walked away, her eyes rolling. He always did that every day as well. He suffered the obligatory good natured jokes from his teammates about getting shot in the butt, while running away, and the humor helped with the stress of the close quarters.

Suddenly screaming came from the yard. Angus rolled over, grabbed his gun and headed for a window, pain shooting from the raw wound as he moved too quickly. Gwenn was already down the stairs and out in the yard, pistol in hand. Her heart stopped. The scene before her shocked her back into the desperate reality of the brave new world in which they lived.

A small dog growled low, its rabid slobber hanging low to the ground, dripping from its snarling face. Joshua stood in front of the animal unarmed, arms at his side, hands in fists, his face sternly considering the lethal threat in front of him. He did not cower or cry. He was backed against the house, the animal had him cornered with no way out. It advanced slowly, seeing its prey and moving like a hunting beast. Gwenn raced out into the yard, yelling at the thing trying to get its attention.

The beast turned and then lunged towards the woman. She could not draw down on the animal as her son would be in the line of fire. She ducked and began to run backwards to get out of the way when a shot rang out and the creature collapsed in a heap, its lunge stopped midway, dust spreading out as it slammed onto the ground of the yard. It had collapsed, unable to move or cry out, blood pouring from its neck where the 5.56mm round had destroyed its spine and right jugular vein.

Joshua's sister Kate still stood stock still, her M4 carbine still on her cheek as she scanned for new threats. She advanced, gun still trained on the dog and kicked it with her long leg. Her boot made a dull sound as the air had already escaped from the creatures chest at the moment of death, an instant ago. Gwenn ran to her son and squeezed him and led him inside. She kissed Kate's forehead as she passed and squeezed her arm. She did not have the words required for this moment and her look of combined thanks, pride, wonder, terror and gratefulness was not lost on her daughter.

"I love you Mom, its O.K. Everything is fine," Kate said, in her usual undramatic tone. Like her uncle, she hated romantic notions and preferred straightforward discussion to drama.

A sob escaped Gwenn as she hugged them both, Kate's gun hand keeping the rifle pointed at the dead dog. When she was convinced it was really dead, she placed the selector switch on safe and then took a closer look at the monster that had nearly killed her brother. As she stared at the beast, she noticed a small, oval scar on its back, a bite mark of some kind. Her mind stopped, shock and wonder flooding through her. The bite mark was clearly in the shape of a human mouth.

Gwenn was staring at the same thing as well, both of them looked at each other and it was as if a light bulb had been turned on in their minds. Kate remembered the dog that had burst from cover and had been bitten by the infected human days before. This was that dog. The animal looked for all intents and purposes like a rabid dog, because... it was a rabid dog.

The drooling of the human infected, the rage they exhibited, the mindlessness of their actions in most cases, it all fit. The infection had to be some form of rabies. Kate suddenly took a knee, her breath knocked out of her. It couldn't be. It couldn't be that simple. She looked up at the gathering crowd and focused on Scott Rees. His powerful forearm was visible where he had rolled up his uniform shirt, the fresh scar well healed from his previous bite. He had told the group about the event as soon as he had entered the compound and had been on quarantine for several days. When he had shown no sign of infection, everyone assumed it was because the person that bit him was just nuts maybe, but not really infected. Kate looked him square in the eyes.

"Scott, when was your last rabies vaccination?" she asked, her eyes narrowed in thought.

The man stared at the dog, understanding dawning slowly on his rugged face. "About a year ago. Actually, I was double vaccinated because my asshole of a boss, sorry ladies, would not accept my previous medical records as valid and I had to go get it again. I got a shot series three years ago and then another one year ago."

The group stared back and forth between the dog and Scott, looking at the bite marks on each. It couldn't be that simple. Angus and Matt appeared at the door, Carlos walked up from the nearest guard post, sniper rifle still in hand.

"I thought you said the rabies tests were non-confirmatory, Carlos," Matt called out to his friend, referring to the barrage of testing that had been done on the infected patients in the hospital before the collapse had occurred.

"I did. But that doesn't mean anything. You see, the tests were never confirmed by the C.D.C. Everything broke down before the samples were received and we never got the final report," Carlos' thick Filipino accent measured every syllable and the weight of his words were like iron. "This could definitely be a form of rabies, especially if it were either a new wild type or an engineered version that we have never seen before." The V in version became a B as he spoke rapidly, his excitement building.

"We will never know, of course, but government labs and possibly terrorists were supposed to have been working on common diseases for use as bio-weapons. This would explain why the assay did not detect it at the hospital. If the virus had been altered to change its characteristics, it might not be seen by the assay, as it required a precise molecular fit for detection. It would explain why the infection doesn't seem to be fatal, at least not immediately. It might just cause insanity for all we know. Clearly, the infected do not have hydrophobia. If they did, they could never eat anything and would die very soon."

Angus chimed in, "There have been cases where people have survived bat rabies in the past, for example. A comatose state was induced and there was a small survival rate. Only one victim was ever really the same though. Everyone else who survived it had terrible neurological aftereffects. The survival rate was very low, less than twenty percent, if my memory serves. Knowing that fact, they could have discovered what part of the genome controlled survivability. If they monkeyed around with it, and altered the code of the virus, they could have produced a non-lethal strain. It's been done before. Hell, Pasteur did it with the damned vaccine. The vaccine is a live attenuated virus anyway. I have never thought of this!"

"But how could it be passed from close contact without biting?" asked Matt, the three doctors having a round table discussion while standing in the yard.

"Dad, it's like bat rabies," said Kate, who had been preparing to start pre-veterinary training after high school, before the world ended. "People can get bat rabies without a known bite. The two theories are either that there is a tiny unknown bite or aerosol transmission. If whoever did this used bat rabies to mess with, couldn't this be a latent trait that they brought to the surface?" she asked, looking at Angus.

"My God," Angus said, thinking back to his Air Force job of clinical response team chief. He had been the disaster prepper for his Air Force base and this idea flung him right back into the mindset. "It is certainly possible. The evidence here is undeniable. Ockham's razor states that the simplest explanation is usually the right one, and that is the simplest explanation. We don't know who did this, or why, but it looks like we all need a rabies vaccine." Angus looked at Scott Rees, his eyes piercing the other man, focusing hard on the well-healed scar. "Maybe two."

*Behold, the eye of the Lord is on those who fear Him,
On those who hope in His mercy,
To deliver their soul from death,
And to keep them alive in famine.
Our soul waits for the Lord;
He is our help and our shield.
For our heart shall rejoice in Him,
Because we have trusted in His holy name.
Let Your mercy, O Lord, be upon us,
Just as we hope in You.*
—Psalm 33:18-22 NKJV

CHAPTER 38

Wallace Farm
Portland, TN
July 24
9:37p.m.

A low glow came from the direction of downtown. Scouts had reported smoke rising from the downtown region just before sunset. Something was going on in town. Sam walked to the old pickup truck parked next to the garage. It had rained today in the morning and the crops were coming along well. The palisade was moving along and repair of the house had been started. Couldn't have bullet holes in the living room, after all, thought the leader. He thought of all of the equipment that they had gained after the dangerous attack that they had turned back just three days ago. They were still going through and function checking the rifles and cleaning the equipment.

Three men and two horses had paid the ultimate price for the attack. It had been a sad day, but the community had come together. The yield of equipment had been astounding. Several undamaged Harleys had been pulled under a makeshift lean-to shelter hastily constructed as a rudimentary carport. The real find had been the second van. Behind the pack of outlaws a second supply van had been found, the occupants shot in the back fleeing after their radiator and tires had been shot out.

It was a treasure trove of stolen goods. Counting the working gear found on the bikers themselves, there were thirty AR-15s of various makes. Thousands of rounds of ammunition for these rifles along with over 300 AR-15 high capacity magazines, mostly thirty rounders, had been found in the van. The ammunition included the .223, some military 5.56mm, 12 gauge slugs, buckshot and birdshot, .45 ACP, 40 S&W, and some 5.56mm tracers, along with several boxes of more obscure calibers for various guns used by the bikers. A Ruger Super Redhawk in .454 Casull, and two dozen pistols including Glocks and various 1911s were found, all in working order. Several of the pistols had threaded barrels and suppressors attached. There had been several local gun stores in the area who had been licensed to sell class III weapons including suppressed and short barreled long guns. These appeared to have been stolen from the stores, as they looked brand new; several were actually still in the boxes. The group also found three 14-inch police shotguns, smoke grenades, tear gas grenades, cleaning kits, and probably two hundred knives, ranging in size from large Bowies to small paramilitary folders.

Hundreds of cans of stale beer and pork beans were in the second van. Of no use to the group, a duffle bag full of pornography was immediately burned on the spot, in the middle of the road, so offensive were the magazine covers that Sam did not want any of the women or children seeing them. Overall, the gear had been a godsend. He wished the price had not been so terribly high. He could not get the faces of their dead out of his mind, and having to shoot three severely injured horses had fallen to him, as he was their owner and also the leader of the group.

Now with news of something happening in town, they had to see what had been going on, as a new threat of wildfire or attacking foes could not be ignored. Groups had been out on the day of the attack and had collected all of the salt and spices and other supplies that they could find from the town groceries. Nothing had been seen in town except the obligatory infected hordes. Some of them seemed almost organized in their movement, if the scouts' stories were to be believed. It worried Sam. Either his crew was imagining this, or there really was a change going on. Whatever was the truth, they had to know as soon as possible.

He walked up to the truck and smiled at Chloe Pearl. She and Pirelli Bledsoe were preparing to head into town with Thomas Bledsoe and Trey Wallace. The team was not looking to collect gear and wanted more people in case things went wrong. Each person carried an AR-15 rifle and pistol. Chloe held on to her Ruger 9mm, while the men had selected 1911s from the gear locker that had been relocated to the house. Pirelli chose a Glock 22 in .40 S&W from the locker. The dining room wall had been converted to serve as a gun storage location as the waterproofing was best in the old farmhouse. Sam had worried about the guns rusting and Carolyn had agreed, without a fuss.

Each person carried a number of extra magazines for both the rifles and pistols in vests newly sewn for the purpose. The women of the group had been at the work for several days, hand sewing the gear from old hunting clothes and camping gear. Trey had a cavalry saber slung along his back, while Thomas' rested on the seat next to him. All had large Bowie knives on their hips and wore Mossy Oak camouflaged shirts and pants that had been specially modified.

One of the seamstresses in the group had been an avid zombie novel fan and had an idea about their clothing. While they lacked ballistic protection so far, she felt that they could at least defend against the infecteds' bites. With this in mind, she had sewn into the clothing a very fine metal mesh with holes of 1/4 inch diameter. It was aluminum and they had found it at a local hardware store. A thin tee shirt material lined the inside of the garments underneath the metal mesh. The seamstress reasoned that they would already have vests and maybe backpacks on and so only the sleeves and pants were protected this way. The outer cloth protected the mesh and the inner fabric protected the skin. They were hot, but everyone wore them as these represented the best protection that they had from infection. These were the first four suits. The seamstresses had sewn up two large and two extra-large sets to start out, and the girls had to roll up the sleeves. Pirelli's set was a little big and Thomas could not fit into the shirt, so he had only the pants on and a tee shirt instead, as these were just the first sets and generic in size. If they were bitten on the cloth, it should prevent the teeth from penetrating. It may not have been perfect, but it was a start.

Each person wore clear plastic safety eye shields and each had a homemade shemaugh, or large Middle Eastern style bandana, to cover their faces. This would provide not only some respiratory protection, but also some protection against splashed blood from the infected. Sam's last ditch use of clorox and soap to prevent infection was not lost on the group.

Each of the 1911s selected for this mission had a suppressor attached to reduce the noise signature. Work had begun on suppressing all of the firearms, but that would take months to complete. The girls had small 18 inch machetes at their sides and the truck bed had extra magazines for the AR-15s and 1911s, along with three extra Marlin 30-30 model 336 rifles, each with an ammo belt holding twenty shells. The rifles had nine round black cordura nylon side saddle shell holders on the stocks. Thomas had a cut down rifle case slung on his back with his Winchester trapper 16 inch barreled .30-30 lever gun ready to pull out when needed.

The group had no method of illumination other than the truck's aging headlamps, and these had been covered with burlap and duct tape to black out the lights. The team readied themselves and said quick prayers to The Lord and nodded at Sam. Chloe and Pirelli hopped in the back while Trey rode shotgun. The team had ARs at the ready, rounds chambered, safeties on. Thomas slowly moved the truck out onto the road, well away from the candle and firelights of the farm and turned the vehicle off. They sat in the dark for twenty minutes silently, allowing their eyes and ears to accommodate to the dark. This was a scouting mission only: they did not want a fight.

Thomas cranked the engine and they rumbled quietly away towards town. The trip was uneventful and they began to see lights and noises emanating from downtown. As they neared the edge of town, Pirelli and Trey got out of the truck quietly. They were the most fit of the group and the fastest runners; therefore, they would scout as close as possible to the activity, while Chloe and Thomas would wait at the truck and defend the others' retreat, if needed. The girls hugged each other and Pirelli and Trey set off into the blackness.

Edge of Downtown
Main Street
Portland, TN
July 24
10:44p.m.

Trey and Pirelli remained under the bushes, frozen in terror. The scene before them was like something out of a movie. A stage had been set up in the center of the street, the shops on the side of the road forming walls like a dark, evil cathedral. The apparent leader of the group stood on the center of the stage, fires in barbecue pits and trash cans arranged around him, the constantly moving light from the fires intensifying the sense of unease and fear. The faces in the crowd were lit by several fires, the flickering flames dancing upon the stage, their blank eyes and alternating expressions of lust, hate, fear and apathy disturbing to witness. Waves of new emotion surged through the crowd as the leader spoke.

"Immortality!" the man cried out as his rambling speech continued.

The crowd growled and grunted as the man spoke, howling in ecstasy at words they didn't even appear to understand. Waves of jumping and howling ran through the crowd like a ripple. The two observers were terrified and perplexed by the scene. All of the infected that they had seen in the past had been utterly mindless, yet clearly here were thinking infected people. There had been reports of organized activity from other scouts and collecting parties gathering goods from the area, but nothing like this. These were, well...thinkers! Most of them drooled some, as was typical of the infected, and they had the unpredictable alternating moods seen as well. Their stares were mostly vacant, but less so than the others that they had seen.

"Brethren, we are called! Called to life through the death of the plague. The 'fection. The 'fection has freed us! Freed us from the bonds of this Earth! The new Master calls us to feast!" the hooded figure continued, his face covered by the dark hood of the robe. The crowd went wild, like apes or monkeys in a zoo, hands flailing about, hooting and yelling out.

"Bring in the unblessed!" The leader commanded. Several of the robed infected brought out a hooded prostrate form, hunching down and half carried by the two infected men at his sides. The hood was withdrawn and the face of the police chief of Portland was revealed. He had clearly been beaten and savaged as his bruised face and black eyes showed. The man blinked and looked around, terror filling his eyes. His lip quavered and he tried to speak, his voice not audible. A huge stone decorative outdoor table had been set up behind the leader and they dragged the helpless man onto the altar-like platform and held him down.

The crazed sermon continued, "We have all been called to new life. The new Master has defeated the old. The old was weak! We are made strong by the 'fection. It has purified the weak from the earth. Now only the strong remain! We are the strong!"

"Strong!" the crowd cheered, waving their arms and shouting.

"We are the blessed!"

"Bless..ed!" The crowd roared out, stumbling on the longer word. Clearly the level of thinking was highly variable.

"We have been purified by the 'fection! Tonight we feast! Prepare the unblessed!"

At this, the roaring started and did not stop. Hands reached out and tore at the clothing of the helpless man, tearing his shirt and pants to shreds, exposing his bleeding skin. Clearly, he had been tortured before this event started. The man sobbed with exhaustion and fear, still trying to free himself from his psychopathic captors. Drool ran in rivulets from the faces of everyone as the group salivated over the horrific feast in which they were about to partake. Pirelli hid her eyes and quietly cried. The police chief had always been a very nice man, and this ceremony was the most horrifying thing that she had ever witnessed, including all of the drooling madness and thoughtless insanity of the time since the collapse.

To her, it seemed to fit together, as some of the very first infected that she had seen were EMS workers who had gone on a killing spree, still able to use their weapons and vehicles. There seemed to be a huge variability in the way the infection affected the brains of its victims, but the one constant seemed to be the extremely violent and aggressive behavior. This news had to reach the farm. The threat was far beyond anything that they had ever faced before. The very idea of thinkers to fight against, the terrifying prospect of fighting an organized mob of calculating, thinking, paranoid, violent lunatics froze her mind with fear.

Upon the stage, the struggling man was held down and the leader, the head priest of this evil ceremony of death, stepped behind the helpless victim and shouted, "Feast!"

"Feast!" The crowd shouted, screaming in a frenzy, drool flinging from their open mouths.

"Feast!" this preacher of Hell shouted again, now raising a long carving knife above his head. The victim squirmed under the hands of the infected horde.

"Feast! Feast! Feast!..." The chanting of the crowd continued, unabated as the leader plunged the knife deep into the chest of the police chief, blood coursing out onto the stone table and the hands and arms of the infected horde who could not control themselves any longer and drove their mouths and teeth into the flesh of the man as he lay dying, his lifeblood coursing out, covering the faces of those that devoured him. The crowd surged forward, pressing onto the stage for their part of the kill, like some hellish wolf pack circling a dead buffalo, caught in its final death throes.

Trey squeezed Pirelli's shoulder. It was time to go before they were caught. The crowd did not notice them leaving, as they crawled back the way that they had come. Pirelli did not vomit, but maintained her composure all the way back to the truck. The two got in and they rumbled quietly back towards the farm, lost in their thoughts. The others had sat in stunned silence as the two reported on the scene. This was the worst news. A new and powerful threat right on their doorstep. As the miles slowly went by, the dark night kept each person alone with his and her own thoughts. As Pirelli and Chloe sat in the back of the truck, facing the dull red lights reflected in the sky over Portland, they squeezed each other's hands and prayed silent prayers for help from The Lord. The men sat silently in the front seat, mulling over the information. It was a quiet ride home. It would not be a quiet season ahead.

Foothills of the Cumberland Plateau
Private forested road
Group property
July 25
10:27a.m.

Margaret Gunn hugged Stephanie Rees and they wiped tears from their eyes and smiled, laughing at the emotional moment. They had been preparing gear for the expedition and the realization that their family members were going into harm's way had simply overpowered them. The team would be in a convoy. Angus, Matt, Darryl Washington and Justin Clearwater would take the Gunn's deuce and a half, while Scott Rees, John Calvin, Samuel Tulley and Donovan Tulley would take the Calvin's deuce. Both vehicles had multi-fuel engines and could run on effectively any modern fuel including fuel oil, diesel, gasoline, kerosene, aviation fuel, used motor oil from abandoned cars, or even mineral oil from downed transformers. It would take some time to armor the vehicles and prepare enough equipment to ready them for the trip.

They would need food, clothing, weapons, ammunition, medical supplies, shelter, communications gear, armor and a lot of luck to fulfill their mission. They would be gone for a long time, and it was very possible that they would never return. The journey would be long, arduous and extremely dangerous. The remainder of the team left behind would have the difficult job with reduced manpower, of securing the compound against enemies. Life would be difficult for both groups, to say the least.

The Bradley fighting vehicle would be kept at the compound as its fuel supply was somewhat harder to find, running only on diesel.

Having the vehicle with its powerful 25mm cannon and advanced imaging technology available to protect the property was a very reassuring prospect to the recon team. It still had over 700 rounds of the deadly 25mm shells and over 1400 rounds of .308 for its M240C machine gun. The equipment scavenged from the attackers was a true gold mine. Several M4 rifles complete with AN/PEQ-2 or newer AN/PEQ-15 infrared/visible laser target designators, Aimpoint Comp M4 red dot optics or Eotech red dot optics would allow for full night operations when used in conjunction with the night vision googles recovered from the attackers. Most had the AN/PVS-14 night vision monoculars, but two of the newer AN/PSQ-20 combination night vision/thermal imaging monoculars were also found.

The AN/PSQ-20 combined light intensification with thermal imaging for a truly remarkable and unprecedented ability to detect the enemy at a distance. Both of these advanced monoculars would stay with the compound and the less advanced units would be divided between the groups. The laser designators, when used in infrared mode, could be seen through the night vision monoculars, but would remain invisible to the naked eye, allowing for first strike capability against any enemy without night vision. Combined with the rest of the gear recovered, the find was truly miraculous and advanced the defensive and offensive effectiveness of the group to a level never before expected.

In addition, several other types of ordinance were recovered from the attackers' vehicles. Two 60 round ammunition cans of M433 HEDP 40mm low pressure high explosive dual purpose grenades were found in the third Humvee. These rounds could be fired from either the M203 or M320 grenade launchers and could penetrate two inches of steel plate armor out to their 400 meter range and inflict terrible casualties in their target areas, as Darryl and John almost found out the hard way. Eight more rounds of the M433 HEDP and 15 more rounds of M406 HE 40mm rounds were found on the vests of the two dead grenadiers. The M406 high explosive rounds were equally impressive and had a blast radius of 5 meters.

The Humvees themselves were not salvageable, but the two M2 .50BMG machine guns on their turrets were undamaged, as the Claymore miraculously had not damaged the machine gun on the Humvee hit in the fight, and the one behind it was also undamaged. The Humvee that had been hit by John's LAW rocket was nearly a complete loss, as was the first Bradley hit by Angus. No gear of any kind was salvageable from these vehicles. The horrifying task of removing the usable gear from the bodies had been conducted by the group members, after a long prayer by Lucien Tulley.

The terrible loss of human life had struck a nerve within the group. They hated the duty and several, including Scott and Margaret Rees and Gwenn Gunn had to walk away during the cleanup, to keep their composure. Several of the Tulleys vomited as did Justin Clearwater. It was an awful experience. As they had worked, Darryl and John simply got angrier and angrier at the unnecessary loss of life. They had both been Air Force and felt that they were burying traitors during the cleanup. Neither man would talk to anyone for days after the event, and each became sullen and withdrawn until the memory of it had faded somewhat in their minds.

From the bodies, several functional helmets and armor plates were gleaned, as well as radios and personal gear such as knives, compasses and binoculars. The sections of undamaged soft armor and plates would be retrofitted to the Deuces along with several plates of aluminum armor from the undamaged sections of the destroyed Bradley. All of the ammunition and reactive armor plates had exploded when the AT-4 munition had hit the Bradley, but there were still salvageable portions of the standard armor left that could be removed and reused. This would prove invaluable in protecting the deuces for the long mission ahead.

For now, the mission prep would have to wait. Despite all of the loss and terror, or maybe even because of it all, life moved forward. There was a wedding to attend. Samuel Tulley and Grace Winifred were getting married today. They had waited simply as long as they could stand now. Both had pledged their love for each other long before the world had changed, long before thoughts of survival blocked out all other peaceable progress. The couple had waited on this day for months. Both were fundamentalist Christians and both had saved themselves for this day. Their purity had been put to the test many times and with the recent loss of life, they would not wait another day.

The group members wore their best clothes, a mishmash of uniforms and civilian clothes, and all were well scrubbed and spit-shined for the event. All of the Tulleys had on their Sunday best and John Calvin gave away the bride, as her father had not survived the first wave of the attacks by the infected. She knew in her heart that both of her parents were looking down from heaven at them. Margaret Gunn let Darryl Washington borrow her Anglican Book of Common Prayer, as this was the only written guide to a Protestant Christian wedding, left to review. The Corpuzes had a Catholic version which frankly was almost identical, but Samuel and Grace choose the Anglican version, though they were both Southern Baptist, as it was the closest thing that they could find to their idea of a wedding.

The bride wore simple clothes, no white gown was available, but she had flowers in her hair and her smile beamed so brightly that her appearance was radiant. Samuel stumbled and coughed while walking to his spot for the ceremony. The wedding was held in the yard, under the shade of a live oak, a beautiful setting for such an event. The women in the group giggled and cried when they saw John walking Grace up the makeshift aisle. Every chair in the compound was out on the lawn to make a rough rectangle with center aisle, and Darryl stood in between the couple, prayer book and Bible held together. There was no one in the clergy here to perform the ceremony and so the Tulleys had prayed about what to do.

In the oldest days of the recorded history of the Bible, a couple would simply announce their intention, receive the bride's father's blessing, and then consummate the marriage. To the group, these times seemed every bit as dramatic and every bit as much of a new start for the world as were those days. Darryl had been a lay minister in his church and after lengthy prayer, Lucien had asked his friend to perform the ceremony.

The bride held hands with her groom and the light filtered down through the clouds and branches, dappling the scene with the beauty of God's creation. The onlookers wept openly, men and women both, so beautiful was the scene. The words of the service took flight, the soaring majesty of the great romance on display for all to see. The union of two souls was performed in this eternal dance of hope and joy: communion of the maker with His followers, under the sky He created for them. For an eternal moment, all was good and right with the world. The worshipers bowed down and took communion with coarse bread and old wine, saved for such an occasion.

There was peace at last, for a short time, a time of renewal, a time of healing. The wounds knitted themselves closed, the memories of evil faded briefly, under the spectacular day that the The Lord had made. The unity of the group members was evident in this most holy of ceremonies. It was a good day.

After the festivities were complete, Lucien and Abigail gave their makeshift bedroom in the barn to the new couple and slept well in the common area. The group would need more lodging and farming would now have to commence. Life would go on as it had for millennia before. The wheel of time would continue to turn in its inexorable pace, the comings and goings of men, small matters in a great universe. The time of rebirth was yet to begin. The time of struggle was still upon them and they would see many days of sorrow, fear and pain yet to come. But for now, the peace which passeth all understanding would remain with them, and they would live in the brief calm which follows the storm.

EPILOGUE

South of Downtown Nashville, TN
Ruins of Golden Hills Mall
Parking lot
September 2
6:41a.m. Just after dawn

Angus stood in the parking lot, gazing out over the shattered bodies and blood soaked asphalt. They had survived yet another attack. He had been waylaid here when scouting for the convoy. He had attempted to reach the mall bookstore for maps when the attack had occurred. He was lucky that he hadn't been killed in the crossfire. They had to find the next Health Department to search for the vaccine. They were close and he could feel it.

He thought back to all that had happened to him and his family and friends over the past several weeks. He thought of the terror and horror of the recent time and his mind wandered back to every brush with death. He thought of the lie, the lie that all atheists believe wholeheartedly. The lie that keeps man from truly living. The lie that we, as humans, are ever really alone.

He thought of every time he should have died, every time he needed help and wondered at the intervention required to keep him here, breathing. He knew people died: he had seen far too many dead recently to ever sleep well again. He knew suffering had come again to the earth, and that it had never really been absent before anyway. Yet, at the same time, he knew he was not alone. He knew that as he stalked the ruins of this once marvelous civilization, that he could never be alone again. Not after what he had seen and experienced. He knew that The Lord God of Hosts must be with him, with them all. He knew that he walked alongside the footsteps of the One, and that no matter if he lived or died, he would never, ever, truly be alone.

John Calvin helped him up into the cab of the Deuce and a half, the rear turret gunner scanning with the M2 machine gun, taken from the vehicles of the failed invasion force months before. John followed into the three man seat and closed the door, pointing his AR-15 out of the window slit cut into the steel plate armor. The vehicle revved up, and they set out down the road, the morning light painfully beautiful as the chirping insects sang a hymn of solitude, a dirge to the former glory of the world, its bones now drying out in the sun.

The road ahead was long and winding and the men of Gallatin could not see the end. The vehicle pressed on, its twin following some distance behind, eyes scanning the ruined terrain for threats. It would be a long fall and a cold winter ahead, but right now Angus felt hope. Hope for a future past all of this. Hope for a better tomorrow. As it had for eons before, the sun drifted lazily in the sky as the woodland camouflaged vehicles lumbered out of sight, the insect cacophony ushering them onward, onward into an uncertain future.